Prism of Purpurine

By Roy Baldwin

Creative Gateway

First Published by Creative Gateway 2015
Reprinted 2017
Copyright © 2015 Roy Baldwin

Paperback Edition: ISBN: 978-1-908636-31-7
Also available in eBook

Typeset in Caslon Bold 11/14

Designed and published in Great Britain
by Creative Gateway, Norfolk, UK

Acknowledgement

Prism of Purpurine came into existence as a consequence of reader encouragement to create a long awaited sequel to my ghost story, Mauveine, which I wrote and published last year for the annual NaNoWriMo writing competition. Once again, I entered NaNoWriMo to supply me with another adrenaline shot of inspiration for an intense block of story writing.

NaNoWriMo is a fantastic opportunity for all writers, new and experienced, to create a fifty thousand word novel within a disciplined timeframe of the thirty days of November, supported and encouraged online by a vast community of other local and international writers. In its sixteenth year, NaNoWriMo anticipates at least half a million people to join the largest writing event in the world, from across seven continents including Antarctica. Through its Young Writers Programme, NaNoWriMo also globally provides free resources and a curriculum to over eighty thousand students and educators in two thousand classrooms. In addition, a host of volunteers provide write-ins and events in five hundred regions, including my own in the UK city of Norwich. NaNoWriMo is an awesome writer movement which I am proud to support.

I decided to attempt another adventure into the horror and paranormal genre, within a landscape of historic characters and plots, and write the sequel which addresses the main question still hanging over from Mauveine. Is the terror finally all over? The new challenge to be met has been formidable. I needed to move my timeline both further back into the seventeenth century and onwards into the future, as I hastily scribbled a rough plot outline in the last few days of October, prior to commencing writing on November 1st. The discipline of writing every day and hitting a set of strict deadlines is amazingly cathartic and highly energising. Fortunately, a goodly flow of words soon materialised, the keyboard sizzled endlessly and unexpected characters past, present and future emerged, ferociously taking over the entire plot and writing process. For thirty days I have lived, once more, in another fantasy world, writing and researching on the go for the entire time to successfully complete the NaNoWriMo challenge.

Prism of Purpurine, like Mauveine, defies simple categorisation. The novel is best described as a fictional mashup of horror, fantasy, history, science, art, romance and adventure. It does, however, follow the complex and challenging emotional journey of three female protagonists who try to support one another and unravel a darkening McKenzie family secret.

Unfortunately, they are joined along the way by others not quite of this time, who threaten and frighteningly defy the expected consequences of death and oblivion.

This novel has benefitted hugely from the inspiration and support of people who I would like to take this opportunity to thank profusely:

§: Firstly, my family for putting up with a grumpy, reclusive and uncommunicative hermit locked away for yet another November month in a solitary writer's dungeon.

§: Secondly, my friends and writer network for the fantastic encouragement and forgiveness that I didn't read or reply to their emails, tweets or blogs for a month.

§: And finally, once again, Rowena Beighton-Dykes for her excellent knowledge of historic fashion and seventeenth century culture to point me in the right direction, and Aliyah Marr, who through her uniquely talented and artistic capability, always succeeds in being a personal source of strength and inspiration for the necessary creativity and inner determination to get the work completed and out there.

Roy Baldwin
February 2015

Chapter One

West Lancashire, early November 2010:

Plunging her arms deep into the dark oak chest full to the brim of cotton and linen dresses, scientist Victoria McKenzie pondered over the vast amount of family items from the past she continued to discover in the attics of Orsbrick Hall. Ancestral belongings, knick-knacks of long gone yesteryears, all kinds of stuff, systematically packed away for purposes unknown and then mysteriously left, completely untouched. She examined the styles meticulously. Her best friend Abby, artist, fashion designer and expert in historic culture had taught her the required fashion pointers. Those dresses were definitely late nineteenth or early twentieth century in origin.

Abby was special, her closest soul mate, and Victoria would be forever in Abby's debt for bringing family roots, Aunt Eveline and the destiny of Orsbrick Hall together for the start of an exciting and meaningful future life. Gazing lovingly at her diamond engagement ring flashing in the new overhead spotlights, she would no longer be plain old Dr Victoria McKenzie, but the new Mrs Julian Endersby-Finnis. The title certainly had an arresting, even aristocratic flamboyance, although Julian was forcefully suggesting that she should keep her birth name and directly maintain the

McKenzie family line. Given the long heritage that went back at least four hundred years, which she and Julian had discovered over the last six months, perhaps he had a point. In fact if she was really honest that little niche of name independence and the lure of remaining her own McKenzie brand well suited her psyche deep inside.

She sighed loudly. It was literally only two months since Julian had gone down on one knee, covered in lime plaster and cement, and proposed romantically in their kitchen whilst she nonchalantly stirred a huge pan of scouse stew for dinner. And how happy she had been to scream a decisive 'yes' one hundred times and promised to love him to bits forever.

Abby's judgement was right.

After all that frivolous time, single and uncommitted, she needed an older man, and Julian had made out to be an irresistible catch of a partner. It wasn't only the great sex and his remarkable cooking but his intuitive grasp of exactly what made her tick inside, something no man had ever previously got close to. Certainly the restored iron bed of Uncle William was experiencing a renewed, and regular energetic airing. Julian had put in extraordinarily long days continuing to make her huge house, Orsbrick Hall, more and more habitable. They now had sorted out a fantastic living quarter and modern kitchen, and she had chosen the large bedroom above as their own. It was the same one they were frightened out of their wits in, on the first day they surreptitiously entered the place and wood pigeons had ferreted inside through a broken window and flapped about like demented demons. Julian had turned the space into a beautiful master bedroom with a new ensuite installed. Down the corridor, he had made another six bedrooms habitable for guests.

But parts of the house still felt eerie, especially the musty, old attic rooms she mooched around in today. Once this part of the house would originally have been servant's quarters and sparsely furnished but at some point, when the servants left for good, the rooms were eventually utilised for storage. The McKenzies were definitely big-time hoarders. There was so much historic junk and paraphernalia lying inside chests, trunks and wardrobes, as well as fascinating scientific equipment that she was carefully cataloguing down in the basement laboratory, which she had finally cleaned out and painted up. Certainly the new lighting Julian installed down there made a huge difference, and she had ideas ... far reaching scientific plans for a new business ... perhaps Mauveine had been giving her inner inspiration. She wanted to talk to Abby first and see what she thought.

Her mobile suddenly rang at the other end, lying on the small antique mahogany table. A piercing echo bounced from wall to wall, accentuated by bare, stained floorboards. The effect made her jump. She still had a few measures of unease in various parts of her mansion, although she was, thank goodness, no longer frightened by Mauveine, who had not materialised once since they solved the mystery of her McKenzie lineage and she and Julian had committed to living together permanently in Orsbrick. Mauveine's restless spirit must have finally become happy and contented, although Victoria couldn't admit to Abby that she still didn't actually believe in ghosts …

Gosh who was on the mobile? It continued to ring and ring incessantly. She grabbed it hastily, saw an unknown number and muttered a quiet hello.

"Hello to you gorgeous," the caller replied softly. "You sound a little subdued? Everything okay?"

"Oh Julian, I didn't expect to hear from you yet?" Victoria said, relieved. She perked up. "But where are you phoning from?"

"Just had to borrow Rula's mobile, my battery's dead again. Mmm … you sound like you don't want to be disturbed. Not found someone new already have you lurking up in the attic?" Julian growled back playfully.

Rula? She wondered.

"An interesting concept … but no chance, I'm afraid darling. Anyway, I don't think my ghostly friend would approve. She'd stalk me again with serious intent! But I am actually in the attic as it happens, fishing through some amazing old dresses which could well have belonged to Mauveine or perhaps even her sister Lydia. We McKenzie's must have got bustier over the years. I reckon these are no more than a size eight, although they are quite long. I'll have to get the sewing machine out. How are you getting on at your house?"

He laughed. "I reckon in your case, you've digested far too many of Abby's giant kebabs during your shared fancy-free days in the wilds of Rotterdam. I can detect a slight Liverpool twang already, as well as a hint of the vernacular, know what I mean Victoria?"

"Ha, ha," she replied laughing and returned hastily to her standard posh English voice. "So how is the former bachelor pad? I still haven't seen your place yet either."

"With the state it's in you wouldn't want to. The house has been well and truly trashed. Furniture was set alight in two rooms causing a major blaze. I'm gutted completely. Those bastard tenants from London, who I thought were nice guys and genuine professionals were apparently off their head on coke most of the time and had some crazy rave there. All hell broke loose with the other tenants, who are from Poland and Latvia and fantastic. They went in, drove out all the party-going vandals including the shit tenants, threatening dire consequences if they returned and have even tried to clean up, bless them. They managed to put the fires out before the fire brigade arrived, otherwise it would have been a complete waterlogged disaster, but it's bad Victoria, lots of physical and smoke damage."

Victoria went quiet. She knew instantly how upset Julian would be, given his dedication to personally restore and conserve the old Grade Two listed building with his own hands over many years.

"Julian, I'm so sorry, really, really sorry to hear that. What are you going to do? I can come over straight away and help."

"No, there isn't much you'll be able to do to be honest. Got to start from scratch and assess the extent of the damage. I'm afraid I'll have to stay over for a few days, maybe even a week or longer and start working on the repairs immediately, and you've still got so much to sort out at Orsbrick anyway. Fortunately, my little living quarter annex is undamaged. A couple of the Polish guys have a construction background, two are carpenters and one is a plasterer and have volunteered to help, which is great, but I'll still have to do lots of it myself … money has got a bit tight of course as we've both sunk so much into Orsbrick Hall and you need to hang onto your redundancy to eke us out for the next six months … and winter's coming. Hey, maybe by then I'll have written a best seller. Could really do with that fillip right now."

"Logically, you're correct, twelve months to go before I qualify for the next phase of my inheritance … Still want to marry me Mr Builder?"

He laughed loudly down the phone. "Deffo!"

"Deffo? What sort of alien language is that for a writer, conservator and prospective husband? Abby and I had better get our double wedding booked quick before you and Lynton get cold feet."

"Not me, and I would say by the size of that ring of Abby's, Lynton is pretty serious."

"Yes, she waves it about a lot these days, but Abby is so happy I can forgive her. I've never seen her so relaxed and together ever since I met her. And, she confided that with Lynton's help, she's even looking at restarting her design business, over at his Southport gallery. She and Aunt Eveline, with of course Gerald in tow, are going to take a look at the empty shop next door tomorrow."

"Sounds great … sorry must go. I'll leave the wedding arrangements in your joint capable hands. I've got to find some lime plaster, not easy to get that stuff locally. I'll phone tomorrow and let you know when I'm back. I'll miss you."

"I'll miss you too, love you, bye and take care over there."

"Love you, I will. See you soon."

She put the phone down and stared mindlessly out of the raised sash window towards the water-lily pond. Amazingly the sashes were still in good repair, one of the few positive things Uncle William had managed before he died. Given the expense repairing those it was just as well. Suddenly something large and black flew past across her line of sight, very close by and made her leap back. She stared down to see a huge black crow had landed on the jutting out gargoyle beneath the gutter. It stared malevolently up at her, squawking loudly. At least she thought it was a crow? Or was it a rook? She had no idea of the difference, but her innate scientific curiosity made her look more closely. The head was quite different from her expectation, oddly shaped with a distinctive bald patch and a jutting, curved, yellow beak, almost like a small vulture.

Despite her former top grades in natural sciences, this bird was nothing like she had seen before. The crow went quiet, looked at her again and flew onto a balustrade on the top of the round tower, near to her at the back of the house. She could now clearly see the square, wooden hatch window opening, which was looking in dire need of a repaint, and through which she understood Uncle William once gazed out with a telescope at the night skies. The crow remained standing, quite motionless and stared back, squawking loudly again, an odd and deep raucous cackle which made her shiver. They'd left that telescope room alone up to then; there was so much else practically to do first and make habitable. Julian intended to go in and sort the tower out later.

A faint whiff of something pungent drifted into her nostrils. But it wasn't like before, that horrible odour of aniline whenever Mauveine had shown her ghostly but beautiful face. This was something far more unpleasant, a bad animal smell, reminding her of wet and dirty doggy fur. She wasn't a lover of dogs, remembering the large, old and smelly hound Rusty, her father had kept at Cinderblack Lane when she was a small child. As usual her mother had vehemently objected, especially because he insisted on taking Rusty for walks every night along the canal at exactly the same time, and she kicked up such an unpleasant, incessant fuss that the dog was eventually given away to one of his colleagues at school. The dog was never replaced. Her father retreated to his spiders in the cellar and her mother continued to drink copiously. What lousy memories of her childhood, she still had after all those years. Little wonder that she ran far away at sixteen to Holland.

Then she realised. The smell must have been that strange crow; perhaps it was old and sickly. She sniffed again but the stench was gone, the light breeze through the open window having cleared the air.

But deep in her mind, she felt uneasy again. Maybe she should go and look inside that telescope room sooner rather than later ... but not on her own. She picked up her mobile and dialled. The number was answered immediately.

"Hi there, where are you this afternoon?" Victoria chuntered. "Fancy a genuine Columbian coffee? And I've made some irresistible lemon drizzle cake which I need to share with someone as Julian won't be back for a few days. Bad problems over at his house in Liverpool. Go on, I know you can't resist."

"I'm just finishing cleaning up after a major conference this morning. Lynton's latest money making venture at the Red Lion, he's renting out the old barn as a conference venue. The first gig has been to a load of boring old senior educationalists from Liverpool City Council, looking for a cheap venue. Lynton of course has been using his Rotary contacts again. But I have to say, it was a great success and they loved my Mediterranean buffet, they will be back! Very tempting, Vikki, but I don't think I can get over. It's a bit tricky. I need to finish this lot off before Lynton gets back.

"Actually Abby, whilst the going's good, let's sort out our double wedding. Also, I need your help ... I don't want to do it on my own. Vultura has pointed to somewhere in the house I need to go and explore."

"Sorry, Vultura? I'm sure that's a comic character I read about during my decadent magazine designer past. Vikki are you okay? Who is Vultura?"

"Err ... a crow ... I think."

"I'm just grabbing my car keys. I'll be there in ten minutes."

Abby rushed upstairs, threw on her best skinny jeans and cardigan over her tee-shirt and grabbed her bag, fluffing up her spiky, pink mop of wild hair. She ran into the rear yard, first yelling at Diane on reception to ring Carrie and finish off the cleanup of the barn as she had to urgently go out. Fortunately, Lynton had gone again on the train to work and left his Merc outside. She really had to get her own little wreck of a hatchback, once she'd saved some money up when her new art and design business gets going. She didn't want to rely all the time on Lynton's largesse, despite his never-ending generosity. She loved him madly but he had already committed to help her get her business off the ground anyway.

But Victoria had her worried. Only Abby alone, with Aunt Eveline, knew the truth about what really happened to Victoria at Orsbrick Hall, two months previously. How, with the ghostly intervention of Mauveine and the intense psychic power she shared with Eveline, the three had neutralised the terrifying evil forces set to destroy Victoria and Julian and in the process reshaped McKenzie history. This had allowed Mauveine and Isi to finally rest in peace along with everyone else in the family affected by that awful seventeenth century curse. Victoria, Julian and Lynton had no memories of what happened or their involvement, because for them, with history rewritten, it never did. The effort very nearly killed Aunt Eveline. It had almost drained out all of her psychic abilities which had become increasingly obvious talking to her, but Aunt Eveline had immersed herself back into textiles art and was encouraging Abby to do the same. The traumatic happening down in the cellar had been pushed far away now in Eveline's mind, the whole unhappy family saga had drawn at last to a close. The full secret would stay that way, locked forever inside Abby's head.

Abby certainly felt at peace within her entire self and looked forward to their double wedding. She and Victoria did need to crack on and sort out the arrangements fully as the male side of the equation was, as usual, conveniently preoccupied with other things. But was Victoria getting a sign of something else afoot in the house? She put her foot down, forcing the Mercedes quicker along the dual carriageway, and arrived at the front gates in ten minutes.

Drawing up slowly on the gravel outside, Abby gazed around the estate. Julian and his two Polish helpers had already done wonders to the front of the house, with the usual bit of weekend input from Lynton acting as general dogsbody. Already, Orsbrick Hall was acquiring a majestic, lived in appearance, akin to how the manor house looked in the nineteenth century. Abby, intrigued with how far they had progressed, was keen to see the restoration of the elegant Georgian ballroom which Victoria insisted would be a priority so they could utilise the splendid setting for their wedding celebration. Orsbrick Hall finally had the aura of a happy place again, something which had not been seen by anyone since the 1920s, when Uncle William, Victoria's uncle, had created a lively epicentre of exciting social events, and propelled Orsbrick as the central milieu for local high society. Sadly that period became short-lived following the day William's girlfriend, Alicia, suffered a suicidal drowning in the Leeds and Liverpool canal at the rear, driven by severe depression after the premature death of their newly born daughter. Perhaps

Victoria sought to revive some of that past grandeur, giving Abby renewed thoughts about the shape of their joint wedding programme.

Victoria slowly opened the large oak front doors and bounded out to greet Abby, pulling open the car door with a wide smile.

"Gosh you've done your hair yet again, just like when we first met in Rotterdam. It looks fabulous, really suits you and goes with that sparkly grey cardigan."

Abby emerged from the car and gave Victoria a big hug.

"Yeh, Lynton loves it, I can't do anything wrong presently ... I'm sure it won't last through, so make the most of it I reckon. Sorry chuck that I've been a bit quiet over the last fortnight. We've been working non-stop on my new art and design business plans."

Victoria grinned as they walked into the grand hallway. "A little bird told me that you're about to sew up a megadeal tomorrow on a set of accompanying premises too — really fabulous for you."

"Ah, now I think I know exactly who that little bird might be ... and I thought she could keep a secret."

"Aunt Eveline was ever so subtle, but I confess I prised it out of her eventually. Her latest work incidentally, the size of a small tapestry, is hanging up in the Appleby Lodge dining room and is quite amazing."

"Actually I helped her with that. I haven't told Eveline yet but I'm going to start work on some of my own textile art, having been inspired by the amazing things she produces. Anyway, talking of little birds, your other feathered friend doesn't seem to be around? At least not perched on your shoulder? Tell me all please Vikki. What on earth is going on?"

Victoria turned pensive. "To be honest it was a bit of an odd thing. But I suppose lots of things in this place have been odd anyway. I've become used to unusual surprises, it doesn't bother me. I'll just get you a coffee and a slab of home-made lemon cake. I can still see plenty of room inside those skinny jeans."

Abby sat down and stared out into the well-tended garden. This was the first time she had been in the drawing room with those gorgeous giant patio windows, making the room so beautifully light, since she watched Mauveine and Isi ride off into the distance on their horses, immediately after the happening ... the cellar incident. She breathed in deeply but felt calm and happy. All was psychically well inside her head, despite Victoria's announced new pet, Vultura.

Victoria returned with a tray of coffee and cakes and immediately relayed the crow incident, and how close he had flown past her face. So close she could smell him, and it wasn't especially nice.

"I'm not keen on dogs either, "Abby said slowly. "Much prefer cats and their independence, although I must admit, in this massive place a guard dog could actually be a good thing to have and the place is well big enough. You could even have a kennel out the back." She handed Victoria her cup. "So where in here haven't you been yet? I would have thought by now you knew every nook and cranny, top and bottom, intimately."

"So did I. But there's been so much stuff to sort out and do as well as the ballroom renovation, you would never believe. Gosh I must show you the ballroom in a minute — I think you might be a little bit amazed. Anyway, we still hadn't got to the observatory tower. I assume the key is still amongst that large bunch hanging in the porter's lodge, by the meters."

Abby remained thoughtful as her mouth was stuffed with a huge piece of lemon drizzle cake. "Mmm, this cake is super. Where did you learn to bake like that? I never saw any such cooking domesticity in our Rotterdam pad of former debauchery. In fact what are we going to do with that Dutch flat? I'm still paying you rent I noticed in my fast dwindling bank account."

"I've already put the apartment up for sale," Victoria replied despondently. "There has been some good interest being in a prime location near the harbour, but the property market in Holland is really depressed now. So by the time I pay my lawyer and do the repairs and ship our stuff back to here, a container incidentally is on its way with all our worldly goods before I forget, I'll just have enough profit to pay for …"

She stopped.

"Well? … Go on. Pay for what?"

"Tell you later," Vikki whispered with a smirk and got up for the other 1920's silver coffee pot. "Anyway, you must stop your standing order. I'll refund you the last payments."

"Every little helps, thanks. Okay, Ms Birdwoman, let's do the tower. I'm getting as intrigued as you. I'll just go and grab the keys then we can unlock the secret chamber … when we've finished these cakes first!"

It took the two of them to push the heavy, creaking door slowly open. A strong, musty whiff of stale air immediately blew back out across their nostrils. The quaint circular room, shrouded in darkness, hadn't been entered for years. The light switch didn't work but they could see a large object, covered in heavy linen cloth, looking like a telescope, in front of the wooden shutters.

Victoria strode in. Orsbrick Hall was her place now; no longer was she frightened or in awe like when she and Julian first crept inside on their first date. "Abby, can you hold the door open. Shit, it's on a large spring, no wonder it was so tough to push. I'll go and open those shutters and let some air and light in." She pushed the sturdy wooden latches up and pulled the large shutters inside. Sunlight flooded inside, for the first time in a very long time.

Abby was already busy pulling the cloths off the large and impressive telescope, still in remarkably good condition. The polished brass tube and support was sat on a track to enable the instrument to be pulled back and forth through the window space. "This is mightily impressive, how old would you say this thing was?"

Victoria perused it carefully, her scientific curiosity now aroused. "Wow, this is a reflecting telescope ... with a mirror ... look at all those brass gears and controls to set the elevation up accurately. Someone in the family must have been quite an ardent amateur astronomer. I would say mid-eighteenth century, looking at the design. Gosh the mirror must be about a foot in diameter. Abby, there's a brass plate on the side. What does it say?"

"Hang on, just need to rub it gently ... err ... William Herschel, 1787. Does that mean anything?"

"Bloody hell Abby, only the Royal Astronomer to King George III during that period; Herschel discovered Uranus around then. Whoever was the McKenzie family head at that time must have had some serious Royal connections. Herschel made a limited number of these reflecting telescopes, which use mirrors rather than lenses, so you can make the magnification much greater as mirrors are easier to accurately grind very large and support effectively. See, look, the eyepiece is near the top, so you need to stand on those steps in the corner. This period of history was a great era of brass instrument making. Julian will be hugely impressed when he sees it."

"A lot of stuff in this place must be worth a fortune. Have you got insurance?"

"Good question, the short answer is ... no ... we've been too busy, which is inexcusable."

"I'll ask Lynton. He's got good contacts in the heritage field and I'm sure he'll get you a good deal for the entire house. Needs a specialist insurer I would think."

"Thanks, Abby, I don't know what either of us would do without Lynton."

Abby grinned. "Absolutely, include me too."

They looked around the room. A stylish, dark oak table with some stools stood at the side alongside a sturdy, matching bookcase with a dirty glass front. The shelves were full of leather-bound eighteenth century astronomical and scientific books in excellent condition. There were also leather folders filled with drawings and sketches of observations, with references to various planets, including a drawing of a section of the Moon, with craters labelled and Saturn with its rings and some dotted moons.

"Somebody in the family at that time was also a very good artist, Vikki, these sketches are phenomenal. What a find."

"Yes, I love the synergy of right brain creative versus left brain scientific amongst the McKenzie's, although sadly in my case, it is definitely all left. There isn't a bone of art inside my body."

Abby sighed. "Never mind chuck, you've got me and Aunt Eveline to make up for it!" They both became giggly when a loud, rasping squawk made each one turn sharply towards the window. A large black bird, with a curved yellow beak was perched on the rail around the little balcony outside, only a few feet away, its eyes dark and gleaming."

"Shit Abby, it's Vultura again. Why is he staring at you?"

Abby stared back, and instantly felt a strange pulsating sensation pass through her head, making her feel faint. She knew immediately, this was no ordinary bird. But she had to stay calm, focussed and especially she had to be non-plussed. This was not a good time to put fresh, alarming ideas into Victoria's head. She had to think on her feet quickly. One thing Abby was very clear about ... they had to search this room thoroughly and now.

"I reckon Vultura is some sort of cross between a magpie and a crow," Abby replied, making it up as she went along. "Rare, I know, but those mating occurrences do happen apparently. Look at the markings. He's a hybrid and probably lonely. It's my big, dangly, gold earrings I reckon — his inner magpie is getting the better of him." She waved her earrings and the crow squawked again. Then with a flutter of large wings, he flew off into the distance."

"Can you smell that old dog? Exactly like when I saw him earlier?"

"Just caught a whiff. The poor thing must be sickly, probably on its last legs. These old houses are a magnet for oddball bird colonies, I bet you have bats somewhere too as well as crows and rooks."

But Abby hadn't smelt the slightest thing.

Victoria laughed. "Yes, I bet there is. Actually I wonder if one of these keys opens that giant padlock?"

"No, but I reckon this one does," Abby replied, having opened up one of the drawers built into the table. She fished out a huge brass key and smoothly unlocked the chest by the window, quite unlike all the others they had found previously, being much older; maybe sixteenth or seventeenth century. "This trunk looks rather like something which has come off a ship," Abby remarked.

She lifted up the heavy lid. Inside were all kinds of medical instruments, measuring scales, saws and various knives, scalpels and contraptions like pliers, tweezers and clamps.

"Good heavens," Victoria exclaimed. "This looks like equipment belonging to a doctor or surgeon, but the instruments are seriously old, earlier I would say than the nineteenth century. I've seen medical implements in the Science Museum of that period and they were a lot more sophisticated and better made. Wonder where this equipment came from? What's this down the side?"

She pulled out a heavy object, carefully encased in thick, grey muslin wrapping, and took it to the table near the window. A large bang erupted as the chair holding the door open fell over and the door closed itself shut on its giant spring. The metal latch fell down on the outside. Vikki ran to the door and began to pull and shove furiously.

"Fuck Abby, we're locked in, oh shit, shit, shit."

Victoria's face had turned very white. She started to shake as if some sort of internal and inexplicable terror had gripped her, when Abby realised. Victoria was immediately reliving the awful disaster in the Ahrendolie refinery, when she was locked inside the inspection tunnel which then filled with gas and finally blew up and threw her out alive but killed her other eight colleagues.

Abby ran across the room and gently hugged her friend, by which time Victoria had buried her head deep into Abby's chest.

"Hey, hey, don't worry," Abby whispered. "There's a metal fire escape at the side of that balcony outside the window. We can climb out and get down there. You're not locked in. Absolutely no problem at all." She gently rubbed Victoria's blonde hair, as her quiet sobbing filled the air.

After a minute or two, Victoria prised herself away. "I'm sorry ... I don't know what on earth came over

19

me. I suddenly became horrendously terrified, that is just not like me one little bit."

"I understand, but I think you were back in that shit refinery for a moment, and you've experienced a very understandable reaction. That explosion trauma will remain in your subconscious for a long time, only natural. But this isn't the refinery Vikki. Orsbrick is your lovely home, which has welcomed you back with open arms. And, your ghostly friend won't allow you to come to any harm either, will she."

Victoria smiled, drew herself up and wiped her tears. She felt embarrassed being so irrational. "Yes, I guess you're right. But it was a horrible feeling for a moment."

Abby had walked over to the door, opened it immediately and laughed. "It might help if you turn the handle the right way too. It only moves one way, admittedly not the intuitive way … so you're forgiven this once. Anyway, if all else failed we do have the benefit of mobile phones and Lynton would have come riding to the rescue, admittedly cursing his head off as tonight is Rotary dinner at the Ship and Mitre. Well maybe not riding. Let's see what that thing is on the table."

Victoria was already carefully unwrapping the muslin. They stared at the strange object finally revealed, a large piece of perfectly shaped, cut and polished glass, semi transparent and displaying the most beautiful light crimson colour throughout; a highly unusual artefact. But it was obvious it was a piece from something larger, one edge was rough where part had broken off.

Victoria thought hard. She held the object up into the light to inspect it better where tiny coppery-looking speckles could be seen running throughout inside. She hadn't seen anything like this before. The artefact was certainly a scientific curiosity, presumably some kind of glass. But was it man-made or natural?

Abby pointed back to the muslin. "Look, there's a piece of old parchment paper inside that muslin wrap. She solemnly read out the handwritten message. "Death holds the key to the light and the gloom, let no man take them asunder soon. Robert McKenzie 1729."

They looked to each other totally mystified. But Abby's brain had whirled into gear, reminded of the old mystic incantations and denunciations she researched and used at the end of the horrific curse enactment down in the cellar. She would say nothing, but resolved to start doing some new research again. She needed a valid pretence to scour through some of Victoria's very old family library books.

Victoria continued. "Well, another example from the mysterious McKenzie family background. I don't know anything about our history before the Mauveine era and the dyeing and textiles period of the 1860s, especially that part of history further back during the 1700s. Still plenty to research don't you think?"

"Yes definitely … I'll help you," Abby responded instantly, thankful for the perfect excuse to also dig in the archives, but do it her way.

"Right," Victoria said looking at her watch. "I reckon coffee break number two is looming and we still need to discuss our wedding arrangements, remember."

"Yes, I agree. Hey, look inside this other drawer," Abby replied, rummaging at the table again. "There's an old, large leather wallet here."

She pulled it open carefully. The wallet was stuffed with various yellowing papers, old sepia photographs and official documents. As Victoria replaced the cloth over the telescope and locked up the ship's trunk, Abby laid out the papers on the table and peered over them. What she saw amazed her. They were all official papers, bills and old photographs of Mauveine's nineteenth century wedding to Isi. She looked absolutely beautiful and Isi was indeed a very handsome and fanciable man, the family likeness of course reflected in Julian's equally good Fazackerley looks.

"Just come and look at these, quick," Abby shouted.

Victoria came over and took a deep breath. "These documents and photos are absolutely amazing," she whispered. "We must take everything downstairs as well as this strange piece of crimson glass. Mauveine looks so stunning. What a gorgeous wedding dress, I wonder whatever happened to it?" She then realised that what she had been rummaging through earlier may well have been wedding apparel. "Hey Abby, this is Mauveine's actual wedding certificate. They were married on December 25th 1866, goodness, that was Christmas Day. Nobody gets married on Christmas Day, well not now."

"Yes, but in those days it was quite popular. Mainly because you had only those two guaranteed days of public holiday, so you didn't have to take time off work and lose pay. Christmas Day weddings are still legal now actually, although most people don't realise that."

"In that case, we've just sorted our wedding day. How do you fancy getting married this Christmas Day coming, if we can fix it? And it will be like a triple wedding then with Mauveine somehow."

"Hey, what a great idea. Why not? Won't be popular with all the guests but who cares. Even Julian won't be plastering then. I shall get going immediately, utilising my unique super-duper organisational talent. First thing will be to chat up the Reverend Wellesby Sutton-Briggs, vicar incumbent of Burscough Parish Church. This is going to be no less than the full monte for us, chuck. I'm sure I can persuade him to allow Lynton in too, especially if I offer Julian's services to patch up the stolen lead on the leaking roof in the nave."

"You seem to know a lot about the vicar with the weird name? And what's wrong with Lynton?"

Abby went quiet for a moment. "Lynton was divorced once, before he remarried and then he became a widower ... mmm ... that doesn't sound right really. Anyway, Welly comes into the Red Lion a lot when we do the folk nights. He's quite a singer."

"Welly? I must say Lynton's packed a lot into his forty years hasn't he," Victoria replied, smirking, looking back intensely at the pictures on the table. "Anyway, it will be third time lucky for him and I must say his smittenness seems decidedly resolute! That isn't right either; I mean a person's state of smittenability!"

They giggled. She sensed Abby behind leaning forward to pick up the picture, except Abby's hand was covered in a black velvet glove. "Where did you find those lovely gloves, they fit you …"

But Abby was stood opposite on the other side of the table, her face kind of paralysed, staring straight at her. Vikki turned and stood back, her mouth dropped. Next to her … was … oh gosh … it was Mauveine, but with a tall man alongside dressed in riding breeches, who could easily have been Julian's younger brother. It was Isi. Abby of course knew, but Victoria had never seen Isi before. They held their wedding pictures and were giggling to each other in ghostly quietness, and then both looked at Victoria and back to Abby and grinned happily. Mauveine held up the picture and pointed at the dress to Victoria, then returned it carefully inside the leather wallet and they walked in silence towards the door, hand in hand. With a quick wave they sauntered through the door and disappeared. Moments later Victoria and Abby could hear a sound of horses galloping off into the distance through the open window. Victoria ran to the window and stared hard into the distance. All was quiet; some cattle were mooing softly in the distance and not a soul or a horse anywhere.

"Oh my God, Abby. I'm so glad you were here to witness that. You saw her too didn't you. Mauveine is still around and I presume that was Isi, but they both seemed so happy. Crikey he looked just like Julian; that feels so very odd. But, I'm not frightened anymore."

Abby drew breath, her mind racing. She hadn't expected to see Mauveine ever again, but obviously they retained some means of returning through those parallel universes whenever it suited them. Victoria didn't know Abby had seen them both before, all part of the secret and it needed to stay that way. But her mind felt very fresh and light, airy and clear, all seemed to be fine with her psychic perceptions. She felt no danger now. Perhaps Mauveine was trying to reassure her as well.

She turned to Victoria. "They're both exactly how you and Julian described them, and in the pictures and definitely they were at peace. I think we've just got ghostly approval for our planned double Christmas wedding, looking at the grins on their faces. I reckon you'll have to track down that former wedding dress of Mauveine. I'm sure she wants you to wear it."

Victoria reflected, things were making sense which must be why she had felt a compulsion to rummage in the attic rooms. "I agree. I'm certain I know where the dress is too. That would be wonderful," she said and fingered the picture again. "But I'll definitely have to get the sewing machine out. Mauveine was a little slimmer than me."

"Hey, Eveline and I will sort all that for you. There's nothing we can't do with a pair of scissors and a bit of fancy linen and silk. Maybe you'll find some other nice wedding dresses there. Like say Lydia's, Mauveine's artistic sister? Lydia, from that picture on your hall wall, is definitely my slim and svelte self."

Victoria hugged her best friend tightly. "Yes, but a lot taller, you'll still have to get the shears out," she replied with a grin. "I'm glad you were here today, something told me you needed to be. Now, let's go and finish that cake."

"Deffo, chuck."

Vikki scowled. Everyone, even the fiercely Mancunian Abby, was becoming scousified.

Chapter Two

Late August 1665: Trinity College, Cambridge.

A heavy banging on the door was followed immediately by a loud bellowing voice, as the head porter made every effort to be heard in his characteristic and ungainly way, a routine which the first year students had quickly become accustomed to. "My Lord Robert McKenzie, are you in there sir? Your hackney carriage awaits you downstairs. Mr Newton is already seated. The driver is impatient, and will not wait a minute longer."

"Heavens above Galbraith, I'll be five minutes, I can't decide on which waistcoat, the dark red or the bright blue. Give the fellow another halfpenny to wait. I'll make it up to you, be sure," Robert McKenzie shouted back. Only two weeks into the term and already he was bored stiff with the lectures, which went at a pace a snail would find stultifying, and especially with the lack of women around in this tedious institution. There was a time to be serious, but playtime was already desperately needed.

His father, Lord Cameron, Earl of Burscough, had also been to Trinity College, and was maniacally focussed on ensuring his eldest son followed suit, like his father before him. The old and established family tradition, now two hundred years past, of all McKenzie males to attend Cambridge University had to be maintained. And natural science and mathematics were mandatory, when all Robert really wanted to study was philosophy. He had learned so much from Greta, his longtime science governess. He smiled and tipped out another box of waistcoats before finally grabbing the yellow and black one, gaudiest of the lot. Having a governess only four years older than himself had provided him, when he was fourteen, with an especially rounded and enriched education, spoiled only when Lucinda caught them at it in the hay-barn. She was mad as hell, but he quickly realised that Lucinda was insanely jealous. She had fallen in love with Greta herself. That was the trouble having a twin sister, and she always wanted to follow him around everywhere. Lucinda had the real scientific talent and ought to be here, not him, if such things were ever in the slightest remoteness possible, but his father had ignored all pleas to give her special tuition. Instead Lucinda had to be presented to court very soon; marriage would be in the air.

McKenzie ran his hands through his long, blond hair and skipped down the rickety stairs, almost knocking over the ponderous Galbraith. He thrust a shilling into the man's large hand before climbing up into the carriage. The horses, steaming and agitated, wanted to be off.

"Here man, that should clear my tab for the last week."

Galbraith tipped his cap. "Grateful, my Lord. And what time will we be expecting you both back sir?"

"When we're done Galbraith and not before. Now be off. I heard that Asquith down the corridor is veritably pissed out of his head with a surfeit of mead and throwing up in the dining room. Better sort the knave out, sir, I beseech you. The wretch stinks to high hell."

Galbraith sighed. Nobility. Too much money, not enough studying and no discipline. The students were not like they used to be. Galbraith turned to McKenzie's companion, sat quietly and gazing intently out of the other side at a notice announcing a forthcoming cantata recital. A serious and quiet student for a change, who was never wanton or begetting trouble. "Mr Newton, sir, please keep an eye on Lord McKenzie here. The last escapade cost the College dear, replacing the annex windows."

At which point the surly driver at the front lashed the two horses, and slamming the rickety door shut, they set off briskly, bouncing onto the main street and down into the town.

"Isaac my good man, why so gloomy? You look like shite, just when Friday is upon us and we can at last have some fun. And the treat, I do proclaim, will be on me this night. Do you like my new waistcoat? Let's see who we can impress tonight. What say you, sir?"

Newton had been scribbling in a small notebook, deep in thought. He shoved it in his pocket and looked over to his friend. So much was going on, his mind was on fire with new ideas, and he was going mad with wave after wave of restless thoughts and hadn't slept for two nights.

He had to talk about it, but could see Robert was winding well off. He too, he thought, must try and learn to relax. He smiled back but felt hugely uncomfortable being thrown roughly from side to side. "I must say Robert you sport splendid attire; your dress will impress the ladies that's for sure. By heavens there must be some better mechanical method to make these carriages smoother, like suspending the axles for a start. This bouncing and rattling around makes my teeth ache. In fact I must see the College barber and have one pulled."

McKenzie laughed his loud raucous bellow, which fellow students had grown to quickly recognise right across the Hall. "A good slug of whisky and the pain will be over in a second, my friend. Methinks that before you attempt some engineering though, you would best first reflect on the sad state of the English road, which is the real problem with our journey. If the poor fellow out there driving in this rain was to fall off, it would not be the descent to kill him, but instant drowning in the mud. Just look at that swathe of filth."

Newton nodded. The logic of the statement was unassailable, but he needed to save his mental effort on the physics which he was fast discerning in the difficult matter of corpuscles of light, to which his latest work was being devoted. "Where are we headed then Robert, you said a fun place, like a library?"

Robert roared with laughter again. "No, good sir, we will shortly land at the Bridge Arms, a select tavern of some repute which my father commends. The ladies are fair and the beer is good, so I am told."

Newton looked out through the window and grimaced. Ladies he had no time for since his broken engagement five years before to sweet Kathleen, and the slut then married another suitor, a damned farmer, immediately afterwards. He would devote his life to intellectual not carnal endeavour. But beer he thoroughly enjoyed, although that nagging toothache was payback for having such a sweet tooth. He should not have devoured six plums before departure. He turned back to McKenzie. "Alas Robert, I am told by the chaplain at breakfast, in confidence of course, of some grave news which disturbs me greatly."

"What man? I haven't been privy of any rumour? 'Tis a veritable quiet morgue in that damned place, with intrigue in such short supply. This is not like you, Isaac, to be distracted by tittle-tattle."

Newton looked stern. "Tis not tittle-tattle Robert. You are aware of the outbreak of the Great Plague in London? Verily, thirty thousand per week are dying presently. Bleeding and the sulphur remedy are making no difference to the foul goitres. The College authorities are concerned of its meddlesome spread to within parts of Cambridge, especially in the poor area north of the river. They will likely close the College soon, in fact all the University, for an indefinite period. I am most depressed by the thought of returning to Grantham. My optical experiments are going so well, and I have not the means to continue them there."

"Well, if that be the case, so be it. I am not conducive to Trinity and would be happy to be back home, find my tutor Greta again and pursue more philosophy." He grinned. "She is a fair woman, Isaac, I must say, strong in mind and plump in body."

"There is more to our calling than mere women, Robert," Newton replied angrily. "You are rich and have the means to do what you want; I must establish my reputation and have so much to achieve yet."

"Then it is done. If we are eviscerated from this dump, I will guarantee your study to continue, my friend, as your intellect is the only one which gives me some convivial pleasure amongst these over-pissed dullards surrounding us, and that is only the tutors! What do you say?" McKenzie cried, slapping his friend hard on the back. "We are now due to arrive, the stench has cleared. Look they even have lit torches in front of the house, it must be well supported."

Newton proffered his hand and shook McKenzie's warmly. "I am indebted, Robert, to your generosity. I will take your offer, but as a loan, then when my researches bear fruit you will be repaid, with good interest, sir. And now, I shall buy us the first two flagons of their best ale, for which I confess I know already I will have particular partiality."

The rickety four-wheel hackney carriage, imported from London, drew to a stop, as they tumbled out onto the cobbles outside the inn door. The rain had finally stopped but as the door slammed, it fell straight off its hinges onto the ground, just missing Newton's leg as he dived to the side.

McKenzie handed a shilling to the driver sat shivering in the front behind the horses, barely covered in a coat full of holes and soaked to the skin. "Here my man, this should cover some repairs too. We thank thee, you will need to devote some maintenance to this carriage I fear."

Newton was carefully inspecting the large wheel at the back, cracked and askew, little wonder that their ride was bad. He was ruminating about circular motion and the exact calculation of varied velocities, when he suddenly had a flash in his brain. He must scribble some mathematics of motion and flow later, a veritable inspiration for a new calculation method had come to him. Flow ... flowing ... flux, a method of fluxions ... by the Lord's Prayer, that title will be a new direction.

McKenzie grabbed his friend away, still deep in thought staring motionless at the wheel, and immediately pushed open the creaking inn door. "Come Isaac, what on earth are you looking at? If the plague is coming and our time is short then let us make with full merriment. Your shout, I believe you said, sir?"

Already on their second flagon of ale, the two students sat at a large table in the corner. Newton, wearing his second-hand dull black breeches and waistcoat, his curly, thick hair long and unkempt, was standing out somewhat dourly amongst the coterie of brightly dressed and smart, well-heeled gentry, many in wigs, laughing and joking with the small groups of rowdy girls and bawdy women, who had equally gravitated into the place for entertainment, fun and some lucrative business before the night fell. It was truly noisy everywhere, with a fiddle player belting out shanties and a group singing in the other corner. Robert McKenzie was at the bar talking to Henry Billings, the landlord, who had just carried out a great pail of logs to put onto the roaring fire. Billings instantly remembered McKenzie's father, Cameron, with a fond utterance of 'by Jove,' although he refused to discuss the unspoken exploits Lord Cameron and his friends apparently got up to, but it appeared that the inn was a selective magnet for many gentry and yeomen with money, looking for a good time, and where discretion was assured.

McKenzie looked around casually. It was an unusually chilly night for the time of year, needing a fire. Even a frost could be felt in the air, but then year after year temperatures were always so damned cold and winter was forever sheer hell. Whatever was the matter with the climate which was decidedly cooling?

Loud peals of laughter were coming from the mixed card tables and some women had already removed vestiges of clothing in their increasingly inebriated states, egged on by the men, grunting and tossing coins into their bonnets. Little wonder that the landlord made sure the drinking area stayed hot like his rooms already laid out ready and waiting off the corridor behind. A whalebone corset was thrown on the table, when some oaf picked it up and waved it around, shouting crazily. Likely some of those buxom Norwich women, who came in regularly in groups of twenty by wagon-carriages for business, would end up naked fairly soon and be whisked off to be fucked. He felt a strong measure of arousal himself and his eye caught an older, pretty woman in her early thirties, dressed in an expensive long, silk green-flowered dress. She was preening herself alone on a stool by the bar. Her hair was deep red, long and stunning, flowing in curls right down her back. He tapped the landlord gently on the arm.

"Henry, who is that fair woman yonder on the stool? She is beautiful but alone in here? I don't understand."

"That, my Lord McKenzie, is a lady by the name of Coleen Fitzpatrick. She lives nearby, in a very stunning, real brick townhouse on the river, with actual glass windows and a wondrous garden, filled with fruit trees of all kinds. She is a widow. Sadly her former husband, a rich wool merchant, had the misfortune of receiving a bale on the head from a broken pulley rope; rumour has it she secretly severed the twine. Now, a wealthy businesswoman in her own right, Coleen likes her independence, despite many suitors, who she selects when it suits her, rare for a woman in these parts."

"And pray Henry, what may be her business? Is it still sheep and wool?"

The landlord guffawed. "Look around you, sir. These girls are carefully selected and managed, so that any with poxes or pustulence of the cunny are weeded out. I get good commission. You see that swarthy, ugly looking bastard over there in front of the King Charles painting, with a hook for a hand? That's Carlos. If she settles on some prey for the evening, he drags them over to her. They don't say no of course. But it's rare, very rare ... The last one who did refuse had mistaken her for a molly house keeper. He was found down the next alley, a hot poker up his anus. She's looking your way my Lord Robert, take care."

McKenzie glanced surreptitiously over to see her smile, a good set of white teeth, daresay, he thought. She was hypnotically alluring but he felt an icy chill run down his body, his ardour shrinking fast. "Fuck me, landlord. I will indeed. Time, methinks, to return to my friend. Here's sixpence for these flagons, keep the change. Veritably my friend has a strong thirst for your excellent ale, which I was previously unaware of."

He looked over to Newton, who he could barely see for the great swathes of tobacco smoke swirling all around the room, and groaned. Not far from their table a great racket was going on as a podgy woman, with short black hair, was fleetingly lifting her voluminous skirts up and down to reveal tantalising flashes of large and bare, white arse in time to the fiddler. The pennies piled into her empty glass. Newton was totally oblivious, staring at the table deep in concentration, and scribbled mercilessly in his notebook, the pages covered in diagrams and mathematical symbols.

"And who sir, may I ask, is your friend? I can see an enthusiastic Cambridge student to be sure. I hope Madam doesn't catch his eye, although that looks very unlikely," Henry Billings remarked with a sly grin.

McKenzie laughed. "Yes, I agree, he is one Isaac Newton, from Grantham in Lincolnshire. He has a sharp intellect, one of the finest in the College, but sadly Newton will amount to nothing in this world. His introversion and unworldliness will be the death of him; I keep an eye out for his well being."

"Quite so, my Lord. Aye, looks like you'd better get over there. We have some new business just entered."

A fresh and welcoming cool breeze fanned across to the bar as the heavy door was slammed shut. Darkness had now befallen and two well dressed gentlemen, somewhat older than either McKenzie or Newton, had walked in. One was short and stocky, not looking especially well, his light brown hair untidy with a large bald patch on his huge head. He stared ahead with a serious expression at Newton, still scribbling hard, alone in his inner world at the table. The other was somewhat taller, decidedly wealthy in appearance with a well fed paunch, but displayed a definite air of flamboyance, expensive clothing and mischief. A man, McKenzie thought, of dalliance and charm without a doubt. After resting their cloaks over the stand, the shorter man pointed to the empty spaces around Newton's table and they decided to walk that way.

The shorter gentleman spoke out, in a coarse, broad Cornwall accent. "I say, sir, may we join you around this table? 'Tis a busy evening in this establishment and spaces are scarce."

Newton looked up, frowned, and waved nonchalantly at the seats before returning, deep in thought, to his notebook scribbles and drawings. As they sat down, the short man spoke again, intrigued by what he saw. "If I may be so kind as to ask sir, but your drawings appear to be of optical prisms engaged with the dispersion of light which I happen to know well. Pray sir, what are you working on?"

His dapper companion was obviously more taken by the surrounding gaiety, laughing loudly at the sight of the plump woman nearby now down to her slip, cradling the bushy head of a drunk and dishevelled aristocrat, who slathered over her very ample, bare bosoms and large brown nipples.

Newton stopped writing and put down his crayon and looked up. At that moment McKenzie had gallantly returned to the table to rescue Newton, carrying two more large flagons of ale. "Gentlemen? May I prevail upon you to join my friend and I in some refreshment, which I say verily you both look in dire need of? The tab is on me. I have brought us an extra flagon to start with. The ale in this inn is mightily potent but of great sustenance. And the landlord will also bring over some pork pies and sweet cakes,"

At the sound of food, Newton decidedly perked up. The alcohol had by then numbed his aching molar. McKenzie added. "And what, my friends, may your names be?"

The taller and older man responded immediately with a big smile and held out his hand to McKenzie. "That is so very kind. My companion and I have indeed travelled far, and have much thirst and hunger, from London in fact, thence to Oxford before finally alighting here." He motioned to his short companion. "This is Dr Robert Hooke, newly appointed Gresham Professor of Geometry and I am Pepys, Mr Samuel Pepys, and Secretary to the Board of the Admiralty in London. We are here to see my old alma mater in Magdalene College. And you sir?"

"Lord Robert McKenzie of Burscough and this is my friend Isaac Newton. We are natural science students at Trinity."

"Lord McKenzie? Ah, of course, now I remember. Your father will be Earl McKenzie. I had much pleasure of discourse with him ten years ago here, at this very inn in fact. You take after him well. And, Mr Newton, I see you are a man of both letters and figures that is highly commendable. You will have to forgive my companion, Dr Hooke, of his prying nature, but he is fastidious of intellectual challenge and certainly knows something about the nature of light."

A serving wench, pretty, but no older than sixteen, commenced laying out a large plate of pies, cakes and fruit at the table and generously topped up the flagons from a huge glass jug. McKenzie noticed Pepys give her a friendly pinch of the bottom and a wry smile as she departed with a giggle.

"Ophelia, youngest daughter of landlord Billings. Last time I saw her she was a lively childe of ten years. Now becoming very ripe and comely, ready don't you think Lord McKenzie?" Pepys whispered, with a wink, his accent very precise and regal, decidedly a man with likely Royal connections, having such a high naval position.

Newton was now in deep conversation with Hooke, the two engrossed with perusing a variety of sketches and equations which Newton was hastily drawing all over the table, whilst Hooke belligerently rubbed out figures and inserted others.

McKenzie pondered his friend, Newton. Damn it, always so hard to read, sociable only when it suited him and usually connected with his work, exactly like then. But McKenzie sensed that the discussion, which he was catching concerning ideas of light permeation, was a topic of intense disagreement. Newton, stuffing his face with cakes, was feverishly postulating some sort of theory of tiny corpuscles. Hooke, meanwhile, an unpleasant sounding and antagonistic individual, but obviously very sharp on mathematics and the practicals, was advocating propagation of light by waves, a preposterous sounding concept, although their depth of argument was already way beyond his knowledge. However McKenzie saw for the first time a side of his friend not perceived before. Newton was clearly, deep inside, a fighter for his beliefs and a persuasive arguer, even philosophical in his mode of attack, quite a surprise. Newton had hidden depths. Perhaps he may have some potential after all.

Pepys meanwhile pulled McKenzie's arm and encouraged him to sit closer. "I think Lord McKenzie that we can safely leave Mr Newton and Dr Hooke to their intellectual ramblings, they will be at it all night until morning. I know Hooke, like a dog with a bone where mathematics is concerned, but your friend Newton is similar temperament, I fear. 'Tis a fair waste of the other pleasures of this tavern methinks, do you not agree sir?"

McKenzie laughed. His assessment of Pepys was accurate. Despite the married ring on his finger, Pepys was a sophisticated man of the world who liked the finer things of life and, like him, shared a love of women. "Yes, I understand fully Mr Pepys. Now as a former purveyor of the benefits of this establishment do you have any suggestions appropriate to a virgin such as me?"

Pepys roared. "Sir, I fear you are deliberately doing yourself an injustice to your status. I must note your statement, anonymously of course, in my diary which I am keeping presently of my life experiences. I hope one day to maybe see it published and make a little money. Although I have to say, much of my writing this year sadly concerns the Great Plague. So many dying, sir, the graveyards are already full all over London. Now they dig huge pits and throw in fifty to a hundred bodies at a time, there is nowhere else to bury them. My friend, a medical doctor named Lucas, has tried all manner of cures with leeches, including ingestions of mercury, arsenic and sulfur, none yet making headway of success, they continue to die. He recalls to me awful things about the foul goitres between their thighs and how quickly the victims perish. I just hope the next winter will deprive the pestilence of its relentless movement for good. Last winter the extreme cold, when the River Thames froze solid and we skated day and night for months on end, caused a huge drop in cases."

"It is a fearful curse, Mr Pepys, especially for the poor, although I understand nobody is spared. But those with wealth can at least escape the eye of the scourge. Newton tells me that he has heard the Cambridge University may close up as a precaution against infections."

"Tis true I'm afraid sir. You will indeed have to be gone by the end of next week. My alma mater warned me ahead of this trip. They have contemplated such drastic action for some time, and events are overtaking them, so they have to act quickly and decisively. But in the end it will be for the best. Cambridge University must survive for the good of England."

"For me, that is not such an imposition, but for Newton, he will be sorely depressed. I will however keep an eye on him and ensure his enthusiasm for study is able to be maintained. But he is such a doleful character. He has no interest in the ladies, and his drive to interact with the necessary social mores to advance his status is sadly limited."

"Good for you sir, I do believe that will be a good thing. Hooke may also be able to help your friend; he has excellent connections in the academic world and access to wealthy sponsors of science experiment. Hooke is a wondrous man of engineering, you should see his new reflecting telescope he built by his own hand. They will advance our knowledge of the natural world ten-fold. Hooke also never partakes of the flesh; however we men of the world cannot all follow such monastic pursuit. Abstinence is bad for the circulation, so my medical friend tells me, and I am very inclined to agree!"

Robert McKenzie laughed and nodded. "I am more inclined to the mental challenges of philosophy and astronomy Mr Pepys, as is my dear sister Lucinda, who shows great talent of the scientific mind and its applications. I should also like to keep in touch with Hooke."

"Indeed sir and it shall be done. However more pressing matters for you and me. We have the eye of the lady of the house."

McKenzie looked across to see the smiling gaze of the compelling Coleen, wending their way. "I truly fear, Mr Pepys, that woman has I understand, ways, according to Henry Billings."

Pepys laughed heartily and swilled down the final dregs of the flagon of beer. "Have no fear, my Lord Robert McKenzie. I know Lady Coleen of old, and I can vouch that she has the most delectable, plump cunny, shaved bare and smooth exactly like Aphrodite," he whispered. "She normally shares her dues with a companion or two, so be bold sir. Your virginity will be put down instantly like a mad dog. We take her together, if you are not a prude?"

McKenzie laughed his deep bellow guffaw again as Newton glanced up for a brief second, frowned, then reverted back into deep academic discussion and argument with Hooke, each stuffing themselves with cakes and neither noticing or interested in the naked, plump lady orally performing, two at a time, at their next table. He suddenly felt a cold object, drift lightly across his hand. The sight of a large metal hook filled him with immediate dread.

"Gentlemen, Lady Fitzpatrick would like you to take sherry with her and her companion, Miss Ophelia, down in the drawing room. A fire is lit, would you follow me."

Pepys nudged McKenzie promptly with a smirk. "Follow me, kind sir," as he slowly walked behind the giant rear breeches of minder Carlos towards the door into the private quarters. "I shall be generous today Lord McKenzie, you may partake of the pleasures of pretty Ophelia first. It is, I duly decree, only right and proper, two virgins together."

They each roared laughing as McKenzie playfully slapped Pepys over the shoulder, swilled his last ale, quickly put a pie in each pocket and both disappeared off into the gloom ...

Chapter Three

They had an enormous job to persuade her into the car, then she was sullen and silent all the way back and now they faced the same challenge getting her out of the car and into the front door. Victoria was amazed with the gentle patience and tenacious perseverance of Abby, faced with such a difficult issue. Eventually, with some careful cajoling, they finally managed to force her to walk inside the Red Lion and up to her new bedroom. Victoria and Abby had travelled down to Oxford University together, following a tearful and suicidal call from nineteen year old Judy, Lynton's daughter, studying in the first term of her second year philosophy, politics and economics course at Balliol College.

Lynton desperately wanted Judy to follow in his own illustrious footsteps. She was outstandingly clever and a gifted student, having gained a special scholarship from a leading London law firm, Conservative party donors and old drinking friends of her father, of course. But Lynton, despite his kind intent and generous support of his daughter, had seriously failed to acknowledge that something was dreadfully wrong from the beginning. After despair, desperate confusion and finally a complete dead-end, Abby had taken charge and immediately decided to bring Judy home, whatever Lynton felt. She would personally look after her. Abby had no intention of taking on any role of replacement step-mother. There was no way she would ever fill the shoes of Lynton's deceased wife, but she loved Lynton dearly and as far as she was concerned his problems were her problems, and she would do whatever it took, seeing Lynton struggle so badly with how to help his daughter. She could at least get onto a closer friendship level, if possible, with Judy. Their initial meetings a few months before had been cordial, although there was then an understandable tension in the air. However, this time Abby quickly prised much more about Judy out of Lynton before she left for Oxford with Victoria.

Victoria searched around the large kitchen for the kettle and some teabags, impressed with the newly decorated walls and kitchen appliances hanging meticulously on the wide lime wood rack, and turned on the gas to make them all a drink. Eventually, after some kind of muffled and long conversation upstairs, she heard Abby quietly close Judy's door and trip down the stairs, giving Victoria a jubilant thumbs-up.

"Progress, at long last. For the first time, she gave me a quick hug and thanked me profusely for bringing her back and listening to her, and she loves the way I've decorated her room. I'm absolutely done in. I'm glad you shared the driving back, it really is a trek down there and back by car in one day."

"Yes, especially with the state Judy is in … so … are you going to tell me what really is the matter with her? This is more than the normal university second year blues starting isn't it. That's very obvious."

"To be honest when I first met her over the summer, I thought she was just a tad neurotic and over-sensitive. Of course she wasn't exactly ecstatic at the thought of her father seriously dating again, especially when she saw me. The usual ... only child, doted on daughter and insanely withdrawn. Certainly Judy is exceptionally bright. Once she knew I had a doctorate she became a little more accepting."

"What? The certificate that says return to Kelloggs if found? 'Absolutely Fabulous' springs to mind actually ... sorry Abby, I'm being unforgivably facetious, but she is a little plain, and really has quite pretty features, which a bit of makeup and some dress sense would help."

Abby poured out the tea and grimaced. "I agree. You're forgiven this time. Somewhat over-protected by her father in her teens, Judy never had much of a chance at boarding school to be rebellious. Mind you I went to boarding school and I loved rebelling."

"Yes, it shows ... seriously, what more do you know about her now?"

Abby opened a packet of ginger biscuits and started devouring them. "Help yourself. Lynton finally opened up last night. He has been very cagey about Irene, Judy's mother, but that's perfectly understandable. Irene died when Judy was thirteen, and it was then she was sent to boarding school until she was sixteen. She did well academically but was hugely unhappy and surprise, surprise, bullied. It appears that Judy was strange from a baby, and at some stage had been diagnosed with Aspergers, the high achieving type, but I don't think Lynton and certainly not her mother wanted to accept it. Judy has real difficulty with gauging emotions and communicating normally. I realised that when I made a joke with her when we first met and she looked back blank, and you know how good my jokes are."

"Well, you make Lynton laugh that's for sure, so she certainly doesn't take after him. No ... more like her mother by the sound of it which doubtless never helped either. So Lynton presumably was stuck between two vulnerable females he loved dearly but couldn't communicate with."

"To a degree probably so. When her mother died, Judy had a complete breakdown. Lynton couldn't cope and was advised about the boarding school in Hampshire, one of those special, expensive establishments, mixed intake, which caters for high level autism, small classes, one to one tuition etc. She just told me now; the one thing she loved about Wingates was running the library, which gave her respect. What she didn't tell me was that at sixteen she became pregnant, refused point blank to discuss the father, although everyone guessed it was the boy who had been constantly bullying her for two years, and had an abortion before her O-levels, and she still got 12A*s. Lynton decided to bring her home and she finished her A-levels at Cradwell.

"What? Where my father used to teach?"

"Yes, apparently she loved it, matured and became, not unexpectedly, a natural for Oxbridge. She won a scholarship, but Lynton insisted she followed him into PPE at Oxford, to harden her up for the real world, when what she really wanted to do was classics and history. A bad move ... typical stupid male thinking. But what on earth do we do with her now?"

Vikki pondered, staring into the circling patterns of tea and milk in her mug as she stirred it slowly. "I've got an idea. Do you remember Yvonne, Eva's ... err ... friend at her school who was Head of History?"

"You mean the one Eva was shagging night and day and eventually ran off to live with?" Abby replied casually.

"That was the Head of English actually," Vikki replied testily. "Sometimes you can be so ..."

"Don't finish it, you're still mad, deep down, about Eva ditching you aren't you?"

"No, I know you didn't like her and she is well out of my system now. I love Julian and Eva knows it, but she was a very important part of my life then. She made me grow up and understand relationships for the first time ever."

"So you think Judy needs the same then, an Eva in her life exactly like you? I bet Eva doesn't turn up at our wedding."

"For fuck's sake Abby, just now and again you can be so damned annoyingly obdurate. Take those Mancunian cloth ears off will you and listen, you're not the only one with ideas."

Abby went bright red. She was raging inside, preparing to fly off the handle, but equally she was exhausted, she had to get a grip. She took a deep breath. "I'm sorry Vikki ... I just feel incredibly knackered and I could kick Lynton for being such an ass over his daughter but I really want to help her."

"Yes, I know you do." Vikki hugged her. "Now have another big mug of tea, you know how much you like it, and calm down. Actually I need another biscuit."

"Yes please," Abby replied slurping down a big mouthful. "Okay, go on then, Yvonne?"

"She went to Balliol College too, to read history. That subject area is a major strength there apparently, but Yvonne also mentioned the opportunity she had of doing additional study at the famous Bodleian Library, in archive work. The big thing now in libraries is digital archiving and information science, especially in the private sector. The way Judy was hammering her iPad in the car she's obviously very adept at computing. That may be a way to get her back on track, by listening and now acting on what she wants to do."

Abby finished slurping and gave her trademark big grin. "Gosh chuck, you're not just a pretty test-tube are you? Judy loves anything with computers. I'm onto it. I think, given the state she's in, she needs a break first, write off this year and then start a new history course next October. And, given Julian's contacts in the National Trust, perhaps we can get her some interning in archive or library work somewhere. The present Provost at Balliol is an old student mate of Lynton's ... with my powers of persuasion I'm sure we could swing it and make Judy happy again ... brill."

"Brill? Yes, actually that sounds like a cool plan. Now that we've solved the world's problems, can I see how you're getting on with the alterations to Mauveine's wedding dress? You looked totally fabulous in Lydia's old dress."

"And you will too, but Aunt Eveline and I had to put some work in on the bust line. It must be all that Dutch milk and cheese you consumed; Mauveine was rather pert in her heyday."

"Okay, I won't shout again that you're calling me fat now. What's that rattling at the back door?"

"Lynton, he's taken the wrong keys yet again." She fiddled with the latch and Lynton came bounding in, threw his briefcase on the floor and rushed over to Victoria to give her a generous hug.

"Hey, I've not seen you for weeks. Sorry, I've been extraordinarily busy with work. I've finally taken on a new partner and we're going to expand our growing specialism in industrial fraud … I must say, a very lucrative addition to the practice. Anyway, to what do Abby and I owe the pleasure?"

Abby intervened smartly. "Your daughter is back Lynton. Vikki and I have fetched her home today, we simply couldn't leave it any longer, and before you go bounding upstairs, let her sleep. She's in quite a state but I think now we'll be fine by the morning. I have a plan for what to do next with her, it might cost you a bit, but I'm happy to take charge and look after Judy, get her back on track. I know I can do it."

Lynton hugged Abby hard then kissed her passionately; burying his head in her chest, moaning, as Victoria gazed on, at first wide-eyed but eventually feeling her feet shuffle about in an embarrassing twitch. "I love you Abby. If anyone can sort her out you can. I'm so grateful. I don't care what it costs."

Abby, squinted back over his shoulder at Victoria and gently pushed him away. "Okay, one problem out of the way. Now, equally important … our double wedding. Have you managed to bribe our illustrious vicar then, especially as the 25th is a Saturday?"

"Pardon?" Victoria exclaimed in disbelief.

"Yes," Lynton replied decisively with a wicked grin. "I've given Welly the top billing at our New Year's Eve sing-along folk bash here in the pub and he's finally agreed to move the Christmas Day morning service to the afternoon. So we've just got time to call the three banns. It's all sorted, organist, choir, the works. The wedding service will begin at ten thirty am prompt. Better get Julian to order his morning suit pronto Vikki. Mine is, I think, still hanging in the wardrobe. We'd better check that Abby. Top hats, tails the full monte will be required. And, you will not believe, but I have booked us the old Rolls Royce at Arkwright's Garage down the road; Arkwright's son will do the driving to take us to the church on time."

He began singing, not very melodiously.

Victoria intervened. "Last weekend, Julian and I finally finished off the restoration and decorating for the ballroom and you will both absolutely love it, all restored back to the original 1920's glory, using Uncle William's old photographs and Aunt Eveline's remarkably sharp memory for colour schemes. So our wedding breakfast will be there. I'm booking the Ormskirk Jazzettes for a bit of fun. You'd better bone up on the Charleston, Abby!"

"I'll get the formal guest list out tomorrow," Abby replied cheerfully. "They've all been forewarned. Okay, there was some grumbling about Christmas day and the kids, but most are coming. I think the novelty of a double wedding intrigues many of them."

"Which reminds me," Victoria suddenly added dolefully. "Who is going to give us away Abby? I can't think of anyone whatsoever? What about your brother?"

"You must be joking, I can't think of anyone worse, but I am working on it ... and it isn't Eva!"

Chapter Four

Early December 1665: at a house in Woolwich near London:

The journey over the last two days had been a long, uncomfortable and hazardous one and he kept his musket, sword and pistol close by his side, but fortunately no highwaymen were encountered. The light grew dimmer, as Robert McKenzie's personal carriage eventually veered off the main road and took a sharp detour left down some very narrow and dirty back lanes, towards his final destination. The house of Mr Samuel Pepys. Following their interesting meeting at the whore house in Cambridge, they had quickly become firm friends and both had corresponded regularly since, culminating in an invitation by Pepys to visit and partake of some interesting social events, to include attendance with King Charles the Second. McKenzie's father, the Earl of Burscough, had insisted his eldest son went at haste to further his social network in London, and receive a rare introduction to the King. He had remonstrated against any objection Robert raised, as meeting with high level politicians was too good an opportunity to miss. This was especially pertinent as the King and Parliament were finally settling to some sort of working harmony together, for the first time since the head of King Charles's father had been parted from his body by the axe sixteen years previously. Without doubt, Pepys was, as Robert McKenzie suspected, very well connected.

But it wasn't the highwaymen that bothered him, he was a deft shot and strong with the sword, but the plague, still rampaging and virulent throughout the capital. There were indications of some respite in the number of new cases, and winter was fast approaching, but nevertheless he had to take real care and not mix with any plebs or paupers. Pepys had assured him that all means of protection of the Pepys household, family and servants had been thoroughly taken and that no member had fallen ill from the pestilence, so he agreed finally to go. Also he was now a relatively idle gentleman. As Pepys forewarned, the whole of Cambridge University did duly close until further notice, and all students were dispersed back to their homes. Some socialising of merit was therefore welcome. But he remained concerned about his friend Isaac Newton, who had returned to his home in Grantham. Although it must be said, Newton was not so ill at ease as expected. Rather he had been enthusing about his new discoveries in some strange, new mathematics he called fluxions, which Newton claimed would change the whole way planetary motions and navigation could be calculated.

The second driver, recruited in London, had insisted on the detour as the spillage of stinking mud, on the usual route between London and Woolwich, had grown vast and was now ten feet deep, full of faeces and other rotten offal thrown in daily, like a giant latrine, that had become impassable, even with the large wheels of the carriages. A man falling in would drown in the shit immediately, which is why they took a special ferry across the Thames upstream and were wending their way east again.

He had decided he would visit Newton on the way back, and sent news of confirmation when they had reached Nottingham. He would provide some additional funds to keep Newton's academic spirit and enquiring mind up. Newton had already written, indicating he had undertaken a wonderful light experiment with his damned prisms to show him. Lucinda was extremely interested in Newton's work, and her passionate persuasion was central to continuing a considerable largesse.

The drivers stopped for a minute to check their bearings on an old map. McKenzie got out and stretched his legs, his stomach was feeling quite sore with the rolling around of the damned carriage. He pulled out a small wooden box, inlaid with a fancy marquetry of pearl and coloured stones, and took out one of his new cigars. They had arrived, specially ordered by his father, from Seville in Spain, and endorsed by King Philip himself. It was, McKenzie thought, interesting that Seville had now become the centre of the booming tobacco trade, certainly a city he must visit as he had been told the women were dark and luscious, and looser than a deer on heat. He loaded his tinder pistol with gunpowder and lit up with a loud bang, as the drivers jumped out of their skin, thinking attack was imminent and finally he puffed away to his heart's content, a much needed respite from this travelling torture.

"Lord McKenzie, sir, may I suggest that you be careful with that device; it will attract brigands in this area and we are tired if forced to fight."

McKenzie looked around. Giles was right, and my God, this place was the absolute pits, all kinds of stinking matter thrown out of the windows and into the street. He was told by Pepys that his grand house had a running water system, brought down from a reservoir through elm and lead pipes but there was little sign of such civilised comforts here. He watched as two old women lugged pails of dirty water into the house opposite, and then on the other side, someone threw the contents of a chamber pot straight out of the window barely missing a passer-by. A fetid stench hung in the dank air. A pack of wild dogs ran past, slithering and skating in the mud, and voraciously leapt onto the rotting carcase of a dead horse, left in the gutter where it died outside the local inn. Not a place, either, he would dare venture into, eyeing the filthy pockmarked faces of a couple of dirty looking whores in ragged clothes lurking outside. He had heard London attracted so many people for work, but he had not seen such acute poverty, anywhere.

"Sir, we must go quickly. Jason says it is not good to stay here," Giles shouted as a rickety cart groaned and creaked to a halt about twenty yards up.

"Just wait man, what on earth is that?"

The light was fading but McKenzie could see it was piled up with at least twenty naked bodies, men, women, old and young, some children, their faces contorted and their bodies bent into grotesque shapes as the stench of putrefaction wafted downwind, causing him to retch up the contents of his stomach over the front wheel. The horses started to whinny. Three bedraggled old women, sores and dirt over their faces, emerged from the house alongside the cart, dragging the body of a young woman by the legs, no older than twenty. After dumping her into the gutter, they proceeded immediately with knives to cut off all her clothing and hack away fingers for rings and jewellery before slinging the mutilated and naked bloody corpse up on the pile. Wiping their hands they proceeded back into the house for more.

"Who for fuck's sake are those old hags Giles? They are like hideous vultures, preying on the dead. To whom do they answer? I will smite them dead with this sword."

Jason grabbed his arm. "No Lord McKenzie, you must not go near them, sir. They are appointed by the City of London, old women whose job is to tend to the plague's dead. Only they are allowed to do what they do. The bodies go to the giant pit in Chelsea. They are allowed to take any assets as recompense for their hideous duties, it is legal and sanctioned. Interfering will get you hanged, but most serious, you may easily catch the dreaded pestilence yourself. Please sir, get back into the coach, we must fly. This place is bad, look more bodies are being dragged out further up the street."

McKenzie gazed in fascinated horror as more carts pulled up near him, the yellow pus and oozing goitres from the freshly dead clearly visible, making him retch once more. He leapt into the carriage as the drivers whipped the horses into life and they sped off down the lane and out into the country onwards to Woolwich, only a half-hour away. He seriously pondered, as the roads levelled out to a pleasing flat and green stretch. There just had to be some kind of cure for this vile pestilence, but most importantly, what can someone of his means do for such dire poverty? He decided there and then, he would end his Cambridge university nonsense, and would enter Parliament as soon as possible. He had the rights of a nobleman, and he would do something useful, and fight injustice and poverty, improve the lot of these poor, working people. Perhaps meeting Pepys and the King would be fortuitous and even a hand of destiny was playing its part …

Following a warm handshake, a smiling Pepys led Robert McKenzie towards the impressive stone house, well detached from the others and with grounds and a stable block to the rear. His servants handled the extensive luggage from the carriage inside. Pepys's wife stood smiling at the entrance, but Pepys took him first to one side.

"Your drivers, Robert, can tend their horses and sleep in the barn, hay is plentiful. A tureen of meat pottage and jugs of whey will be provided and a warm brazier. 'Tis a cold night. I trust your journey was bearable?"

"For the first time, in a godforsaken place called Lambeth, I saw the effects of the plague in the streets. We kept well clear of the bodies but the whole thing troubles me. I would like to discuss some politics with you after dinner, if I may, Mr Pepys."

"I suspected you may, sir. Such discourse is welcomed. Yes, the pestilence still prevails everywhere, although much less in Woolwich, but rumour has it that cases are indeed slowing down. But I fear the only way to remove the scourge is by fire. The whole of London would need to burn down and eliminate the evil. Please, call me Samuel in our private quarters, no need for formality here. I have a meeting arranged tomorrow at the naval headquarters and an inspection of a new ship to trade with the West Indies. The King will be in attendance. I pray you will accompany me as my honoured guest, sir? Then you will be able to avail yourself of some important contacts, who will ease your way to more influential power, my Lord Robert. Now, let me take you to meet my wife Elizabeth. I married her when she was a young girl of fifteen and love her dearly, but my wife is of a fiery temperament. If she mentions Betty Lane, of Westminster Hall, please allude that you have never heard of such a name."

"I understand Samuel. Truly Elizabeth is a handsome woman if I may say. And your children?"

"You may say Robert, but sadly we have not conceived. She has deep sadness over that. I fear the removal of the stone when I was young has prevented me such pleasures. Ah ... Elizabeth dearest, may I introduce you to my friend Lord Robert McKenzie of Burscough in Lancashire. He has come all this way for a visit; we must treat our honoured guest well."

Elizabeth stepped forward. "Come, Lord McKenzie, let me show you to our guest room. I have prepared it myself, and I think you will enjoy the new paintings on the walls. We have even procured some splendid pictures by Diego Velázquez himself, direct from the court of King Philip in Castille. You will find fresh linen and towels, a jug of mead and hot water to freshen up. Dinner is being prepared for seven thirty; you may wish to rest for an hour or two?"

"Thank you madam, I will indeed — the journey in those wagons is not conducive to much sleep."

He commenced the long climb up the winding stairs behind Samuel's wife. Her long dress skirted over the stairs to reveal a neat and comely shaped ankle. Various thoughts percolated into his mind when she had first looked at him with those beautiful doleful eyes. There was, he reflected, much complexity in this household to be sure ...

The morning was bright and cheerful on the dock. Pepys was busy scuttling along the quayside, chatting to all and sundry. The landing bay teemed with fashionably dressed noblemen and gentry of all kinds, as Pepys shook hands and discoursed from one to the next. A comely and well dressed young woman walked alongside him and very close, arm in arm. A strange set up, Robert McKenzie wondered, to be sure. He gazed at the new ship, with gleaming brass cannons poking through the sides and wallowing gently in the dock. Its tall masts were loaded with hanging ropes and the brown decks newly painted with tar and wattle. The sailors were gadding about with buckets and artefacts of all means to put the finishing touches to the decking and rigging.

He had been quite disturbed by the odd incident of the night, waking in a sweat on his side to find his cock, hard and willing, gripped and manipulated until he came with force into the bedding, a dream of substance like his youth to be sure, except it was no dream. As he turned and rubbed his eyes in a daze, a tall woman in a flimsy night dress tiptoed quietly to the door turned and smiled back. Those eyes, they had it. She was he was sure, the lady of the house. Over bacon breakfast no indication of anything untoward materialised, all smiles and bonhomie, as Pepys whistled happily with the news in his paper that the Dutch trade war was going blindingly well for the British who had sunk a further troupe of ships off Amsterdam and taken some key trading ports.

Pulling up his collar, he felt the breeze up the Thames had become quite chilling. McKenzie suddenly realised a tall gentleman, of well manicured disposition with a natty moustache and fine clothes was standing beside him, also gazing at the frenetic activity on the quayside.

"The work has made fine progress sir," the man remarked nonchalantly to McKenzie, who had pulled out a cigar and offered one back to him.

The man examined the cigar carefully. "Thank you, sir; I will keep such a fine smoke for later at dinner. You are certainly a purveyor of worthy and selective trade, my friend."

"Indeed sir," McKenzie replied, warmly. "The war effort being made to secure England as the rightful centre of all traded goods, and eviscerate those Dutch interlopers is sound and just. The King of this fair land has it correct; I fully support such a move. We will win this second war and quickly that's for sure."

His companion laughed. "I do believe we will. And your name sir? Are you connected with this new venture we see before us? The Half Moon is certainly a fine ship, with new designs which I think I have influenced a little within the Admiralty."

Robert McKenzie smiled. "Indeed. I am Lord Robert McKenzie of Burscough, sir, and you are?"

"Lord McKenzie, of course, I knew your father many years back. A man wisely committed to the cause of the time, we were very grateful."

McKenzie looked back puzzled. "The cause? I pray your forgiveness, but I am perplexed, sir. Sorry, I didn't catch your name?"

"I didn't give it but it is Stuart, Charles Stuart. I masquerade occasionally as King of this realm as well."

The colour drained from Robert McKenzie's face. He felt a flush and chill simultaneously flood through his body as he took a swift and highly gestured bow, lowering and sweeping his cap. "Your Royal Highness, I beseech thee with profuse apologies for my gross stupidity."

The King roared laughing. "I tease you Lord McKenzie. Pepys over there told me you were here. I would request a small favour. I now have to do my duties and launch this fine vessel." He beckoned towards a stack of barrels of molasses and a young girl, no older than her mid teens, walked from behind and then stepped forward nervously towards them. "Would you please take care of my ... err ... niece. She will bring you later to the celebration dinner at the Admiralty. I have just assigned urgent duties to Pepys, so he will not be going. He must immediately order more provisions and muskets for the war effort. We will win this war as you say, sir. I would like you to meet

Lord Devering, Parliamentarian and Second Lord of the Admiralty, a distinguished seafaring man but advancing now in years, his father was instrumental in the Armada battle. I wish to set up a separate Board of Trade; the venture needs some young blood. Ah … I must go. A pleasure to meet you Lord McKenzie, please give my regards to the Earl."

Four of the King's Guards had appeared and escorted Charles Stuart briskly to the ship's gangway to join a coterie of assorted functionaries and noblemen. As they departed, McKenzie felt an arm slip lightly into his and looked down at the smiling face of the King's niece. She had long, blond hair and stunning features, her face carefully made up and her nails manicured. Her teeth were remarkably white. She buttoned her coat from the breeze and tucked in her scarf tightly around her neck. McKenzie was mesmerised by her beauty and poise for someone so young.

"Good morning Lord McKenzie, 'tis a cold air around us to be certain." She had the slightest lilt of origin from the Principality of Wales, which quite perplexed McKenzie. "My father is thankful for your kind escort. He has given me some tasks to fulfil on your behalf, if I may. My name is Bella, Lady Bella Scott of Haverfordwest, my Lord."

"Your father?"

Bella blushed gently. "My mother is Lucy Barlow, she has acquaintance of my father for a very long time, I was born in the Hague, indeed I must in theory be Dutch, which provides my father with much merriment, given we are now at war with them! You will of course be discrete, my Lord."

"Of course, Lady Scott," McKenzie replied thinking immediately of Queen Catherine and the many rumours that the King had a personal life, even more divisive than Pepys. That certainly was the likely case, but such was the plight of most noblemen. Obviously and unusually, the King was happy to acknowledge and support his varied offspring. But McKenzie couldn't get her beauty from his mind, as she pointed southwards to the end of the quay and they walked towards a splendid carriage nearby, sumptuous with padded red seating and a tier of six well kept black horses, a far cry from his own beleaguered carriage which needed upgrading in comparison.

"So Lady Scott, what interests you the most in this world? Please excuse my presumptions, but I am an inquisitive man by nature."

She laughed a gentle sound, and her eyes danced with fascination of the handsome man whose arm she now gripped tightly. Mr Pepys was right; this Robert McKenzie already appeared much more acceptable than any of the knaves at court she had been introduced to. And, he was clean shaven and smelled sweet for a change; his clothes were fresh and fashionable, certainly a man of standing and taste. At sixteen she was already one of the few in her inner circle who was not yet married, and was intending to stay that way, but perhaps …

"I too, sir, am inquisitive and love to learn. My studies are presently taking me far into astronomy and mathematics, as well as natural philosophy and religion. I live at Oxford with my mother and have regular tutelage by the Honourable Robert Boyle, Fellow of the new Royal Society that my father has recently chartered. Do you know that Mr Boyle has already proven that Adam and Eve were Caucasian? And his experiments on light with diamonds, I am privileged to work with him on."

McKenzie was startled. He stopped and stared into her deep set, blue eyes. "Please, Lady Scott, call me Robert. You mean the actual Boyle, discoverer of Boyle's Law and proponent of the gaseous experiments?"

"Of course, and you may call me Bella." She giggled momentarily then continued with a serious expression. "The essential mathematics is easy but I need more powerful tools to describe the changing fluid flows better. I have been hard at work on such things, but presently remain baffled, but am confident of a breakthrough when I understand more."

McKenzie contemplated for a moment. "I think, Bella, I may know someone who is on to this, please leave it with me," as he helped her carefully into the carriage, noting her temptingly slim waistline. But more important, he knew, for the first time, after all his wasted energies on constant debauchery and licentiousness with vacuous, and flippant, aristocratic females and drunken whores that he had unexpectedly met a woman with the match and standing of his beloved Lucinda, his twin sister. And he was already in love. Lady Bella Scott had a fire in her eyes, lit with a burning intellect and fierce ambition. He sat beside her, feeling the warmth of her lithe body close, and drew breath quietly, his ardour rising fast. The drivers whipped the horses and they set off at a smooth pace towards the Admiralty.

"I look forward to that Robert. Now when we arrive, please stick close by me and we shall land you with the most advantageous seating, so you may pursue discussions of an appropriate political persuasion over dinner and port with the King and others of influence, once the ladies of course retire."

Bella was undoubtedly, McKenzie mused, a remarkable and sophisticated young woman. His father had been correct. This trip was becoming an opportunity he could only have dreamed of. He would though need to act quickly. Suitors for Lady Bella must be aplenty. He would have to decide and secure his legacy and the future generations of McKenzies with a wife worthy of such a challenge, and deep in his heart he was sure there was indeed such a thing as love at first sight. His long-held scepticism and contempt for such talk had vanished, although he would desire Lucinda's approval first …

A good hearty meal had been hungrily devoured by the two friends and a second flagon of strong home-made ale placed on the table. A roaring log fire burned cheerfully in the huge grate, in front of which the large hulk of Caesar, the family dog, a massive mongrel wolfhound, snored contentedly, having finished off the remains of bones of lamb thrown upon the floor for him. The three had been out on a successful hunt together, riding over the vast, flat fields surrounding the modest manor house at Woolsthorpe in Lincolnshire, having caught numerous rabbits and game to be boiled for lunch the next day. Robert McKenzie already felt light-headed and quite giddy as Isaac Newton's mother busied herself with serving them the large portions of apple pie and farm cream to finish. It was, for her, a pleasant change to feed men again, following her recent second widowhood and the unexpected return home of her only son Isaac, following the announcement of plague in Cambridge. She looked contentedly at Isaac, who scribbled manically on the table, trying to convince his new friend the very pleasant Lord McKenzie, of the importance of those silly experiments he was conducting incessantly in the farm buildings at the rear. Although money was tight, she was glad to return to farming after the death of her second husband, an evangelical vicar, whose wifely duties she had not been cut out for. The sheep were now doing well for them but she had given up on persuading her son to become a farmer, his inclination was zero. Certainly, at The King's School, Isaac had shown much academic promise and talent, but he was such a shy boy. Whatever would become of him was a nagging worry.

"Here, Robert, finish that flagon of ale, then you must come out to the yard and see my latest experiment in the building yonder. It will astound you, believe me."

"Okay, anything for some peace and quiet, but my head swirls. I see your love and capacity for strong ale remains undiminished. But before we depart into your laboratory, I must tell you of my lovely sister Lucinda. Verily, you would like her." He winked surreptitiously at Hannah, Newton's mother, who raised her eyebrows glumly. Young ladies she had also long given up on.

"And why would that be?" Newton replied, quite disinterested, as he assembled a collection of pieces of glass from a box under the table.

"She is an ardent student of astronomy, Isaac. Her talent with mathematics is good enough for Cambridge, far better than mine. But father deplores the idea of women being educated, sadly. His generation are so out of touch with the needs of modern England. Lucinda would very much like a copy of your recent binomial theorem discovery, such a neat method of expansion of a series, formerly so clumsy after the cubes."

"And, it is pleasing you are in touch with my work, but I will provide your sister with a copy," Newton muttered, rummaging for a final piece of equipment.

"I am. Lucinda shares a love of the findings of Galileo with Lady Bella too, although I worry still about the influence of those damned puritans around, still trying to trumpet such scientific facts as heresy and having people denounced. But Bella assures me that the King is intent on removing their offensive power quickly. Already, would you believe, the theatres are reopening in London after his recent decrees. That is progress, my friend. Culture, the arts and common sense will win out over those religious bigots and fundamentalists. Indeed, we unfortunately have on our land, a firebrand of an Abbot named Rimmer who resides at the old Orsbrick Priory. He hates our family because we have enlightenment and don't adhere to medieval religious views. My father once called him a fool to his face, although equally provides Rimmer with safety and anonymity from the King's Guards."

Newton looked up and became thoughtful. A faraway look engulfed his expression. "I agree with you Robert. But pray, who is Bella? You see so much cunny I can't keep up with them all," and immediately blushed. He had forgotten his mother was sat near the fire. She stroked Caesar, coughed and quietly left for the kitchen.

McKenzie smiled. "Lady Bella Scott is now the true love of my life, Isaac. I have firmly decided. I will visit her soon at Oxford and ask for her hand … I can't say how royal is her connection at present, but let me assure you it is very secure. Her beauty and science intellect are uncanny my friend, the equal of my illustrious sister. Bella wishes to know of your strange work on fluxions. She is tutored directly by Boyle and helping him with further experiments on the fluids."

Newton stood up, his face bright red. "Boyle? Did you say Boyle? He is a close associate of that idiot Hooke who maintains the most preposterous ideas of light consisting of waves," he thundered. "By three in the morning that night, I had veritably worn him down; Hooke had not the stamina to press his case any longer. I cannot yet pass your lady friend my work on fluxions, the mathematics is so radical and I need to pursue more refinement. I passionately believe my work will change the face of calculation forever and that imbecile Hooke will not get near it. I will see that man cursed into Hell, he is so foul of temper and goodwill for other's theorems." He pulled himself together and forced a smile, patting McKenzie on the shoulder. "Come now, and see my work with prisms, I will set it up quickly, the candles are ready. You too Caesar, come on both of you."

McKenzie sighed as they all trotted to the farm building, then he remembered, rummaging in his pocket. He had something to show Isaac too, a wondrous and rare sight, an opinion of which he would seek. "I'll be with you in a second; I just want to fetch something from my room to show you."

"Okay but be quick, I can't always reproduce this effect."

McKenzie squinted at the large, clear glass prism on the table which had been laboriously ground to precise angles by Newton, who then pulled across heavy, black curtains on a rail around them so that only the bright light of the special candle flickering behind could be seen. Caesar, bored, had loped off outside to his kennel. Newton then placed a blackened board with a slit before the prism and they both stared at the profusion of a full spectrum of colour, clear and bright on the white paper, emitted from one edge.

"You have produced a genuine rainbow, my friend," McKenzie exclaimed. "That is truly amazing. I have not seen such a beautiful thing so simply made."

"That's not the end of it, watch carefully."

Newton placed a similar prism to intersect with the spectrum and a faint ray of candlelight could be seen emerging from its edge.

"By heavens Isaac, what does this mean? I feel witness to a fundamental discovery. Your findings, sir?"

"Indeed Robert. What I believe I have shown is that light is composed of the constituted colours of the rainbow, which obviously have different properties which the prism is able to recognise, split up and reconstitute. I call the phenomenon refraction. I conclude with a simple theory of colours my friend. Your jacket is red because the material absorbs all these colours in the light but reflects just the red part, or any other colour you see. Black objects absorb all the colours and reflect none. As for white? Such objects reflect all of these colours; it is logically sound, my theory, is it not? I realised that oaf, Hooke, was already onto this too with his work on telescopes but I intend to beat him to publication. Yonder, the clock says time for another beer."

"I'm done with the beer tonight, Isaac, I don't know where you put it, and I must rest my weary bones. But this result has, I know, huge implications for all kinds of further study. I will see to it, you will have the funds here to pursue more experiment along with your mathematics. A yeoman's income is not sufficient for such complex contemplation. I have the means and want to help. Heaven knows how long the Cambridge University will be shut. The pestilence sadly continues unabated, but Woolsthorpe will now be your new laboratory, properly funded my friend."

Newton rose from his seat and with an uncharacteristic grin hugged Robert hard. "Thank you, I didn't want to ask but I am so grateful. I have been sick with worry about the funds, my mother is just making enough for us to live and board here at the farm."

"You are welcome, but before we go I must show you this rare thing, which I acquired whilst in London with Bella. We were relaxing at dinner in Pepys's house and he had invited a strange young man, no older than eighteen, but with such amazing artistic talents by the name of Grinling Gibbons."

"A peculiar name I must say."

"Yes, the man is Dutch. Both Pepys and Bella, interestingly, have strong Dutch connections. The man is an odd individual, but already a genius wood carver and stonemason and had brought with him all manner of amazing and intricate decorative Baroque garlands and other small plaques for our perusal and opinion. We were truly entertained all evening. Pepys was so taken, he intends to introduce Gibbons to the King, try and get him some commissions. However at the end of the evening, Gibbons pulled this artefact out of a box, and insisted it needed a new owner ... and offered it to me immediately as a gift."

McKenzie, opened up his satchel and took out a large heavy object, wrapped up in oilskin. He unfolded it carefully on the table, as Newton lit some more candles.

"What on earth is this thing?" McKenzie exclaimed, gently rubbing his finger over the surfaces. "Tis like your very own prism, but the colour and markings are so strange and it is so polished smooth and finely cut, as precise as the work you have done yourself on glass."

They both stared mystified at the peculiar pale crimson hue of the translucent, prism shaped glassy solid. The tiny flecks inside were permeating throughout, like copper but shimmering iridescent in the flickering candlelight.

Newton picked it up carefully, to look more closely with his magnifying glass. "I do declare, Robert, the background of this manifestation and its origins defeat me. Is it natural or man-made? Certainly there has been an uncanny skill used in creating the shaping."

He pulled out his callipers and made a careful measure of the side angles. "Perfect symmetry and the prism angle is correct to ten seconds, even I can't achieve that exactitude. And so very strange, the body generates slight warmth to the touch, like it is a living organism, very strange indeed." He looked up, serious and contemplative. "You say this Gibbons artist was odd? Please define odd? Sometimes people say I am odd ... but I'm just curious about the world. I merely stand on the shoulders of giants already passed."

McKenzie stared back and nodded. Newton occasionally had the profoundest of language when he wanted. "The young man Gibbons was nervous. He spoke often in a faltering tone and his concentration was poor except for when we attended to the wood carvings, then he became highly animated. I know artists are eccentric but I caught him shiftily observing me, and then looking at Bella and back again throughout the evening at dinner, saying nothing. I found the man somewhat unnerving, but a youth of course and probably not yet mature in mind or body. Bella said she had known him since a child in Holland. He intimated that its origins were likely Mediterranean and then mumbled that it must never under any circumstances be broken ... that the whole object must forever remain intact ... but he didn't expound on why or the consequences, but that I must have it for good fortune. It certainly looks pretty. What happens if we shine a light through it I wonder? Will it affect your spectrum Isaac?"

Newton looked pensive for a moment and replaced his plain glass prism with the crimson one and increased the lighting fivefold, carefully replacing the shielding. The light beam clearly went in - but nothing came out. No matter how much light was used or how the crimson prism was oriented, the beam disappeared.

"This is not an expected result," Newton proclaimed loudly, angry with the outcome which he couldn't explain. "The light is absorbed into the body of the prism but never returns, yet the prism remains the same colour, which is not black. This is an outlier to my theorem. Nature, dear Robert, always likes to keep us on our toes. But I will dwell on the matter, believe me my friend. I will concentrate hard on it."

"Enough excitement for one night methinks. I must attend to my bed before I am forced to drop here onto the floor. Your mother makes a very strong beer."

Newton slapped him on the back. "You'll get used to it. Anyway, tomorrow we ride into Grantham first thing with your carriage; my mother wishes to visit my sickly aunt and she will stay for a week. She has cooked and stored a cupboard full of pies for me, and I will show you my old school too before you depart. I can walk back. I love the solitude across the fields but will stop at the Dabbling Duck for refreshment on the way home."

They headed back into the house, McKenzie whistled, thinking fondly of his beautiful Bella at Oxford and decided to write to her before sleep. Caesar came loping behind and spied two large, brown rats lurking near the privy. He shot off into the blackness after them, a cacophony of growling and screams emitted. On his return, Newton remonstrated and threw a pail of water over his bloodied head.

As they prepared for bed, Newton casually picked up a large letter, freshly delivered at dusk and left on the table. He shouted up to his friend who was rummaging for his flannel night-wear and bed cap.

"Robert, come down here, there is something been delivered for you, with urgent scrawled over the front."

As McKenzie stumbled down the stairs, his gaze fell on the crimson prism which Newton was carefully wrapping up with the oil cloth. His eyes were indeed playing tricks with the tiredness upon him, as he was sure he discerned peculiar and hazy spectral phosphorescences flickering like marsh gas surrounding it. The air suddenly gave him an odd chill, despite the remnants of the logs still red and glowing in the hearth. He rubbed his eyes. No sign now of any glow as he picked up the letter, whilst Newton shifted the large bolts across the door, and carefully unpicked the wax seal. The stamp revealed it had been sent from home. His face turned white with horror and dismay at what he read and he threw the parchment down fiercely with a cry.

"Robert, what on earth is the matter? Do the contents pertain of severe news?"

McKenzie was in bad distress. Tears ran down his cheek. "I must return home, now immediately, there is no time to lose. Please unlock the door, I must rouse my drivers and prepare the horses for immediate departure. Where is my pistol?"

Alarmed, Newton slid back the bolts and McKenzie shot out of the door over to the barn. Newton picked up the letter, written two days previously.

December 10 1665, Orsbrick Hall
My dearest Robert

By the time you read this all may be lost. I have escaped the turmoil and managed to get this letter away by our black crow messenger and fast cart. There has been a serious riot in Orsbrick at our newly opened Hall, incited by that evil Abbot, Rimmer, who, with a group of friars, roused a mob from Burscough and denounced us as pagans, witches and unbelievers, citing Lucinda and her astronomy and demanding the same justice as Galileo.

I am so sorry, my son, but your sister is gone, burned alive at a stake in our cellar with her assistant by Rimmer's own hand before we returned from a hunt. Your father and his men drove them out and are barricaded in, fighting the mob with musket and pistol from the windows. I am trying to rouse the local Guard but fear it will be too late. Those evil men of the Priory want your father alive for a full hanging. Please come quickly, but take great care my son.
Your dearest mother.

Newton grimaced with fear and rage. He ran up the stairs and picked up McKenzie's bags, shoving in as many personal belongings as he could, and carried them to the door, as McKenzie re-entered, his cloak drawn around him and his face haggard and white. The carriage and the horses were outside, agitated and whinnied gently, steam rising from their mouths as the drivers pulled the rest of the luggage on board. McKenzie grabbed the letter off the table.

"I must be off now, my good friend. Thank goodness it is a clear night with near full moon. We will make good progress; I shall sleep as well as possible on the journey."

He jumped into the carriage and the horses were whipped. Newton shouted back as the giant wheels slowly turned, Caesar at his feet looking equally glum.

"Take care Robert and good luck, I am so, so sorry. Write me when you can." He ran alongside the departing wagon and threw in a large bag of pies and a flagon of mead. "Your need of sustenance this long journey is far greater than mine, I wish you well."

McKenzie forced a smile and a wave and they were gone, mud flying into the sky.

Back in the kitchen, Newton looked at the table and cursed. Robert McKenzie had left behind his precious crimson prism. He would get it sent on forthwith, despite the costs.

Chapter Five

A smiling Victoria unlocked the large oak double doors and showed them straight into the ballroom. Abby and Lynton sighed loudly in amazement. Hanging from the ceiling were four magnificent chandeliers, found from a local antiques shop and fully restored. Poised majestically from the high ceiling, they were all sympathetically wired up with modern but authentic electric candle light bulbs rather than being hosts to the former fire hazard originals. The ceiling, whose original magnificent ornate divisions had been painted over by Uncle William in a dull, uniform green, had been redecorated back to its former glory. The intricate and raised plaster covings were delicately covered in a mottled, dark cream, surrounding a series of pale duck-blue rectangles.

Abby gasped as she inspected the twelve foot, reddish-grey velvet drapes which voluptuously surrounded the massive six bay windows at the far end, and matched the side walls to cover the arched floor to ceiling windows fully. Unusually patterned and speckled red and cream rich period wallpaper adorned the walls, and the huge marble mantelpiece and fireplace had been freshly renovated and cleaned spotless. The old, worn carpeting had been lifted away and removed to reveal a beautiful and now polished dark, Italian tile floor, in excellent condition. The black Steinway baby grand piano, which Abby and Victoria had found forlornly resting with cloth covers in one of the bedrooms, had been carefully brought down the wide staircase, and was sat in its obvious place, in front of the windows on the raised semicircular floor, between two grey, fluted pillars. The broken wall lights had all been replaced and new ones added, providing a fantastic lighting effect along the side. Apart from the piano, the room was empty.

Julian pointed up to the ceiling. "We were really lucky actually with those. These original 1910 chandeliers had been lying in the back of Rustin's Antiques in Ormskirk for years. Nobody wanted them so we bought them with a bit of bargaining for a song … well relatively speaking."

He looked at Victoria who grimaced. Abby could sense that relatively meant a lot, and she knew money was becoming tight, especially as Ahrendolie, Victoria's former refinery employer, had suddenly gone into an abrupt administration, and the rest of her agreed redundancy lump sum was withheld to pay off the angry Dutch bank creditors. She really must do something to help. Victoria had to last the next twelve months, but stubbornly would not accept any financial help from Lynton, who had generously waved his cheque book on numerous occasions.

Julian continued. "Given the height and weight, Kacper and I used an old medieval crane and winch technique to lift the chandeliers up onto the ceiling, after we restored them in my new workshop here."

"Kacper?" Abby asked, puzzled.

"Yes, he's one of my loyal Polish tenants, a trained heritage building decorator and restorer and an amazing worker. I would never have finished without him. Eastern and Central Europe, especially Poland, have been much more steadfast in maintaining their old building craft and conservation skill bases, much of which is disappearing in the UK because of those damned stupid Further Education Colleges, who bow solely to the modern and unskilled training diktats of the influential house building lobby. All they're interested in is easy money, wherever it comes from, not losing a precious local skill base forever when the oldies die out."

Lynton laughed. "Like you, you mean! I sense a soapbox coming on. But how did you get this tile floor to look so original, like new? Hey Abby, I reckon you and I can really do the Charleston and Tango here?"

"Didn't need much, once I pulled that worn carpet and revealed a treasure of a base then …"

Victoria cut him off. She knew that Julian would happily drone on all afternoon about plaster, varnish and electrics if let. The food was ready. She had actually cooked special Greek kebabs, with her own seasoning for a change, definitely as good as Abby's best. "So you two really have been practising then? Preparing for a little showing off at your wedding breakfast are we as usual?" she said with a hint of cynicism, and jealousy because Abby had always been a far better dancer.

Abby blushed and grabbed Lynton's hand. "His fault chuck. He insisted on paying for a few dancing lessons and I must confess, this man, although you wouldn't guess it, is remarkably light on his feet. Anyway we'll have to rally the troops somehow to enjoy themselves and allay all the moans and groans about the celebrations being on Christmas Day."

"Yeh, my quasi-aristocratic upbringing again, I'm afraid. Formal ballroom dance was de rigueur when I was a kid." Lynton replied. "Hey I can smell some great food. And I have a surprise for everyone to be revealed when we eat."

They walked towards the dining table. Victoria looked sheepish and softly mumbled, "Mmm ... so have we. Julian can you take Lynton down to the cellar and bring a couple of bottles of that 1982 claret up please? Abby, let's get that food on the table and don't you start squealing, I can occasionally cook as well as you, okay ... almost."

Sitting back from the table, they were all quiet and stuffed, especially following the extra helpings of the early Christmas plum pudding, an old McKenzie recipe, which Victoria had found in one of the chests.

Abby poured out tea into the china cups. "So Vikki, what's your surprise then?"

"Me first," Lynton interrupted, pulling out a wodge of tickets from his jacket pocket and waved them around. "And before anyone says a word, this time I won't take no for an answer. This is my treat and we've made a ton of money this month from Chinese land investors. This, ladies and gentlemen, is our joint honeymoon in my hand. See ... I knew nobody had thought about what happens immediately after the wedding. This is a guided trekking holiday through the

Brazilian Amazon jungle for a week. We all deserve a treat after the hard work."

The air became noticeably muted. The silence could have been sliced up with a carving knife.

"Really?" Victoria stuttered, breaking the deafening lack of sound. "Oh Lynton, what a wonderful thought — Julian and I do appreciate it. Abby, I can see from your face this is as much of a surprise to you."

"You bet," Abby replied, glaring at Lynton for not telling her first. She looked like she was about to immediately sound off.

Victoria had become subdued and thoughtful, and then with a glance at Julian, who was irritatingly staring down at his boots, she interrupted. "Lynton ... actually ... oh well, I'd better say it. I'm afraid, very sadly, we ... well me ... err can't accept your kind offer of trekking in a hot jungle because ... we're expecting. I mean I'm expecting, like twins. I'm nearly two months."

"Vikki, that is so absolutely and fantastically wonderful," Abby shrieked excitedly, leaping up to give first her and then Julian a big hug. "You kept that one quiet," and ran through the mathematics in her fast brain. "Mmm ... I think I know when that might have happened," she added with a huge grin.

"Yes, I'm sure you do," Victoria blurted out laughing.

Julian blushed red to his boots, rubbing his glasses desperately. The memory of him and Victoria both naked, surreptitiously celebrating the firing up of the new central heating boiler, but in reality being watched first by ghostly peeping tom Mauveine and then by everyone else, was still etched in his mind.

Lynton shook Julian's hand warmly and kissed Victoria on both cheeks as Abby poured out three large glasses and one small glass of the prime claret for a celebratory toast.

"You really should have asked first Lynton, before booking," Abby remonstrated.

"Actually folks," he declared, with a grin. "I do have a back-up, just in case you didn't feel you had the energy for a deep jungle trek. I was particularly concerned about Abby being fit enough of course," he replied with a laugh, receiving another glare and a hard kick under the table. He pulled a second set of tickets out of his other pocket. "A thirteen night luxury cruise around the Caribbean. First we fly to Barbados, and then sail relaxed into and around St Lucia, Antigua and finally Jamaica, where you will enjoy, in the warm and pleasant weather, swaying palm trees, golden beaches and turquoise seas, with beautiful forests and teeming coral reefs. Plenty of sight-seeing, eating and drinking in the various coastal ports, and of course Julian, don't forget the rum, being a seafaring lover."

This time smiles all round immediately ensued. "Both trips are booked, but I can now cancel the Amazon with no charges. Arianna, the new Russian travel agent in Burscough, owes me a favour, like her lease and visa being sorted with no questions asked."

"That sounds fantastic, Lynton," Victoria replied. "Yes please, and thank you so much. We really could do with a good break. You can put your rucksack and hiking boots away now Abby."

Abby smiled and mouthed menace playfully back to Lynton.

"Yes, thanks a lot Lynton, we really appreciate that," Julian said. "In fact talking of rum, I have something interesting I found last week in the other cellar, let's just go and have a look …"

Abby got up and cleared away the dishes into the kitchen whilst Victoria loaded them into the washer. She spoke tentatively. "I can see money is really tight, Vikki. Lynton is very happy to give you both a loan to tide you over, especially now your Dutch pay-off has gone up in smoke."

"No, thanks Abby, we'll manage somehow. We've just had to spend more than we originally estimated, getting everything ship-shape to live here comfortably. Uncle William lived a very spartan existence. And now all the arrangements for the wedding and a luxury honeymoon too. Honestly, Lynton has been generous enough already. The advance from the trust and more has unfortunately well gone on the renovation and paying for the extra labour. We just have to see out the next twelve months and live here come what may, then problems should be over. Lynton's a lovely man actually, now his true self is coming out. Anyway … your turn next!"

Abby looked uncomfortably away. "I'm really pleased for you both, honestly I am. But Judy is still not well, although she's getting out now; we've been going for long walks each morning. I'm determined to make her better."

Vikki pondered and said no more. "I see you've brought the dresses. Whilst those two sailors drink the rum barrel dry, let's go and check our fittings, hopefully for the last time. I shouldn't expand any more in the next three days should I?"

Abby cackled. "I don't think so, but I wouldn't want to do this in six months."

Morning of the 25th December and the harmonious bells of Burscough Parish Church were pealing loudly. How Abby had persuaded the ringers, the whole choir and even the organist to turn up on Christmas Day nobody knew, although some free kebab nights at the Red Lion had likely changed hands. Victoria and Abby looked splendid in their brilliant white linen and silk dresses. Lydia's dress, which Abby wore, was overlain with all kinds of intricate flowers and patterning, Lydia, the artist, having originally been at work. And whilst Mauveine's dress was plainer, Victoria, all made up, looked equally stunning. The males, they hoped, were safely at their seats and looking respectable.

Julian, they learned, had been particularly worse for wear in the morning, having been thrown into Sefton Park boating lake by his Polish tenants and Lynton. This followed a heavy intake of stag night frivolities on Christmas Eve, which started at the Ship and Mitre in Liverpool with the best Captain Morgan's demerara rum. Kacper and Roland, Lynton's new law practice partner, had offered to be the two best men and they all finished the evening, a heady mix of lawyers and construction workers, celebrating Polish style, dancing arm in arm down Dale Street, with vodka bottles tucked into their trousers, and huge sausages draped over their necks, before being cautioned by the police. Luckily, Lynton still had enough legal wit and working intellect to dissuade the police sergeant of any further need for action in the direction of the jail, as they hastily hauled Julian away muttering drunken obscenities of a fascist dictatorship running the City Council and the Police Board.

"Here comes Ali, his timing is always impeccable … when I threaten him nicely of course," Abby whispered to Victoria, as they sat demurely in the Rolls Royce outside. Ali had been Abby's kebab house boss and owner in Rotterdam. A Christian Orthodox Turk, he had graciously offered to give both of them away.

"You first Vikki. Listen, we're on, they've just started the wedding march. Once you're at the altar, Ali nips out the side and comes back for me and we repeat it. Fun, aren't they, these double weddings? I'm quite excited are you?"

"Of course," she replied grinning happily. Ali opened the door. The booming of the organ resonated through the open doors, and he held his hand to gently help Vikki out. They could see a large congregation had gathered inside, but from where heaven knows. Fortunately the earlier drizzle had subsided.

"You look wonderful Vikki," Ali remarked, "and you too Abby, although you should have got tanned up on my machine first."

Abby put her tongue out at him playfully; he'd seen her nude on that machine often enough in the past. She whispered quickly to Victoria. "Judy is there with Angela and the rest of the Red Lion team. I bought her a lovely outfit which she chose herself in Zara. Fingers crossed, but I feel normality is coming back."

Victoria put her arm deftly into Ali's, which felt strange, and for the first time for a long time, she momentarily thought about her father and wished that he had actually been there and walked her down the aisle. He hadn't always been such a weird oddball, especially when she was a child. But Ali certainly had an unexpected poise and sophistication in his splendid morning suit which matched the occasion. His new and gorgeously sultry Lebanese wife, Nelva, had changed him dramatically.

Taking a deep breath, Victoria turned to Ali, arm in arm and smiled. "Let's go, I'm ready."

As the two couples emerged from the ancient church, the sun finally peeked out from the clouds and lots of photographs were taken whilst confetti was being thrown everywhere. Victoria, still the ardent and staunch science atheist, was not comfortable sat inside a church, but watching Abby totally entranced, she played along and made the effort. The entire service became very special. Aunt Eveline, her voice firm and clear, gave a distinguished eulogy to Uncle William and her father Jack, Aunt Eveline's two twin brothers who were the last members of the McKenzie family to have attended the local church. Finally, with Gerald playing a moving solo cello version of 'Ave Maria' they signed the marriage register together.

A number of children were running about shrieking loudly amongst a lot of hubbub as people gathered in groups to watch and wish them well. Apart from their forty invited guests, mainly friends including Julian's two sisters, Abby's brother and some distant relatives of

Lynton, at least a hundred other locals unexpectedly turned up from around the parish, having heard that a McKenzie family wedding from Orsbrick was taking place for the first time in a hundred years.

Abby looked around but there was no sign of Eva anywhere. On the one hand she was glad but on the other she knew Victoria would be terribly disappointed. She did, though, see Marlies with a new girlfriend, so something had clearly moved on. Both were chatting happily to the Reverend Wellesby, alongside Victoria and Julian. Lynton was standing with Judy, talking to some of his family.

For some inexplicable reason, Abby tucked in her dress and decided to go back into the church, now silent and empty, for a quiet moment and carefully sat down on the hard wooden pew in the front. She gazed up at the reflecting and twinkling red, blue, green and yellow colours of the splendid stained glass medieval scene, lit boldly by the sun behind the alter. The air was still. A slight musty odour of damp furnishings and old prayer books permeated the air, when a rustle beside her made her jump as something touched her hand. She turned, expecting Lynton or the vicar, but instead was startled at the sight of Mauveine and Isi, smiling and sat right next to her, both in smart, nineteenth century Sunday best outfits. No purple shawl or riding gear this time, her long mousy hair neatly piled up into a bun. Abby turned fully to look, for the first time at Mauveine's entire face. She had such lovely, sharp features, exactly like Victoria, but with a small mole on her forehead.

Mauveine began to speak. Abby felt her mouth drop wide open in total disbelief. This was the first time

Mauveine's voice had been heard. She never thought that would have been possible. Mauveine's accent was a soft and distinctive Lancashire, not dissimilar to her own, but broader and very clipped.

"Don't worry Abigail, nobody can see us only you. We came for the whole service and it was lovely to see you and Victoria married, and our dresses fit you both perfectly. You both looked so stunning. Where are you going for your honeymoon? Victoria and Julian appear very excited."

"Err ... the Caribbean ... I mean the West Indies, for a cruise."

"Ah, that is a long journey. When does the ship set sail from Liverpool?"

"Plane actually?"

"A plane? Isi replied, his voice deep and rich.

Mauveine giggled. "He forgets he is not of this time sometimes, Abigail, please ignore him. In which case, Isi and I wish all of you a lovely time. Goodbye for now. But just one thing. One day, ahead in the future, Victoria will need to know what happened, Abigail. You must tell her when the moment is right, and you will know that moment. Promise me?"

"I do promise Mauveine."

Abby turned, hearing a clattering sound of footsteps behind, but when she looked back Mauveine and Isi had vanished. It was her brother Edward, with wife Eleanor behind pushing baby Luke, snug asleep in a buggy.

"Hey sis, who on earth were you talking to? Haven't started secret praying have you? I remember you used to solemnly say the Lord's Prayer twice every night when you were ten before you went to sleep."

"Yes and you were an idiot, even then at six and you haven't changed much. I was just humming that aria quietly to myself that Gerald played."

"Aye, as I remember you did have a good voice once in the choir. Anyway, everybody is heading back to this Orsbrick mansion which Vikki and Julian own. So get lively chuck, you have to lead the way."

She grinned and punched his arm playfully as they walked back out and jumped quickly into the Rolls Royce to head for Orsbrick Hall and then she could get changed into her flapper gear guaranteed to surprise even Victoria. She had designed and made her own 'little black dress' in honour of her deep admiration for and hero worship of Coco Chanel and her influencing liberation of women from the strictures of the Victorian era. She came up with a perfect replica of Coco's 1926 short drop-waist creation which shook the fashion world at the time, to be completed with topical pencilled in eyebrows and bright painted nails. A top up tan at Ali's would have been a good idea though.

The special, old Lancashire wedding breakfast and rapid-fire speeches and toasts progressed like clockwork and even the long awaited best man speech finale, delivered in a haltering Polish accent, made the guests roar with laugher at the antics of Julian on his stag night. Victoria held his hand tight and kissed him on the cheek, his glasses were being rubbed so much the lenses nearly dissolved away. Abby had organised an excellent outside caterer through the Red Lion, and once the tables were removed and the floor cleared, the jazz band arrived and the bar quickly set up in the adjoining room. The large ballroom easily accommodated the guests, now joined by the rest of the congregation as Victoria had announced outside the church that everyone was welcome to come in the afternoon, as they swelled the throng of revellers. The ballroom had the perfect atmosphere and she wanted it filled again, with people, laughter and fun, just as Uncle William had regularly done when Orsbrick Hall was the social mecca of West Lancashire during the 1920s. The sight of Abby and Lynton, dressed in their period gear, with everybody crowded around clapping them on dancing the Charleston to perfection, was worth every effort they had made to finish off the ballroom in time, and arrange the party which soon got into full swing ...

Late evening had finally crept upon them. Guests with children including Edward and Eleanor were ready to pack up and leave but Lynton and his lawyer friends and Julian's Polish tenants, with associated wives and girlfriends, were livening up for the karaoke disco, which would round off the evening Red Lion style, and finish whenever the last guests remained standing, which usually meant six in the morning. Orsbrick Hall fortunately was well detached. Julian was already belting out his variant of Robert Plant again, not a good sign.

Victoria sat down in the study, highly in need of some peace and quiet and a breather. She had helped Marlies and Joanna in with their overnight bags and laptop cases, both wanting to go to their room and rest.

Victoria had received a telegram, amazed that such things still existed, from Eva who wished her and Julian well. No mention of Abby, but Eva had to be with her ailing mother in Leipzig. She and Julian had managed to ensure fifteen bedrooms were in a state fit enough to sleep in and allocated them to special guests for the night. Eva's room was hastily reallocated to Ali and Nelva.

Staring half-heartedly at yesterday's newspaper, a voice shouted to her from the doorway. "Vikki have you seen Judy? I can't find her anywhere and I've been all over the house, just no sign of her for ages. Shit I hope she hasn't gone missing on me."

Victoria turned to see Abby, changed again into a smart red evening dress and six inch heels, but looking uncharacteristically disconcerted. "I saw her about an hour ago, actually. She was with that group of young lawyers and looked pretty happy to me. She's probably popped to the loo or maybe got a breath of air outside, it's frosty but clear. You worry about her too much Abby; she's fine I'm sure. After all Judy's twenty now and can please herself, can't she?"

Abby ignored Victoria. She had to find Judy, something wasn't right, she could feel it. She didn't know what it was but had learned now not to ignore her inner voice. "Yes, you're right Vikki; I'll just pop outside anyway. I could do with some air to be honest. Jesus, that disco is booming away in there and Julian has moved onto Black Sabbath at the microphone."

Victoria groaned. "Crikey, okay see you later. I'm just going to show Marlies her room."

Abby slowly opened the front door and crept out, her fur coat wrapped over her shoulders. The air was sharp but the wind had died down and the night was crystal clear. She stared at the myriad of stars twinkling brightly. The moon's profile half visible behind the roof line lit up everywhere around. The rest of the guests and visitors remained partying inside as she strolled between the rows of cars, feet crunching along the wide gravel driveway. She was grateful for some fresh country air, and headed towards the McKenzie family graveyard at the end of the house. She felt like a cigarette for some reason, although she gave up smoking many years back, along with the drugs. The security lights went on. It was then she noticed something huddled up next to Uncle William's grave. Still wary after encountering the last happening there, she walked forward tentatively and heard loud sobbing. She immediately recognised the coat. It was Judy, curled up into a ball, wailing and moaning uncontrollably on the ground; there was no time to go back for anyone.

She ran forward and called out loudly. "Judy, Judy, it's me, Abby. Everything is alright, you're safe, I'm coming, so don't worry, you're going to be fine."

On reaching her, Abby knelt down on her haunches and held Judy tightly. Violent shivers ran in waves in her arms. Judy looked up, her eyes wide and her stare manic, petrified, almost hysterical with fear, and clung to her like death. What on earth had happened?

"Please don't let them come for me, Abby. Please, they are truly so horrible, please Abby, keep them away, I can't bear it. Someone has to put those fires out quickly, the smell, those people are burning alive, oh my God Abby, keep them away."

Abby peered towards the blackness in the woods but could see or smell absolutely nothing. "You're fine now Judy, there's nothing here whatsoever, believe me. Whatever or whoever it was has vanished. Honestly, you're safe now I've found you." She stroked Judy's head buried in her chest, gently for a minute or two, as Judy's breathing slowly returned to normal and the sobbing finally stopped.

"Now," Abby said firmly. "Tell me exactly what you saw."

Judy nervously raised herself uneasily from the grass and pointed towards a small clump of ancient oak trees, further to the east of the main woodland. "I was just getting some air on my own; I'd been having a nice time with Reginald and Jarvis, and feeling fine when I heard a load of noise coming from over there. Curious, I walked towards the end of the house, when suddenly everywhere became enveloped in thick, acrid smoke. There was noise, lots of it, gunshots all around and screaming; people were shouting, men's and women's voices. I could see huge fires burning, great flames, leaping into the sky. I stood terrified, rooted to the spot, not knowing what on earth was happening. Then the most horrific thing imaginable happened …"

"What Judy? Go on. I'm listening."

"I saw people running, but they were not of this time, Abby. I know my periods of history very well. I could tell by the way they were dressed, they were poor people, wearing dirty, ragged clothes and holding pikes and staffs and axes. Some were monks in long brown robes, but there were also gentry, well dressed, on horseback and on foot, fleeing towards me, holding muskets and pistols, and firing back at the crowds. It looked like a reenactment of the English Civil War in the early seventeenth century, I saw one performed in Newark at school, and also I studied that period for A-level History so I'm sure. It was definitely during that timeframe. Then ... what I saw you would never believe ... only ever before in pictures, wood carvings you know ... I actually witnessed three women set alight, fully clothed and tied up to stakes, side by side in a bonfire. People were hysterical, shouting witches and denouncements. The women screamed hideously as their hair went on fire and their faces melted and the horrible stench of flesh and wood burning filled me with nausea. Nearby other people, badly beaten, naked and tied up, were being thrown down a well one by one, over there."

She took a breath and stopped, concentrating hard on how to describe the next scene. "I looked towards what the gentry were fleeing from; they were heading for the house, badly outnumbered by the mob. Another naked man, blood pouring from between his legs and wriggling, was being lowered, hanging on a rope from a tree branch. Then he was held upright, still alive, as those monks took out long knives and started slicing open his stomach, pulling out his intestines as he screamed for mercy. Finally they started to hack off his arms and his head dropped. I just watched someone being hung, drawn and quartered Abby, exactly like it was described in our textbooks. Some monks in the mob pointed towards me and shouted, 'get that other witch, burn her, burn her,' and they started running towards me. I ran into the graveyard here, stumbled and hid behind the two large stones. I could hear their voices getting nearer and nearer ... then you came. Oh Abby, what on earth has happened? Something absolutely awful took place here a long time ago, I'm sure of it. You believe me don't you? ... I trust you ... because I'm like you aren't I."

Abby, stared deeply into Judy's earnest face and realised instantly. She attuned her mind differently, concentrated and felt the signs for the first time. Then she remembered. Of course, Lynton once talked about his younger sister being psychic, although she had died in that terrible drowning accident at Brighton when they were young teenagers. Poor, poor Judy, who not only had the burden of being autistic but she had the 'gift' as well. It was obvious from her expression this was the first time Judy had told a living soul. She had likely hidden her secret from everyone, all those years as a child and a teenager, especially from her parents and school friends because she was convinced they would laugh at her even more, or decide she was definitely totally nuts, and have her locked up and sectioned.

"I believe you Judy, no you're not alone. Some of us have been born with a special ability ... to cross into different parallel universes and see and hear things others have no idea about. I do very much understand, I hadn't realised until now. I think you and I probably have differing wavelengths or communication patterns, which don't always interact or tune into the same periods of time. Which is why I haven't seen such terrible things myself, but I have seen other manifestations here, not bad things, but during a different time, Judy, later. It's nothing to worry about; they are only visions, ghosts of a time past which can't interact physically. You were there momentarily, as real as it could get and sometimes you will dream it too. The Civil War period in the 1640s, and before then, was riven, as you know, with daily violence, huge social changes, disease and hideous wrong-doings. That was all part of English life sadly. I promise something here and now Judy. I will tell your father, no, not about your abilities, you need to do that yourself in your own time, when it is appropriate for both of you. But I will tell him I will look after you, Judy from now on. I promise and will help you to cope, every day, our way."

Judy hugged her tight and smiled. "I feel like a silly child, but equally something seems to have flown straight out of my brain, like a great weight lifted off. I'm so grateful to you Abby. But I'm determined that I'm not going to be a burden to anyone, you or my father. Tomorrow, I get back to my history studies and will take that archive internship that Julian kindly fixed up in English Heritage. It will be interesting to fish around old attics and catalogue Georgian wallpaper in Preston Castle. There must be no end of mystery and stories and lots of fun too immersed in that Regency period, well for me anyway. I intend returning to Oxford now Abby, at the latest by next year. My father says that the College Procter can be flexible for when I'm ready. Gosh I'm totally drained. I really need to go to bed. I can hear the party though is still in full swing."

Abby grinned and kissed her cheek, which was warm again, and they walked slowly back to the main entrance. "Yes, your father has a canny knack of pulling strings whenever it's needed. That's more like it. I can see your colour back, and I feel your contentment. Not a word of this to anyone, Judy, especially Victoria. Something tells me it won't happen again. When you go in, I suggest you head for bed. I'll tell Victoria I found you getting some fresh air, had too much to drink and it reacted with your medication which you're going to sleep off."

They stopped near the front door and gazed at the full moon. Abby looked into Judy's eyes. She was not so plain at all, quite a vivacious young woman when she was done up like today, but most importantly Judy had experienced a sea-change they all had to go through at some point, as she herself only knew too well.

"Before I go up, Abby, I haven't said it and I apologise, but I can see how much you love my father and he dotes on you. You've done wonders for him. I think at last both he and I can put the sadness of my mother's death out of our lives, away to one side, and get on with the future properly. I'm really happy for both of you, truly. I'd like to think of you more like an older sister than a step-mum, if that's okay?"

"Thanks Judy, that means a lot to me. Now tell your father the same too, he really needs to hear it. I'm definitely not the step-mothering type. Anyway, I'm not that much older than you and I never had a sister, and you've met my awful brother, so that sounds great. Time for bed, I won't be far behind but your father still has the partying stamina of an ox. Thank goodness tomorrow and Monday are holidays to recover, then we're off to the Caribbean, yippee."

"I'll be fine at the Red Lion. I'll help Angie with the folk night on Tuesday and sort out my job at English Heritage. Gosh, the vicar here is the top slot, hope he's good."

"He'd better be." Abby said, laughing. "Goodnight, love you, see you tomorrow."

"Now what are you two cooking up? Not a party murder mystery I hope. Julian has moved onto Leonard Cohen and is sounding most morose." Victoria suddenly appeared out of the shadows.

"I don't think so, we've had enough madness for today I reckon," Abby replied and winked at Judy.

"Goodnight Vikki," Judy chirped and kissed her on the cheek. "I'm off to bed, I've had it. Just to say, I'm so pleased for you and Julian and Abby and my father. It was a wonderful double wedding today. I know you'll all be amazingly happy. Bye."

Watching Judy trot off into the house, Victoria turned to Abby. "You found her then, exactly as I said, getting a breath of air. She seems very happy. Do you know whether she's going to take that internship Julian fixed up?"

"Yep, starting next week, all sorted."

"That is progress. Now, are you going to tell me what's been going on? You've seen her haven't you? I can tell by your face Abby, so out with it."

"Yes, briefly, both of them again, they seemed happy with the wedding. Approved! Let's have a good natter when we get on that beach in St Lucia."

Victoria laughed. "I thought so, me too; in the kitchen when I was opening some more bottles of wine, the bar had run out. They were both scrutinising the new washing machine would you believe and shaking their heads. Then I got a big smile and thumbs up, like happy domesticity folks."

"I suspect Mauveine already knows it will be regularly filled with nappies in the not too distant future. She and Isi had it tougher a hundred years back, all that boiling and scrubbing. I'm done in. Lynton can do this party thing all night and more, how, God knows at his age. Hey, do you want to watch Black Swan in my room with a big pot of tea? I've got the blu-ray in my bag."

"Yeh, why not," Victoria chuntered. She grinned and linked Abby's arm. "They've thrown Julian, who finally descended into a very bad Bob Dylan and passed out, onto the couch in the sitting room to sleep it off. Some honeymoon night. Just like old times, Dr Abigail Grey. I'm keeping my maiden name ... the family heirloom and all that. Julian can remain his very own aristocratic brand."

"I like being Mrs Grey, but I think you're right. Now, how do we work that damned video in there?"

A quiet knock on the study door disturbed her concentration. "I'll get it; probably Judy wanting one of my famous hot chocolate night caps ... Gosh, Mrs Grable, what a pleasant surprise. What are you doing here?"

"She's come to pick up Aunt Eveline and Gerald before they wear themselves out," Victoria shouted, rising from the armchair. "Their impromptu concert in the ballroom was the star turn of the karaoke tonight."

"What concert?"

"The one, my dear, you sadly missed whilst you were mooching about outside for Lynton's daughter."

Suddenly Aunt Eveline, arm in arm with Gerald, hobbling with a stick, appeared in the doorway.

"Eveline, I hadn't seen you all night, hope you had a good time." Abby replied, wide-eyed.

Betty Grable, the Appleby Lodge warden, took Gerald firmly by the arm. "I'll just get him down into the Range Rover, Eveline; I've already put the cello in. Congratulations both of you. Sorry I couldn't make the bash, only one on duty this afternoon, but a beautiful service this morning. It makes a welcome change to see a McKenzie soiree as it were. It has been a very, very long time since this place buzzed with people enjoying themselves. Come on Gerald; doing the cha-cha at eighty-eight is not the wisest thing to attempt now is it."

"Ah, but I feel good," Gerald replied in a slurry voice and gave Eveline a wicked grin and a wink, as he was led off.

"Marvellous time my dear, wonderful day and about time as Betty said. It felt just like 1925 again. I'm sure William was smiling out there. You missed our duet on the grand piano, Abby, such a shame. Gerald is quite talented on that too. We did a few Vera Lynn war songs, like 'We'll Meet Again,' and got everyone singing along … see, the old ones are always the best, not that awful Rolling Stones noise. I wasn't too impressed with Julian's Mick Jagger."

"No, neither was I actually Aunt Eveline," Victoria replied glumly as Abby stifled a laugh.

"That old fool thinks he's on a roll tonight, but the state he's in, it will be at least a week."

Victoria blushed as Abby giggled loudly. "Anyway Victoria, you look worn out so the three of you had better have a good lie down now, I think."

"The three of us?" Victoria looked puzzled, and then her fast brain cottoned on. How did Aunt Eveline know? They had agreed to keep her pregnancy a secret between the four of them, at least until they all got back from honeymoon.

"Sometimes we older women can simply work out these things." Eveline replied casually, kissing Victoria on the cheek. "I'm pleased for you, a good time to propagate the McKenzie line don't you think? Enjoy your honeymoon to the Caribbean, very nice I must say. Anyway, must go. Abigail, will you see me out please."

"Of course Eveline."

The two of them had just reached the front door when Eveline stopped and looked deep into Abby's eyes. "Now Abigail, I must say something important. I know why you were outside; I sensed the whole, full picture. You will have to tell Victoria and Julian and Lynton too, what happened that dreadful night in the cellar."

"You mean now Eveline?" Abby whispered, feeling acute anxiety.

"I don't mean now my dear. No, no, only you will know when. But what happened to Judy was a signal, all may not be done. I don't feel anything worrying, in fact quite the opposite. I feel exactly as I did when William and I had that wonderful picnic around the pond on his hundredth birthday and I painted those waterlilies, a second release, which is excellent."

"You know what happened outside?"

"Of course, although my senses are weakening, Abigail, and the detail eluded me, except it felt pretty awful and a long time before. The future will be down to you and now, I believe, Judy too. When I met that lovely girl over the summer, I knew she was one of us immediately, but I realised you didn't. Her wavelength is different, but sharp, so very sharp. She is picking up enactments in time well before you and me. That, I fear, is one of the reasons her mind has been so troubled. Modern medicine may say one thing now and define her mental condition within some convenient psychiatric box, but the true picture is quite a different order. You understand me, my dear?"

"Yes, indeed Eveline. Tonight I realised too, somehow I tuned in like you, but not sufficient to be scared witless as Judy obviously was. I intend to look after her fully from now on."

"A noble calling and wise, Abigail, but don't neglect your art whatever you do, you have so much talent. I am so pleased your new gallery we chose together is coming on, especially as you intend to try textiles. You must come over again soon to the Lodge. I want to teach you some new techniques whilst I have the energy, and I have a special painting for you, nobody has seen, and then you will understand."

"Thank you so much, I'll be over once we return from sunning ourselves."

"Excellent, have fun, I would if I was sixty years younger. Now I can see Betty waving, must fly. Gerald needs putting to bed, his own tonight. Bye my dear."

As Aunt Eveline shot off up the drive and out the gates in the bright glare of the security lights, Abby stared into the clear night sky and pondered. Of course, Mauveine didn't appear either tonight because her paranormal universe is not the same; she probably is ethereally unaware of what Judy saw. Powerful and often tragic events can leave a paranormal record imprinted on the place where they once took place, like has been seen at several old battlefields. Abby thought hard about her own knowledge of history, thinking about Judy's comment on the Civil War in the 1600's and Newark, a particularly grisly and tumultuous time across England. She then remembered, after the battle of Edgehill near Liverpool in 1642, ghostly re-enactments full of the sounds of battle, horses and fighting had been regularly witnessed since. Even it was said, King Charles's own officers were able to recognise friends who were there. She had also read about phantom soldiers and horsemen from the Duke of Monmouth's defeated army in 1685, seen on a particular night in July fleeing from the famous battle of Sedgemoor, with even Monmouth himself riding furiously away from the battlefield.

As Abby made some hot chocolate and a large pot of tea to take upstairs, Judy, she concluded, had been inside some enactment similar, but right here at Orsbrick Hall. Her mind went quickly over the original research which she had teased out of those old and rare books in the library upstairs. About when Abbot Rimmer, Head of the original Orsbrick Priory, on the land on which Orsbrick Hall had been subsequently built, instigated the burning of Lucinda McKenzie in the cellar followed by the centuries-long Rimmer curse which triggered the subsequent terrifying happening with Victoria and Julian. That warp in paranormal space-time had been healed, put to rights forever, thank goodness, and Mauveine was finally rested. Judy's description had definite similarities to that Rimmer period, possibly earlier, but there were no older books or records available at Orsbrick. It would be a challenge to find out more.

Abby decided to leave all those thoughts to the back of her mind. There was a reassuring calm around, the party had subdued a little but plenty of lively noise in the ballroom could be heard as the disco continued quietly. She looked forward to finishing the evening quietly and a gossip with Victoria on the best double wedding day they could ever have wished for. Abby breathed a sigh of pleasure. And she had a present for Victoria, a nice bracelet; after all it was still Christmas Day. Hopefully, there were some decent shops open on Boxing Day as they needed to restock their holiday wardrobes quickly, given Lynton's surprise holiday announcement, and she was desperate for some new bikinis.

"Tea has arrived Lady McKenzie, now have you got that video working?"

"Of course Lady Grey, time for discourse and scurrilous gossip," Victoria replied with a giggle as they sat down on the large sofa.

Lynton was taking a quiet breather from his boozy lawyer friends and antics, the drinking contest between England and Poland still rowdily pouring forth at the bar, despite the time of three-thirty am. A scantily clad Latvian girl by the name of Rula staggered past him out of the front door and threw up over the gravel outside. He sighed and placed a thin blanket over Julian, snoring peacefully on the couch. He yawned and casually picked up the local Christmas Eve newspaper, the weekly Ormskirk Gazette, still unopened on the coffee table nearby. He flicked through the car advertisements, looking for something he could buy Abby, now she would need to travel back and forth to Southport. He still had that silly habit picked up from his mother of perusing the births and deaths section of the classifieds, and peered over at anyone he knew when a large and bold entry caught his eye.

Died tragically, 20th December 2010, the loving grandchildren and great-grandchildren of Mrs Agnes Rimmer, inconsolable in her grief. May they live forever and fulfil their destinies. Donations only please to the Ormskirk Boatpeople in Need Trust.

He scratched his head and reflected for a second. His brain was not wholly tuned in following all the consumed alcohol, but the name was vaguely familiar. Directly underneath was a second entry.

December 21st 2010, died suddenly of a broken heart, Mrs Agnes Rimmer, aged 96 of Canal Street. May Judas Fine repent his gross misdeeds in the next world.

A peculiar entry he thought, his legal mind immediately intrigued with the tragic set of family coincidences. Who on earth was the oddly named Judas Fine? Then it hit him, of course, the bizarre Rimmer family. They were the oddballs who caused serious trouble with Julian and who he had covertly photographed with his mobile phone, that night the four of them ate in the George pub. The head of the family had violently accused Julian of being somebody else they knew, someone who was clearly bad news. Bloody hell. Sad cases though they were, that lot had endured a tragic family set of events you wouldn't wish on anyone, and just before Christmas too. He flicked back to the main newspaper and finally caught another article.

December 20th: Reported by James Steward. A tragic accident occurred today at 12.15am on the main road out of Parbold village, when a family estate car, driven by a Mr John Rimmer, dock worker, aged 46, from Canal Lane Burscough, was in a horrific fatal head-on collision with a JCB digger. Mr Rimmer, who was thrown decapitated onto the road, died instantly and his wife and three teenage children subsequently died of burns at the scene, despite the heroic efforts of ambulance paramedics and fire crews who arrived quickly from Ormskirk. Eye witnesses described the vehicle as having become instantly engulfed by a huge, crimson like ball of flame, and confirmed that the unharmed driver of the JCB, which had careered out of a side road, bucket forward onto the wrong side of the road, giving the car driver no chance of avoiding it, calmly got out of his cab and ran from the scene into the woods nearby towards the canal. Despite being chased, he completely vanished. Police have since named the man as Judas Fine, aged 53, a Dutch national, working for Borigg Farm on casual agricultural work. Despite an extensive manhunt of the area and a diver's search of the canal, no sign of Mr Fine was found and an international arrest warrant has been issued, with fears he may have fled the country already.

Lynton drew breath. A tragic and horrible scenario, although nobody had mentioned it and it happened so close by. Something nagged at him about the whole incident, but his brain was far too fuzzy to concentrate. He would discuss it with Abby tomorrow sometime. Downing his definite last glass of whisky, it was time to throw his friends and Julian's tenants, out of the ballroom bar and up to their rooms and call it a night.

Chapter Six

Easter 2011 at Orsbrick Hall:

Peace and quiet but Julian was back in Liverpool again, this time for a long period of extended scribbling to finish off his novel. For some reason he simply couldn't write at home. Victoria was surprised. Not especially with Julian's writer block, but very surprised, that Judy had been allowed to return to Oxford University at the beginning of February and start her new course in History and Classics early. From her wide knowledge of universities that shouldn't be possible mid-term. Still, she pondered, Oxford and Cambridge operated by their own rules, and of course Lynton had been his usual persuasive self with the hierarchy down at Balliol College. Most importantly, Judy was finally off her medication and the archive internship had done wonders for her self-confidence and social skills. It was as if Judy had become a totally transformed young woman, from the train wreck she and Abby had brought back home at Christmas. Judy was though improving from a low base and remained seriously reserved and highly introspective, but that was how it would have to be. It was her character and the way the genes fell, certainly Judy didn't take after her father one little bit. Abby had given a lot of dedicated time into constantly looking after Judy, cajoling her back onto her feet, this way and that way, all credit due. How Abby managed that and simultaneously got her new art and gallery business off the ground, again demonstrated Abby's formidable organising skills once she got her teeth into something she cared about.

Victoria, tired, sat back down on the couch and picked unenthusiastically at the pile of exercise books. She really had to finish that tedious marking. If anyone had ever told her six months previously that she would be teaching at Cradwell, in her father's own former laboratory, they would have been laughed out of court. But financial needs must. Her redundancy money and profit from her flat sale were well gone. Julian was badly in debt with the restoration of his Liverpool historic town house after the fire, as the insurance refused to pay up on some bizarre technicality, and his writing had stalled. Despite Abby going on a persuasion tack every night, Victoria staunchly refused any loans from Lynton or the bank. She hated the idea, despite the logic, determined as before to pay her own way and be independent and debt free come what may. So when an unexpected call came from Dame Rowena Bayswell-Hart, headmistress of the private Cradwell School for Girls, desperate for someone urgently to teach maternity cover A-level science until the summer, then she instantly volunteered. They took her on, amazingly with a cursory interview and a smile, despite her lack of teaching experience and her own growing maternity state. Rowena liked her former industrial experience as a senior polymer chemist and her array of qualifications. Nepotism reigned supreme at Cradwell. There was still a bizarre fondness in the school for Dr Jack McKenzie, her deceased father and former Head of Science for donkey's years. But his reign was too way back for most people there to now remember him. Actually she had to admit the teaching was turning out to be very enjoyable. At least the students were all girls, very well behaved, bright, and extraordinarily enthusiastic about science and ultra hardworking. She smiled. They certainly were the complete antithesis of the dumb slags from her old comprehensive school at Parbold High. Cradwell girls were the self-selective, paying cream of the crop, a majority heading for Oxbridge, with most parents very well-heeled, and generous school scholarships for the few kids who weren't. It was like managing a group identical to her when she was seventeen, quite unsettling until she became used to it. She had finally fired up enthusiasm to mark the kinetic theory of gases homework assignments when her mobile rang. Peering at the screen, it was Christine Summers, her jovial senior laboratory technician, who had been at Cradwell many years, and worked even for her late father.

"High Christine, what's up? Have we run out of mercury again?"

"No, no, all is ship-shape for practicals tomorrow, and the new retrieval machine means we shouldn't need to order any Hg for a long time, goodness me, that metal has become so expensive. No, why I phoned is I was having a clear out of the old stock cupboards, and you know that tiny desk, buried for years under a pile of boxes? I found something in the drawer, which I had long forgotten about, but I think you should have. It belonged to your father. He was very attached to the thing, although why heaven knows."

"Mmm ... I'm afraid my father had many strange attachments Christine," Victoria quipped, hearing Christine instantly laugh like a drain at the end of the phone, whilst Victoria could only think of the dreaded, overweight potato woman in town he visited every Friday night. "Okay, I'll pop in early tomorrow before classes and you can show me."

"I think you'll be surprised, bye."

Victoria put down her mobile and recommenced marking, when it rang again. "Shit," she cried out angrily, "I'm destined not to finish this," then seeing it was Abby she relented.

"Hi chuck. What's new? Sold any pictures for a vast profit yet?"

"Actually, Ms Cynical, I have as it happens. That rather gorgeous looking canal scene I painted down at Appleby Lodge in January? Well it's gone for a pretty penny, the buyer insisting that I was the new J.W.Turner himself."

"Mmm ... anyway, I'm sure you didn't call to boast about your income generation did you. You know early evening is sacred work time for teachers. I have some seriously hard marking to do, unless you want to solve fluid flow equations of rapidly moving particles colliding with themselves and the sides of their container?"

"Sounds ultra-tedious to me. Anyway, to relieve your worn out brain, I intend to pick up Judy tomorrow at the station and we've decided to come to Orsbrick, after school of course, and treat you and Julian to a McDonalds dinner. Lynton is still in Hong Kong. He's had to stay on and pamper his Chinese clients a bit more."

"Okay that's fine, I've got the afternoon off anyway tomorrow, a Governor's discretion day or something, so if there's no answer I'll be in the cellar. No Julian either, he's scribbling again down in his Liverpool basement and walking aimlessly in circles around Toxteth trying to get some inspiration for his ... err ... blockbuster novel. He says it's the only way he can conquer writer's block which has bedevilled him since Christmas."

"Why he seriously can't write at home in that lovely place I do not know. I thought he would savour the environment. You are still very determined to restore that laboratory down there aren't you. Are you really going to replicate Mauveine's dye experiments?"

"Julian says he's too close to the atmosphere here ... don't ask me about the peculiarities of writer sensitivity, anyway he's promised to return for Sunday lunch, I expect his last tin of baked beans is running out. Actually, I've brought together all my old Leiden University organic chemistry notes and Mauveine's journals, bought a few chemicals from my meagre teacher's pay through the school and already created one of her unpublished aniline dyes, a fabulously beautiful yellow. I intend to distil coal soon and get truly authentic eventually. But I must get on with my marking Abby."

"I'll try and paint with some of that stuff if you can make a solid precipitate like they used to do, if you like. I reckon Mauveine herself would be impressed, if she isn't alongside helping you anyway. Okay, enough banter for one day, we'll see you tomorrow, Bye, bye."

Victoria strode into her school laboratory. The atmosphere almost felt like being back in Ahrendolie again, except in here it was a lot less sophisticated. She peered inside the ancient fume cupboard and noted the materials prepared for her class at nine o' clock, with lab coats on the wall hooks and the apparatus for her ten scholarship students already laid out on the benches. She hoped she wasn't going to get into another argument with Danielle again about pinning her waist-long hair up; she was as feisty as Abby.

Christine was in her prep room, early as usual pottering about. She worked extraordinarily long hours, sheer unblemished dedication over many years to the job.

"Hi Victoria, come in here and take a look at this. Your father was quite obsessive about it. He brought the thing out of its box every day and polished it, like a sort of ritual. Warding off the evil spirits no doubt, particularly Dr Edith Marples, who ran the school with an iron rod in those days!"

Victoria stared at the object lying on the bench. Shit, it was a twin of the same weird glass artefact that she and Abby had found in the telescope room. Yet another large glass prism, but a more startling blood red in colour. She touched it, and it felt oddly warm. "Good heavens, I've got a twin of this prism that we found before Christmas, also when we had a clear out. Actually, apart from a slight variation of colour, this one is the same, slightly rough on one edge. I wonder whether they are pieces of the same original. Have you any idea what it is or what it means?"

"None whatsoever. Your father refused to discuss 'crimmy' as he called it, although I did gather the prism was some kind of long-standing family heirloom. Rather than cluttering the place up, you may as well have it, or I'll put the thing in the skip."

"No, no. I'll take it home. Maybe I'll get to the bottom of the puzzle sometime. I reckon there's a third piece too, from the shape." She put the prism segment carefully back into its blue, velvet-lined, wooden box and placed it into her bag.

"Well if I find that as well, I'll keep it for you. Now, we've just got time. How do you want your demonstration set up at the front? And if that silly girl, Danielle creates again about her lab coat being too unfashionable, I shall personally strangle her, especially as this experiment will be under test conditions."

Victoria laughed. "Don't worry. After my one-to one with her last time, I think she will be quite chastened this morning. I was used to some unruly male graduates in my lab at the refinery. Danielle received the same treatment, works a dream. I can be quite severe when I want."

"Take after your father, Victoria. Jack was the same, never did his pupils any harm. I still miss him … finding that glass thing brought him all back."

"Really?" Victoria said, as she watched Christine go atypically quiet, into a slight dream and a little flushed. She pondered, and pondered again and smiled. There was a lot about her father she simply never knew.

Maybe he and Uncle William were not so different after all …

They sat quietly having tea before heading off to McDonalds in Burscough. Victoria fancied doing something different for a change on a Friday night. Julian had become quite tiresome. He was constantly fretting and brooding about his damned novel which would never likely get anywhere, although his other backlists, to be fair, still sold slowly. And she had picked up Aunt Eveline on the way home so it would be a girls quartet night out. Victoria had fished out the prism object from its ornate box and placed it on the table, with the unwrapped twin she and Abby had first found. They gazed at them curiously. She had been right; the two were definitely pieces from some larger one. Eveline had gone very quiet and thoughtful before she piped up first.

"Good heavens above, Victoria my dear, you have two of those things. It has been a very long time since I saw the one that just came out of that beautiful box. Abby, take a closer look at the markings and the marquetry design. Seventeenth century?"

Before Abby could reply, Judy, who had been staring non-stop at both pieces, answered in a monotone. "Yes, the box was definitely made in Holland, probably Rotterdam, I would say sometime in the 1660's, probably by a woodcarver and stonemason called Grinling Gibbons. I recognise the style from a museum exhibition I visited two years ago in London."

They stopped and stared at Judy, immersed in her academic historical element, as she continued about the unique and wondrous work of Gibbons and his eventual rise to fame as a wood carver in the court of King Charles the Second. Abby now realised the significance of the origins, feeling relieved, because this was the first time Judy had returned to Orsbrick Hall since the wedding day. Judy had definitely fought off phobic fears since her fearful ghostly enactment sighting.

"The two pieces are indeed part of the same object," Judy continued. "There's a small third element missing, then, if assembled together, you would have a perfect prism. At one time the whole artefact, before some catastrophic accident, would have snugly fitted inside that box, which has obviously been specially made for it."

"Why catastrophic, Judy?" Abby retorted.

Judy's eyes shifted uneasily about, like she had been caught out doing or saying the wrong thing at school. "Sorry, inappropriate literary expansiveness, I was getting carried away. I should have said unfortunate."

Aunt Eveline, still deep in thought, glanced at Judy, and interjected. "Yes, I remember clearly now, I must have been about six or seven. When Jack was an adolescent, just before he boarded at the Bluecoat School, he would keep that box and the glass piece you found, in his childhood laboratory, Victoria, religiously under his pillow, along with shells, dead insects, and other collected boy-items. It became a bit of a family joke for a while, and William, as ever, would tease him mercilessly, but Jack would never ever say why it was so obsessively important to him. I quite forgot, because of course, they both disappeared at sixteen, after winning those scholarships to Cambridge University.

He must have kept the damned thing with him all that time and finally it, or part of it, ended up at Cradwell. How odd, but then Victoria, sadly as you know, my brother, your father, was always somewhat strange and temperamental."

Judy was still concentrating and thinking. Abby had gone to refill the tea and returned with a fresh pot. Suddenly Judy grimaced and reiterated loudly in a deep whisper. "I know exactly what it is, I've worked it out."

Abby looked at Eveline who appeared somewhat perturbed. But Victoria, her scientific antennae twitching, was simply eager to hear.

"Well Judy, explain. What are your findings?" Victoria asked.

Abby instantly thought Victoria sounded exceptionally officious and school-marmish.

"I recognise the object now from my classical history studies," Judy said. "The pieces are very old, by that I mean this material was known about going right back to early India, at least two thousand years BC. It's a man-made glass with likely origins in Rome, originally they called it obsidian. The Romans used it for dishware and the crimson colour and slight speckle inside is copper, with I believe some lead and magnesium oxide and carbon mixed in. People once called it blood glass and then eventually, especially after production, the process became a refined manufacture in the Vatican. They called it purpurin, later with an 'e' at the end ... so purpurine. I've seen some beautiful, late nineteenth century mounted purpurine bowls, with gilded bronze beading applied using the same technique, made at the imperial glassworks in St Petersburg. These were in the

Walters Art Museum in Baltimore. My mother took me when I was six. I remember the exact conversation, my mother was an amazing Russian historian and …

"Have you been to the Walters Art Museum, Abby?" Victoria interjected blithely, conscious that they needed to shut Judy up or she would never stop, her photographic memory was going off into overdrive.

"Err … no, but I've heard of it? Did you say the technique was refined in the Vatican, Judy? What sort of period would that have been?"

"Not totally sure, but the evidence would point to probably the late fifteenth and early sixteenth centuries."

Abby pondered. Her brain whirred like a dentist's drill, once more assembling dissociated historic data but as yet making no sense.

Victoria continued. "Well, now I think we've solved the prism of purpurine mystery, Judy. I'm seriously impressed at your detailed grasp of science and geology. I wonder if the third piece will ever turn up? Would be nice to have the lot then perhaps using modern adhesives and Julian's adept conservation skills we could join them together." She looked impatiently at the slow-ticking grandfather clock in the corner. "Well, looks like it's time to eat … I'm ravenous, and girls, because today is payday, then double burger and fries with salad are on me all round."

They stood up and Abby helped Aunt Eveline, who had become very stiff, out of her chair. As they put their coats on, Judy out of the blue started again, her face now contorted in a deep frown.

"I'm very adept too Victoria. I've been making and selling jewellery at Oxford to earn some extra money so my father isn't paying for absolutely everything. My new friends love the creations. But I wouldn't want to touch those purpurine things."

They all stopped. Aunt Eveline glanced sideways at Abby who immediately replied. "Well, why not Judy? What's wrong with them?"

"I saw the glow, they are positively evil. My advice Victoria is to throw them out and get rid, immediately."

Victoria was thrown by the remark and a little flummoxed, but thought fast. "Actually, I shall test them with my portable Geiger counter. I reckon there may be a smidgen of radioactive mineral thrown into that mix, yellowcake, for example, a common uranium ore, was used for years as a paint. Anyway these bits of glass are family heirlooms, so I intend to hang on to them for the time being ... and I'm curious why my father felt so extraordinarily close to them. So, enough of prisms for one night. Shall we drive into town in the Beast, Abby? He hasn't been out for a long time."

"The Beast?" Judy piped up, now having fortunately moved off her purpurine agenda.

"Yes. The black Beast has an interesting Liverpudlian history, of wanton women and bawdy shanty songs, isn't that so Victoria? We'll tell you over your French fries," Abby replied gaily, shoving Judy through the front door gently. "In fact Vikki, I'd better drive, and then we can all get in the mood?"

Aunt Eveline laughed. "Really Abigail my dear, you do make me laugh sometimes, almost as much as Gerald. Help me into the front will you."

120

Chapter Seven

The sitting room door creaked open as Victoria peered up from her afternoon Sunday snooze. "Oh my word, the wanderer returns, and to what do we owe the honour of your presence kind sir? Like two days down in the Toxteth dungeon seem to have stretched into two weeks. I expect the quill is now a mere smoking stump."

"Cheeky, I sent you texts every day with big smileys and hearts all around them."

"Gosh, were they from you? And there's silly me thinking I had a husband once upon a time who suddenly went permanently awol. Good job it's been mock exams period, otherwise I might have had a slight twinge of loneliness rattling around here on my own."

"You have lots of good, friendly ghostly company," Julian replied with a wide grin. He was glad to be back. "Anyway, the good news is, following a last minute spurt of deep, street wandering inspiration, I've finished the errant novel. Manuscript went off this morning to Sara, my editor in chief. All finito, done, afgewerkt as they say … and I'm taking a break for a day or two, but then it's back to sawing and plastering. What's for tea?"

Victoria scowled. "As my mother used to say, when in a whisky-sozzled 1940's reverie, which was usually most of the time ... Bread and dripping. You can spread some connie-onnie on it."

"Connie-onnie?" What the hell is that?"

He gave her a big hug followed by a long desired, sloppy kiss, and by her vigorous response she was not really angry with him, at least not at that moment. Although the euphoria could easily change in five minutes time if he carried on being obnoxious.

"Never mind, I can warm up the remains of a chicken casserole I made earlier. I'm now down to bartering food and veg at the Burscough market, with the stall equivalent of Abby's Ali. Waitrose is but a distant memory. Funds are becoming a little tight dearest. My payday just about covers the overdraft payments and that's it. Do you think your garrulous and loquacious editor, the great intellect on all matters bookish, detestable Sara, could be persuaded to offer a little sub on your meagre advance?"

"Mmm ... doubt it. You know how publishers are these days, as skint as us or so they tell their authors. This is what they mean by being property rich and cash poor, like those London pensioners with houses worth millions they bought fifty years ago. I'm thinking of putting an ad in the local shop, odd job man for hire, will tackle anything legal."

"Well I agree with the odd, only joking darling, we've just got to last until next December then hopefully my inheritance will come true and our worries over."

He smiled. He could work in Waitrose too if necessary and do the garden section, and Victoria did have a job for the next two months so life could be worse. "Actually, the other good news is that I'm back with a full set of Polish and Latvian paying tenants, so after I pay off the bank loan for the renovation, I should have some profit over end of next month. Okay only fifty pounds, but that will buy a lot of bread and dripping! One slight problem though ... err ...I just need to go and fetch something outside."

She knew that look and he'd wiped his glasses three times. She immediately had the feeling she wouldn't like what was coming and a minute later wasn't disappointed. She stared at the sight in front of her, as the sight stared back, both immediately weighing up the other in reverential silence.

"Err ... meet Rocky, Victoria."

She couldn't believe her eyes and gaped incredulous. At the end of a great, thick leash held firmly by Julian appeared a massive dog, at least three and a half foot high at the shoulder and that was before his great, shaggy head was taken into account. He had a huge, dark brown coat, with a pleasing mottled cream fleck running through it, neither smooth nor bedraggled. He stood panting, wary but obviously disciplined.

"Where the fuck did you get that ... err ... animal from, Julian? Dogs are not exactly my forte. You know that, especially as I was bitten badly by an alsatian as a child and have been very wary since. Jesus, he's absolutely massive. What is he?"

"Rocky belonged to my erstwhile seafaring tenant, Sebastian, who unceremoniously did a bunk with six months rent and left him behind. What could I do? He just sort of looked at me in his room with those sharp eyes, so over the last two weeks he's followed me around and kept me company in the basement. I couldn't leave him there. He's nine months old, really well trained and no bother, honestly, but I must admit he eats a lot. However, we can buy his food in bulk at one of those pet wholesalers in twenty five kilogram packets like cement, a lot cheaper than tins of dog food."

"And how long does that last?"

"Almost a week so it's not so bad.

"Jesus Christ, Julian."

"Now, I'm going to let him off the leash and the two of you can make friends. He's quite calm, he won't bound over. Rocky understands his size and strength and is quite gentle and very loyal. On his hind legs he's nearly seven feet tall and weighs about sixteen stone, I have had him with his paws on my shoulders licking my face once, even I can only just hold him, but he won't do that, unless asked. Anyway, we have the right sized house for a dog like him, don't we?"

"Your last sentence was the only thing I feel comfortable with Julian. It's not easy for me, especially him being the size of three alsatians. Why couldn't Sebastian have had a poodle or a corgi or something? No, sorry, that's daft."

Victoria looked askance at the prospect of the leash coming off, although Rocky's tail was wagging now and he looked much friendlier, perhaps a positive sign. But she knew she had to do this and cope. Julian was obviously a sucker for animals, and shit, think of the logic, what a guard dog, Rocky would make. "I won't ask for the shoulder treatment, so how do I make friends?"

"He'll come to you and nuzzle, just stroke his head and he'll be fine."

Julian unclipped the leash, mumbled something in his ear, and she took a very deep breath, eyes fixed on that massive head. He lolloped quite gently across the room; only taking what seemed like a couple of very long-legged strides.

She had never seen such a huge dog, bigger even than a great dane, which one of her school friends had kept. He stood next to her, stiffing curiously and his long tail wagged furiously, sending a draught into her face. Then he pushed his warm, wet nose into her hand and she tentatively stroked his head, hearing a quiet, rumbling growl in his throat. He looked up at her and let out a couple of deep barks, and nuzzled her more strongly, his tail continuing to wag furiously. Julian smiled. Relief and drops of perspiration showed clearly in his face.

"He definitely likes you, he knows you're apprehensive, as are most people to be fair, and is making allowances but I reckon now you've got a friend for life."

"Look Julian, he's rubbing his head against my stomach and sniffing, I think he knows there are some more family members gestating in there."

Julian laughed. "Probably does. Wolfhounds are a sensitive and intelligent breed. I'll give you the full history, which I've researched, over dinner, but they were once used extensively, many centuries back, as hunting dogs by the nobility to catch wolves and bears. They have the strength and agility to kill a wolf outright. I wouldn't be surprised if dogs like Rocky were even kept here at Orsbrick Hall, centuries back. I'll just bring in his bowl of water. Don't worry, I'll take him for a walk later through the woods, he's quite habitual like me and has a big bladder."

Victoria watched as Rocky ambled over to the window and dunked his head into his obviously favourite huge metal drinking bowl with his name stamped across it and slurped it dry in seconds. Then well satiated, he gave a large yawn and slumped on the rug in front of the fireplace, the burning logs now down to a warming red glow, taking the chill off the room. He was soon gently snoring.

"I'll feed him later, he eats religiously twice a day, breakfast and dinner, same times as us, he never wants to snack or anything. I've calibrated his food against his weight and height and think we've got it right now; he was a bit underfed before. Sebastian would leave him on his own for days on end. I'll just bring in the two food sacks I've brought on the pickup truck into the kitchen."

Victoria went into the kitchen to heat up Julian's casserole, still eyeing Rocky warily, although she had to reluctantly admit, he was unexpectedly growing on her already. Small yappy dogs never appealed anyway and this dog fitted the house very suitably. He seemed contented in the abode already; maybe Mauveine had owned dogs too. As she dished out Julian's meal from the microwave and poured out two glasses of white wine, he struggled in with a great big bed-basket and some food bowls and carefully placed them at the other end of the kitchen come former scullery. It was a big room, even for Rocky. Thank goodness they weren't living in her Rotterdam flat. Orsbrick Hall would be paradise for him, although how they were going to afford him as well only heaven knew.

As they settled down in front of the ten o'clock news, Victoria felt a renewed contentment filter back. The inaugural walk around the woods with the three of them really had been fun, and even though dusk was approaching, Rocky was hugely playful. He bounded about, fetching big sticks and very much enjoying exploratory sniffing around their favourite pond. He also seemed very relaxed when Julian gave her a passionate kiss, as they all sat on a giant log and watched the fish peck around the emerging early water lilies, so that was a hurdle out of the way. A jealous Rocky would definitely not have been a good idea. He seemed quite an independent animal and enjoyed making his own fun having lived in a shed all year round in the rear yard at Julian's house in Liverpool and obviously relished being outdoors. Julian insisted that the following day he would make a kennel for Rocky out of the pile of old wood she had brought up from the cellar after she cleared it out.

"So, what about the completed epic then that you've been so secretive about?" she murmured, snuggling her head into his chest. "Are you going to tell me what it's about now?"

He took off his glasses for a quick rub. "Once Sara and her team have finished editing and tweaking, Cut and the Cuticle should hopefully be published sometime next year. The story is a fictionalised steampunk account of high society politics, science, romance and the arts in West Lancashire in the nineteenth century and is set on the seafront, in a huge Victorian townhouse in Southport."

"Strange sort of title, darling? So were you really inspired by the entire goings on in Orsbrick then and me?

"Of course, you heard me tapping enough in Lynton's attic eyrie in the Red Lion, but I wanted to include something of the sea into the plot as well. You know how much I like the coast."

"That's true," she whispered, stroking his thick, grey hair. "But publication still seems an awfully long way off. Why on earth does it take so long?"

"Sort of traditional I suppose — lots of processes to sort out. I don't know to be honest, but … well … I've quietly leaked a couple of chapters, slightly modified as a short story, to one of those online fan-fiction sites springing up. I reckon these new eBooks are going to be the next big thing."

Victoria sat up. "Fan-fiction? Beyond me, especially if it doesn't have a ring of carbon atoms around it, but Sara is going to go full-ape, Julian, she could quite justifiably cancel your contract. What a stupid thing to do."

"Don't worry, she has to find out first and she won't have a clue. Sara knows nothing about digital. The fan-fiction is well camouflaged, but it might help to bring my name to a wider audience."

"Your name? You mean you've used your actual name, not a nom-de-plume? Shit Julian."

"Yeh, well," he muttered, frowning. "I hate pseudonyms, anyway it's done now … probably won't be read anyway, so forget it …"

Early evening and dinner in the Ship and Mitre restaurant was always busy, especially on Fridays. Half-price happy hour drinking hauled in the street trade, especially the many young office professionals working on Dale Street. But Lynton, as usual, had booked his favourite oval table by the large window, as they gazed down at the throng of shoppers and early revellers scurrying about outside.

"So, Abby, how is the new art gallery going?" Julian asked as the waiter brought over the wine and an apple juice for Victoria, who would drive the Beast back home. "Sorry, I haven't been over yet but I've been really busy with the observatory restoration. Guess what, after a major struggle and a careful cleanup, I've got the telescope working and also motorised those wooden window slats. It's like Jodrell Bank in there now, fabulous views of the moon. The experience took my breath away."

"Wow, Julian, no problem — that is so impressive. It sounds wonderful up there. I really liked the view, didn't we Vikki? The gallery is doing fantastic, thanks to Rockefeller here getting me started, but is already paying its way and the punters are queuing up for my new textile pictures. Aunt Eveline is a great teacher."

"We've finally sold my luxury pad in Southport and decided to put all the profit into launching Abby's business," Lynton interjected. "I didn't want to go back there, too many memories and neither did Judy. She loves coming home to the Red Lion, so that will be our home for good, as it were."

"And plenty of room for a future pattering of feet then Abby?" Victoria chimed, with a smirk.

Abby looked back. Unexpectedly her face turned quite serious, and she gripped Lynton's hand. "Actually there's ... well ... something we want to tell you, so we may as well ... I suppose ... tell you now." She took a deep breath. "Lynton and I have agreed not to have children, we ... err ... we just don't want our lifestyle to change and we both feel we've got enough on with Judy anyway. No disrespect both of you, and I'm sure you'll make amazing parents but ... well, kids are not for us. You know me Vikki, never been one for babies much."

"Listen, you'll change your mind once you get pregnant, as I've done, and I was even more anti-baby than you remember ..." Victoria replied brusquely, feeling quite irrationally irritated with her best friend.

Julian grabbed her hand under the table. "Leave it Victoria. I think Abby and Lynton have obviously given their decision a lot of thought, we should respect that. I certainly understand where they're coming from."

Victoria glared at him and yanked her hand away.

Abby and Lynton smiled back weakly; both felt a little uncomfortable. Lynton got up. "Just popping to the gents. Abby can you get that menu off the bar please? It's a special a-la carte evening, all on my tab guys, business expenses."

As Abby strolled slowly to the bar, Victoria turned sharply to Julian. "What's all this 'I know where they're coming from' bit? I wasn't happy with the way you patronised me then. I'm expecting twins, you're going to

130

be a father soon, and you sound like you're regretting it already. Well are you?"

"No of course not, I'm sorry Victoria, it's just … I could sense Abby wasn't finding it easy to tell us and you especially, just let them be."

"Let them be? Abby's been my best friend for twelve years now, we've been through all kinds together. I've a right to persuade her to …"

"No Victoria, you haven't and she's not you, they're happy with the way things are. Leave it out please … let's not have a row here. This is like a celebration," he whispered, looking around at some people staring over. "Abby's coming back, now cheer up for fuck's sake."

"Okay, for her sake, but certainly not yours, arsehole …"

Abby could see the red faces, but Victoria smiled as she handed out the menus and Lynton bounced back into his seat and immediately changed the conversation altogether to another topic about his international work and progress on Victoria's laboratory renovation, as normality returned to the conversation once more.

The journey home in the Beast, however, was not quite as smooth. Her rancour with Julian quickly returned and they argued continuously about children until eventually Victoria shut up, and they continued out of Liverpool in total silence. This was, she thought, by far the worst row they had suffered since being together, and she felt quite upset Julian remained silent. Finally she decided it was better to ride out the storm rather than continue stirring the embers. He said he loved her and happily anticipated the birth of the twins, boys according to the recent scan. She and Julian needed to start thinking through names.

But he kept his peace, and looked forward to taking Rocky out for his evening stroll once they got back. He was also concerned about the texts he had received earlier as they walked to the car. When he switched his phone back on, Sara had sent him five angry messages, one after the other. Somehow she had found out about his illicit moonlighting and discovered his stories on Adriana, the big bad fan-fiction site. Victoria was right. Sara was obviously livid and was indeed threatening to sever his contract. But there was an unexpected respite, at least for now. The free stories had apparently been going viral; he had no idea, too busy renovating. Apparently thousands were being downloaded and had circulated online all around the world. Sara, therefore, had insisted and decided to bring forward the publication of Cut and the Cuticle drastically and ordered him to start immediately on the revisions and rewrites. He would be sued if he didn't meet the new deadline. He couldn't tell whether that was all good or bad, and her texts were very vitriolic, but at least he was still in the game of being published sometime … of sorts.

Silence ensued for the rest of the evening. Victoria went to bed early and Julian decided to read for a while. He crept into bed around midnight. At least Rocky had been jovial to see them back, preferring now to sleep in his new kennel at night. He would have to start reworking that damned novel and he still needed to tell Victoria about Sara's discovery. She would be livid over that too.

Victoria had been restless. The night felt massively too hot for the thick duvet on the bed. She was upset about rowing with Julian, but for some reason she also hadn't slept well generally, especially since the revelation from Judy about the prism of purpurine. Although she had tried to put it to the back of her mind, the almost calm and resolute 'pure evil' expressed by Judy over a mere piece of triangular shaped red glass still nagged.

Suddenly Julian was woken by a sharp slap over the face, as he jumped up in bed to see Victoria, bolt upright, waving her arms around and covered in sweat, her eyes wide open. "No, no, we have to stop them, they must be killed." She shouted. "We can't let the wolves eat my babies, stop them, Julian, please stop them …"

He shook her gently and held her tight. "Wake up Victoria, come on. You're having a bad nightmare, easy now, you're okay. It's just a dream."

As she groaned and came to, she looked vacantly at him, pushed her long hair back over her face and wrapped her arms around his bare shoulders. She was sweating profusely and felt horrible; Julian had already discarded his pyjama top. She really should have changed the bed earlier. But the pains in her stomach had grown awful and then she felt it all down her leg, wet and trickling. She threw off the duvet and they both stared in horror at the bloody mess all over the sheets, her nightdress equally covered. She screamed out in terror, this was much more than a nightmare.

"Oh, Julian, oh my God, help me, please help me, I'm having a miscarriage. Oh fuck Julian, do something," as she tore the sheets off and ran hysterically, blood pouring from her, into the bathroom.

Julian stared, immobile for the moment. His brain had stupidly seized up, and then he heard the deep, loud bark of Rocky outside. Something had disturbed him too and it made him spring back to life. He grabbed his mobile and immediately rang 999 for an ambulance. Thank God they weren't far from the new regional hospital in Ormskirk which had recently built a specialist maternity unit. He pressed Lynton's name on the spur of the moment, not knowing who else to contact, as Abby answered sleepily. He could hear Lynton in the background mumbling what the hell was going on.

"Just come please Abby," he cried down the phone. "Its Victoria, something terrible has happened. I think she's losing the babies."

"I'm coming now Julian. Lynton get your arse out of that bed, Jesus, have you phoned for an ambulance?"

"Yes, yes they're on their way, in fact I can see the siren light flashing now, Christ that was quick. I must go downstairs and let them in and make sure Rocky is secured. See you shortly Abby, thanks, thank you so much. I just wish to fuck I could do something, it's terrible."

"We're on our way, let the ambulance in. See you in ten minutes …"

As Abby ran in, she saw Victoria, now sedated, being brought towards the door on a stretcher. The blue lights of two ambulances flashed incessantly outside. "Julian, I'll go with Vikki in the ambulance. Don't worry she's sleeping and the paramedics have everything under control. She'll be in the maternity ward in no time and in fantastic hands. You've got to find Rocky first and lock up. Lynton can you help him? Have you no idea where he's gone?"

"None, I heard him bark terribly when Victoria and I woke up and she was … in such a state … but when I got downstairs he'd vanished. It's not like him he's such a calm, predictable dog."

"We'll find him, don't worry Julian, he's probably gone off chasing a fox or something," Lynton replied calmly. "Then I'll take you straight to the hospital."

Abby waved as the ambulance, lights still flashing, drove off quickly down the drive and onto the main road and the rear red glow disappeared fast in the mist. Everywhere was an eerie calm with the mist swirling around the trees, a strange night being so warm and misty at the same time. Julian found some torches and they walked briskly towards the wood, Rocky's favourite spot. But they had only wandered about thirty yards when they saw a huge black shape leap out from behind the trees, out of the mist and run towards them at enormous speed.

"Jesus, what the fuck is that?" Lynton shouted, grabbing Julian's arm, terrified.

But as it got nearer Julian smiled. "It's only Rocky. You forget how big and fast a dog he is. Come on boy, where on earth have you been? You've got to come inside now for the night."

"Bloody hell, he looked like the proverbial 'Hound of the Baskervilles' running like that. Shit, what has he got in his mouth?"

They looked down and shone their torches onto his head, as Rocky finally bounded up to them and then obediently dropped some object defiantly onto the floor, like a hunting dog that had caught a game bird. Rocky's eyes blazed. He was panting hard and his muzzle covered in blood."

"Don't pick it up Julian, it's a large piece of some animal, but it sure isn't a fox. I used to do a lot of hunting in my misspent teenage years on Grandpa's estate. Definitely the wrong colour. Fuck, it looks like half a head and a pointed ear, look at the fur, bits of black and grey and the eye has been chewed off. Whatever that was, it certainly isn't alive anymore. He's all pumped up. He must have chased and killed it, the size of him. I can't think of any animal that could out-run such a large wolfhound. It looks maybe like a large badger."

"Whatever," Julian replied. "Let's get him inside into the kitchen. Got to hurry."

At the hospital, Victoria was finally comfortable, drowsy and being comforted by Abby who was holding her hand. They had put her in a private room, quiet and airy. The on-duty consultant quickly confirmed that she had lost both babies with no obvious cause. Abby felt bereft, and guilty, wrongly but she felt it badly, after the tense discussion over having children earlier in the evening. She would willingly have swapped places, but she couldn't. Fate had dealt such a cruel blow to her best friend who had cried so much in the ambulance.

Suddenly the door opened and Aunt Eveline walked in, by which time Victoria had gone off to sleep. Eveline put her fingers to her lips, walked over and gently stroked Victoria's head on the pillow, muttering poor thing. She beckoned Abby to the window.

"Eveline, how on earth did you know? We've only just got here by ambulance?"

"I just knew, Abby. I was still up, I don't sleep much these days, and felt the wave, you know how it is. Woke up Betty Grable who thought I'd gone as gaga as Gerald, but my face probably gave away the seriousness and she kindly brought me immediately. Betty is downstairs with a tea, she'll be fine. I understood that particular feeling, I've not had it for a very long time, dreaded it, but it's happened."

"I don't understand Eveline," Abby replied softly, "Are you saying that you …"

"Yes, my dear. Never told a soul before, not even William but in 1941 I had a miscarriage of twins too, after a secret affair with a Liverpool Member of Parliament. It was the only time in my life I ever truly felt in love. He was killed in a bomb blast at the docks, and then my miscarriage happened, about the same time as Victoria, sadly. He never knew."

"Gosh, Eveline, I'm so sorry."

"Water under the bridge now at my age, although a day doesn't go by when I wonder how they might have grown up. But conceiving twins and losing them, has been, I'm afraid, a recurring and unfortunate legacy for many McKenzie women."

"Really?" Abby replied, her mind searching for some potential comfort for when Victoria woke up.

"Lydia, my grandmother, also lost twins the same way. They were her first, but she went on to have other babies. My mother too was a twin, my dear, the other, as they often did then, died at birth so I believe. But people never talked about such things of course. Lydia's own mother, Susanna McKenzie, also lost twins and had more children, although sadly she died prematurely from smallpox."

"Gosh."

"Did Victoria mention anything in the ambulance here?"

Abby looked puzzled again. "Not really. She was hugely upset of course and by then the sedatives were kicking in. She did mutter in a drowse something about a bad dream and wolves eating babies. She seemed to be in a nightmare when she woke up by the sound of it, but the miscarriage had already happened whilst she was asleep, so Julian said. In fact, I'm going to pop outside and phone Lynton, they should be here by now."

Aunt Eveline went back over to Victoria and stroked her head again on the pillow and put her bare arm back under the blanket gently. She pondered long and hard, frowning. She wouldn't say anything further to Abby but needed to read over her war diaries again.

The door opened again and Abby walked over, exhibiting an irritated expression.

"Is Julian on his way then, my dear?"

"Yes, eventually. When Lynton answered, he was completely out of breath. They're cycling here, would you believe, in the pitch black and cold with no lights between them. I heard a car hoot as he was talking!"

Eveline laughed. "Two determined young men, my dear, we should be proud of them."

"Apparently they eventually found Rocky outside in the woods, locked up Orsbrick, and jumped into Lynton's Mercedes but that wouldn't start. So they ran to Julian's old pickup, which had two flat tyres, and Vikki's car is in the garage being serviced. They then discovered those two old 1920's bikes I found in the boiler room, pumped up the tyres and started pedalling. Lynton was complaining bitterly as Julian, despite being ten years older, is much fitter with all the building work and was many yards ahead but he complained even more about the Merc, which is only two weeks old."

"You have to laugh really, don't you," Eveline replied, stifling a further quiet giggle.

"Anyway Eveline, I know something is bothering you. As you said ... you know how it is. So are you going to tell me?"

Eveline sighed. She didn't really want to say, but Abby, who she was extremely fond of, had her insistent look on. It was impossible to keep secrets from each other.

"Come over here, my dear, this is for your ears only. But all those years back I had a similar wolf nightmare to Victoria, that awful evening. At the time I put it down to an odd and frightening situation that had been going on and was playing on my mind. Over the previous six months of the war, a number of people nearby had been savaged and killed at night and half eaten by packs of abandoned feral dogs, starving and roaming about in the neighbourhood. Given the dire war circumstances prevailing, I suppose not that unexpected. Food had become in extremely short supply. The packs of dogs were seen jumping out from bombed out houses and factories. There were many bomb drops then, the blitz was relentless, night after night with no respite, like London. That period was the height of aerial bombardment. But survivors described their canine attackers, not as dogs, but as large wolves with black, iridescent fur. The authorities ignored or ridiculed them as lunatics or drunks. However, armed men did eventually go out and rounded up a large number of feral dog packs and shot them all. They were big dogs apparently, and it stopped ... that was that. Peculiar isn't it, after all this time, to be reminded of that coincidence again, which I had truly well forgotten, as my life of course moved on."

Abby reflected. Another item she would park into the far recesses of her mind, but as Evelyn said, a coincidence and no more. Anyway, she didn't feel especially alarmed, just sad, so wasn't unduly concerned. Her priority was to ensure that Victoria could get back on her feet and move her life on too like her Aunt Eveline.

Time did move on. Even though the daily encouragement of Victoria out of her inevitable depression felt like a lifetime of walking on eggshells for Abby, autumn eventually came around. She and Lynton had taken both of them, plus Rocky, for a seaside summer holiday in Cornwall that everybody hugely enjoyed. Victoria and Julian were noticeably better; time was slowly healing the pain and grief. Each of them had furiously immersed themselves into work, to stave off the pain. Julian was revising away his perpetual novel with his publishers standing on his neck, and Victoria finished off the cellar laboratory refurbishment and commenced serious work on nineteenth and early twentieth century undiscovered coal tar dyes. In addition, as Victoria's circumstances had dramatically changed and she had been doing so well teaching and achieved outstanding examination results for her A-level students, Cradwell Girls School offered her a permanent job as Head of Science, and follow boldly after her father.

Judy had finally settled into Oxford. At long last contented and off her medication for good, she seemed to be stable and doing fine. In fact life for both couples appeared to be gradually heading for an extended period of welcome calm and normality. Abby's paintings continued to sell well, Lynton's business was expanding, Aunt Eveline and Gerald maintained their happy relationship and Victoria and Julian were trying again for more babies. It was a mere two months further to go before Victoria would be able to sign her deeds and confirm that she had lived in Orsbrick Hall continuously for twelve months to trigger her long awaited and significant cash inheritance that rested quietly, gathering interest in Aunt Eveline's special McKenzie Trust bank account. Their lives could only become better …

Chapter Eight

A Saturday morning in early December 2025 - Southport, Lancashire:

Despite the time of year, Abby emerged from her all-electric BMW sports car, the top down, still dressed in only a flimsy tee-shirt and jeans. She first plugged into the pavement bay, noting that her monthly charging period was due, and triggered the automatic account with a wave of her mobile phone. It was good that parking meters had finally been replaced by charging meters over the summer, the four-party coalition government having struck a last minute deal between the energy companies and local councils to cover the lost income. But of course over the last five years, electrical energy costs and associated power generation expansion had become so cheap owing to the massive shale output, pumped from the huge Bowland Meridian Field discovered nearby. By itself, Bowland was producing more gas and oil than the whole of the UK even needed. The country was once more fully independent of all energy imports, with a prognosis to last well into the next century. North Sea oil was but a distant memory. All wells had been mothballed as uneconomic, used as national repositories for the carbon dioxide pumped in from the myriad gas power stations everywhere.

She wandered down a side street towards the sea front, and caught the unexpected sight of throngs of people, young, old and children, sat on the beach in deck chairs, digging sand castles and eating ice-cream. A real bustle was evident. Without a doubt, the big beneficiaries of the continuing heat wave in England, since the end of September, had been coastal seaside towns, once long viewed as end of the line communities for intractable deprivation, poverty and unemployment. Now these places boomed with tourism over the last four years, when the climate suddenly flipped from those awful, extreme weather periods of continuous rain, gales, floods and snow to a relatively calm, balmy English summer, extended to almost all year round. It felt to Abby the same as people talked about early last century, with summer cricket, warm beer and quiet picnics. Temperatures were definitely on the rise, and global warming was accepted as a fact. But it remained a wing and a prayer whether the predictions of unstoppable and world-end calamity by the year 2125, as the climate change pundits now bemoaned, were facts or fiction. As far as Abby was concerned she would make the most of it, by then it wouldn't matter.

Finally she reached Starlings the florist, tucked away into a small courtyard, where she could enjoy a large pot of tea outside in the little cafe next door ... and wait for Judy and the children.

"Good morning Mrs Grey, we've got your order ready. Would you like some roses and iris mixed in with the waterlilies? They took some finding I must say but we got there in the end, special order from Rotterdam."

"No thanks Dorothy. Just the waterlilies please, with some ferns if you can."

"No problem. That will be eighty-five pounds and ten pence, including the new VAT rate. Lord knows what we small shops will do if it rises about this thirty percent. Just swipe your phone over the reader."

Abby picked up the flowers and sat down in the cafe. It was ten tears to the day that Eveline had died, aged 103, exactly the same age as her brother William. She was found dead in bed with Gerald who had also passed away alongside her. Whether one expired with shock, seeing the other had died, no one would ever know, although Betty Grable said they looked so wonderfully peaceful and serene entwined in each other's arms. Victoria had insisted that both be buried side by side alongside Uncle William in the McKenzie graveyard, a fitting end that Aunt Eveline would have been very happy about. Poor Betty though. That awful osteoarthritis was forcing her into early retirement from Appleby Lodge in the New Year at seventy four, despite her recent graphene hip replacement.

She expected Judy to arrive with Caroline and Toby. Toby had just started walking, but Judy really had to make more effort to discipline seven year old Caroline from bullying him all the time. Abby sighed. At least Judy was, by and large, coping well as a single mum, as long as she remembered to take her medication. It would have been better if a father had materialised, but as neither father was known, nor would ever be discussed, following Judy's two and only obsessive emotional flings, then she would need to maintain a caring, background role to ensure stability. Judy's job as

Chief Archivist at the County Council headquarters in Preston at least provided her with a good independent income, and her small town house in Ormskirk was always spick and span, more than could be said for the Red Lion. The pub had become a little run down again. She needed to take a deep breath from the international demands of her successful art gallery and get the place sorted. Lynton, never home much, seemed to have become oblivious, especially as the buying and selling of art in Europe had become his great obsessive passion, too often, sadly, at a financial loss despite her constant attempts at rebuffed advice. Thank goodness Edward Jacobson, his long suffering senior partner, had kept the law business in Dale Street and the other Lancashire franchises well ticking over, or they would be broke and bankrupt by now.

A loud giggle and cries of 'Auntie Abby' resounded in her ears as Caroline, in a pink summer beach dress, ran into the courtyard and gave her a giant hug, quickly followed by Toby, a huge grin across his ice cream covered mouth, staggering along behind in his romper suit.

"Sorry I'm late," Judy panted. "We got here early and I couldn't get them off the beach. I could do with a green tea. They can have a small milkshake each."

Abby smiled, pulled out a ten pound note and waved over the young girl serving. She didn't give Judy a hug. Judy didn't do touching these days.

"I like your cotton dress Judy, really suits you that colour. Gosh your legs are still tanned from the summer. This balmy weather I suppose."

"Yes, but things will change soon, it will be exactly like the fall of the Roman Empire, swift and brutal. Actually this dress is a bit too crimson and gives me the willies to be honest, but I hate throwing things out, especially when they were presents from my father. He meant well."

Abby smiled again. She was long used to Judy's clipped style of conversation, and reflected for a second. She knew Judy still had something bizarre lurking in her subconscious from that afternoon at Orsbrick Hall, aeons ago, when they all examined Victoria's two strange pieces of purpurine glass prism. The third piece never did turn up and probably never would, but fortunately there had been no ghostly repeats of reenactments. Judy had, for the first time in fifteen years, been back to Orsbrick Hall several times since the summer and seemed relatively calm and normal there. Well, who wouldn't be the way Victoria and Julian had transformed the entire place. Those two really had done exceptionally well between them since the dark days of 2011. Once Lynton had signed off Victoria's twenty-five million pound McKenzie legacy, they were on their way, but the national celebrity status they had both acquired since, one would never have guessed.

Judy continued to ramble on incessantly as the children ran wild around the courtyard, about her latest huge digitisation project she was leading, a mass of newly discovered archived records of five thousand Lancashire canal boat people, dating back to the 1770s. Abby was half listening then remembered. She had forgotten to remind Judy about the special Sunday

146

lunch Victoria had invited them all to, for celebrating the original print publication launch of Julian's novel, Cut and the Cuticle, the book that then went on to change his and her world completely.

Abby interrupted, giving Judy time to wind off her incessant diatribe, like slowing down a thirty thousand rpm flywheel. "Don't forget you and the children are invited to Vikki and Julian's celebratory Sunday lunch. Cut and the Cuticle reached its one hundred millionth copy sold this week since it launched in 2011."

"Will all of those children be there? They make me nervous."

"Come on Judy, of course they will. It's a family celebration, anyway they're growing up fast and Caroline and Toby love playing with the dogs."

"Okay, but I would prefer it if I sit next to you and Dad this time."

"Lynton won't be there. Sorry to say but he's decided to stay on in Bucharest, he thinks he's found a long lost Goya. Some chance of that. So you can sit with me, okay?" Abby patted her hand reassuringly.

Judy pulled her hand away, nodded and smiled, relieved. Conversation with Victoria's teenage children was so hard.

Once Abby had paid the bill, Judy departed with her children for the train back to Ormskirk and Abby sauntered down to the beach. Now that Lynton would not be back for the weekend, as promised, she had some rare time to herself, especially now her lively new gallery manager, Jessica, had taken charge so brilliantly from day one. It was midday and the temperature was nudging a balmy twenty five degrees centigrade, with just a slight westerly breeze blowing in from the Irish Sea. She decided to buy herself a cornetto ice cream and sat quietly in the shade, alone, under a large umbrella on the sand, and mulled over the changes that had taken place since she opened her gallery in 2011, an auspicious year for her as much as Victoria and Julian ...

Orsbrick Hall, still in private McKenzie hands, had been fully restored a long time back. But what was astounding being the way the place had become the high society social mecca and focal point for everything lush, opulent and extravagant, an art and culture powerhouse venue for Lancashire, visited regularly by all kinds of rich film and literary celebrities across the world. That was just Julian's contribution. She would never forget his face when that cantankerous literary agent Sara, still representing him, told him that Cut and the Cuticle had been shortlisted for the 2012 O'Geary Book Prize, and then amazingly it won. The achievement launched Julian into the literary world he had dreamed about, but never expected to embrace in a million years, so often of course, for writers, a matter of luck, circumstance and the full moon being out that night. One hundred million copies later, sales across thirty five countries and twenty seven languages, eight further bestselling novels and three Hollywood films, he was comfortably worth two hundred million dollars.

They never in the end really needed her inheritance. So Victoria used it to amuse herself. She left teaching and Cradwell, and invested her time in getting her science laboratory project up and functional, trying to discover Mauveine's original dyes and colours outlined in those old papers they found. She succeeded, and a lot more. The McKenzie dye factory, a niche and lucrative business, was built five years later on the new industrial estate in Burscough, and exported special coal tar dyes and historic paints to textile manufacturers and artists all over the world. The McKenzie's, just like in the 1860s, had once again become the largest employer in the locality, with a renewed respect from the general community.

Victoria and Julian had done so very well between them. Even she, Abby, was one of Victoria's best marketers, using the special paints extensively in her textile arts, which also sold steadily around the world and kept her own feet at least on the ground.

She smiled. Despite all that wealth and fame, their friendship had stayed strong and special. Julian remained the same old Julian, witty, caring and constantly rubbing his glasses. In between writing, he restored old churches, using his special charity heritage fund. He was a little older, certainly greyer, but still remarkably fit and lithe for his sixty-eight years. Victoria still enjoyed regularly gadding around the world with him on book and film tours and loved her successful business. But most of all she enjoyed her family and especially, their four children, two sets of twins.

Bel and Maddie were sixteen year old kick-ass scientists like their mother and the boys, fifteen year old Ned and Zak, technology nerds with a penchant for building and riding powerful motorcycles around the estate. They sported the latest 1950's fashion craze, in their drainpipe trousers, quaffed, gelled hair and wide sideburns. Without a doubt, Victoria was having it all; securely confident, self sufficient and relaxed.

Abby reached up to pull the front door bell-rope, anxious because she was late, and she was never late in her life for anything. Lynton had kept her on the phone too long and she didn't like the sound of his relentless cough. Clair the housekeeper saw her come and opened the door immediately with a huge smile.

"Don't worry Abby, dinner won't be for another half an hour. Cook is taking her time today with a traditional McKenzie recipe, including vegetarian for Judy, who is already here. Give me your coat. Everyone's in the drawing room."

"Thanks Clair," she replied, spotting Rob, the Orsbrick Hall estate manager, drive past in his tractor and gave him a wave. Danielle, the cook, was his wife. Victoria came out of the kitchen and marched towards the entrance to give Abby a big hug.

"Hey, how are you doing? Judy is here with her children; I was surprised she arrived on her own. They're having a great time with Jeb and Kai. Is she okay Abby? She's a bit withdrawn today?"

"Usual Judy I'm afraid. She was a little anxious, ever wary of large family gatherings which still make her nervous. She'll be fine once I go in."

"Is she coping? I mean at home, the kids look … well normal."

"They are, and so is Judy, Vikki. Just some days she needs to escape, but she's doing fine and holds down a responsible job so … well … I'm much happier."

"Great. Julian has gone to fetch the boys. They're still out on those wretched motorbikes in the woods."

"Knowing Julian, he's probably on one too now."

"That's what worries me. Hey, Maddie and Bel got top marks in their Christmas A-level science exams, Maddie was just one point ahead of Bel and they're still only sixteen, so it's now scholarship preparation. Putting them a year ahead at Cradwell has paid off. All that teen angst and boredom disappeared overnight being amongst their older peers. I want both of them at Cambridge University this summer."

"Don't you miss being at Cradwell, as Head of Science?"

"Sometimes I really do, but so much has happened over the last ten years ..." Victoria replied wistfully. "Anyway, I didn't want to end up like my father, part of the furniture!"

They laughed, just like old times.

Walking into the drawing room, glancing first at Aunt Eveline's painted pond picture on the wall, Abby looked instinctively out of the long garden windows. Sometimes she wished she saw Mauveine and Isi again. It had been so long since the last sighting, at their double wedding. Obviously they finally were both at peace. Judy, looking prim in her short skirt and top, smiled, pleased to see Abby, as Jeb and Kai, two young wolfhounds, and grandsons of the sometime deceased Rocky, loped in, chased playfully by Judy's two children, before they settled their huge sizes in front of the log fire. Bel and Judy resumed an intense conversation as Abby looked on. Both were similar introspective and academic personalities. Maddie, despite being Bel's twin and a minute older, was a more definite clone of Victoria, independent, sassy, gorgeous looking with that sharp McKenzie female stare and effortlessly clever. They began to gather for lunch. Everything was informal exactly as Victoria liked it, as Julian and the boys strode in, guffawing and bellowing over some joke or other.

"I hope you three are going to clean up first?" Victoria shouted, scowling at the mud following behind them.

"Sure Mum, sorry, won't be long," Zak replied cheerfully.

Julian walked over to Abby and gave her a hug. "Lovely you could come Abby, I haven't seen you for ages. These damned book tours again recently and I'm directing the latest Hollywood film would you believe this time. No Lynton? I've brought a special malt back with me from Edinburgh for us today. Never mind, I'll have to drink it myself."

"Sorry Julian, he sends abject apologies, got tied up with business in Romania?"

"Good Lord, not a place I enjoy frankly."

"Hey Dad, you can share that Jack Daniels with Zac and me instead," Ned shouted loudly, Victoria glaring at him, before he spotted Abby, her spiky red hair, slim figure and pencil skirt as short as Maddie's attracting his adolescent gaze. "Abby, you are just way too cool to be my aunt," he burbled, openly leering at her up and down and laughing loudly to Zak who went a brilliant and embarrassed red.

Maddie immediately gave him a hard shove, as he tumbled off balance and glared back at her. "What the fuck was that for, err … sorry everyone, just slipped out, Maddie's crazy as a newt."

"You're just gross Ned, fancying your aunt and older women all the time … you think you're God's gift and you're just a creep."

"Yeh," Bel chimed in, jumping out of her seat. "Are you going to tell everyone about those old Parade magazines which belonged to Great-Uncle William, stashed under your bed then? I wonder what he does with them all."

"How do you know …?" Ned retorted before Maddie cut him off sharply.

"Ned's bored with his new 3D iPhone20 already, as he has the attention span of an amoeba. All he wants now is retro porn, ha, ha, isn't that so Zac?" she cried out, her eyes flashing with victory, seeing him squirm in public. Zac stayed discretely sullen. Everyone laughed, especially Abby.

"Okay you four, that's quite enough thank you," Victoria intervened but felt inwardly pleased that Maddie was proving as adept as she was in her teens, at fighting her own corner. "Will you boys get cleaned up please immediately? Time to eat and we have a very special venison pie dish today, with spinach and pasta alternatives for Judy and Bel. Clair and Danielle are serving now in the dining room. Julian, can you fetch the high chair from the study for Toby … let's go everyone!"

Chapter Nine

Julian picked up his plastic electronic newspaper and tapped from the morning BBC News app and into his Ormskirk Gazette subscription, pleased that the supernet wifi problems they had always experienced through the thick walls of Orsbrick Hall had been finally eliminated by their new hundred terabit per second optical cable line and boosters. His euphoria ceased immediately, as he grimaced sternly at the headline, stark in bold, black print.

Gruesome discovery in the Leeds and Liverpool Canal.

Last night the body of a naked young female was found floating in the reeds near the lock at Parbold by a holiday cruiser. Speculation that the body may be that of the missing sixteen year old, Sally Savage, who has not been seen for the last two weeks, was denied by the police until forensic tests are completed. A further update would be provided by the Police Superintendent later in the day.

He felt some indisposition about leaving with Victoria for another book tour in Tennessee that afternoon, although they had agreed to take a week's holiday, as they had never visited Nashville before and wanted to indulge in some authentic country music. He tapped around the other news apps for a local blogger who tracked stories far quicker than the press and found Canal Worm immediately. A post on this headline was already up. It appeared that the American holidaymakers had discovered the torso after berthing for the night. The female's head had been neatly severed off. Then a video clip of Superintendent Hargreaves appeared who had released an update quicker than expected. The body was indeed Sally Savage, a classmate of Maddie and Bel who they said had not been in school for over a month. The girls mentioned that everyone assumed Sally Savage had run off with her twenty year old boyfriend to London as she had been sick and tired of living at home and especially attending school. That had not obviously been the case.

Suddenly the door opened and Victoria hurried in, flustered. She was having breakfast with Abby in the dining room.

"Morning darling, what's up?"

"Have you got any of those painkillers handy?" Victoria replied, rummaging in drawers to no avail. Abby is suddenly feeling quite unwell for some reason, with a terrible headache. I do think it gets stuffy in there sometimes, the triple glazing is too perfect." She smiled and then noticed he wasn't himself either.

"Yeh, there's some in my man-bag over there. Shit, that friend of Maddie, Sally whatever her name is, who was missing? A body has been found in the canal near Parbold and looks like it's her. Knowing Maddie, permanently glued to her phone, she probably knows already. Where are they all?"

"In their rooms still asleep. Half term starts tomorrow remember. Listen, you over-worry about them, they'll be fine with Clair and Danielle, they are all very sensible. You know the girls especially hate being fussed."

"Yes, wonder who they take after!"

"I'll talk to Maddie later. Must see to Abby first, she's on her way to meet Lynton from the airport and fetch a stack of new paintings from customs."

In the dining room, Abby still felt peculiar and hastily swallowed two tablets.

Victoria quietly closed the door. "Okay Abby, out with it," she whispered. "We've known each other for far too long and I've got a long memory. The last time I saw you like that was when I was lying in hospital in Rotterdam, after I described that terrible incident in the refinery. You've had a turn haven't you?"

Abby knew already but was reluctant to admit it. Something was very wrong. She had felt her head implode like a bolt out of the blue and that awful sickly weakness come over her, not a sensation she had experienced since all those years back. "I don't know, Vikki, maybe, or more likely it was the effects of too heavy a meal last night. Anyway, the pain's going now, I feel much better already." She changed the subject, needing to think more on her own. "Are you all packed then for Nashville? Wish I was heading out there for a bit of Leanne Rimes too."

"Yeh, the concert is all booked. We're staying at some Great Western lakeside hotel. Should be fun. Your normal colour's coming back, chuck."

They laughed warmly, now seemingly back to normal. More than likely, Abby thought, the damned menopause was starting early. She had odd symptoms already. Better visit her doctor.

Two days into half term, Ned was mooching around the shed, bored. He was already well ahead with his school assignments. He switched on his phone and looked for a new Chuck Berry rock and roll music video then found Zac peering into a tablet and playing some war game. "Hey, fancy a lunchtime bottle of beer again at the Cabbage Inn? I've just phoned Ade, he's up for it and he said he'd bring his sister Dottie, but we'll have to take the girls too. Come on don't deny it, you fancy her rotten."

"Okay why not, I'll just ask Maddie and Bel. They're in their rooms doing their homework."

"Fucking hell, it's only half term! Maddie really is like a permanent swot on steroids. Her brain will explode one day." He stared back at his phone screen. "Ade's on his way. We can cycle along the towpath, weather's smart. It'll be a good ride for a couple of hours."

Grumbling, Maddie and Bel fetched their mountain bikes out of the shed and joined the others outside.

"You're not bringing those two are you?" Maddie groaned, seeing Jeb and Kai stood patiently in the yard panting.

"Yes, why not?" Ned replied curtly, already irritated that Maddie and Bel were coming, but that was a necessary part of the deal to bring Dottie along. "They need the exercise, and will love a long run along the cut. Anyway sis, I'm only thinking of you. They can fend off any molesters, although looking at that 1980's frizzy hair of yours, any groper would freak and run a mile anyway."

He laughed loudly, joined by his best friend Adrian, as they both smirked at Zac, unusually talkative, chatting up Dottie energetically at the side.

Maddie grimaced. Adrian and Ned were well suited, both real oiks. "Actually, that's not very amusing Ned and you know why," she said.

Ned went quiet for a moment, thought about Maddie's former classmate and apologised. "Let's go folks," he shouted, changing the tone and waved two twenty pound notes in the air. "Drinks are on me at the Cabbage, the landlord is actually a mate of Ade's brother, so we'll all be fine. Anyway Bel, the way you dress you look thirty-five already, especially with those glasses."

"Ha, ha," she replied, grimacing at her idiot brother.

They set off quickly along the gravel towpath towards Liverpool. The two large wolfhounds easily maintained the pace behind, happy to be out running. Apart from a couple of walkers who promptly dived behind the hedgerow seeing the dogs, an imposing sight at the front of the gaggle of bicycles, all was quiet and deserted along that particular stretch. A great crowd of gravelled dust flew up behind them as they made steady progress. Although generally the local council maintained the canal well, that initial stretch still had no asphalted walkway. Large trees and bushes dipped over the side and into the deep water as they passed though green fields, the occasional pair of noisy wood pigeons and doves flying clumsily across their path.

The Cabbage Inn was about ten miles further on, one of the old and original canal pubs that were built for barge and farm workers to refresh in. The red-brick, imposing building stood nestled alongside the sloping, cobbled stone bank. The public house was a former popular watering hole and resting place for weary boatpeople in the very distant past, who hauled their slow, horse-drawn and gaily coloured barges up and down the towpath from Yorkshire to the docks in Liverpool, carrying huge quantities of coal, cotton, sugar and all manner of traded goods.

Maddie remembered that Great-Aunt Eveline had said the area around the Cabbage Inn had once been miles and miles of flat, empty, rural countryside, nothing but woods, ponds and farms, not a council house to be seen. Hard to believe now, Maddie thought, when one looked at the vast, suburban, concrete sprawl of Liverpool that imposed an ugly facade of identical housing estates nearby. The inn was reputed to be haunted by the ghost of a former boatperson, who in the 1870s had fallen in drunk and drowned after a hard night in the snug. Occasionally he had been seen in the bar late at night on the anniversary of his death, dressed in a top hat and merrily playing a fiddle in complete silence. Bel of course, didn't believe in such nonsense being the cold, rational scientist like her mother. But Maddie was more open-minded and became quite agitated last time they drank in there and Ned started to fool around, whooing stupidly. They all liked the Cabbage, but were sworn to secrecy that nobody must tell their parents they went in, although Abby had once secretly confided to Maddie that Victoria was caught a number of times in the George at fourteen, but that place in Burscough really sucked.

They had just reached Harrison's Bridge, about half-way along and decided to stop for a breather and a swig of water. The dogs sat, panting patiently, and looked as fresh as they left. Everyone was making fun of Zac and Dottie, who didn't play sport like the rest of them waiting, and were struggling to keep up the pace. Around them the woods had thickened up. The old brick, humpbacked bridge, now supporting a main arterial road, rose up majestically in a long semi-circle. Zac had taken Dottie to look down at where the canal had been originally built over the River Old, an unusual sight of still water sat over flowing water. The river acted as an overflow sluice feed, managed by the local water board, further on. The weather was suddenly turning. A chill breeze had set in and dark clouds gathered overhead. The girls were concerned they had no coats then someone mentioned Sally Savage. They fell silent for a moment as two leisure boats chugged slowly past, one behind the other. Zac clicked on his net-watch to synchronise the 5G mobile broadband signal and then put on his iGlasses to check the local weather forecast. They groaned again. Zac was such a perpetual nerd.

"Weather should be fine, probably just a quick blip in the air." he mumbled, fiddling with his watch.

"Hey, what's that lot doing over there?" Bel suddenly shouted, pointing at something strange near the bank in the water about fifty yards further down, almost completely camouflaged under the thick, overhanging willows and bushes, which had grown wild, covering almost a quarter of the width of the canal. Ned, showing off his bicycle one wheelers and doing a selfie with his new phone at the same time spun round.

"Seems like the remains of a large boat to me. I'm going to take a look," he replied and cycled furiously towards it. The others, except Ade, had trailed way behind. As they approached they were immediately met with an odd and foul smell in the air, like a mixture of wet dogs and rotting compost.

"Jesus," Adrian cried, beating Ned by five seconds. "What the fuck is that stench? Hey Zac, you haven't shit yourself have you?" he called back, laughing as the others braked and skidded on the gravel. They dumped their bikes on the side and stared into the thick tangle of foliage in the canal.

"I wish you'd put a sock in it Ade, your stupid jerk comments all the time make me sick," Dottie, his sister cried, red in the face with annoyance.

Ned waved everyone back to order, smirked, and said solemnly. "Can you all calm down please? Dot, after all, is only standing up for the man she loves. See, she does fancy you Zac."

Maddie seeing Dottie embarrassed gave him a sharp push as he fell off his bike laughing. They all turned to Zac, totally oblivious, who had his iGlasses on again. He was concentrating hard at something and grimaced. The two dogs had suddenly stiffened and growled menacingly, then both jumped into the bushes on the other side, sniffing and searching for something.

"Hey, shut the fuck up you lot, sorry Dottie not you," Zac spluttered. "I've just done a quick search and

161

a database match. Look at the side of the boat. I know everywhere is pretty burned out but you can just see three quarters of the name."

They all turned and looked down the side of the vessel at the white lettering, the former yellow painted surface now black and scorched. The rotting hulk, half sunk in the water looked like it had been there for a hundred years.

"Mmm, the Dutch …" Bel started to say, fingering the shape of the letters in the air.

"Dutch Tulip," Zak finished off. "That was the name of the holiday boat which found Sally Savage, I reckon this is it. But how come it's got into such a state?" He quietly continued his iGlasses search, looking for more information.

Ned by now had jumped onto the deck, followed by Ade, big and muscular like his brother, six inches taller than the rest of them and with a reputation in the school for being a hard bully when it suited him. "Ade and I are going to take a look inside, after you Ade."

"Be careful you two, there might be someone hiding, I think we should phone the police first," Maddie urged, now feeling very concerned and agitated, especially as her idiot brother always did before he thought. Bel and Dottie had followed the dogs into the bushes to see what on earth they were searching for.

Adrian smiled. His thick biceps rippled in his tee-shirt. He winked at Maddie, pulled out a knife from his belt and started pulling strongly on the locked cabin door which eventually after more tugs and a sharp kick by Ned gave way.

Adrian was only inside the black hole for five seconds, when they heard him shout and scream, loud and fearful, followed by a horrible, deep growl and a scuffle as something inside leapt on him. The girls screamed. Ned was stood at the door rooted to the spot, his eyes wide. He stared at the scene with incredulity and terror, for what seemed an eternity. But it wasn't. In a split-second, the two wolfhounds ran, barking like crazy, and leapt onto the boat, knocked Ned over and tore headlong into the cabin. An enormous fight ensued, furniture flying everywhere, followed by a second ear-splitting and curdling scream. The dogs emerged, covered in blood, dragging a large and very dead animal out onto the deck, its throat torn and severed. Ned ran in and started struggling to pull Adrian, now unconscious, out by the legs. Zac jumped onto the deck to help him, followed by Bel and Dottie. Maddie, still standing by the side, pulled out her phone from her bicycle bag and frantically dialled the police.

Bel immediately took charge on deck, calm and collected as ever. She had completed a first aid course recently at school and was putting a plan of action into place. Adrian's face was black and cut all over and his clothes shredded. He was bleeding badly, his upper arm half severed, the pain having caused him to pass out. Ned was white and shaking. They stared in disbelief at the bloodied mass of fur on the deck. It looked impossibly like a huge black wolf.

"Ned, Zac, don't just stand there, bring me that sheet in the cabin and the blanket on the floor, quickly," Bel shouted, Dottie cradled her brother's head in her arms, as he came to, moaning in severe pain. She gently wiped his face. He shook violently. Ned came back with a handful of sheets, followed by Zac who held a pile of blankets and pillows from the wreck of what was left of a former sleeping quarter.

Bel grabbed Adrian's knife and quickly cut up shreds of sheeting to apply a tourniquet and arrest the awful bleeding from his badly bitten arm, whilst Dottie, helped by Ned and Zac, covered him with the blankets to keep him warm, propping his head comfortably with the pillows.

But whilst they were occupied with Adrian, wolfhounds Jeb and Kai had begun to drag the dead animal towards the edge of the boat. Finally, coordinating their joint strength, they hurled it headlong into the canal. It landed with a great splash. The water bubbled and hissed as the matted, furry mass immediately bloated up and then slowly disappeared in a cloud of steam. A fetid stench filled the air.

Maddie, still on the towpath and having successfully reached the emergency police and ambulance services, watched, mesmerised and fascinated. It was as if whatever that thing was had dissolved away like white chalk in sulphuric acid. Staring at the water, where all was now calm, she realised the sun had returned and that foul smell everywhere had vanished, but something out of the corner of her eye disturbed her. She looked up and over Harrison's Bridge to see a woman on a bicycle, perched on the top and watching them, quiet and impassive. Maddie blinked and stared again, concentrating harder. Although the woman had some sort of old and dirty looking hoodie pulled up over her hair, the face was clearly visible. She gasped … that was impossible, surely not … it just simply couldn't be. The face was the exact image likeness of Judy's, the same long features and staring eyes, even the colour of her hair.

She shouted up but the woman hastily jumped onto her bicycle and pedalled away furiously, disappearing into the distance.

"What the fuck?" Maddie muttered to herself, shaking her head.

Ned was now beside her whilst the others remained with Adrian. Bel's tourniquet had successfully worked for the moment. Both dogs lay beside him quietly, panting. Dottie was giving Adrian a drink from her bottle of water.

"Are the police and ambulance coming? Who were you shouting to, sis?" Ned asked, staring up at the bridge.

"Nobody. I thought I saw someone but they seemed to have cleared off. Ambulance is on its way, shouldn't be long and the police too. Christ, I wish Mum and Dad were here and they're not due back for four days. We'll probably have to give some sort of statement."

"I hope they can save Ade's arm, shit he's in a bad way," Ned replied, watching his sister and Dottie on the boat deck. "Bel has been absolutely brilliant, I don't know what we'd have done if she wasn't here. Reckon she should become a doctor or something. She's actually stopped all the bleeding. Ade went into like shock which isn't surprising. Jesus, Maddie, if it hadn't been for Jeb and Kai, that wolf would have had all of us. Where's it gone so we can show it to the police?"

"The dogs shoved it over the side, but it just disappeared under the water." She decided to keep the surreal dissolve and bubble aspect to herself. She needed to reflect, especially after how she had felt beforehand.

"You're joking?" Ned replied in disbelief. "That's really weird, sis."

"You said wolf. Really Ned, do you actually think it was a wolf? They've been extinct for many hundreds of years in England, although this area apparently was one of the last remaining haunts for wolf hunting. It was probably a large and wild feral dog, hanging out in the remains of this boat."

"Honestly Maddie, the others will back it up. They saw it closely as well and Ade of course. It was definitely a wolf, and a big one. I saw those eyes stare at me just before Jeb jumped on it. They were yellow and evil."

"Listen," Maddie replied thoughtfully. "The police will be here in a minute, and we've got no evidence of a wolf carcass. We must all stick to the same story, because nobody is going to believe us, or all this boat stuff which Zac found. I'm going to call Aunt Abby."

"Good idea, I'll just tell the others. I can hear a siren. Look down the road, there's the ambulance, thank God."

The paramedics examined Adrian carefully and gave him a shot of antibiotic and a sedative. Now dozing quietly, they brought a stretcher out and strapped him in, before carefully manhandling him over the side. Ade was a dead weight on the slippery deck, as they finally struggled along the towpath into the back of the ambulance, helped by Ned and Zac. The dogs sat obediently and quietly by the bicycles, and drank water from their bowls. Bel had quickly washed the blood off their mouths. The police meanwhile were questioning the three girls. They were stern and certainly disbelieving that a wolf was on the prowl, especially when Maddie reiterated numerous times that the animal had sunk into the water. A second patrol car, lights flashing, drew up below the bridge and a more senior police inspector in his early thirties jumped out and immediately took charge whilst the others were told to look inside the boat.

As he started up the ambulance, the senior paramedic shouted over to the inspector. "Colin, don't be too hard on that girl there," pointing to Bel. "She did a superb job of first aid, as professional as I've ever seen, even in accident and emergency. I reckon she's saved this lad's life and hopefully his arm."

Bel smiled back at the driver and muttered thank you. The ambulance shot off quickly, with all sirens and lights belting out. Ned, after checking the dogs who now seemed remarkably relaxed, sauntered over to rejoin Zac and the girls. The inspector and a young female detective sergeant, having first established that nobody else had been injured, took over the questioning, whilst the other offices were instructed to search around the vicinity of the boat and in the shrubs. Another large police van drew up. A team of half a dozen forensic officers, in white suits and protective clothing, jumped onto the deck with electronic devices and commenced a thorough search of the inside of the cabin, collecting all kinds of samples and bagging up bits and pieces. Maddie hoped they would find something which would corroborate their statements.

The inspector turned to Ned, having ascertained he had been the closest to see what had happened to Adrian.

"I'm Chief Inspector Colin Sullivan, so start again lad, for Detective Sergeant Wilkins here and me, slowly and carefully, from the point that you got the cabin door open."

He waved at one of the officers who perused Jeb and Kai with some trepidation, but they remained seated, calm and untroubled, once Zac had called over for them to stay and lie down. "Constable, can you phone in for a diver from the Preston search and rescue unit. I want one of the team over here immediately."

"Yes sir," he replied, and walked briskly back to the car.

Maddie, carefully watching the forensic activity with interest as they roped off the scene thoroughly, turned to Inspector Sullivan, who looked her up and down in a way which gave her a chill in her stomach. What was wrong with these guys? "So, err … Chief Inspector Sullivan … do you believe us then, that the wolf disappeared under the water?"

"I don't think I was talking to you young lady," he replied testily, in a thick Liverpool accent, as she bristled at his rude arrogance, the bastard. Yet another misogynistic police idiot. The female detective shot a glance over to Sullivan and he took a deep breath and recommenced, sensing the expression on Maddie's face that this could be someone troublesome. He really wanted to get back to the station for a salary review with the Chief Constable. "Assuming that something did end up in the water, then whatever it is, we'll find it down there. Your name, miss?"

"I'm Madeleine McKenzie, this is my sister Belle and my two brothers, Edward and Zackary," she replied formally and precisely, emphasising her posh accent even more. The others stared. Nobody ever used their proper names.

She continued unheeded. "Our injured friend is Adrian Agnew and his sister Dorothy is the person who has accompanied him in the ambulance to the hospital. I can give you where they live if you need it now. Our address is Orsbrick Hall."

Maddie had decided the group needed a leader and some clear speaking and she was the best and the oldest, just. "Edward, can you relate to the Chief Inspector exactly what you saw, although we have of course already given a description to the two officers over there."

Sullivan immediately thought posh snobby gits, probably with influential parents. He'd better go a bit easy, not really the normal scum he usually saw on a Saturday night fighting and vomiting drunk in the street. But all young people were hoodlums in his book, moneyed or not. "I'd like to hear the story again, for my own ears, please."

Ned continued slowly, reiterating as much as he could, although it all happened so quickly and in a blur. The ones who really saw and understood couldn't speak, Jeb and Kai.

After some further bland questions by the detective sergeant, Chief Inspector Sullivan turned to Maddie. "We would like you all to accompany us back to the police station for further questioning and to look at some pictures of other potentially related boat crime. There's been a lot of vandalism with canal boats lately." He pointed to the second large police van, thick bars over the windows, which had just arrived, which Ned stared at askance. "I also want to ask your cooperation for some blood tests."

"But we don't do that stuff, officer," Ned stuttered, glancing at Zak, who said nothing, but was looking stupidly guilty before he had even be charged.

Sullivan smirked. "You mean drugs? That isn't the reason for my request but now you've mentioned it, and having heard these bizarre explanations, we'll do that check as well."

Maddie gripped Ned's arm tightly. He was looking unhelpfully belligerent, standing to his full six foot height and squaring up to Sullivan. "Are you charging us Chief Inspector?" she said. "If so I would like to request our lawyer to be present," calmly, thinking on her feet about what they always did in crime movies. Bel turned open-mouthed to Maddie, whilst Ned and Zac looked blank.

Detective Sergeant Wilkins was now very uneasy with the situation, which was getting out of hand, especially with her boss who had a reputation for going hard on any young person brought to his attention. Her instinct was that the kids in front of her were telling the truth. Something distinctly unusual had happened, even though the story was so outlandish. This incident had nothing to do with vandalism or drugs. A message pinged loudly into her phone. She read it then drew Sullivan aside immediately and whispered something hastily in his ears. He frowned and departed at haste, with no further comment except to say that Detective Sergeant Wilkins would accompany them down to the station.

Ned and Zac leashed up the two dogs. As they walked with all the bicycles, including Ade's and Dottie's, to the police van, Sergeant Wilkins stopped. "You were right about one key part of your statement. Headquarters have just confirmed that the pleasure boat here does indeed belong to the American couple who found the missing dead girl, Sally Savage, your classmate Madeleine. It had been assumed and told to us by friends that the couple were boating in some other part of the country. We will be putting in a major effort to find them quickly."

Zak punched his hand in the air and shouted 'whoa' immediately receiving a glare back from Bel, before he meekly apologised to Sergeant Wilkins, who grinned.

"Now, before we go down to the station," she continued, "Just to confirm, there won't be any need for blood tests or lawyers Madeleine, but I do want to show you all some other pictures and get your evidence properly noted. And I think Chief Superintendent Hargreaves, my boss, will wish to talk to you directly. Your parents should be present however. Do you wish to call them now?"

They looked at each other sheepishly, and shuffled uneasily as Maddie again piped up. "They are both out of the country on business and not back for three days I'm afraid."

"So who is looking after you, in loco parentis as it were?"

Maddie instantly sensed a potential problem looming. The last thing they wanted was for social services to suddenly swoop on Orsbrick Hall, and her parents landed in court for child neglect, ridiculous though it seemed, but such a thing had once happened to her best friend Lucy. She looked up to the bridge and pointed.

"She is, just coming over, our Aunt Abby," thankful to see a familiar figure marching towards them.

At the police station, Abby arrived separately, very uneasy. Sam Hargreaves, she knew of. He was the grandson of the former Sergeant George Hargreaves, who Victoria revered as a child and whose picture was still hanging up over the fireplace of the George pub in Burscough, they all used to visit and eat at, way back in 2010, when Victoria first learned of her Orsbrick Hall inheritance. In keeping with his family, Chief Superintendent Hargreaves had maintained the tradition of policing through the generations but had done especially well, having worked up quickly to become one of the most senior ranks in the County, after being the first Hargreaves to graduate from university.

Following the temporary placement of Jeb and Kai into special kennels, Abby and the four teenagers undertook further questions and the recording of statements. After a warming police lunch, they were finally ushered into a large room as Detective Sergeant

Wilkins returned with a tall, round-faced jovial man, but somewhat overweight, Abby thought, for a copper. However, he was very friendly and informal from the outset, introduced himself as Sam, insisting they called him that, and confirmed that the somewhat unpleasant creep, Chief Inspector Sullivan had been taken off the case and assigned to other duties in Liverpool. Chief Superintendent Hargreaves confirmed he would personally lead this investigation, as circumstances had changed. It also turned out that Sam had been a friend and classmate of Victoria, commenting on how well she had done, bringing Orsbrick Hall back as an economic and social hub of the local community. He was also in Lynton's Lodge of the Brown Bulls in Southport, which was typical of Lynton. Who didn't he network with? Abby breathed a sigh of relief. Sam had seemed unexpectedly pleased with the information provided and was very positive, not flinching even over the wolf story. She had dreaded what she would say to Victoria and Julian over the phone. Undoubtedly, knowing them, they would head back on the next available plane if there was any problem with the children.

They sat down around the conference table with coffees and coca-colas, as Sam Hargreaves commenced.

"I hear, Madeleine and Belle that you both want to be scientists, same as your mother. An excellent choice, I must say. We need more women in science in this country. Forensic technologies in the force have advanced so well in the last fifteen years that in the old days we would never have been able to confirm results as quickly after the event, only four hours ago. You might want to think about forensics when you get to university, excellent career prospects."

They both smiled and Bel nodded. Maddie though had other ideas.

He continued. "And you boys? Both strapping lads, you'd make good coppers, never did me any harm. Your fine detective work on identifying the boat, Zackary, has brought together a lot of progress. Belle, the hospital contacted me earlier to personally say they were extremely impressed with your professional first aid. Not only has that young man's life been saved by your prompt action, but, so it appears, has his arm. They've managed to sew it up successfully and done a stem cell skin graft. The injuries will take some recovery and physiotherapy, but eventually your friend Adrian should be back to normal. The hospital wishes to put your name forward for one of their outstanding young people awards, Belle, which I will wholeheartedly support. Well done."

They all clapped warmly with cheers all round as Maddie kissed her sister on the cheek and Abby gave her a giant hug. Bel beamed, she had never won anything in her life before, always been quiet in the background grafting away.

Sam Hargreaves continued. "Okay, now here's the nub of things. I'm addressing the media immediately after we finish. You will all be anonymised, but I want you to personally hear the report first. Forensics did indeed find evidence of wolf fur around the boat, and on swabs taken from the dog's mouths, but we couldn't find anything in the water, as yet. There is a trough of deep mud down there so they will have another look.

We also found wolf fur on the body of Sally Savage, discovered tragically in the canal a few weeks back. At the time it made no sense, but now things have suddenly come together. This morning, after an unacceptable reporting delay, the owners of a private zoo confirmed that a couple of wolves have escaped on the Rattenheath estate north of Ormskirk. Heaven knows why people want to keep them. You can neither tame nor train wolves like dogs, and once back in the wild they revert to type immediately. It's pretty clear to me that your dogs killed one of them, and by the matching we suspect the same one sadly had found the girl's body and butchered it further. It was understandable for a wild animal, but of course for Sally Savage's family this has been a very difficult and distressing time."

They nodded. Ned felt queasy again at the thought of that wolf eating a girl's head and how lucky they had all been, and sipped his coke steadily.

"Our attention is now firmly focussed on finding the American owners of the leisure boat, which they obviously dumped and tried to destroy evidence which we have found of Sally Savage in the cabin. In addition some sheep have just been reported killed, and a farmer has claimed he saw what looked like a wolf lurking at the end of the field, but missed when he shot at it. So an organised hunt will be on for the remaining one. We have more work to do to close Sally Savage's case, but I feel much more positive we can envisage the scenario that probably unfolded, very tragic though it has been. Now, I have to leave and tell the press what I've told you. Detective Sergeant Wilkins will take you back to the kennels for your two dogs and arrange to get you and the bicycles back home in a van.

"That's fine, thank you Sam," Abby replied. "But I came in Victoria's pickup truck and we can all fit into that so I'll take them home straight away. I'm sure Detective Sergeant Wilkins has a lot to be getting on with."

"Good, excellent," he replied and rose stiffly, shaking all their hands warmly. "If you can depart out the back way please, I can hear the press baying for me in the front!"

Chapter Ten

Clair pulled open the heavy front door and they stumbled inside, exhausted, and flopped instantly into the armchairs. First girls, then boys followed by dogs, whilst Abby and Rob unloaded the bicycles from the rear of the pickup and wheeled them into the triple garage.

"Where on earth have you all been?" Clair gently asked. "Your mother rang after lunch and when I said I had no idea where you were, I'm afraid she wasn't at all happy."

"Don't worry Clair," Abby replied. She walked in and gazed at the slumped teenagers, already gorping aimlessly at the television. "They've been on the canal. A bit of a long bicycle ride today and in the end I had to pick them up from Liverpool. I think they've overdone it, even the dogs haven't had so much exercise before," watching them stretched out and yawning on their favourite giant rug in front of the fireplace.

Danielle bustled in, her face red with running down the stairs. "My goodness, I heard the door go and hoped it was all of you. We were getting worried. I'll just rustle up some homemade cheeseburgers and chips."

"Cool Danielle, I'm starving. Mushy peas too thanks," Ned replied with a grin, pulling open a can of beer out of the fridge.

"Is your father happy with you drinking that beer, Ned?" Danielle uttered sternly. "Last time I was not sure, he went fairly apoplectic if I remember?"

"We sorted it and Dad chilled, as long as we stick to only one with a meal. He's just glad I don't smoke. Guinness goes well with a burger doesn't it Zac and beer's good for you."

Zac stared up momentarily, and then his head flopped back into his tablet. He was checking the local news press releases. "Whatever, bro. I'll stick to this coke thanks."

Searching for anything on the Sally Savage murder, Zac soon found a short video clip of Chief Superintendent Hargreaves, released earlier. With his headphones on, he ran through it and smiled. True to his word, Sam Hargreaves had relayed the facts to the media exactly as he had told them in the police station, only saying that a group of cyclists spotted the holiday barge on the towpath and then called the police as it looked suspicious. Indications of blood and animal remains found on the boat showed that one wolf was likely dead, but they were still trying to find the corpse. Zac felt great relief. No names, thank Christ, or their parents would go ape shit. A police hunt was apparently ongoing nationally for those missing Americans, and local farmers were organising some shooting groups to track the remaining wolf still on the loose. The zoo owners would be heavily prosecuted. He pondered. They all had to keep schtum at school for the moment. But what about Adrian?

"I'm going to feed the dogs, Aunt Abby, and then walk them in the woods for their nightlies," Ned chuntered, never able to keep still for long and waved the beer bottle he was drinking from. He disappeared, with Jeb and Kai lolloping after him hungrily. "Come on Zac, give me a hand will you."

"Yeh, I need a shower and get changed too. See you guys over dinner in twenty minutes," Bel added, walking to the door, as Abby nodded. She looked across the room at Maddie, who was staring nonchalantly out of the window in deep thought.

"A penny for them Maddie. Want to come and tell me?"

Maddie turned around and smiled. She had always really liked Abby and knew now this was the time to confide. She settled down in a chair and they both picked up glasses of home-made lemonade that Clair had brought in earlier.

Abby broke the ice first. "You know Maddie, when I look at you now and especially after today, you remind me so much of your mother, it is quite uncanny. I think you've taken after her much more than any of the others, temperamentally and academically. Despite you two being a twin, Bel is more like your father. Hey and Ned and Zac could be anybody's I guess!"

Maddie laughed. "Yes I agree, Ned especially. Bel and I may be twins but we're not identical, just fraternal. It's all about which eggs get fertilised and how."

Abby sighed. "That sounds far too complicated for me. Never was too hot on biology, but then I was a rebel at boarding school and much more into punk rock at your age."

"Aunt Abby, can I please just call you Abby now? I know Mum insists but it just seems sort of naff at my age."

Abby smiled. "Yes please, I'll have a word with Vikki. The word aunt makes me feel terribly old and now I am getting terribly old even more so."

"Gosh, I never think that at all. You always wear the most fashionable gear and I love the way you do your hair and makeup, you look fabulous. Will you show me some time?"

"Yes of course. But it was a bit wilder when my hair was pink."

"Really, I never knew. I wish I understood more about Mum when she was younger. She never wants to talk about when she was my age at school or even being a scientist, yet she's a fantastic role model for girls at Cradwell. I know you two shared a flat in Holland once and that's when you met. That's about it. I know very little about my grandparents, except Mum's father had also been a science teacher once at my school a very long time back. I got a little bit of info from Great-Aunt Eveline but that was ages ago. I was only seven when she died."

Abby always felt a strong bond with Maddie. If she ever could have chosen a daughter, Maddie would have been it. "I suspect Vikki sees in you a clone of her at the same age. You are so very alike in temperament and ability. Your mother had a tough time in childhood and had to fight hard to complete her education and climb up the career path to become a senior scientist in the Netherlands, when she and I first met. They were good, carefree years then. Everything changed when she got word of inheriting Orsbrick Hall. The rest, including all of you, as they say is history!"

Abby suddenly found herself struggling to concentrate, the more she gazed at Maddie who had moved onto what happened during the day again. Then it hit her like a bolt out of the blue. She understood for the very first time ever, like some weird tuning in had taken place, probably triggered by the day's events that she had been uneasy about ever since. It was now obvious that Maddie had the same thing.

"Is there something you want to tell me?" Abby uttered slowly and deliberate.

Maddie went thoughtful for a moment. "Yes, I need to tell someone, badly, and neither my parents nor the others would understand. They'd really think I was bonkers, but I saw something more today, a couple of really odd things, Abby."

"Yes, I thought you did. So?"

Maddie started to explain tentatively, unsure at first whether to confide, as she described the strange sinking and dissolving away in the water of the dead wolf enveloped in a cloud of steam, followed by the sighting of the unknown woman on the bridge, a woman who looked exactly like Judy. "But there's something else Abby that goes back, like ages ... as far as I can remember. I once confided in Great-Aunt Eveline as a small child. She was like that; you always wanted to tell her all your deep secrets, as if she already knew them anyway. Great-Aunt Eveline said something just before she died."

Abby grinned and nodded. She knew very well and missed that all-knowing aspect of Eveline terribly.

Maddie stopped for a few seconds to gather her thoughts again. "She said it was fine and nothing to worry about, but never to mention it to anyone. Except, when I got older one day, I should ask you ... as you would understand."

Maddie sighed and continued slowly. "For as long as I remember ... I sort of see things occasionally ... maybe two or three times a year, outside in the grounds. I'd describe them as visions of a life long ago past in history, with lots of noise and bustle going on around me. Men, women and children are working in the fields and going about their daily business, tilling and gathering hay, even skating on the pond in winter, covered in ice. All happy stuff, and I'm like an observer in a dream, but I can't participate. It's really weird and always I relive the scenes in the same sort of time period. Then, after a minute or two, everything around me dissolves into a mist and vanishes, and I feel a sort of deep peace inside my head, for hours afterwards."

Maddie stopped and looked up to gauge Abby's reaction who continued listening with intense interest, no sign of ridicule in her eyes or her body language. Maddie continued, now feeling confident for the first time to describe her own reactions. "Curious, as ever, I secretly researched the style of clothes, the activities and the scenery both online and down the library and used the excuse for a history project. I quickly concluded that what I see always happens in the seventeenth century. I've now rationalised the experience ... sort of to cope really. It became in my mind the same as having vivid dreams, except I was awake. But a month ago, one night, I was locking the front gate and the visions all changed and became very upsetting and scary. Guns were being fired and people were running about distressed, and then I saw something horrible. Women were tied onto stakes and set alight. They were screaming, awful sounds and smells, presumably being condemned as witches. Logic makes me feel that those last visions and what has happened today are connected somehow. What does it all mean Abby? Are they sort of like ghosts?"

Abby pondered hard. This was extraordinarily tricky, something in Orsbrick Hall was certainly amiss again, after all those years since 2011. Plus, the mantle of knowledge and psychic capabilities was being passed on to the next McKenzie generation. She instantly decided. There would be no faffing about. She had to be direct and absolutely crystal clear with Maddie. Thank goodness she was so bright, grown-up and stable, unlike her own step-daughter, who shared the same abilities. "No, I wouldn't describe them as ghosts, not in the way people usually talk. You were born with a special type of psychic gift Maddie, which often runs in families, especially on the female side. You're able to perceive what I would describe as different universes in alternative phases of space and time, and you are a kind of connecting rod, a communications channel. I call it a wormhole."

"Like in physics, you mean?"

"Yes, you're a pathway which can bridge the now and then. Your paranormal sight is attuned to the specific period you describe, we all tend to be different, I don't know why. Eveline was very sensitive, and she and I were close. I do miss her so very much still, but your mother doesn't share it. Vikki has always been tolerant when something has arisen that she can't analyse and argue away, but deep down she is still sceptical, especially with her very strong left-brain scientific, logical and rational view of the world."

"You mean tolerant with you? You have it too Abby don't you."

"Yes, the same thing runs in my family strongly, and is also in Lynton's too coincidentally."

Maddie reflected for a second. "So Judy has it as well. I knew it, I always knew and couldn't work it out, but I can't connect with her like I know, now, I am connecting with you. Don't take it the wrong way, but Judy's always given me the creeps, and then I see a clone of her on that bridge this morning. It makes me feel very nervous."

Abby sighed. Maddie was already so very mature and grounded for her age. But Abby knew Judy's routines, religiously mapped out and recorded well in advance, day by day, so she could step in immediately if a sudden crisis blew up, especially with the children around. And Judy was definitely working at the archive all day. "I understand about Judy, but she is truly a very kind and gentle person, massively clever and caring. She just has to battle daily against her lack of connection with the emotional world. It's why she struggles to understand jokes and ironies, which you and I take for granted. People over the years have taken advantage of her, sadly. Sometimes the world gets too much and she shuts down, and then I try and catch her."

"Like with the non-existent fathers I presume," Maddie replied with a frown, realising she had badly misunderstood Judy and should have known better, and would try harder to develop a relationship.

Abby continued. "I can't explain what or who you saw this morning, but it certainly wasn't Judy because she was at her desk in work. Sometimes sightings get a bit warped, a confused manifestation, probably as that psychic space-time bends and moves around ragged edges."

Maddie laughed. "I like the eloquent way you put that Abby, but I understand now, and I can't tell you the relief I feel for the first time that I'm not worryingly bonkers. Who is Mauveine?"

Abby looked up sharply. "Why?"

"I was doing some science work with Mum and she mentioned her as the inspiration behind developing and experimenting with all the dye business she's developed. I surreptitiously checked in some of the family records in the library and I've read Mauveine's original papers, an amazing woman of the time. I now realise. Was she a distant relative? Does science run in the family too?"

"Yes and yes, Mauveine is the person in the painting in the hall alcove. But there's a big family split. Either the McKenzie women did science like you and your mother, which was hugely challenging in those days because of the patriarchal society and lack of support for women's education, or they became artists like me. Great-Aunt Eveline and Lydia, her own grandmother, were amazingly creative visual artists in their day. You come from a talented family, Maddie, and your father is a pretty cool dude too."

"I agree, for an oldie he's not bad still."

They giggled and Abby gently patted Maddie's hand affectionately. She immediately remembered that remarkable day when Julian, shirt off and bare-chested, sledge-hammered into Mauveine's laboratory in the cellar all those years back, and had wished instantly that she, rather than Vikki had found him first. But Lynton turned out to be a great catch in the end and she had been genuinely happy for all those years since being with him.

"Abby, are you okay, you've gone into a daze?"

Abby grinned. "Yes, just thinking ..."

"You've got a lot of happy memories haven't you of those times before we were all born and you first met Mum, Dad and Uncle Lynton. I'd love to hear more about that. I do love reminiscing and am always curious about the family and history and stuff. I'm not as Mum seems to think, all science day in and day out like her. It's not a criticism but she does like to keep very focussed in the present, and gets impatient with the past, unless it's science of course."

"I will, Maddie, I promise. You and I have crossed a new threshold which is great. Oh, and call him Lynton too, he's become worse than me these days, obsessing about getting old. He likes to believe that fifty-five is the new twenty-five. You're much more rounded and curious, like Great-Aunt Eveline and me. Anyway, our food should be ready. We'd better see how Clair is getting on."

Abby realised that a new and fundamental beginning for the two of them had transpired. But equally she and Maddie needed to help each other, to try and find out what was suddenly going on in Orsbrick Hall. Whatever the occurrences were, Mauveine and Isi appeared to be outside this continuum or they would surely have made themselves known.

As they got up, the door opened with a clumsy bang and Ned strode in grinning. "Hey you two, your dinners are in the oven keeping warm. Guess what, something really weird has happened?"

Abby and Maddie, in turn, looked sharply at Ned, concerned instantly in their own way. There had been enough weird occurring for one day.

"It's Ade. Zac and I have eaten and we were about to head off for the bus and visit Ade in hospital, see how he's doing. I was going to sneak in a couple of beers. But he's completely disappeared. Neither Dottie nor the hospital have any idea where or how he got out unseen and where he's gone and his arm is like all bound up. So Zac and I are cycling round to Dottie's, who lives with her aunt, to check out what's happening and see if we can find him."

Abby pondered. "Okay, but take care both of you. You've got your mobiles I assume? Where are Adrian's parents?"

"Zac doesn't use his mobile, he talks through his iGlasses these days. Sadly, Ade's mum and dad split and both did a bunk years back, so he lives with Jonny, his older brother who takes care of him. He's like never had a proper home. But he's my best mate, so I gotta look out for him. See you later."

As Ned shot off, Bel walked in. "I've still got to eat too, and then an early night, I'm totally done in. You guys want to watch The Matrix with me, like food on laps and stuff? Aunt Abby, Dad has installed a new plastic plasma TV screen with built in sound, which looks like Georgian wallpaper on the big wall in the sitting room, until it fires up. The picture is awesome 3D, you really must see.

"Yes, okay," Abby replied. "Gosh I haven't seen that film for years."

"The Matrix?" Maddie queried, puzzled.

"Just up your street Mad," Bel cried. "A futuristic sci-fi where people are controlled by computers, the film was way ahead of its time when it was originally made in 1999."

"Sounds more like a Zac thing, but yeh, my brain needs to switch off too."

"Great," Bel replied grinning, before twirling around to march out. "I'll just fetch the burgers from the kitchen and switch on. It took a bit of fiddling to link the film stream up last time."

On the way to the sitting room, Maddie suddenly stopped and picked up her rucksack. "Gosh I almost forgot. I've got something I wanted to show you that I found in my room the other day, stuck behind one of the old desk drawers. I have no idea what it is, but it looks interesting."

She reached in and pulled out something wrapped in tissue. When she unfolded the paper, Abby felt a pang of irrational fear run up and down her spine. It was a crimson and translucent small piece of shaped glass.

"Why did you want to show me Maddie?"

Maddie thought for a moment, screwed up her eyes and shrugged her shoulders. "To be honest, I don't actually know why, I just did. But looking at your face you know what it is and you don't look especially cheerful."

Abby held it and looked closely. The glass felt slightly warm to the touch, just as she remembered the others. "No I haven't a clue, but ... well many years back, soon after we had our double wedding and your mother had just become ... err ... shit where was I ...?"

Maddie, sharp as a bullet her fast brain still on overdrive immediately reacted. "Was Mum pregnant before she had Bel and I?"

Abby felt sick inside. For whatever reason, Victoria had obviously never told the children. There was no way she could lie to Maddie at this moment. She took a deep breath. "Yes. And I've well and truly put my foot in it."

Maddie touched her arm gently. "Look, don't worry. I won't mention a thing to the others and when Mum's ready she can tell us, as and how she wants. But what happened?"

"Sadly, Vikki miscarried. There was no reason it just happened. Both babies were lost, boys."

"Babies, you mean another set of twins? Gosh, there could have been six of us ... like three by twos, almost a Noah's Ark."

Abby laughed. "Yes, I suppose that's one way of thinking of it, but you and Bel were conceived immediately afterwards. They were very keen to have you. Listen Maddie, I'm going to tell your mother in the nicest possible way that I've spilled the beans accidentally. All of you should know anyway. When Vikki gets her head into those test tubes, all else gets forgotten about."

"Yes, don't I know it, but you still didn't finish your sentence about this glass object, did you."

"Two others like it turned up, fifteen years ago. The first one Vikki and I found in the telescope room. We had just opened the room up for the first time. Then your mother, soon after she started teaching, discovered a second one which your grandfather had kept in the science laboratory at Cradwell for many years.

"Really?"

"Vikki's science technician found it after a clear out and gave it to her. But we all realised they were part of a whole at some time with a piece missing, and I suspect you've finally found that third piece, by Jove, after all this time. Judy identified what the material was. A very rare piece of Roman glassware called purpurine and this, plus the others, formed a special triangular shape of crimson glass."

"Gosh, you mean like a prism of purpurine?"

"Yes, I suppose so, what on earth ...?"

They both turned startled, hearing a rattle and banging on the patio windows. In the fading light, pressed right up to the pane and staring in with sharp, pinpoint eyes stood a large, jet-black bird. His crooked and curved yellow beak was banging rhythmically on the glass.

"Oh my God ... Vultura."

"Vultura? What on earth is that?" Maddie cried, puzzled. "He's just a lone crow, but obviously injured, I need to help him."

She ran to the window. But the crow stopped, stared hard at her for a moment then, with a squawk, flapped its wings and disappeared fast, over the woods and off into the distance. Maddie turned around. "He's obviously fine, probably flew into the glass by mistake as they do and got momentarily dazed. Thank goodness, I hate it when birds injure themselves."

"He wasn't injured Maddie. Anyway, let's get our food and watch this film before Bel thinks we've done a bunk too. She's probably fed up waiting. Actually, I know where your mother put the other two glass pieces in the telescope room. Do you have any super-glue by any chance? After that, before I go home then …"

"You and I need to join them together don't we? I know, but don't ask me why. I can feel the need and I agree, these pieces definitely want to be one whole item again for some reason. Why is this piece slightly warm? Do you think all this stuff today is connected Abby? Only you and I seem to get it, although we each have slightly different perspectives."

"Yes, I think they are connected and I need to talk to your parents tonight too on the phone. You and I have to stay quiet and observant, but leave the talking with me Maddie."

"Fine, lips sealed shut with a big zip."

Abby laughed. That was exactly the same phrase Vikki used when they shared a flat together, usually about the men she ravaged and ditched daily.

"Hey both of you, are you eating or what? I've put your food back in the oven again and the film has been on pause for hours. What's the big secret all about that's so important? Are you going to let me in on it then?"

Bel was indeed quite irritated.

Abby stopped, pondered for some seconds, glanced at Bel and decided. "Yes … we are."

Maddie nodded.

"Cool, I love secrets, so let's eat first then."

Chapter Eleven

Abby crept on tiptoe into the bedroom. Lynton was sleeping like a baby in their Regency bed, obviously dreaming sweet dreams with that silly smile on his face. It had better be about her. She had stayed up until three in the morning, buoyed up by copious cups of organic camomile tea and tossed around the myriad thoughts and events of the day. Lurching from one mental receptacle into another, she mixed and layered them onto a logical palette to try and produce something which had even a vague meaning.

In the end Abby did what she knew best. She grabbed a pile of extra-large sheets of art paper and her tubes of paint and began to create pictures furiously, determined to physically force answers, any answers she didn't care, using her innate and heightened right-brain. But no matter which way she applied various coloured washes with a bold stroke of the brush, the results were the same; dark, chaotic and void of simplicity and order. Somewhere in that visual chaos she was capturing there had to be a deeper meaning. It was as if her brain was targeted to prevent truth emerge inside her subconscious however murky and remain locked inside the deepest recesses of her imagination. She had to break down those barriers and unlock the necessary psychic coding. She persisted for a further hour. Gradually, new shapes materialised onto the paper, very unpleasant looking images which made her tremble until she looked closely at the final painting ... at long last, she knew. Totally exhausted, sweat poured into her tee-shirt. Her body felt drained to the point of collapse. But having put off the necessity all night, she now had to phone Victoria.

Her thoughts returned to Maddie and Bel earlier. They had applied a strong, transparent resin-glue from Julian's workshop to the three pieces of purpurine glass, which as predicted fitted against each other perfectly, like they were waiting to be joined into an obvious larger prism. She put the object down vertically on the bench to allow the glue to dry unhindered. Then the strangest of phenomena occurred. Before their eyes, a peculiar and pulsating orange glow emanated gradually from the top, spreading downwards until the whole prism became enveloped. The effect was, as Bel succinctly put it, like the way the corona surrounds the sun at a total eclipse. They could feel a wave of heat also transmitted and stood back, petrified. After half a minute the glow slowly faded away before disappearing completely, along with the heat.

Maddie moved forward tentatively. Her scientific curiosity would not be stopped and she picked it up, despite Abby pleading for her to leave it alone. Meanwhile Bel found Victoria's portable Geiger counter, still sat in the bathroom cabinet next to the aspirin and shampoo, and waved it carefully overhead. Reading was zero. But they gasped as they looked carefully at the glue lines. They too had completely vanished. The piece was a complete whole, as if brand new and undamaged. The slightly flecked, reddish copper variations in the three colours had melded into one perfectly clear and beautiful pale crimson colour. Also gone was the residual warmth of each separate piece. The whole object had become quite normal and cold to the touch becoming the most perfect glass prism shape, which Maddie immediately confirmed, after she did a quick calculation and then measured using her father's angle callipers.

After an intense discussion between the twins and a hasty scribble of exponential equations on Julian's scrap pinewood about the possible occurrence of a form of fast and rare radioactive decay to a half-life of zero and the heat melting the glass together, they all agreed the end result was very aesthetic and pretty.

But Abby had been fascinated to watch Bel's reaction to everything, consistently calm, casual and matter of fact, as if she already knew or expected the outcome. Abby had agreed with Maddie that they should gather together Bel, Ned and Zac first thing in the morning and have a truth and tell session, before Victoria and Julian actually returned. Maddie was now determined to come out, as she saw it, alongside Abby to the rest of the family that she 'saw things' and also about the wolf 'dissolving' in the water. Abby kept silent about Bel. But she now suspected that Bel, as sharp as or even sharper than Maddie, was also psychic and had equally kept the fact to herself.

Concentrating hard on her recall of the exact shade of pale crimson, Abby painted the prism as perfectly as she could. It was perched alone, prominently in gloomy light on a dark wooden bench with a candle at the end, bathed in a spectral rainbow of coloured light. She was inspired by paintings she had seen in the Royal Society Hall of early light experiments conducted in the seventeenth century. Having an excellent visual memory, Abby finally brushed in her recollection of a picture of Isaac Newton, to complete the historic setting.

Casually she stood back and observed the result as the crimson paint unevenly dried, but then she gulped hard. The wet and dry areas in the prism were congealing into a clear and discernible shape; first the eyes, then the beak and finally the wings and feathers. The object looked back at her intensely. Vultura the crow, or whatever he was, had manifested there, directly inside the prism. She couldn't take her gaze away but slowly, as the paint dried, Vultura simply vanished away, until the finished picture was perfect, one of the most simple and powerful she had ever done, as good as an original Turner or Constable.

The phone rang and rang. Finally Victoria answered, her voice echoing in the background.

"Abby, this is very late your time to be calling me? Gosh it must be four-thirty in the morning, UK time. Julian is already in bed fast asleep, can't take the pace poor thing, and I'm just about to have a shower? Is everything okay?"

"Yes and no ... and I couldn't sleep."

Victoria went silent, her brain quickly going into gear. "It's Judy isn't it? Is she, you know, unwell and err ...?"

"No, it isn't Judy, she's fine."

"Okay, just let me go into the lounge and quietly shut the bathroom and bedroom doors. We're in this huge condo that Julian booked." A moment later, she was back on the phone. "Out, with it. Shit Abby are the kids alright?"

"Yes, no need to panic, they're all fine. But something happened today, in fact a huge lot of stuff has happened which you need to know about for when you come back."

"So?"

Abby, as precisely as her fuzzy and tired brain would allow, relayed the incident from the beginning, starting with the holiday boat, the dogs finding and killing an escaped wolf, the police and the link with the murdered Sally Savage. But again, clearly, she affirmed the children were fine.

Victoria listened quietly before reiterating firmly. "We'll be on the earliest available plane back in the morning. I'll see to it first thing, all the book business is concluded anyway."

"No, Vikki you don't have to spoil your holiday, just come back when you expected to."

"I know your tone intimately Abby. How long have we known each other? There's more isn't there. Have you been feeling alright yourself?"

Abby took a deep breath. It didn't matter how many years had elapsed, Dr Photographic Memory, was never going to be fooled. "Okay, yes there is more, and I'd better get this out quickly."

"I don't need embellishment, the facts that's all, quick, sequential and precise."

"I wish my brain right now was as together as yours. I've accidentally put my foot in it about your miscarriage to Maddie. I'm really sorry Vikki, we were chatting and the words just started to slip out without thinking. She's as razor sharp as you and immediately guessed the rest. She's really fine about it, not a problem."

Victoria laughed. "Sorry, no, I'm not laughing at you, just how much Maddie is like me, too mature and self-sufficient for her own good. She's really scary some days, but at least Julian and I have brought them all up properly, well loved, balanced and happy, not like the shit environment and childhood I had. I was going to tell them anyway soon, I'd already decided. I've just been too busy. So?"

"How do you mean so?"

"The rest, Abby, that's not all, don't obfuscate."

"This is a bit tricky. Basically Maddie confided things to me?"

"Things? What kind of things?"

"Listen Vikki … she's strongly psychic, exactly like me and … well … I can't put it any simpler, she's … seen visions regularly … ever since she was a small child but always kept it to herself. Maddie's rationalised the sightings to the back of her mind, as I also did at her age. But her paranormal reach is linked to another era, at least two hundred years before Mauveine."

"Fuck Abby, I had no idea. Has she seen Mauveine?"

"No, she can't. Mauveine's spirit occupies another parallel universe that doesn't join up."

"You're talking all this psychic and ghostly mumbo-jumbo again, same as fifteen years ago. You know how I feel about all this, and I haven't changed … rationally and cynically I remain very agnostic."

Abby now felt she had to be firm again, a repeat of the last time. "And remember your promise fifteen years ago, after you saw Mauveine in the back of the Beast. I want you to make that promise again Victoria, have an open mind please once more. I know it's harder, but you saw Mauveine then and Julian saw Isi and we all found out since why there was the family connection. So promise?"

There was a pause and Abby took a decision, because her sixth sense and deep intuition had kicked in and was shrieking loudly in her brain. She must leave the full grisly details of the terrifying Mauveine and Rimmer cellar happening exactly as it was. The passage of McKenzie history had been changed forever, memories never existed including Victoria's, Julian's and Lynton's. Only she was left, now that Aunt Eveline had passed on, and Mauveine of course, who knew the true story. There was enough brewing up in the present to think about, but Victoria had to be brought back on board with Julian, come what may. Their lives had been changed once. That scenario may be about to repeat itself again.

"Okay, yes you're right, just as you were then. I do promise. But what about Bel and the boys? Are they … err … similar?"

"You mean psychic. I don't know yet, but Maddie and I agreed last night that we will discuss the matter calmly and sensibly with the other three first thing in the morning. I'm better at this than you, so let me get on with it, please. Deal?"

There was a further silence as Victoria pondered. "Yes, deal ... I can see that makes logical sense. I'll speak to Julian first thing, but we're returning home tomorrow, whatever. I'm going to love you and leave you. Get some beauty sleep, especially if you're talking to the horde early in the morning. Good night Abby."

Abby laughed. "I will, time to snuggle into Mr Dreamy, snoring away peacefully. See you ... well ... when we see you, Bye."

"You mean Uncle Lynton has actually gone on a hunt for the other escaped wolf?" Ned asked excitedly, as they gathered mid-morning around the dining room table.

"Yes," Abby replied. "The animal was spotted again stalking sheep half a mile from Harrison's Bridge. All the farmers and the police are using horses so they can get across the fields quicker, so he's taken Jet."

Abby smiled inwardly and thought fondly of their two expensive bought horses which they recently acquired and were housing in the old stable block at the back of the Red Lion. Lynton was riding regularly for exercise on Jet, his black thoroughbred gelding, whilst she had begun to join him on Snow, her white mare, now she had got used to them. Lynton was a natural, having grown up on his parent's estate with horses since a baby. It had taken her a while to get used to riding after so long, one of the few tangible benefits of her boarding school education, but she loved the experience again, especially owing her own horse. The added benefit, apart from the fresh air, was that she and Lynton were back close together again. The horses had at long last forced both to rebalance their constantly busy lives and find proper time with each other. The recent Sunday morning ride along the beach and surfing the edge of the waves at Southport had been quite exhilarating and romantic. Riding seemed to get Lynton fired up again with unexpected passion when they got back home, after what had been a somewhat prolonged and quietly encroaching absence. Thank you Mauveine and Isi. Now she understood their former horse devotion together.

Bel piped up. "Wonder if Mum and Dad might buy us horses? I loved those riding lessons we all had when we were younger."

"Yeh, I reckon we all did then," Ned replied wistfully. "Do you fancy that Zac? Shit, he's got his iGlasses on again, sorry Aunt Abby."

"There are four ex-race fillies for sale on eBay, really cheap," Zac muttered, tapping his tablet, phone and iGlasses in order one after the other.

"On eBay? You must be joking ..."

"That's enough thank you," Abby intervened. "Maddie and I want to talk about something very important, concerning yesterday. There are some things you all should know and try to understand. From today, we will see each other in a different light. And, starting with no more Aunt and Uncle please, just call us plain Abby and Lynton from now on. It makes us feel old and past it."

The others, apart from Maddie, stared blank and Ned grunted, "Ugh?"

"I suspect Ned," Abby continued with a smirk, "You had already decided that was not the case anyway."

The rest roared laughing with the joke. Ned went an immediate red with embarrassment, before muttering that it was all cool as far as he was concerned.

Maddie drew in a deep breath and slowly and carefully described how she had been seeing seventeenth century enactments in the Orsbrick grounds outside, ever since she was a little girl. They listened wide-eyed. Abby did her usual paranormal interpretation, with references to the usual parallel universes and wormholes and then admitted that she too had the same psychic senses. Abby finally looked at each one. Apart from Ned scratching his head and screwing up his face, Bel and Zac were remarkably nonchalant.

Bel spoke up. "That's cool Mad, and I understand totally why you kept it all to yourself, especially with those dumb-arses in school. Sorry to disappoint, but your talents aren't unique in this family. Whilst you've been passing the time with witches and men holding pikes, I've had regular fun waving at two guys on horses who trot around the woods. I never felt frightened. This house is old and full of family history; you'd expect the place to be haunted."

They all turned in astonishment to Bel.

"Horses? What kind of people?" Abby asked. Intuition the previous night was proving correct. Bel was quiet, deep and very surprising.

"Well, I even know who they are. I could tell from their dress the likely period, I've been top in history for three years running and realised they were ghosts. I did some extensive reading and photograph research in Mum and Dad's family library upstairs. She is Mauveine McKenzie and he is Isaac Fazackerley. They got married eventually and Mauveine is our, let me get this right, Great-Great-Great Aunt from the mid nineteenth century."

"What?" Maddie exclaimed. "You've actually seen her? The Mauveine, the scientist who Mum goes on about as the great inspiration behind her dyeing business? And you've seen her husband Isi?"

"Whoa there sis," Ned butted in. "How come you and Bel have these ghostly fun jaunts with folk long dead and I never hear as much as a clank of a chain? Reckon I'd better stand naked outside in the full-moon, seems werewolves are going to be my bag."

Maddie glared at him. "Just occasionally Ned, I wish you weren't so fucking idiotic and grow up. Sorry Abby, but he can get right under my skin. It's like the throw of a dice Ned. As Abby says, some in the family have it and some don't, fact, get over it. And the thought of you naked anywhere makes my breakfast come up."

Ned grinned, he loved winding his sister up. "This just confirms, all you girls are weird man, just leaves me and little old Zac here as normal regular guys, thank God. Ain't that so Zac my man? I could do with a fag. Sorry Abby, don't tell Dad."

Everyone laughed again.

"I've seen Mauveine and Isi too. They're a couple of cool dudes. Jeb and Kai love them, they run around the pond together playing. But only with these on. Hey, that other wolf has just been shot dead, near Ormskirk.

That's one less problem to worry about. Wonder if Lynton bagged him Abby?"

They turned in unison to stare silently at Zac, twiddling again with his iSpecs and large net-watch. Even Abby was dumbfounded.

"The dogs too?" Ned cried. "Jesus, I just don't believe it."

They all looked down to see Jeb and Kai, sat under the table quite unperturbed, their tales wagging again.

Maddie had gone thoughtful. "You haven't mentioned Mum and Dad, Abby. How do they fit into all this?"

"Vikki saw Mauveine a few times when she first got the house, back in 2010. The period was a stressful time, but since then all has been quiet. It took some detective work to find out who Mauveine was and what everything meant. Your father is like you Ned, so you're not alone in the household and Lynton too."

"Thank goodness for that." He smiled, with inner male relief. "When are they flying in, Abby?"

"Tonight, early evening. Now, they know all of this and that we've had a conversation. My advice is to keep every bit of it quiet in the family, at least for now."

"You bet," Ned replied, nodding vigorously. "We get enough flak simply living here and being posh without adding to it. Even I'm not that thick Mad."

"I know Ned," Maddie replied gently. "Actually, what's happened to Ade? Has he turned up yet?"

"Yes, forgot to mention it. His brother said he came wandering in about three am, quite dazed and then lay on the couch and went straight to sleep. He'd walked all the way back home through the woods and fields and along the canal on his own in the dark. Says he can't remember any of it or why he walked out. Probably some sort of shock after-effect. Christ, I'm glad that other wolf never spotted him. Some doctors from the hospital have been over there and checked him over. Apparently his arm is almost healed up already, they're all amazed and he's fine now. Zac and I are going to meet him and his brother after lunch and we're going to the Liverpool-Everton derby match this afternoon."

"I can't believe that," Bel said. "Not after the state he was in when I bandaged him up. That's really bizarre."

"It's this new laser stem cell treatment I reckon, sis, so Dottie was telling Zac. They took samples from his nose and formed like a new skin in record time. Apparently it's been used a lot with burns, but this was the first time it had been tested on like a severed arm. I've already filled him and his brother in about the police and the press and to keep their mouths shut."

"Yeh and I've spoken to Dottie," Zac added.

Bel wasn't convinced but said no more.

"Ned, what's Adrian's surname?"

"Err ... Agnew, but his dad's name is Rimmer. It's sort of complicated. Why Abby?"

"Nothing Ned, I just wondered, so we know in case he did get a mention in the papers anywhere," Abby replied, thinking on her feet but inside suddenly feeling a severe and chilling alarm. She needed to talk to Lynton, quick.

At the newly opened Morecambe Bay Island international airport, Abby and Lynton picked up

Julian and Victoria, tired out from the travelling which had been delayed out of the US over bureaucratic visa and inane security issues. After piling their bags into Lynton's Merc and a quick coffee, they drove straight to the Red Lion for a chat and some much needed decent food.

Whilst Victoria and Julian were sat comfortably around the best table in the empty restaurant lounge, Lynton wandered back in holding a rare 1979 Chablis he had been saving in his kitchen for something special. Abby had rustled up one of her old favourite kebab meals, and ran in with a tray of hot plates, the spicy food adorned with her patented trimmings.

Julian grinned. "This is just like old times Abby. Gosh it is simply ages since we last had these ... mmm ..."

"That's what I like, a man who appreciates my food. Yeh, an Ali speciality this recipe, and he's still making them big-time in Rotterdam would you believe."

Victoria smiled and gave her best friend a gentle hug. "Thanks for picking us up. Now I'm assuming we're going to talk about the kids and all this stuff going on."

"Yes, but after we've eaten first, consumed a couple of glasses each of this fabulous Chablis, and relaxed," Lynton chipped in, raising a toast.

"Hear, hear," Julian replied, "Let's start, I'm ravenous."

They clinked glasses, and tucked into their meal, winding down and talking excitedly about the book tour and Lynton's recent find of two genuine Goya paintings which he had bought in a backstreet shop in Bucharest for a song. Once Abby served coffee, she decided it was time to pull them back to the events on the Leeds and Liverpool canal. She had thought of a suitable way of telling the background of the terrifying 2010 summer ordeal in the cellar. She intended to achieve closure and bring more understanding of what was going on presently, without generating alarm. Especially she needed to avert any disclosure of the horrific activity, now obliterated from their memories and history, which Victoria and Julian, as well as Lynton, had been forced through.

Julian cleaned his glasses slowly. "I've been thinking hard as we flew back, Abby. Let's speak candidly. We're all open-minded and the four of us have known since 2010 about Mauveine and Isi, and subsequently my Fazackerley family connection and the tragic sadness of Uncle William and Alicia with the death of their baby in the 1920s. Once Victoria and I decided to settle down here, understand the family history and restore Orsbrick Hall that seemed to finally settle the roving spirits of Mauveine and Isi. They've never reappeared since then, so job done as it were, and everything and everyone are happy ever after as they say in the romance genre. So what is this entirely new paranormal disturbance all about? Why now? Strange black crows? And the kids finding that pleasure boat and helping to solve the mystery of Sally Savage, the poor murdered girl in the canal? Wolves everywhere? The scenarios are taking the shape of something out of one of my thriller novels. And now we learn that three of our four offspring have also seen Mauveine and appear to have the same psychic sensitivities as you! I'm not taking this in too well if I'm honest."

"I don't have the answers Julian. Actually, only Bel and Zac claim to see Mauveine, Maddie sees other things, much earlier, in a different time altogether. But ... well ... I'm going to fill in some other aspects. And you listen Lynton too because you don't know this. Can you open that second bottle please?"

"Eva died a couple of months ago."

They all turned and looked at Victoria who had started crying, not sure what to say.

"I didn't want to tell anyone or talk about it. She passed away with an inoperable brain tumour. Marlies rang me a while back and took me over to Eva's house. She'd been living alone for many years, I had no idea. We were both there and Eva died in my arms. Marlies and I buried her a week later. That's the reason I've not been myself and distant, not because I've personally felt anything bad or wrong with Orsbrick in any way."

Abby got up and held her gently for a moment. "I'm so sorry Vikki. You should have told us."

Victoria wiped her eyes and breathed in deeply, returning to a smile. "Eva was private, but it's over and time to move on. I think we're going to have to depend on you Abby to try and pull together some logic and rationale around what is happening, although this recent sequence of occurrences makes me uneasy."

Abby sat down and Lynton refreshed each wine glass. "Not just me but also Maddie. She is far, far more sensitive than Bel or Zac, so much like Aunt Eveline was ... the same McKenzie perceptions and calm acceptance. I'm still amazed at her maturity, Vikki. She really is a chip off the old block. But Maddie is psychically attuned to another era, around two hundred years before, in the mid 1660s. It was around the time the McKenzie dynasty and Orsbrick as we know it really began shaping up. She hasn't seen Mauveine and probably can't and won't. That's the way it works."

Both Victoria and Abby were as usual immediately and intuitively reading each other's minds. There was a third party in the mix, also tuned into the same era as Maddie. Judy was not going to be discussed, especially in front of Lynton.

Abby continued. "There is another factor which none of you are aware of and which played a critical part of the eventual settling down of uneasy spirits in 2010. Only Aunt Eveline, me and Mauveine were involved." She was aware of her forehead sweating. She really had to think and word this next part right.

"Mauveine? But how?"

"I'll get to it Vikki. Julian, do you remember that big argument way back in the George pub with a family of unpleasant people?"

"Yes, I certainly do. They thought I was someone else; a distinctly unsavoury bunch, especially the father. That little incident came close to a major brawl in the bar, and I was quite prepared to take that guy apart, there and then."

"Fortunately, you kept your cool. They're all dead incidentally the whole family, bad car accident in Parbold. Happened just before our double wedding," Lynton added, as Abby glared at him, feeling impatient but also irritated that he'd never, over all those years, mentioned that fact.

"Really?" Julian replied, his eyes narrowing. "Sorry Abby please go on."

"I did some digging in the McKenzie family archives when we were sorting out the huge pile of stuff discovered in chests and drawers. I focussed on records, papers, and eventually the extensive library of family history. To cut a long story short, with Marlies's help I found old online records of the local press. That family in the George were called Rimmer, and they had ancestors who were boatpeople and who fought for generations with your boatpeople ancestors, Julian, the Fazackerley's. A particular accusation, also made in the George but in the 1870s, involved Mauveine's father, James McKenzie and led to a massive skirmish and deaths and finally revenge which went on and on, tit for tat with following generations of the Rimmer and Fazackerley families. The present day Rimmers recognised your family resemblance Julian, certainly the old great-granny matriarch there did. This dispute was a factor which had led to Mauveine and Isi remaining unsettled spirits. Aunt Eveline and I, together with Mauveine's subtle guidance, managed to psychically distort the related universes and change the space-time so effectively that the dispute ended. It had never been possible before, especially because of that long, desolate and isolated period of Uncle William which ensued inside Orsbrick Hall. It was then that Mauveine and Isi could finally rest happily, alongside the comfort that Orsbrick Hall would continue with another McKenzie and Fazackerley, united in love once again ... you two!"

Abby stopped and took a deep breath. At last she had told the story, as Eveline and Mauveine warned she must. But the details of how she did it and what actually happened must remain with her, not as a burden but a sensible obligation. Her heart was thumping, she hoped desperately that nobody would want embellishments.

A silence filled the air for a good half minute.

"But Abby, why after all these years haven't you mentioned it before?" Victoria whispered with her voice edgy and her mind veering towards her usual scientific dissection mode, exactly what Abby dreaded.

Julian put his glasses back on. He had become thoughtful and pensive, making associations with his own past. "Because there was no need Abby, was there," he said. "The issue became closed, job was done and all of us could get on with our normal lives. This is the same reason my grandfather moved from Burscough to London, changed his name and re-married. You, Mauveine and Aunt Eveline aligned some distorted, paranormal tectonic plates back into shape and brought together a long awaited harmony of the system between past and present within the McKenzie and Fazackerley families. But why were those plates distorted in the first place? That is an interesting question."

Abby nodded.

Victoria turned to Julian and Lynton. "You two believe all this? Try as I always have, I can't explain it using my best science and my trusted logic," she said, her voice faltering. Once more she was irritated with her own frustration of having to confront things she didn't understand or couldn't explain. But she had promised Abby, and would keep to it ... open mind, open mind, open ...

Victoria continued. "But ... I do accept there are things in our universe ... energies, connections, timelines, which we don't yet fully understand. Already mathematically, multiple universes have been proven to be theoretically possible and time travel too. In fact Maddie and I were only just talking about all this in the lab recently. Theoretical physics is her big love these days, which I think she wants to specialise in and I'm encouraging her. Mmm ... now I realise why she was asking, but she didn't understand at the time, but now probably she will and should too. Abby, you are so incredible as a friend and much more ... you really are one of the family."

A tear trickled down Victoria's cheek, as Abby gave her a warm hug, followed by Julian and then Lynton.

Abby sat down, relieved. Lynton poured out a third glass of wine for everyone and mouthed taxi to Julian, who nodded back. "One final thing," she said, "and I don't have answers, but Julian's question I believe is the link to what has happened in the last few days. Why was the space-time distorted in the first place? Because something two hundred years before Mauveine was a trigger that still lingers, and the ripple may be returning, so all of us, including the children, will have to be observant and help each other wherever we can."

Suddenly the door bell rang loudly, making them, still tense, jump. "Nearly forgot, pub opening time shortly," Lynton said, going to the door. "I think that taxi I texted Julian is here early."

Victoria quickly drank the remains of her wine. "That's fine we need to get back home, relax and talk to the kids now. Thank you so much Abby for the amazing food and … well … for everything and being my best friend. We'll see you both in a few days."

"Yes, I'll save you a piece of my special Edwardian spotted dick and custard," Abby replied, feeling light relief on the one hand and a level of apprehension and anxiety beginning on the other. She had serious research to do tomorrow.

Lying in bed, her arms wrapped around Lynton, Abby took a deep breath, her brain still buzzing with thoughts, trying to stimulate her subconscious and her dreams to help find more answers.

"I can hear your brain clanking away," Lynton murmured, stroking her hand. "You're really quite some woman, Abby aren't you."

"You reckon?" she murmured and snuggled in closer.

"Of course, but you did forget one other important factor didn't you."

She sat up, screwing her eyes. "What factor?"

"Judy of course, but I understand why."

Abby squinted. "You know? … I mean you know she has …" she replied, flabbergasted, as Lynton cut in gently touching her lips with his finger.

"I've known since she was a child, as did her mother. Remember my sister too was very psychic, I wasn't surprised but I also knew Judy had and still has innate difficulties with the normal world. So keeping tabs on that was always our priority. I reckoned her paranormal abilities would take care of themselves, as it did with Diane. And since I realised all those years back you were the same, I knew and felt assured that Judy would, if necessary, have a safe cushion to fall back on."

"My goodness, Mr Goya," Abby replied with a smile. "You really are the sensitive creature you always claimed you were, aren't you."

"Mmm … now how about a little celebration then of my new found inner male?"

"What, two nights in a row? Gosh, okay then, hope you're up to it," as she rolled on top of him, yanking off her nightie, laughing and giggling, then groaned happily as his warm hands ran right up her naked body.

Chapter Twelve

First day back after half-term. Ned and Zac had to maintain a sustained knocking on the front door but eventually they heard a shuffle of feet and someone coming down the stairs behind. Ade's elder brother, Jonny, by now late for his morning orderly shift at the mental hospital, had asked them to make sure they got Adrian to school with them because since he returned he was, in Jonny's words, 'acting kind of way out, man.'

Certainly, Ade had been unusually quiet when they went to the football derby match, but that wasn't surprising as he wasn't long out of hospital. Physically he seemed remarkably recovered and his arm, whilst bruised and painful, could move almost normally already. The large and deep wolf bite that had virtually severed it down to the bone had miraculously healed over, with barely a tiny scar visible. Ned, Zac and Jonny were amazed — the miracle of 2020's modern and individualised gene medicine again.

Adrian opened the door aggressively. His tall bulk filled the space, seemingly very irritated that he was being disturbed. Ned looked up at him with some concern.

"Hey, Ade, what's up? Go and get your bike, pal, we're all going to be late. Hutcho the Head is on first thing with a careers pep talk and I know you haven't finished your maths project yet, but I'll help you sort it later this morning. We can give private study in the library a miss, boring anyway."

"Ain't going, I've got other plans?"

"Eh? "What sort of plans? You've been top all year in technology alongside my little old brother Zac here. You've got your engineering place agreed at the College, as long as you get your exams passed, Ade, that should be a doddle."

Adrian almost snarled. His bottom lip was all curled up horrible and he raised himself up to his full six foot six, towering over them. "Are you two paying attention? I'm not going to school, not now, not ever, got it?"

"C'mon Ade … that's fucking stupid, get your bike and shift yourself," Ned pleaded, totally mystified. What had been going on in Ade's head? It was like talking to a different person. Was he in shock still?

Ade suddenly grabbed the six foot one Ned by the front of his coat and half-lifted him off his feet and pulled him closer, until his face was just a few inches away. "I'm not saying it again. Now fuck off the pair of you," and shoved him hard, as Ned stumbled off the front door step.

"Cool it Ade," Zac retorted, coming to the aid of his brother and standing in between. "I know you like to bully the shit out of some of the kids in year ten but we're your mates remember, like we just saved your fucking life on that boat especially Bel. What the fuck is up with you?"

"Piss off."

Ade turned around, walked in and slammed the front door hard as both boys muttered quiet obscenities and got back on their bikes, cycling furiously down the road towards school. Out of sight of the house, Ned pulled into the side of the road.

"Bloody hell Zac, Jonny was right. Way out is a major understatement. It must be some delayed reaction or something. He was alright when we saw him the other day. What has Dottie said?"

"She hasn't seen him since we went to Anfield. She said she really felt scared. He talked to her like she was some lowlife and told her not to come round, as girls and whores weren't welcome. I know some days he sort of gets a bit temperamental, but I agree, this isn't like him. That boat stuff must have fucked up his brain more than we all reckoned. I think you should phone Jonny and tell him, I've got his mobile number here in my phone.

Ned grabbed the phone and dialled, now feeling increasingly puzzled. A short conversation ensued with Jonny on his tea-break. He finally turned to Zac who was carefully polishing up his iGlasses before putting them on. These were the very latest model. To everyone else they looked like a pair of cool Ray-bans but for Zac, they enhanced even further his formidable IT skills and access to immediate online information, communication and data.

"Man, Ade is definitely acting odd, now having talked to Jonny. You'll never guess what his plans are?" Ned said slowly.

Zac was reading from his iGlasses. "It's quite common in cases of trauma, like accidents or assault, for people to either become very withdrawn or get aggressive and out of character, according to this recent report from MindCare, the local mental health charity where Jonny works. If I had to put money on it, then Ade would more likely fall into aggressive given his cocky nature and his size."

"I think that's a tad simplistic," Ned replied. "And Jonny being in the trade would recognise it anyway. No, Ade has decided to ditch school and not only head for Ireland but become a priest as well, so, quote, 'he can help rid the world of evil.' Jonny says they have family over there in Dublin who'll take him in. Ade is getting a night boat this evening from Liverpool."

"A priest? You've got to be joking. Ade is the least religious person I've ever come across. Remember? When he was about twelve and he pissed over the altar when we all broke into the local Catholic church at Parbold and nicked the communion wine? Jesus. But he's only sixteen?"

"Jonny says good riddance. Ade's been a pain in the backside for some time at home … never does anything or cleans up after himself."

"You mean like us?" Zac replied, quick as a bullet. They both laughed. "Nothing strange about that!"

"Well, looks like there's nought we can do about it. Goodbye to a good friendship, although let's be honest, Ade was heading for the tech' and we're a shoe-in at the sixth form college so we'd have gone our separate ways anyway. But he was shit-hot at engineering, such a waste. However, there's always a silver lining, Zac. I reckon Dottie will need some tender loving care and lots of comforting now that her little brother, she dotes on, is doing a bunk — in with a chance there definitely."

Zac punched his arm playfully. "Eh, pack it in, she's not that sort of girl, on the other hand ..."

Laughing loudly again, they swigged their cokes and pedalled off furiously to get to school.

By the end of their first school term week, an extensive police search nationwide had begun in earnest for the American owners of the holiday boat, keeping the crime talk maintained in the local press and on TV with further media speculations of guilt. Maddie and Bel were having their own problems at school. Despite keeping quiet and their heads down with their studies, an insidious rumour was circulating that the two of them were involved in the finding of the holiday boat as they owned large dogs. They suspected that Dottie may have accidentally said something to her aunt who gossiped with the mothers of other kids at the school. Whatever the cause, the four teenagers and Dottie, bolstered by support and advice from Victoria and Julian, diverted the attention away to gypsy traveller families who had camped around Harrison's Bridge. They also kept big dogs, but had conveniently vanished from the area, back onto the road. Adrian had by then absconded well away into some apparently run-down enclave of Dublin.

Maddie was suffering from bad headaches and strange feelings of dissociation, initially putting it down to exam stress and overwork. Victoria and Julian remained heavily preoccupied with major book and business matters. Following a quick phone call, Maddie decided to quietly catch the bus after school and see Abby at the Red Lion. Quickly, two large cappuccinos were made and they sat chatting on their own in the snug, where a log fire still burned from lunch time.

"I can't get that wolf or whatever it was out of my head, disappearing into the water like it did. The others, especially Bel, have put the whole thing out of their minds already and are just getting on with school stuff and what have you. What's the matter with me?"

"Nothing whatsoever Maddie. I know incidentally what you're sensing. I can feel the pain lurking too. I've learned over many years to live with these things. Best way to deal with an onset of sensitivity is to find the cause and then confront it. I've got a suggestion. Vikki rang me earlier and said she was doing an overnight in London tomorrow with your father. Shall we do some digging in your family library? I'll pop over when you're back from school? That has helped me greatly in the past, to find explanations. Let's see what we can find in the seventeenth century period you're sensitised with. Two heads are definitely better than one."

"Oh Abby, yes please. Mum's incredibly busy at the moment with a big dye contract coming off, although to be honest I think she's trying to put what happened out of her mind, and I sense irritation when I bring it up."

"Yes I know the syndrome, believe me I understand that very well …"

They giggled and devoured the last of the carrot cake before looking upstairs at some pretty cotton dresses which Abby had decided she very much wanted to give to Maddie.

Maddie picked up her phone. Both she and Bel were now getting into a panic; they needed to do something quickly.

Abby, over in Southport, was busy moving the latest batch of new pictures into prime position for a weekend sale at her gallery. Struggling with Lynton to lift a heavy framed painting into position, her iPhone started rattling around the polished coffee table like a demented rabbit.

"Shit," Lynton shouted, panting on the ladder, the ringing echo bouncing continuously from end to end. "Just leave the damned thing Abby, your phone always goes off when it shouldn't. If it's important they'll ring back."

"Hey Mr Grumps, just take a breather will you, let me take a look." She picked up the phone. "Hi, what's up? Still okay for this afternoon?"

"Abby, things are really bad here. It's Mum. She came in from the lab late last night not feeling so good, but overnight she's gradually become really terrible, coming on with like a fever and getting delirious followed by vomiting and diarrhoea in the last half hour. Bel and I are with her. Dad's just called the doctor but he's panicking. Can you get over?"

"Yes absolutely, we're on our way. Lynton's with me, we're at the gallery so I'll be about twenty minutes. See you later, bye."

"Who's that?"

"It's Maddie, something's happening at Orsbrick, Vikki has become very sick. Let's go, we can finish this later." She called over to Gillian her assistant manager. "Have to go out urgent, Gill, you should be alright for the rest of the day. Can you lock up at five? Seems quiet today to me."

"No problem Abby, catch you tomorrow."

They jumped into the Mercedes and shot off. Fifteen minutes later, the car screeched to a stop outside the front doors. Bel let them in and led Abby up the wide staircase in the direction of a guest room where Victoria lay shivering in bed. Lynton meanwhile distracted Julian, who was pacing up and down the living room in decreasing circles of serious distress. Victoria seemed to be getting worse and worse. Halfway up the stairs, Bel stopped Abby on the landing, whilst Maddie emerged from the door with wet towels and a tray.

Bel spoke first. "We want to explain something before Dad comes back. Ned and Zac are just sorting the dogs out. Following some leads from Zac, we've all searched the internet for clues ... the doctor should be here any minute. Not only has Mum got this awful fever, but her lymph glands are swollen and her neck's all puffy. Then she pulled her nightie up and showed Maddie and me these horrible things at the top of both thighs, like right at the top."

"What sort of things?"

Maddie intervened. "Big red weeping sores, she has some smaller ones now on her arms too. Listen Abby, this may sound totally far-fetched but we took close-up photos and Zac did some image matches on the web, with the symptoms etc, comparing pictures four hundred years ago. They look exactly like goitres."

"Goitres?"

"Yes," Bel added. "Horrible body swellings, now normally reserved for the thyroid gland. She has that too. A defining characteristic of a disease not seen in this country for hundreds of years. It looks like Mum has bubonic plague!"

"Oh my God! How can that be? Okay, first thing to do is we keep this to ourselves until the doctor arrives. Not a word to Vikki, she's stressed enough. What about your dad?"

"None of us have said anything, at the moment that doesn't seem wise," Maddie confirmed in a whisper. "Listen, the door bell is ringing, it must be Dr Lee. I'll bring her up. Abby, can you and Lynton keep Dad distracted for a minute? He's in the study with Lynton."

"Yes, no problem, go and fetch her quick."

At the door Maddie was greeted by a smartly dressed and smiling woman as tall as her, with an untidy mop of curly black hair, mid-thirties, with beautiful high cheekbones and the most perfectly tanned, smooth skin. Maddie's mind suddenly went blank as she stared stupidly, flushed and thrown by her own unexpected feelings for a moment.

"Hello Madeleine, I'm Doctor Jennifer Lee," the woman said confidently, thrusting her arm forward to shake hands. "I haven't seen you for such a long time, must be at least ten years. My word, you've shot up. I believe Victoria is too ill to get to the surgery with a bad fever and flu symptoms?"

"Yes, please come in Dr Lee, I'll just take you upstairs," Maddie replied, glancing nervously to make sure her father was still in the study. Thank goodness, she thought, for living in a very large house. She led Dr

Lee inside whilst Lynton and Abby kept Julian occupied.

Arriving at the bedroom, Dr Lee asked to go in alone to give Victoria a thorough examination.

Abby came back up the stairs. "Your father is sitting quietly with Lynton, each having a whisky. I've said Dr Lee will come down and talk to him when she's finished."

"Good," Bel replied, the three of them standing outside the door. "Then Maddie, I think you'd better tell Dr Lee what you reckon it may be because I'm pretty sure she won't have a clue."

After ten minutes Dr Lee emerged, holding an optical instrument and quietly shut the door behind her. "I've given Victoria a sedative ... I must admit I'm not happy with her temperature and her semi-delirious condition. It may be a very bad flu but otherwise I'm just not sure, especially with those nasty swelling sores, which I've put some lotion onto. It's unusual nowadays for bedrooms to have washbasins, but in there it was very useful."

Maddie drew a deep breath. "Dr Lee, is that a dermatoscope? Have you checked the sores against the international database? We have excellent super-fast wifi in here."

Dr Lee looked long and inquisitively at Maddie, amazed at her recognition of such a specialist instrument. She pressed the search button, having indeed taken some images herself and continued to grimace ... either no result or one she didn't want to see. "Mmm ... the scope is still searching, can't understand it ..."

Maddie cut in, now was the time. "We're ... like ... good at science, especially physics. I actually know how your dermatoscope works using polarized light ... Sorry, we've done some researching and ... well ... Mum has all the symptoms of ... I can't say this any simpler, like ... bubonic plague in the Middle Ages — look." She handed her one of Zac's tablets.

Dr Lee reacted totally incredulous. "Sorry but seriously Madeleine, that hypothesis is somewhat far-fetched. Bubonic plague hasn't been seen in this country for many hundreds of years and hardly ever elsewhere in the world either. In fact plague was fully eradicated, along with polio, in 2017. Last known case was in Senegal. Has Victoria been anywhere exotic, like West Africa?"

"No, only to the US, well Nashville actually, about twelve days ago. Please, Dr Lee," Maddie pleaded. "Just take another look at the pictures and the information entry on the tablet."

Dr Lee looked hard again at the tablet images and carefully read the summaries and sources which Zac had meticulously laid out. She stayed silent for another minute but her expression gradually changed. "Who else is in the house presently?"

Abby interrupted. "Apart from Victoria and Julian and the four children, there's Clair the housekeeper and my husband Lynton ...oh ... plus the two dogs of course. Why?"

"Because I'm going to call the special emergency ambulance right away, as well as the County Special Response Unit for notifiable infectious diseases. Incredible though it sounds, you girls may be right.

Whatever it is, I believe Victoria has to get to an isolation ward in the main hospital fast, and we simply can't take any chances."

"So what do we do?" Abby replied visibly alarmed and Madeleine and Bel wide eyed.

"I'm putting Orsbrick Hall into immediate quarantine. Girls, can you tell your brothers and bring the dogs inside. The response unit will bring a vet to check them over. Abby, I think you'd better now tell your husband and Julian and the housekeeper. Nobody from now on is allowed to leave or enter except the medical teams, and depending on what we find, we will also have to then check everyone Victoria has been in contact with over the last five days, and maybe quarantine them too."

"Actually nobody I think, Dr Lee, apart from us." Maddie replied. "She's been hugely busy in her laboratory here finalising a new dye. Mum likes to work sort of intense and solitary at such times."

"Good, that may make our job a whole lot easier."

Maddie glanced at Abby and they both looked at Bel. The three instinctively understood that they needed to chat further about other matters, but amongst themselves.

"The positive aspect is that we have a large freezer full of food, loads of space and plenty of beer and could hunker down for ten weeks if necessary," Julian joked, trying to lighten everyone up as they all sat glumly around the dining room table. Clair had gone to make tea and find some fresh walnut cake. Julian had already gone upstairs with Dr Lee to tell Victoria that she needed to go to hospital for further tests and had nothing to worry about, whilst Maddie and Bel packed a case with some things.

Dr Lee remained with Victoria, making sure she was comfortable and alerted her that the infectious diseases unit would take charge, as a precaution. Victoria remained sanguine and calm. As ever, the inner scientist kicked in, intrigued with what was wrong with her. But nobody mentioned bubonic plague.

"Looks like the guys are here," Ned exclaimed, calming the dogs. He pointed out of the window as three large vehicles, with no blue lights or sirens drew in anonymously and quietly. "NASA has arrived."

"Ha-ha Ned. Are you going to try and be sensible, I won't say normal, for once?" Maddie cried, glaring hard.

Ned laughed. "Lighten up sis. As long as nobody has been touching those swellings on Mum's legs, bubonic plague never spread person to person like say flu, via airborne contact, only by handling and touching."

"I had my thick flannel pyjamas and bed socks on last night," Julian added, "Although after an hour your Mum went into the other bedroom."

"Good, good, that's very useful" Lynton added, realising how daft he sounded and glanced surreptitiously at Abby, who was thinking of the stark contrast with their previous night's bedroom antics, complete with videos and sex toys. She had a fit of giggles stupidly, setting off Maddie and Bel, who immediately understood the joke, leaving Ned to mouthe, 'Eh?'

"Don't forget the fleas," Zac piped up, totally absorbed elsewhere, the micro-fans in his iGlasses emitting a strange whirring like a swarm of bees overhead, overheating through excessive use. His head was simultaneously immersed into three linked tablets, calling up every bit of information he could find. "It was finally determined that bubonic plague was spread by fleas from infected rats, jumping from person to person."

"Quite right Zac," a voice sounded, as they all turned to see Dr Lee at the doorway. "There is one other factor we need to watch and that is bubonic plague can quickly turn into pneumonic plague, if the respiratory system gets infected and then is spread easily air-borne. I can't see any signs of that and she isn't coughing, but I've given Victoria a shot of antibiotics just in case."

They looked behind to see Victoria being stretchered out to the first ambulance by two men, covered from head to toe in protective suits and helmets. She gave a tiny smile and a wave as they all waved back, shouting good luck, and then she immediately vanished in a cloud of dust as the ambulance shot up and out of the drive.

"Dad, I think the vet has arrived, that woman there outside in a green suit. Zac and I had better be on hand, we'll take the dogs into your big workshop. Expect she'll want to check them over, especially inside their fur and maybe take blood samples or saliva. See Mad, I'm not so daft. In fact, for everyone to hear, especially my big sister, I've decided now to take chemistry and biology A-level next year with double maths and physics. I want to train to be a vet not an engineer. And,

I'm heading for Cambridge University. You're not the only one with brains in this family, sis. Zak, bring those dog leashes out will you. Hey, that vet has a cool looking blonde assistant; she only looks my age, great."

"Good idea Ned, go for it," Julian replied smiling. "At last, some focus on what you want to do for the first time."

"You have to pass your exams first," Bel countered, grinning.

"Listen you two, you're not the only ones with talent here, so you can take passing exams as a done deal, isn't that so Zac?" Ned replied.

"They used to employ old women to strip the bodies, hack off any jewellery for payment and shove them into carts for huge burial pits, thirty at a time," Zac murmured, still fascinated, zapping through an original account of the Great Plague of London in 1665.

Everyone turned to stare at him quietly. Maddie shot a glance to Abby; they really had to find some privacy and talk.

"I don't think we're at that stage yet Zac," Dr Lee replied crisply having donned a protective suit, striding back in with a bag containing giant syringes and bottles of a special antibiotic, brought by one of the units. She was accompanied by two male doctors, equally suited, with more bags. "My colleagues, Dr Jones and Dr Remington and I have just created a makeshift examination room in your study Julian. I assume that's okay? Then we can examine all of you thoroughly and take some samples."

He nodded, sanguine, only wishing he could have gone with Victoria in the ambulance.

"You first Ned in you go, followed by Zac, and then you boys can help the vets Dr Gill and Nancy with the dogs. Men next and ladies last." She proceeded to prepare a syringe with a needle around a foot long filled with antibiotic as Ned suddenly turned pale. "Quick push into the stomach for males, doesn't hurt, and females in the upper arm. What's the matter Ned? Get in there please and all your clothes off."

"Hey Ned, just think of England and Nancy and you'll be alright," Zac shouted after him as he trotted disconsolately towards the study. "Ned and Nancy, sounds like something out of the Sound of Music, that ancient film they showed at school, Bel, doesn't it?"

Everybody roared laughing until Dr Lee confirmed there would be no alcohol for the rest of the day. Julian and Lynton returned once more to their own glumness ...

Chapter Thirteen

Early March 1666: Woolsthorpe Manor in Lincolnshire, England.

A cold wind whipped over the flat, muddy fields as Newton trudged warily homeward. The winter was once again harsh. Snow had lain deep on the ground for ages but was finally beginning to melt and a few swathes of freshly appeared green grass had broken through the mush.

He had ventured on foot to see Judas Vine in Grantham for the purchase of new shoes for the horse, which hobbled badly. Vine as usual ranted on about evil, redemption and the devil, a real Dutch odd-ball if ever there was. The journey was an unwanted distraction from his deep mathematical thinking to refine the general binomial theorem further and perhaps solve the difficult equation of the cubics. He was excited, although as yet, the wider publication of a paper was still eluding him. It was so difficult to do proper scientific work in this outback at Woolsthorpe. He desperately needed to return to Cambridge, but the Great Plague continued to ravage all before it, and the opening of the university was not yet granted for the foreseeable future. However, the advantage of not having tedious distractions, especially rowdy, drunken students rampaging around the college halls pleased him greatly.

As he walked back with his replacement horseshoes, he threw his thoughts into some reverie, thinking wistfully not only of Trinity College, but of his friend Robert McKenzie. He had not received any letters back since the distressing and outrageous news arrived of the heinous burning at the stake of Lucinda, Robert's twin sister, and the barbarous butchery of Robert's father, Cameron, following the hysterical denunciations by their local Abbot. However he had gleaned from Pepys, who wrote him at the end of January, to say that Lord McKenzie, on returning to Orsbrick Hall, successfully mustered together a contingent of the King's Guard and drove the vile perpetrators out, restoring order and civility back to the estate. The Abbot had apparently fled, but Pepys had learned that much of the village, shocked by what had happened, rounded up the remaining priests and they were despatched off to hell by the sword and the axe. Robert had now inherited the title and become the new Earl of Burscough. He immediately promised to provide good paid employment for all of the local artisans and peasants who had supported the McKenzie family, through work on the restoration of the damaged Orsbrick Manor back to new. However Pepys made no mention of the lovely Lady Bella, whom Robert, when last he was in Lincolnshire in happier times, had intended to pursue for marriage.

Newton felt ashamed that devotion to his own intense scientific studies had made him forget for far too long about his friend and resolved to write duly that evening, over a warm fire and a large flagon of home-made ale. It was certainly now highly unlikely, he conjectured sadly, given Robert's new status and responsibilities, that the new Earl would ever return to Cambridge if and when Trinity College reopened in the future.

Two and a half hours later, his feet frozen inside his inadequate boots, he ended the nine mile journey and saw the big house standing tall in the distance, always alone and desolate. On approach however he felt first disquiet then alarm. Things did not look as they should to his ordered mind and keen experimental eye. There was first no smoke from the chimney, highly unusual as his mother, almost by clockwork, would have a good fire blazing by then. The ten sheep, recently let out of the barn to graze in the fields could not be seen anywhere. As he came closer, he saw the door was wide open but hanging forlornly from a couple of broken hinges, two of the windows either side broken. That did not look good. Perhaps highwaymen or vagabonds had entered and were still about. He crept stealthily, first picking up a long axe from the barn, took a deep breath and rushed in shouting loudly.

At the back of the room, half-hidden behind a heap of dining chairs, his mother cowered, ducking down her head as her son stormed inside. But seeing it was him, she pushed the pile of chairs over and ran out to hug him in great distress, her clothes torn and dirty.

"Isaac, Isaac, thank God you've come back, terrible things have befallen us, see over there."

He looked under the large dining table to see the huge form of Caesar, lying there asleep on his blanket, except immediately on seeing his precious, huge wolfhound closely, the great love of his life was not breathing but lay lifeless and immobile, his eyes closed. Caesar's fur was matted with deep cuts and his body bloodied. Newton never cried, but this time his emotions overcame him. He rushed, howling with immediate grief to his animal, and hugged him tightly, the blood of the wolfhound covering his new jacket. Caesar was still warm.

"I tried so hard to save him, my son. I bathed his wounds which were terrible but he had paid a heavy price defending the house and me. Both of us knew. At the end he looked into my eyes, growled defiantly for one last time then lay down quietly and died in his favourite spot, where he always laid at your feet to receive his bones at mealtime."

"But mother, what has caused this travesty? I shall take the musket and shoot the devils dead, all of them."

"It has been done, look, towards the kitchen door."

Newton turned and stared incredulous at the four huge, black canine bodies, lying on the kitchen floor. Looking around the room, the evidence of a great fight was now to be seen as his mother lit half a dozen candles. His favourite armchair had been overturned and was ripped and torn, the ornaments on the sideboard smashed and curtains pulled down. Great pools of blood lay everywhere including massacred chunks of animal bits, fur, a head and a couple of ears. The dead canine carcasses, throats torn, consisted of a bloody mass, heaped on one another where they fell. She opened the kitchen door and the ten sheep ran out, baaing like crazy through the living room and on through the front door into the fields.

Feral dogs, he thought. What a terrible thing, but Caesar bravely had killed all four of them. But on approaching to inspect them precisely, he felt his blood run cold. They were definitely not dogs. That was now obvious from the size and shape of their chewed up heads. They looked exactly like pictures he had seen in the Trinity College library. Wolves!

He called to his mother. "But this simply is not possible. Wolves have not been seen in packs like this for over eighty years in England and certainly not in this area, although some old-timer shepherds over in the Dabbling Duck, when they have downed a good fill of ale flagons, claim still to have seen the occasional one."

"There were six, Isaac. Caesar killed four in this very room, such a fight I would never have seen or believed possible. I managed with your musket to shoot another. It crawled outside, and lies dead near the barn. The last one Caesar chased out and I also shot and wounded that beast. I could see it slow severely as it ran through Arkwright's field into the woods, I am sure it will now also be dead."

"Six?"But how did they get in?"

"I first heard them howling in the distance, a sound so evil I have never heard before and wish to never encounter again. It was like the devil himself was baying. I saw their huge shapes way in the distance beginning to circle the other field where the sheep lay. Caesar was growling mercilessly but he ran with me and we chased the frightened sheep towards the house.

Then the wolves ran, baying and howling down the hill towards me. I got the sheep and Caesar inside and managed to shut the door but four of them leapt fifteen feet in the air and threw themselves, coordinated together, at the door which broke with the great weight, whilst the other two jumped straight through the glass windows. They all went straight for Caesar who fought them so hard. Where he found the strength I do not know, I would never have believed it. Finally I managed to grab the musket and got one. Three were already dead and Caesar tore the head off the fourth. He lived for two hours my son but his strength ebbed until we both knew it was too late. He was a very brave hound.

"I shall bury him with dignity, in front of his favourite kennel," Newton whispered, convulsed with grief and unbelieving of a pack of wolves appearing in such a manner.

"I know this may not be the right time Isaac, but Annie Pilchmayer at Ferney's Farm only told me this morning, when I took some fresh milk round, that Beth their own wolfhound has just given birth to five puppies. They were angry at first that Caesar, unknown to us all, had sired them but his puppies are apparently adorable. There are two males both with his unusual crème and black markings."

"Then mother, we shall have them both. I shall do more work on the farm in between my experiments and mathematics to pay for them. Caesar will not have died in vain, his lineage will continue here. I am heartbroken but there lies hope with his two sons. I'll get everything cleared up mother, board up the door and windows and then request Jacobson out tomorrow to glaze. Damnation, I see amongst our precious ornaments smashed, is another but not belonging to me. I will attempt a repair and send it on. Now, if you are able to warm the remains of that pie for us, I will pour us some mead then I must rest and study and write."

March 3rd 1666. Woolsthorpe Manor
My Dearest Friend, Robert, Earl of Burscough
It was with great sadness that I finally received, via Mr Pepys, the confirmation of the dire news you received at my abode about the terrible death of your sister and then your father at the hands of religious fanatics. However I understand from Pepys that on return you managed to wrestle house and land back from the mob, and now hold the full Earldom. I pertain that this will come with massive responsibility and I am already accustoming my expectation you will not be returning to Cambridge, although when or if the College reopens is still perchance anyone's guess. Pepys believes the Great Plague is waning now in London and is beyond its peak but I am not so sure.

However I do hope you may find time still to pursue hard philosophy, undoubtedly in my view, like science and mathematics, excellent to stave off atrophy of the mind, although I wish it fared as well for my teeth. Three more pulled since we last drank ale together. Wooden ones loom large on the horizon.

My experimental and theoretical work has continued well here, despite our continuing income challenges. I do not need the company of others to find inspiration. Solitude suits my psyche and here it is in abundance. However I do have some upsetting news. Today I returned home to find my great love,

Caesar, dead, savaged by a pack of wolves in the house although he killed four but died later from his wounds. The behaviour of these beasts was not one of logical expectation, I forsook it being of the devil himself. My mother shot another two, but we are safe now. I read that some wolves are indeed still seen in your area of Bowland Forest but not here in Lincolnshire for nigh on eighty years, it was so very odd. Sadly too, your precious ornament, the unusual prism of crimson was smashed into three in the fighting. The wolves so my mother described, leapt on it fascinated, again strange. I have attempted a repair as best as I can with boiled hoofs glue but it is not I am afraid perfect. However, I enclose it in this mail and hope the prism arrives safely.

As always, I remain your good friend and you will always be welcome at our home anytime. I also hope that your expectation of romance with the lovely and gifted Bella you described last may bear success. Now as master of the estate, you will want, I am sure, to look to your male successors.

With best wishes
Isaac

Sunday September 2nd 1666 at Woolwich in London:
Early September arrived. Autumn was always a time for taking stock of the year's progress for Robert McKenzie. The last ten months had been exceptionally tumultuous, a major catastrophe for his entire family, especially for his ailing mother who now lay permanently sickly in her bed. She was overcome with unending grief, refusing to rise and wished to die every day. Sadly that may not be long. He still mourned the loss of his beloved and talented sister, Lucinda, whose death had taken her from him at far too early an age.

But Robert McKenzie, like his father and his father before him, was practical and realistic. Already, he had worked relentlessly to bring the vast estate of Orsbrick Hall back to become the central life and wellbeing of the Burscough community. Only days before his journey down to London, he had toiled with his farm labourers to direct the sowing of next year's wheat, a veritable hoard of grain having been thrashed out of the extensive summer crop. Bread would be plentiful in Burscough that coming year and he would personally see to an increase in provision of food and support to the poor, old, and sick, a cause he felt called by God to undertake now that the priory was completely razed and being built over with the new house. As he said many times during the year, at Orsbrick village meetings, the job of the friars to help the needy had long been lost in unjustified, scurrilous plots. They used extreme beliefs to wage war and gain clerical power at the expense of the working community. The McKenzie family would replace that expunged religious cancer and provide directly for all.

Alighting from his ten-horse carriage, protected by a bevy of armed soldiers, he took himself straight into the Moorfields Inn and was immediately led by landlord Jarrold Cocker to their best table aside the large bay window in the lounge. He was early but happy to wait for Pepys as long as necessary. Today he would be inducted into his new position and work alongside Pepys in the Admiralty to set up the new Board of Trade for the West Indies. King Charles had personally insisted that 'a certain Robert McKenzie now Earl of Burscough has the right gumption to lead the business,' so duty to the Crown, as powerful an incentive as any man ever needed must prevail. Fortunately, his younger brother Edmund was a capable fellow to manage the estate effectively in his place, as he would need to be much in London for the next twelve months. Pepys already had a splendid residence lined up for consideration.

After being served a large flagon of best ale, he pulled the letter out of his coat, which he had not had time to read from his friend Newton and opened the seal.

August 25th 1666. Woolsthorpe Manor
My Dearest Friend, Robert, Earl of Burscough

I was so pleased to hear of your recent engagement to Lady Bella Scott and I am most humbled to receive your invitation to the planned wedding in November at Orsbrick Hall. Of course, I accept warmly. Your recent science gift to me of fifty guineas has been greatly welcomed and has been put to excellent use, and I will bring with me my prototype of a new reflecting telescope which uses a mirror to enable much greater light and magnification. I admit that buffoon Hooke, with whom on his insistence I maintain correspondence, provided me with the design concept, but his limited imagination was easily and quickly surpassed by me in the workshop with a radical design, not before seen in the world. I shall be pleased to credit you with rights to first manufacture if such applications are of interest.

Finally I have another speculation to share with you, which came about in a most unexpected way in the summer. I was quietly drinking tea in the garden under the shade of that large apple tree in front of the house, under which my much missed Caesar would relax often from the sun, and where now his offspring, Helios and Mars take his place. An apple fell before my eyes and verily it has sparked such profound ideas about the nature of the drawing power of the earth and how it must work. I am focused relentlessly, with great detailed thought on this hypothesis, and will present you with such philosophical findings as soon as I am satisfied and then publish. It will make Drs Hooke and Boyle very jealous!

Your honoured servant
Isaac

Robert McKenzie smiled and pondered Newton's bold proposition on the manufacture of the telescope. He liked the business idea. His genius friend Isaac Newton thinks through great innovations and he Robert McKenzie funds such research into practice. There could be much money to be made in applying science by that unusual method, there was no doubt. His reverie was interrupted by the sound of a female voice from the inside doorway.

"So Robert, you made it in one piece? And my new axle design for your carriage, lighter and stronger, held out well exactly as my mathematics said it would, despite my sister's objections? Ha ... I can tell by your face you have lost the bet ... so five pounds please."

He looked up startled then forced a smile, although he had to admit, inside his loins wasn't forced. She strode over, ever the confident, ultra-fashionable young woman, and plonked herself down next to him, gazing unnervingly into his eyes.

"Lady Warren. What a pleasant surprise, you look ... really ... quite err ..."

"My dear Robert, you don't have to be so coy with me. I think the word you look for is ravishing is it not? And as we are soon to be related, then it really is time you called me Katherine."

He had to admit Katherine's long, dark, curly tresses, and red blusher on her beautiful face and that tight silk dress displaying her ample figure made her almost irresistible. It had to stay almost. His weakness for cunny must not take over, especially in this circumstance.

"Pray Katherine, has your sister not arrived yet?"

"We actually got here early but she has gone by carriage with Mr Pepys and his wife Elizabeth to look at a grand town house on the Thames, in Greenwich, just come up for sale and not too far from the Admiralty. From the description and sketch I saw, and knowing my sister, then she will likely fall in love with the place immediately, darling Robert. You may have to dig deep inside those pockets of yours."

McKenzie laughed as Katherine asked the landlord to bring two plates of his best pigeon pie with vegetables and a large bottle of Spanish claret.

"So I am afraid poor Bella will not be back from her house-hunting until this evening but Mr Pepys has asked me to convey his sincerest apologies. Of course we are all invited to his splendid residence for Sunday lunch tomorrow. I believe there may be a special guest, darling Robert ... my father."

"The King? What, the King himself may prevail to lunch with Mr Pepys? But I thought the Royal entourage had all relocated in the summer, due to the Great Plague in ..."

Katherine interrupted him, her voice a clear whisper, her tone perfected from her stint as a regular actress on Drury Lane. "Oh Robert, don't be so priggy. The King loves to get out of that boring nonentity of a place, Salisbury, and he needs to keep a quiet eye, in disguise of course, on the many plotters about in the Palace of Westminster. Some already anonymously hang on the gibbet in Pudding Lane, having been identified by his watchful eye. Anyway, a tiny bird told me that my father, as well as Mr Pepys and yourself have a little business to conclude?"

McKenzie sat up startled. His potential appointment was a strict secret, especially from the Parliamentarians. "Who pray, Katherine, are the tiny birds?"

She giggled, coquettishly. "My baby sister, don't worry. Actually Bella and I are half-sisters, which is why I am titled Lady Warren of course. We are privy to much greater secrets, Robert, than you could ever imagine. Ah, our food has arrived."

"On my bill please, landlord."

Katherine raised her arm. "No, Mr Cocker, this will be my treat for Lord McKenzie."

"As you wish milady."

Cocker returned with a second bottle of claret and generously refilled the glasses. McKenzie was feeling a little light-headed but his female companion seemed to have the drinking stamina of Isaac Newton.

"Ah, poor Robert, I can see you are not yet used to the high living of we Londoners, but you will soon get used to it."

"I must admit this pigeon pie is delicious," he replied, tucking into the meal, having missed breakfast as they were running late. "Very different from anything I have tasted, amazingly spicy."

"Yes, a special recipe brought back from Morocco by the traders. Cocker here has made it a speciality. They come from all around London for his fayre. Now Robert, I have something to show you. My sister and I may share a love of science but she is my half-sister and so I have other inherited talents."

"Well, I must say your reputation as an actress has even reached the distant West Lancashire."

"Really? How splendid. No, I mean the visual arts, dear Robert. Unlike Bella I paint, in fact such work is my true great love, well ... almost." She giggled again. "And, to hang in the drawing room of your new Greenwich town house, I have produced a special panoramic of the City of London. The view is taken from a high hill just over the Thames, where I drew and then painted the scene. Now, drink that last glass please, and then you can follow me to my room to show you"

He was feeling decidedly woozy and a period of merriment and detachment was enveloping him again, exactly as he regularly indulged in at Trinity College as a student. He was weak, always weak, especially with drink, but he had to remain strong. Anyway, Katherine, as well as being Bella's sister and daughter of the King was a married woman, but she was of such compelling beauty and talents. Her husband, that decrepit codger Lord Warren was over sixty and she not yet twenty ... although, none of that had ever stopped him before.

They rose from the table and he stumbled behind her towards the stairs ...

McKenzie spent the evening detached from the rest of the world in a delirious haze of befuddled reverie before passing out totally in Samuel Pepys's finest guest bedroom. Fortunately, his liverymen eventually discretely rescued him from the Moorfields Inn and whipped the horses through the driving rain, mud and stench, as quickly as possible to Woolwich.

Pepys meanwhile had returned Bella in another coach, back to the hotel to rejoin her sister. On arrival, Katherine insisted to Bella that Lord McKenzie had to give his apologies and had left for a business appointment, and would then be heading for Woolwich. But Katherine remembered to add that he was looking forward to seeing her the following day.

Bella of course was incandescent, blaming her sister for deliberately muddling the arrangements. Pepys quietly sneaked out the back, after downing a quick half-flagon of ale, and left the two sisters at each other's throats in a screaming match in the middle of the bar, with poor Jarrold Cocker attempting to pacify both of them.

Before Pepys arrived back home, Elizabeth, with the help of some servants, got McKenzie upstairs and onto the bed. She gazed over him, a fine figure of a man, snoring gently in a boozed out haze. A pleasant reminiscence of his previous visit filled her mind and then her desires. She waved away the servants and removed his high-heeled boots, unbuttoned his shirt and took it off, finishing with slowly pulling down his fancy ribboned breeches. His wig had already been carefully placed on the dressing table. Seeing his endowed naked body again, his wavy blond hair billowed over the pillow, made her breathe heavily. Before anybody distracted her, she lay over him and unbuttoned her dress, then rubbed her hands and bare breasts, starting with his muscular thighs, slowly up to his chest, not missing any important part. Finally, with a departing kiss, she pulled a thick nightshirt over his head, shoved his arms through, put on a woollen cap and finally covered him over with a smile. The gorgeous Lord Robert McKenzie needed a real woman for a wife not that waif of a sixteen year old girl who knew nothing yet of life. Elizabeth pondered further, annoyed. Although admittedly pretty, Bella was still the King's bastard offspring, her head always tediously stuck inside a science book and her tongue too resplendent with unbecoming philosophy, which nobody understood ...

Elizabeth sneaked back to her room and lay down besides Pepys, already to bed and wheezing loudly with that damned chest, which made her wince, knowing he must have enjoyed yet another heavy smoking session. She grinned to herself, and looked forward to renewed sweet dreams ... but this was not to be. About three in the morning a loud knocking on the door woke her with a start as she shoved Pepys in the back hard.

Groaning, he came to, his head heavy. "Elizabeth, what on earth is the matter. Why is all that banging going on? Come in for Christ's sake damn you."

Their head maid, Jane, tentatively opened the door. "Sir, Madam, I truly apologise for disturbing you but please come quickly, there is a great fire in the City."

"Good heavens above," Pepys grunted. He forced his legs from the bed, wrapped a gown around himself and staggered to the landing window, Elizabeth behind.

In the distance, a large red glow lit up the sky. The tall, wooden buildings all around were heavily crowded into each other and only separated by narrow cobbled streets. Their jagged profiles stood clear in the light, peculiar at that time of night, normally pitch dark and foreboding except for the odd street lantern still alight. "Tis some conflagration, to be sure, and that pitch used in those buildings won't help. I estimate it to be at the back of Mark Lane or thereabouts. I expect they are pulling down houses now to break the fire. We shall return to bed my dear. The flames will doubtlessly be out before dawn."

"Sir," Jane pleaded. "Some of the servants request permission to go and see to their families who live around there, they are fearful, sir."

"Yes, yes, tell them to go but be careful." Pepys replied, waving his hands in the air. "Many of the buildings in that neighbourhood are so old and rotten they will go up like gunpowder."

"Thank you Mr Pepys."

They returned to their bed and resumed sleep. Pepys was snoring again immediately, although Elizabeth lay for a while and pondered how far the fire may spread, thinking of the area to the west, enclosing the Moorfields Inn where Lady Bella and her even more loathsome sister were staying. She decided not to bother waking her husband.

Pepys being an early riser was awake by six and looked out of the window, the early dawn now lighting up the sky. Flames were still visible although the fire appeared further away. Dressing, he walked briskly down the stairs for breakfast, when Jane, plates clattering in her hand, greeted him, still very alarmed.

"Mr Pepys, sir, it is disastrous along the river front. Already over three hundred houses are burned down and a strong wind has been rising, whipping up the flames and sparks. Mr Johnstone says it is getting out of control and panic has set in. People flee in boats onto the water. The fire-fighters are completely overwhelmed, they don't know what to do."

"My word Jane, fetch me that mug of coffee quickly. I must walk to the Tower and find the Lieutenant. Hurry girl."

"Sir, Lord McKenzie is still sleeping. Do you think I should rouse him?"

Pepys laughed, he knew his friend had overdone it badly, but there was nothing McKenzie could do. "No, we can let him ..." but Pepys suddenly stopped. He had completely forgotten, his head still woozy too. Lady Bella Scott and Lady Katherine Warren were staying in the City that night ... His face darkened as he turned to Jane, grabbing the mug from her hand. "Tell me Jane, the servants who returned, how far has that fire spread? I mean to the west?"

"Pudding Lane is completely destroyed. The fire leapt across Fish Street Hill, engulfed the Star Inn, would you believe it, then spread over into Thames Street, where all the river warehouses, bursting with oil, tallow and other combustible goods, Mr Pepys, went up immediately. Mr Sales also was told there had been a delay pulling down houses in the path, there was much grumbling of rebuilding cost and then it was too late. The fire is engulfing everything down there and is unstoppable."

"Heaven forbid, Jane. Go and get Lord McKenzie now and Giles and Christopher. We have to get our boat out and go up the river to avoid the pandemonium in the streets. We must get to the Moorfields Inn. Hell and damnation."

"Oh Mr Pepys, Lady Bella and Lady Katherine ... I'll fetch him now ..."

Pepys finished his coffee and with the servants and a horse started pulling their boat to the water's edge, praying it was still watertight, having stupidly left the pitching work that year. They looked up to see Robert McKenzie run down the path, his cloak flying around him, accompanied by two of his own footmen. The smell of smoke now filled the air and the conflagration in the distance clearly raged fiercely.

"Fuck all this, Mr Pepys, what is the cause of this disaster? Let us row, pass me an oar. Which direction to the Moorfields Inn? Is it near the water's edge? My precious Bella, we must get there, I pray she is safe."

McKenzie sat inside and rowed furiously with the others, his stomach so bad it was indescribable either from the terror of his beloved Bella being burned alive or the drink or likely both. He reflected on the evening and could remember nothing, after meeting Bella's sister Katherine, so badly had he consumed. As they moved slowly up the river, the lamentable fire drew closer. The stench in the air was almost unbearable. Showers of fire drops hurtled through the air from building to building in the wind. Everybody was endeavouring to remove their goods, laden with everything imaginable alongside sick people carried away in beds, all thrown in a jumble onto lighters in the river. They watched poor people, stay to the last minute trying to save their homes in vain, until the very fire touched them and then they hastily clambered down steps to the waterside and flung themselves into boats. Even the poor pigeons, reluctant to leave their loft homes, hovered above the windows and balconies until their wings burned and they fell down into the flames. Staring at the warehouses burning like torches, Pepys reflected, not only on the copious amount of oil and tar going up but the huge loss of fine wine and brandy stored in thousands of barrels along the quay. He also pondered at the effect on the Great Plague. The pestilence was also being burned alive with the many likely victims who could not be saved.

As they rounded the next corner and approached the river edge, Pepys pointed forwards, shouting and coughing to the oarsmen.

"There, the Moorfields Inn, between those two houses. Ye gods, the place has just caught alight."

"Hurry men, hurry, McKenzie screamed, as the boat pulled alongside the jetty and he leapt onto the bank with Pepys behind him.

Pepys grabbed his arm. "You can't go in there man. Look, the roof is already ablaze, you'll kill yourself for certain. Surely Lady Bella and Lady Katherine will have been rescued already and be gone, they must be in boats on the water."

McKenzie pushed Pepys away hard, who almost stumbled into the river. Then they both turned to see two figures, a man holding a dog and a woman, all blackened, their clothes and their skin scorched but they were still alive, crawling along the mud to safety. Pepys shouted out. "Cocker, sir! For God's sake men, help those two. Where are Lady Bella and Lady Katherine? Are they safe?"

Landlord Jarrold Cocker staggered forward, coughing badly, his clothes smouldering and smoking. "She saved us, Mr Pepys, me and my wife and dog, Lady Bella she is a true heroine sir ..."

McKenzie looked up to see a blackened figure hanging from an upper window, screaming for help ... his beautiful Bella alight ... "Fuck it all Pepys," McKenzie screamed and with his cloak sodden full with water wrapped around his face, he dashed towards into the blazing building. Pepys, shouting it was already too late, tried to grab him again but McKenzie leapt out of the way.

"Follow him, you three, try and stop the fool," Pepys shouted to his oarsmen as they dashed in pursuit but fell back. The heat was too fierce. Everyone watched as McKenzie jumped straight through the burning doorway and into the flames.

As Pepys stumbled towards his oarsmen, they saw Robert McKenzie emerge, carrying Bella in his arms. His large cloak, with copious clouds of steam pouring upwards, covered them both. Rushing quickly, they helped both of them down to the boat and laid Bella gently on some thick blankets. McKenzie sat down on the bank breathless, coughing and spluttering, his gargantuan effort having worn him out. Bella was breathing, covered in soot, her clothes torn and smouldering and her curly hair singed on one side, the smell perceptible. Her cheek on the same side along with one hand though, was with visible, nasty burns. Slowly she opened her eyes, smiled, and arose. Despite being in obvious pain, Bella walked slowly and gracefully to McKenzie, who gazed at her in wonder, as she threw her arms around him and kissed him passionately. Everyone, even the badly injured Cocker and his wife, clapped joyfully. A hero and a heroine both.

Pulling herself away, Bella, looked around the scattered contents from the warehouses, some thrown from carts heading to the water, others spewed from the burning upper floors as they fell and buildings collapsed. She pointed to a couple of broken barrels nearby and small earthenware pots clustered together still intact inside a wooden crate. "Quickly Mr Pepys. Fetch me those pots, I can see they contain honey. And you man," pulling the arm of an oarsman, "Grab some of those plants from that barrel, verily of incredible luck they look like witch-hazel traded from the Indies. And also that liquid tallow dripped into that bucket."

McKenzie stood up smiling, his breath had returned. His Bella was alive and still beautiful. He would love her forever, even if she was scarred with the burns on her face. "Why do you want these things my love?" he called out.

But Bella wasn't listening. Already, with the oarsman, she was furiously shredding the witch-hazel and mixed it together with the honey and grey ash into a thick paste in a bowl. Dipping the water from the river into her hand, Pepys handed her a cloth from the boat and she started to gently wash off the soot, first from her hands and face and finally her hair, shouting in pain. McKenzie held her firmly.

As the black came off in swathes, he breathed a sigh of relief. She was not as badly burned as he first thought. Bella had been terribly lucky, especially as the fire, by chance, had enveloped the back part of the Moorfields Inn first and she had finally run to the front bedroom and slammed the thick oak door shut, providing a temporary fire break.

"I must do this quickly my love, my studies of science and physic will be put to use. Hand me that tincture please." Carefully, Bella applied the paste to her cheek until it was covered and then did the same on the extensive burns over her left hand. "That tallow, my hero Robert, is cooling and beginning to set." She pulled a makeup brush from her dress pocket. "Take care and gently wipe the thick liquid over the paste so it will set as a cover, keeping the remedy tightly on my skin. I have studied this method, as old as the Romans and their armies, and very effective at healing wounds. My dear Robert and you Mr Pepys, as I can see from your faces, you are most intrigued. If applied quickly, which I have done, the burns will remain superficial and should disappear in time."

McKenzie kissed her good cheek. "Verily, my Lady Bella, despite your young age you already are a woman of the most compelling and deep intellect and foresight. I am truly a lucky man that you are alive and will be my wife."

She grinned and kissed him back, alongside cries and clapping of hear, hear. The pain was throbbing badly but already much relieved with the tincture.

Pepys suddenly went quiet, his face contorted. "Oh my God in Heaven, Lady Bella, we have forgotten about your sister, Lady Katherine."

The men stared back, forlornly, towards the burning Moorfields Inn, now a great inferno of a bonfire, the roof and first floor having collapsed totally, with the two adjacent buildings also well alight. The strong heat could be felt even from their distance of fifty yards.

Bella smiled. "It is fine, there is no concern to be had gentlemen. Katherine left last night Mr Pepys. She will now be lodging safely in the Saviour Inn at the docks in Woolwich, and preparing for the maiden voyage of the Half Moon."

"You mean she is ... for the sailing to the Americas, Lady Bella? But that includes a group of thirty Puritans, who head for the growing Massachusetts Bay Colony on the east coast of New England?"

"Yes, I know. Katherine, I am afraid, joined up with the movement recently, in secret. My father was told and he was not happy as, Mr Pepys, you will fully appreciate. The King has approved her departure, with of course sufficient means to allow her to set up a new life in Salem. She will be wed again enroute, as is the custom."

Pepys, his political antennae twitching strongly, was totally flummoxed, already convinced there was something else afoot. He looked at landlord Cocker who looked away.

"But she is a famous actress, my lady. It makes no sense to …"

"No longer. It is done Mr Pepys and of no further concern. Now pray, I must tell you and Robert here that the Lord Mayor of London, instead of leading the fight against the fire was seen gibbering like a baby and galloped past us earlier in the street, heading for safe sanctuary. I am told that he refused to make the decision to pull down the houses before the flames, which incidentally started in a baker's house in Pudding Lane, now sadly no more including all the great theatres. Thence the inferno became uncontrollable. London City is in danger of burning down totally if left unheeded. We must alert the King immediately, who is in residence in the Chapel at Whitehall with the Duke of York, to command the necessary demolition and mobilisation of soldiers to quell unrest. Can we get there by your boat Mr Pepys?"

"Yes of course, and then with horses nearby. Let's get to it. Come everyone, this intervention is vital. Thank you so much Lady Bella. I will tell the extent of the crisis to his Majesty personally, after seeing this dreadful tragedy so close with my own eyes."

As they rowed mightily downstream, Pepys looked down the river, lit from end to end with huge flames, the sky orange for miles. "This day in London will be remembered forever in the annals of history of this fine country as one of the darkest ever," he muttered gravely with a sad heart.

Bella looked up from her seat next to Robert McKenzie, who had his arm wrapped tightly around her to keep out the cold wind whistling along the open water of the Thames, the waves choppy and rough. "But Mr Pepys," she cried earnestly. "From this disaster will surely emanate a silver lining. It is obvious, by the speed of the fire, that London has been vulnerable, overcrowded and dangerous to the flame for too long. Much rebuilding will be required and the opportunity can be taken to plan and use better brick materials. In fact a veritable great spring-clean will emerge, with much needed work for the poor. Also we must end the Great Plague, which I predict will be eradicated within the embers. I am sure the terrible outbreak of the last two years will dissipate fast and is now effectively over."

"By heavens Lady Bella," Pepys retorted. "You have the vision and clarity of a true Parliamentarian. Don't you agree Robert? Although society sadly will never in our lifetime see a woman ever so elected. Lord McKenzie and I will discuss these matters further with the King. In fact I know a man whose aptitudes should be brought to bear. I shall recommend that Wren be given the task to examine a design of a new London and rebuild all the lost churches.

"Wren, Mr Pepys?" Bella queried loudly, "You mean Wren the physicist and geometer of Oxford?"

"Yes, Christopher Wren. He is also a great architect," Pepys mumbled, "Exactly the man for the job."

He began furiously scribbling in his notebook, as the rowers, groaning with the effort, increased speed. All

256

that had happened since he awoke this fateful morning would join the other notes on the Great Plague from the previous year. He was pleased with his writing. A true set of potential diaries were coming together to record this momentous period in English history. He would publish the lot in due course. Perhaps, he mused, the memoirs will even be appreciated by historians of the future.

Bella turned to McKenzie and snuggled closer into his warm body. "However, my dear Robert," she whispered into his ear with a sharp gaze, the wax on her cheek and hands now set white and looking odd, as if she had some awful skin lesion, or worse the pox. "I am not finished with you yet. There are things concerning my darling sister Katherine that you and I need to discuss and clear some air. Do you agree?"

He could feel a cold chill trickle slowly down his gullet and deep into his stomach. Bella knew. Now his mind was cleared after the drunken fog of sin of the previous night, he had to tread very carefully. He could have kicked himself for his loss of discretion, he must not lose her. He looked back into her clear blue eyes, smiled weakly and nodded. She snuggled deeper into his chest. Her delectable man was well and truly snared for good.

She would wait later to also tell him his precious crimson glass prism, which he left in the tavern, had reverted back to its three pieces, after she threw it in a rage at her sister. Sadly, his friend Newton was poor at restoration, the glue being weak and ineffective, although she did throw it hard. Her artist friend Grinling Gibbons, who had given Robert the damned thing in the first place as he was glad to rid himself of the monstrosity, even once mumbled in her ear that the crimson prism would ward off evil spirits. That was after a drunken escapade and a grope, when of course she pushed him away with that awful bad, garlic breath. Katherine, in contrast, gave in to Gibbons's lecherous whims, but then her sister gave in to most men after encouraging them first.

Bella grimaced for a moment but then smiled again thinking of Katherine, her silly powdered face bewildered, and hastily picking up the three broken pieces and stuffing them into her bag once the pronouncement of her imminent Atlantic departure was made clear. Katherine would need all the warding off of bad luck she could find, once on board that ship and out of her life for good ...

Chapter Fourteen

Victoria, tired and weak, peered up from her bed through the plastic window in the pale cream roof of the dome-like structure placed over her. Above, she could see the ceiling of the hospital ward she had been placed in. She was inside a sealed hemispherical chamber, comparable to a Mongolian yurt, totally alone and isolated, with only half a dozen robotic, gloved hands sticking out from the perimeter as company. An eerie quiet pervaded this inner sanctum, punctuated only by the rhythmic, wheezing sound of a ventilation pump outside, ensuring she could breathe purified air. Every hour, nurses would come into the main room and press a multitude of buttons and flip switches. Dials would be rotated and the rubber gloved hands at the end of arms swivelled in response like cranes inside a fun-fair sweet cabinet, and do all manner of things by picking up objects from a tray at the end.

RoboYurt, as she decided to call her new incarceration cell, would gently take a saliva sample, open pill bottles, pass her food and take away the remains. One hand, with a smiley face drawn on it and with red glowing laser eyes, even administered the occasional antibiotic injection, which she initially viewed with great trepidation, but it was definitely less painful than her annual flu vaccination. Various sensors were strapped onto her body, monitoring all kinds of bodily parameters that were wirelessly transmitted to the desktop machine outside, which would print out long reams of results regularly in response. The doctors and nurses perused them hourly with deep interest. She even had a small toilet, with privacy curtains around it and a very quiet flush that piped off into another outside machine from which her waste was immediately analysed and a variety of graphs in different coloured inks plotted straight off.

Victoria was under the direct care of the rather prim and taciturn Dr Rosanne Yardley, a former American Chief Medical Officer of the World Health Organisation, specially flown in from New York. Rosanne had used her unique network of contacts to acquire a very rare form of serum vaccine for bubonic plague, developed and retained in a WHO laboratory in Paris, the only one in the world. The serum had only previously been tested on black rats, which didn't give Victoria a huge degree of comfort. But, she, Dr Victoria McKenzie, was the only person in the world who had now been confirmed as having a unique strain of bubonic plague, last seen in England in 1666 in London, so supervised human pre-trials were not exactly a luxury on offer to her.

In the enthusiasm to confirm such a rare find, Dr Yardley had even supervised the digging up of an old burial pit, preserved under a theatre in Drury Lane, to exhume some seventeenth century victims to check viral DNA. A pale white skull, with a few teeth remaining, sat alone on a lab bench further down.

Victoria had peered hard to try and catch the last print-out through the glass but it was too far away to make anything definitive out. Despite their obvious scientific affinities, Dr Yardley still refused to discuss any findings, irritating Victoria intensely. There was nothing which raised her hackles more than being taken for a fool who knew nothing of science. Rosanne's logical reasoning was on the grounds it was early days and she needed to prioritise on getting Victoria's condition to stabilise.

And it was certainly evident that her fever had subsided from the two evenings previously, but her temperature was still raging too high and she felt very weak and debilitated. The swellings on her thighs and arms remained red and painful but the nurses were able to manipulate the robots to dab some sort of soothing antiseptic cream over them and the oozing pus had stopped under the dressings.

She picked up a bowl of chicken broth and some bread which had entered the airlock hatch and dabbed her spoon unenthusiastically into it. Victoria knew that Julian was next door. He had taken an adjoining room offered and was being monitored, but was not allowed into the outer area of RoboYurt yet. The hospital was taking massive precautions. Was she really such a deadly threat to the mankind of West Lancashire? She was also not allowed electronic devices, on the grounds that sensitive monitoring equipment may be affected. That old hospital chestnut still did the rounds and there was no accessible internet wifi either, but at least she had a couple of old-fashioned printed novels to dip into. Most of the time she lay on the bed, dozed regularly and vaguely perused her books or listened to the radio through a set of headphones as the hours went by between nurses seeing to their tasks in protective clothing.

Day two moved into late evening, and a drip had been attached to her arm to provide the first measured doses of the WHO special plague vaccine. She lay staring at the ceiling. Once more her mind was fast disappearing into hazy oblivion. The lights had been turned right down to allow her to sleep. She had named the four robots, Sylvia, Sly, Sourpuss and Surreal. Sly had earlier brought her a note and a card from Julian and the kids with lots of silly get well messages, kisses and jokes which Ned had assembled, sealed inside a decontamination container. She also received a card from Abby with a note that said the dogs in particular had no fleas and were perfectly healthy, as it seemed was everyone else. The decontamination unit had found nothing at Orsbrick or in her laboratory either, so the source remained a complete mystery, but the family were still under observation just in case.

Around three am, she felt herself woken up from another groggy sleep, her eyes refusing to open. Her hand was being held and all she could think of was Julian had broken in and was rescuing her, and muttered in a whisper how thankful she was he was there.

A whispered voice answered, but softly and with a strong Lancashire accent, a strange, echoing sound. And the voice was female. Victoria, still weak, finally opened her eyes, and with a cough struggled to raise her head up to see, when she took a very deep and unexpected breath. It was Mauveine, wearing a white laboratory coat and her hair in a bun, with Isi standing alongside inside the tent, in a black suit and a top hat, both smiling. And heavens above Mauveine could speak!

"Hello Victoria, sorry I'm not Julian but don't worry. Isi and I can't catch anything!"

Victoria could feel herself wanting to laugh, when Mauveine put her fingers to her lips. The night nurses were not to be disturbed. She looked at her hand which Mauveine was still holding and caressing. She could feel the pressure but there was a gap of some millimetres between Mauveine's hand and hers.

Mauveine continued in that soft whisper. It was interesting how her voice had the local, broad accent but was spoken in a very clear and clipped, posh way, just like in very old English films, and how the intonation had subtly changed over the last hundred odd years.

"You mustn't try to speak Victoria, please just listen, very carefully"

She nodded then looked around and through the glass. Except there was no glass, not even a tent. Her surroundings were those of a room in an old 19th century hospital. A couple of gas lights flickered on the tall-ceilinged brick wall, and her bed a high, metal framed type had starched, coarse and pristine white sheets carefully tucked in over her.

"The circumstances of time and space, and our universes, Victoria, in which we are all held and inhabit have finally come to a special conjunction. But the consequences require you to unlock the powers hidden inside you, the exact same powers of Abigail and your Aunt Eveline. And now you are aware that same ability has been passed on to your children, as happened with Isi and I. But only Madeleine, along with Abigail has the psychic strength and capability to act. They will need your help. You need to believe now Victoria, use your amazing mind and help them. If the wolves of Hades emerge, they must be fought to end our family curse for all McKenzies and forever. You will need to direct Abigail and Madeleine with your mind, you must believe you can do it and you will know when and how. Solutions inside your head will unlock, exactly as you are used to in the laboratory. Do you understand the task ahead?"

Victoria nodded, petrified and mesmerised. What on earth was Mauveine talking about? Was this why she was here and was it all connected?

"You have three days only, when you must unlock the secret of the prism of purpurine, and for the three of you to fight the demons. Lose and your life in your existing space and time will end immediately, the Great Plague will suck in its next victim. Good luck Victoria. Isi and I will help you where we can."

Victoria nodded again as Mauveine and Isi smiled but then they gradually dissolved and vaporised into thin air as the light went a dazzling white, forcing her eyes to close. She opened them again and she was back in RoboYurt, a nurse smiling at her and pointing with Sylvia to begin her six am tests and measurements.

Maddie squeezed her bottle of honey hard into the bowl and golloped down the porridge, simultaneously tapping away at her new iPhone Illustrious, the first model in seventeen years to depart from the same, boring old consecutive numbers. This one had a proper three dimensional screen unlike the others.

"My goodness Madeleine, don't wolf your food like that, you'll get indigestion. I can see my new recipe is going down a treat!"

"Sorry Clair, this porridge is amazing, like nothing I've ever tasted. Just sifting through these messages, Dad sent last night from the hospital. He's finally been allowed into the isolation room and says he's been playing with robot hands, and tried to give Mum her breakfast. They're able to talk of course through an intercom. He says she's looking better and the sores haven't increased or got worse but she's still very weak. Crikey, Mum even calls the robots by silly names. Sorry, what recipe did you use?"

"I'm sure we'll all be relieved to hear Victoria is making progress, even if slow. I found a recipe from that old McKenzie cookery book. All that talk of plagues and the seventeenth century made me look right back. The porridge is from the 1660s, very popular then with oats, some wheat, berries, molasses, nuts and spices not usually used."

Maddie raised her head, thought and then uttered, "Really? Mmm ..." before being interrupted by Bel, Ned and Zac who sat down noisily.

"Hey Mad, can I try your new phone out? Looks really cool," Ned shouted, grabbing at it as Maddie swiped his hand away sharply.

"No, absolutely not. This is from my hard earned savings working. Get a job and buy your own."

"No way am I doing a naff Sunday job in the cafe at Waitrose serving tea to those oldies. Joanne, I mean Dr Gill, and Nancy said I could help them over the Christmas holiday at the vets, with operations and stuff. They get really busy then."

Everyone guffawed.

"Hey you lot, can't you just see it? The Ned and Nancy clinic for hamsters, but bring your own wheels for workouts. Lots to talk about on your first date with Nancy tonight then eh Ned? " Bel shouted, setting them off again.

"You think you're so fucking funny Bel don't you," Ned retorted, going bright red, "How do you know I'm seeing Nancy tonight?"

"Edward? Language at the table please?" Clair retorted angrily, bringing in huge plates of toast and marmalade.

"Sorry Clair … forgot. Wow this porridge is super."

Zac slurped his coffee and looked up. "Now, talking of more important things, despite what the hospital said I am still convinced of the link, rats, wolves, dogs, fleas, bites as the logical chain of events through which Mum caught this bubonic plague. I saw a couple of dead rats in that cabin after Jeb and Kai pulled that wolf out. Think of the logic guys, the men from Mars found nothing whatsoever in the house. Ned's lover, Nancy and co, cleared the dogs of anything, only joking Ned, fess up will you? Mum and Dad haven't been anywhere unusual. We'll discount the country music bars in Nashville they visited, crikey Dad has weird tastes like his dancing. That virus was definitely carried by a flea, probably dead now with all the disinfectant, from the boat, and onwards to Mum. It just missed everyone else."

"Yeh, okay Professor Zackary Turing, but isn't there something fundamentally flawed in your reasoning?" Bel replied, quick as lightning. "That strain of bubonic plague hasn't been seen for over four hundred years. We're like living in 2025 not 1665."

"No, hang on a minute," Maddie said slowly, and thought hard. "Zac has a point, he's actually thinking out of the box here. What if we stretch that process a bit more? I mean in relation to what we all discussed with Abby the other night, as a way of explaining the things we've all seen, sorry Ned, except you."

"You mean all that psychic ghosties crap and colliding universes of time? Come on sis," Ned said out loudly. "No, I haven't a better explanation but it's all just too way out, man. But, I suppose, yeh, maybe we have to start thinking the unthinkable."

"That's more like it. The most sensible thing you've said for ages, Nancy is having a good effect on you after all," Maddie replied.

They all laughed loudly, including Ned this time.

"Explain further then Maddie?" Bel asked as they shuffled their chairs closer, whilst Jeb and Kai ambled in and lay down under the table.

"Let's assume Zac's right. Then the question is how did fleas with bubonic plague from London in 1665 end up on a boat on the Leeds and Liverpool canal now? What if there was a connection between London at that period of time in the height of the Great Plague and here at Orsbrick. Mum said once that this house was originally built over or near a priory or something, and then it burned down around the time the Leeds and Liverpool canal was constructed. Orsbrick Hall was then rebuilt here, which is where we live now of course."

"I can see where you're going with this, Mad," Zac chuntered, firing up his tablet. "What if there has been some kind of time bridging, between then and now? That's like sort of cool isn't it?"

"Not if everyone catches the plague like Mum!" Ned added. "There's also the question of those wolves. It seemed very odd to me that the big black bastard which chewed up Ade was hiding in that boat in the first place, and we conveniently come along?"

"Hey guys, maybe not so odd," Zac cried out very excited. "Just looked through WikiGoog on the history of wolves. They were getting extinct, late 1500's, hunted like crazy for hundreds of years before. But this area, when it was covered with the Bowland Forest was one of the last places for wolves to still be prowling about in England. Occasional ones were spotted right through to the end of the 1700s. Makes sense they could have been around in 1665, not in London but actually here."

"Oh shit ..."

They turned to Ned, his face all screwed up, who was looking straight back at Maddie. "Talking about Ade, he went kind of weird after that incident and cleared off. But Zac, remember what his brother said about what he suddenly decided to do in Dublin?"

"To be honest I wasn't really listening, never liked that freak of a brother."

"He said Ade had decided to become a priest, it was a big joke."

"Yeh, I remember now."

Bel tapped Maddie's arm. Her face was looking dreamily up to the ceiling, her thoughts clearly distracted inside her own mind. "Maddie, those things you saw? Not only were they in that same period of time, but didn't you say, last time, a few months back when you saw something, it was all pretty dreadful with witches being burned or something?"

Maddie gazed at them, momentarily tuned out of the discussion, which was not like her.

"Holy shit, that's it, priests, priories, wolves? Some of this is adding up," Ned replied. "Sis, are you okay? You look a bit funny?"

"Yes, just thinking, sorry I felt a bit odd then. Apart from that awful scene, there's something else you guys maybe should know now. When the body of that wolf vanished in the water, after the dogs shoved it in, and I watched it? The remains didn't just sink. The whole thing bubbled up and fizzed, exactly like a chemical reaction, steam came up and it dissolved, not sank. I'd kept it to myself, who would believe me? Certainly not the police. I think I'd better call Abby."

She picked up her phone and dialled, Abby answered immediately. The others had gone quiet, all reflecting hard, trying to join up the dots which didn't make any real sense.

"We need to do some work?" Bel suggested. "We have a library of books and old records up there which no one has really looked through in detail. I wonder, now we've pulled some initial information and facts together, whether something horrible happened here in 1665?"

"And might be repeating itself in 2025? Fuck, Bel, it's hard for me to buy it, but that is so scary … I mean very, very scary." Ned replied.

They nodded their faces glum.

Maddie returned to the discussion. "Abby is on her way. Lynton has gone into work today so she's on her own, which given everything we've discussed, maybe that's not such a bad thing. She and Mum, donkey's years ago, did start looking through that lot upstairs so she's going to help. Oh shit, my head … it's really pounding now like anything, in sort of pulses. I need to take a painkiller. Maybe I'm having a migraine or something?"

Zac pulled open a sideboard drawer and handed her a packet of ibuprofens. "Here Mad take a couple of these with that apple juice. They work really quickly. All the excitement probably. We're going to have to skip school today, but who cares, this is way too important. I'm going to get all my tablets and head upstairs to the library, at least the wifi works decent everywhere now."

They nodded and followed Zac, the dogs ambling behind.

Clair suddenly appeared around the corner. "Hey all of you? Shouldn't you be getting on your bikes for school? You're going to be late."

"Clair, we need to all do some work in the library for one of our class history projects. We've all got private study today with the exams coming," Bel replied deadpan. "Abby is coming to help as she knows a lot about the records up there."

"Okay, if you're sure, but I will mention it to your father when he gets back."

They disappeared up the stairs quickly.

"Fast thinking Bel," Ned uttered, leading the way. "Best to keep Clair and Danielle out of this."

Maddie followed slowly behind. The painkillers had relieved most of the pounding headache, but the strange background pulses continued in waves, feeling almost like a kind of Morse code. It was at that moment she knew. Instinctively, she realised exactly where this peculiar feeling in her head was coming from. How it was coming she couldn't work out, and it annoyed her hugely not to be able to reason the logic through scientifically. But the psychic pulses were telling her, deep inside her mind, unmistakably, and she was now convinced. Whatever terrible things she had witnessed that former night, the whole lot was coming back to Orsbrick Hall once more. She had to confide immediately in Abby, the minute she arrived.

An email message pinged into her phone. It was Abby again, but saying she would now be half an hour because she was picking up Judy as well as the children, who she suddenly had to babysit. The school and nursery were on strike and Judy had been requested to lead a special local history event for County Councillors, early evening. Judy would take a direct bus into Ormskirk from outside later.

Maddie took a deep breath. Despite what she had said to Abby about making an effort with Judy and to get to know her better, she remained uneasy … especially after the strange Judy lookalike woman seen on Harrison's Bridge. But on the other hand, a grown-up approach, Maddie decided, would be to make a decent effort, take a lead and be mature. Judy, despite being difficult, was a grown professional woman with a good job and struggling as a single mum with young kids. Judy was also a historian and an archivist. Her skills might actually be useful. So she would stay positive with Judy. She just wished she was feeling better.

Up in the library, the four had begun searching through the myriad volumes of McKenzie family history which sat alongside books of engravings, diaries, local histories of Burscough and memoirs of the Leeds and Liverpool canal. There was certainly plenty of information about boatpeople. In other cabinets, the neatly filed folders and notebooks of various science activities were stacked, including all of Mauveine's original dye discovery papers and those of her own father, James McKenzie. There was a huge amount of written material for the period from around 1830 up to the late 1920s but a large gap existed either before or after that time. Maddie and Bel knew enough of the tragic life of Great-Uncle William and also their grandfather, Jack, his twin brother, to understand why there was nothing written after 1929, except formal legal papers relating to the house. But the period before 1830 seemed to be missing apart from a few tomes concerning the development of the Leeds and Liverpool canal, after it was built in the 1770s. All very interesting, but not relevant to what they were looking for, which was anything a hundred years before. Yet Abby had mentioned there was a record of Orsbrick Hall in the 1660s, when it was first built before the great fire in

1799. Where on earth was that? They needed to wait for Abby.

Ned returned with some bottles of brown ale and cans of lemonade. "Reckon we need some charging up of the old brain cells," he called up, laughing, to Bel and Zac, both precariously perched on wobbly step-ladders and looking at books on the top shelves. "Hey you two watch yourselves up there, time for a break."

"Isn't it a bit early for that, Ned? Not with my head thank you. I'll just have lemonade please," Maddie replied.

A familiar crunching sound of gravel and a slight screech drifted through the freshly opened window. The heat in there was becoming quite considerable because Zac had turned both of the giant iron radiators on.

"It's Abby, with Judy and the kids. I'll just go and let them in." Maddie was anxious to get hold of Abby before she came up the stairs.

"Judy?" Ned replied, screwing his face up. "Fuck, what's that headcase doing here?"

"Listen Ned, Judy is fine, you should show some respect," Bella hollered down. "She's a single mum with two kids, a good job and serious responsibilities. Just because she's shy doesn't make her weird. What do you think they say about you, if you think Judy's strange?"

Maddie and Zac laughed as Ned grunted, chewed the metal top off a beer bottle and started to slurp noisily.

"If only Nancy could hear him," Maddie yelled. "I'll be back in a minute."

Downstairs, Clair had beaten her to it, as the two children, Toby and Caroline, ran in followed briskly by

Abby with Judy who trailed behind, carrying a large bag and looking very serious.

"Hey you two," Clair called out, grabbing the children's hands. "Aunt Abby says you haven't had time to eat yet so how about some brunch including some of my fabulous porridge and a blob of honey."

"Yes please Aunt Clair," they both yelled in unison.

"In that case, follow me to the kitchen."

Maddie, determined to make a good start to her new plan, held out her hand to greet Judy with a generous smile.

"Hi Judy, let me take that bag, it's really nice to see you. Abby tells me you've got to …"

But Judy, oblivious, walked straight past her, muttered, "Hello Madeleine must see to the children," and marched onwards towards the kitchen, struggling with the heavy bag.

As she disappeared, Abby gave Maddie a large hug. "Hi, I came as quick as I could. I can see you're trying. Don't worry, Judy will, in her usual way, be resolving your change of approach to her and will return much more convivial, I hope. She has to work it out in her own good time and slot the change into her head. She still struggles with spontaneous. But well done. Judy will appreciate it, believe me."

Maddie smiled and breathed a sigh of relief. "Thanks, I'll stick with it. What's in Judy's giant bag?"

"Toys!" Abby replied, raising her eyebrows.

"Abby, before anyone comes back, I need to talk to you in confidence. Shall we go into the study?"

"Yes, and before you speak any further, I know exactly what you want to say … and I can feel it too. I knew as much when you phoned. Bad head? Throbbing pulses and waves?"

Maddie stopped. "How on earth did you know?"

"This has happened before, once, and only once, a long time ago, but it's something you never forget. Close the door."

Inside the study, they sat down in the adjacent lush, leather armchairs. Abby continued. "You remember a few weeks back when all of us had that discussion about psychic capabilities, paranormal happenings and different universes being bridged in space and time?"

"Of course. That revelation has brought me, Bel, Zac, and even Ned now, closer together and between the four of us we're beginning to make sense of what's been going on. It's a bit scary Abby. I haven't mentioned this yet to Dad and of course we can't say anything to Mum in isolation."

"No don't, not to either especially now. What I didn't say was what happened when Aunt Eveline and I manipulated the psychic distortions and effectively ended the terrible curse that had affected Mauveine and Isi. Now that Aunt Eveline has passed away, only I know the true picture and can remember everything ... a consequence of being the facilitator to make the change of history happen.

"A curse? What was it?" Maddie asked, her mouth open.

"I had decided never, ever to tell anyone, Maddie. But now I know the time really has arrived, which Mauveine said it would, because you and I will be the ones to face a new threat, or maybe still the old threat, which hasn't been completely resolved as I thought."

"Mauveine speaks? You've talked to her, but she's a ghost?"

"I was amazed too, I have no explanation, but I remember it clearly. It was the day we had our double wedding and I was sitting afterwards in the church alone, just reflecting and happy, and she appeared next to me. Mauveine warned me that one day I would need to tell Victoria what happened. But now I realise, even Mauveine doesn't get it all correct and has limitations. You weren't born then. What she really meant was not Victoria but you, because only you in the family has that powerful capability, the same as Aunt Eveline and me. What I promise, Maddie, is to tell you everything but events presently are moving too quickly. What happened was horrific, in the same way your last sightings were horrific too and I don't want to divert either of our concentrations. But through me we can be better pre-armed and organised, knowing the likely psychic challenges we may face. When I do tell you, it must only ever remain between you and me, and I mean for good. We must first meet this next enactment head on. And you will need to trust me Maddie. You and I may see and experience things which you will simply not believe, and we must ensure that we can assist and support everyone else, because they will have a part to play, I'm sure. All the signs are coming together.

"I trust you totally Abby. Was my Mum directly involved then last time, but she doesn't know?"

"Yes."

"Gosh ... oh my word Abby. This is why I know where these waves pounding in my head are coming from. It's Mum isn't it? She's somehow warning us from her hospital bed. So she is psychic too, but she's never said and is so … well greatly secular and cynical deep down. That is obvious from her semi-dismissive reaction to your discussion the other week and the way she's always been, the hard-nosed and disbelieving scientist."

"Because she doesn't know and likely still doesn't and never will. I suspect Mauveine has returned to help us again, all of us. Vikki is replacing Aunt Eveline, who gave me much more psychic strength and direction last time, which I needed desperately and now you too, Maddie. The three of us are pooling our capabilities."

"But what's next? There are still missing pieces, lots of things don't make sense, and upstairs, we can't find anything recorded before 1770. Do you remember where the book was you found of the 1660s here?"

"Yes, I hid it, because the contents were fundamental to understanding the original curse. Let's go and find it and see what else is written. How are the other three with all of this?"

"Really on board, honestly Abby. Considering our many differences, we're working well as a family team, even Ned, for the first time!"

Abby laughed. "Excellent. One last thing. I've asked Judy, before she catches the bus, to help us. Because … well … she's a historian but … I can't say it any other way … she's one of us and will be useful. Goodness, I sound like one of those sci-fi horror movies. Is that okay with you?"

"I knew today, for the first time. Judy and I don't synchronise like you and me but I sensed her properly. Am I getting better at recognition now Abby?"

"Because you're older, wiser and far more clued up than I ever was, so yes. You've a head start on me when I was your age, I had no idea. So you can manage the rest of your life now properly, which is great. Hey it hasn't done me any harm!"

Maddie smiled, feeling more relaxed and confident again, now Abby was alongside. "So, back to Judy?" she replied.

"She saw something once, a happening, a long time ago here in the grounds outside. I eventually found her in a bad state and ... well ... that's the reason why she doesn't come to Orsbrick. She becomes very uneasy. It was a breakthrough today to be honest to bring her over. Let me explain, because her enactment and yours overlap, so the significance is the period of time. We must concentrate on that time, because whatever this is about, that 1660's period is becoming the key focal point in the same way the 1860's period was with Mauveine. I'm sure that time frame will be the connecting factor, and ... there is a family link to witch burning, depicted inside the missing book which I hid."

"Okay, let's go and join the others," Maddie replied thoughtfully, trying to discern tangible links between herself, Judy, the 1660s visions and the sighting of Judy at Harrison's Bridge. They were leaving the study just as Judy strode out of the kitchen to meet them.

"Maddie, I do apologise for being so rude and running straight past you when I came in. I'm so sorry both of you, I wasn't thinking. Just got a bit tied up in my head with the kids and their toys. I've given Clair a copy of their routines, Abby, and she seems very happy to keep an eye on them."

Judy smiled warmly at Maddie, who blinked, certainly not expecting this reaction. It was like talking to a different woman from the flustered one who first came in.

"Now, I've got an hour before the bus," Judy continued. "I understand you want to learn more about your early family background? What exactly, Maddie, do you want me to help you with? History or archiving?"

Abby observed first Judy and then Maddie, saying nothing but smiled inwardly. Her earlier supposition was right. Judy had also got a sixth sense.

Upstairs in the library, Abby, followed by Ned with the stepladder, went immediately to another bookcase at the far end which had nothing on the shelves except books of a typical 19th century collection, some in a poor condition. They were brown and leather bound including old fiction. Even a couple of valuable Jane Austin first editions sat there, as well as travel, cookery books and politics; a very interesting collection which had been lovingly assembled over many years by their McKenzie ancestors. But near one end, on the top shelf, Abby pulled out three books of 17th century copper plate engravings.

They gathered around as she put them carefully on the book trolley. "These are in excellent condition and the only ones I found last time that went back to the 1600s. Now the middle one has specific references to the very early McKenzie family history. Being an artist, I recognised the engravings, and could then work out the unfortunate and tragic event which happened at the first Orsbrick Hall, so don't be shocked. I'm afraid the explanations are in Latin and my Latin isn't so good and I couldn't follow much. Perhaps, Judy, you could explain more of it?"

Maddie decided to intervene. "I've also done Latin for the last five years. Judy, shall we put those books on the table by the window in the light, and take a closer look together?"

Quickly, both of them earnestly examined the pages, chuntering and translating, neither showing any signs of alarm or despondency about the burning of Lucinda McKenzie and her companion, which is what Abby was risking and banking on. But each had experienced the visions already so were preconditioned. So far so good. Bel, Ned and Zac recommenced another search of that same bookcase, to see if they had missed anything, as the next half an hour passed.

Bel, back up the ladder suddenly looked down. "Ned, what are Jeb and Kai doing?"

Everyone turned to see the two dogs sniffing and whining around a large trunk in the other corner, in fact one of many which Abby and Victoria had long ago searched through and found old clothes and papers in from the 19th century. The clothes had been carefully repacked back in the chests. Abby insisted there was nothing of relevance in any of those trunks.

Ned called to the dogs. "Come on both of you, stop that stupidity. Get over here now." But they were undeterred and continued to whine and scratch at the box base. "Perhaps something has got in there and died, I think I'd better take a look."

He opened the lid carefully, after a hard tug to free it. There were old dresses still inside which he pulled out, consisting of white crinoline, linen and silk, all neatly folded.

Abby straightaway recognised them. "My goodness, Ned, be careful please. Just lay them all carefully on the floor. Those first two are the dresses which Victoria and I wore at our double wedding. They originally belonged to Mauveine and her sister Lydia. We had to have them both altered, they were a lot slimmer and shorter than us! I did wonder where Vikki had put them."

"What, like in those wedding photos Mum showed us?" Bel shrieked, almost sliding down her ladder rungs. "She just said they were one of our past relatives, she never indicated exactly whose."

"No that's true," Maddie added. "Who wore which one?"

"Vikki wore Mauveine's original wedding dress and I wore Lydia's. It seemed appropriate. Lydia was an artist and Mauveine a scientist. Lydia was Great Aunt Eveline's grandmother. I'll leave you to work out how they relate to you."

Maddie and Bel, very taken with the arrangement, lovingly caressed the fabrics.

Zac, his iGlasses primed, already had been spitting out the result on his small portable printer. "Wow that is a cool family tree. I'm pretty good at art too, okay, I admit, only computer art."

They all chortled, except Ned who was staring again at the outside of the chest. He looked inside once more. "This trunk isn't totally what it seems, I reckon there's a false bottom. Zac, can you fetch a screwdriver from Dad's workshop? One of his wooden handled old fashioned ones with a straight blade."

Zac returned and Ned, huffing and panting, undertook a process of careful leverage of a thin wooden cover out, which revealed a second and thicker cover underneath. But it was held down with a series of hefty screws. Some of the heads sheared straight off but most came out, needing a lot of strength. He was glad he went regularly to the gym, and hoped that Nancy might like his growing six-pack too. With a final tug he pulled the board up, as everyone crowded around to stare inside, their eyes popping out of their sockets. That false base had been made a very long time back. At the bottom were more books, and letters, all very old, handwritten on parchment, and the books were covered in identical, lettered, dark red leather.

"Let me take them out," Judy said. "I'm used to handling very old paper artefacts, but I can tell you now, just from the appearance, these go back much further than all the other 19th century collections. I would estimate at least a hundred years or more."

Slowly and carefully, Judy took the five books out in order, one by one in silence and laid them meticulously on the large table, followed by the letters, all spaced out so they could be read without touching. They were in amazing condition, almost looking freshly written. The paper was still supple and incredibly well preserved for such a huge length of time. She turned her head to read the bright gold lettering on the spines.

"They are diaries of a Robert McKenzie, dated from 1665 to 1669. Each volume is a different year, a little like the famous diaries of Mr Samuel Pepys, who lived around the same time. I assume Robert McKenzie is an ancestor, Maddie? Perhaps he was the father of Lucinda who was burned as a witch?"

Bel looked up. "Burned as a witch? You mean one of our ancestors? Gosh."

Abby watched Judy, who was her usual impassive and unemotional self, as she explained the details of the heretical denunciation, which she and Maddie had just read and translated together. The denouncement had been initiated and made by priests at the time, because Lucinda was an astronomer who believed in the teachings of Galileo and the sun being the centre of the solar system, which was then deemed as heresy, in opposition to the teachings of the Catholic Church.

Abby listened intrigued. She hadn't really understood all that part, and her history of science in the period was a little vague. This was good, she thought, but Judy's calm manner didn't square in the slightest with the dramatic state Judy was in fifteen years ago when she last had visions of burning witches in the Orsbrick grounds. Perhaps Judy's mind, maturity and consciousness accepted that she had psychically seen something not unusual in that period, and now being with Maddie, some kind of calming down inside her head was occurring. Whatever it was, the change was a welcome relief. Hysteria from Judy right then would have been a very difficult distraction.

"Wow, this revelation is definitely bringing history to life, Judy." Ned chipped in. "Makes you feel sort of important knowing all that has happened in your own family."

"This house stands on or near the site Lucinda was burned on. It talks about an underground room, like a cellar, where wine was made and stored, which would probably have been part of the original house."

"Gosh," Bel added, with a slight shiver. "Sort of spooky isn't it."

"You should know sis, you see 'em," Ned replied light-heartedly, before seeing a sea of disapproving stares. "Sorry, lighten up everyone. We just have an interesting family history of ghosts, cool really."

Abby noticed Judy jump slightly. Obviously she had no idea … and thought.

Judy continued. "I must leave in a minute. Let me show you how to open and read these books, but take great care not to damage the binding, all the glue will be brittle." She opened the first one. "Everything is in the quaint English of that period, and is printed, not in Latin, so it should make sense. But let me warn you about the writing style which you'll find odd. Nouns are all capitalised and spellings can be quite different, although phonetically, if you say the word, the meaning will come clear if unsure. Read slowly and think latterly and you should understand and find lots of things out. The letters are handwritten in English, looks like some are to this person, Robert McKenzie, and are dated later. Suggest you read them on the table without excessive touching, and transcribe them onto one of Zac's tablets over there."

"Thanks Judy, that's great, we really appreciate it." Maddie replied, noticing Jeb and Kai had started once more. This time they stood stiffly to their near four feet in height around the pile of dresses, their hackles raised, and deep growls emitting from their throats.

"Shit, I bet now they have smelt a dead rat."

"Oh God, Ned, not inside the dresses surely not?" Maddie whispered, horrified at the thought.

Ned went over and carefully removed the top two wedding dresses. Sat on top of the rest of the pile was the large purpurine glass prism, shimmering like a crimson diamond in the sharp reflected light through the windows. It was the very same object they had assembled two weeks before. Everybody stared, mesmerised.

"Bloody hell, how did that piece of glass get here?" Maddie cried in disbelief. "I thought Mum had put that thing back in the observatory?"

"So did I," Bel replied. "Maybe Clair just found it first in Dad's workshop and tidied it away up here. You know how she is, hates things out of place. Judy, are you alright? Judy?"

They turned to see Judy, stood some way back and turning a distinctly white colour, clutching her stomach. "Oh God, I feel so sick," she spluttered, looking around for somewhere to throw up.

Bel, as ever lightning fast, grabbed the plaster bucket her father had left and ran to Judy, bending her over and her head into it. "Be sick in there Judy, don't worry I've got you, come on get rid of it," at which point Judy vomited her breakfast up violently inside. By then Abby was at their side and they helped Judy to sit down on a chair. Zac brought her a bottle of water and gave her a tissue to wipe her mouth.

He stared in the bucket, shooing away the dogs as Ned grabbed each one by the collar. "Gosh, Judy, what did you eat for breakfast?" screwing up his face and looking inside at the contents, bright purple.

"I'm so sorry all of you, I don't know what came over me. It must have been the blueberry pie I ate in a hurry. Leftovers, been in the fridge too long and didn't taste too good, I should have thrown it in the bin. Usually I throw everything out religiously after one day. Thanks Zac." She drank a little water and put the bottle in her bag. "I really must go, I feel better now. Thank you too Bel, you react like a real medic. I'm really, really sorry, that was so embarrassing. Abby, I'll see you and the kids later this evening back home."

"They'll be in bed by then. Don't worry have a good day and hope you feel better soon," Abby replied.

Judy glanced nervously at the purpurine prism as Ned offered to walk her out. "I'll just see you to the bus stop, Judy. They've put a seat there now so you can rest until the bus arrives, no problem. At least you didn't throw up over the books."

Bel and Abby glared at him.

"Sorry Judy, just a joke, let's go. Put your arm into mine."

Maddie picked up the prism and placed it on the table with the books and letters. "I'm going to put this thing downstairs later, so we know exactly where it is." She glanced at Abby who nodded. They were both beginning to think very hard again.

Bel picked up the bucket. "I'll just get rid of this. Gosh Zac's right though, never mind the colour, there's a funny smell in here, like paraffin gone off. What does she put in her home-made pies? Zac can you grab those dogs again, God knows why they're interested in a pile of sick."

Maddie shook her head, but Abby's brain was flashing back in time, inside her own mind only, to memories for so long buried deeply. She remembered those first instances when Victoria and her first saw Mauveine, always accompanied by what Victoria had described as a stench of aniline. What did this mean, if anything? Whatever, she was uneasy once more about her step-daughter. Time for a break and then a mass read of these new books and letters. Perhaps something important would be revealed. She looked at Maddie again who nodded and smiled. They were tuned into each other's thoughts perfectly.

Chapter Fifteen

April 1st 1672: Salem, Massachusetts, US

*L*etter: *To The Right Honourable Lord McKenzie,
Earl of Burscough, Lancashire, England
My Dear Robert*

I am writing to you to give my sincerest condolences for the death of your dearest wife and my cherished sister Bella. I received news yesterday from our mutual friend Mr Pepys with whom I have kept in correspondence. It saddened me greatly to hear that she gave birth successfully to the first five of your children but that the sixth and Bella did not survive past his first hour in this world. I was also saddened to then hear that due to the spread of the pox, only you and your daughter, Eliza, now remain at Orsbrick Hall. It is a terrible burden to lose so many, in such a short time. My heart goes out to you.

It has been many years since we last kept company, that lovely night before the dreadful fire in London. A night of wonderful discourse and beautiful memories I have never forgotten. I understand that the London City is being reborn, and that a new vitality is already in place especially now the plague is finished. It took a long time for me to forgive my sister for what she did, and I suspect why she did it. Yet the long and dangerous voyage to the Americas and the close company of the healing Puritan clan helped me reassess my bile and displeasure and dispel the torment and anger of the heart. Although I eventually wrote to Bella, numerous times, I never received a reply but I will remain forever saddened by her untimely death. She had much to live for and to give and I am sure you were both very happy.

My life too has had its troubles. You may have heard, my husband the night we met, died in the London flames, they say he threw himself in. I indeed set sail in the Half Moon a widow, and a week later was married to the Reverend Hawbank from Lincoln, intent on setting up a new parish in the colonies to convert the natives. But sadly, at the end of the next six weeks, conditions became so bad on board and like many the scurvy took him, despite my constant administering to his needs. I therefore landed again a widow, but with my means and his means to my name was able to quickly build a place in the town of Salem. I have founded a new school which fosters the ethic here of hard work and serving God but engenders too, a sense of culture, art and the sciences. And we run plays, of course with religious themes, but children are learning to act and have fun. There are many good things here Robert. People live better and longer including children and the populace have much hope for the future, but we still fare badly with the native Indians, with whom we seem unable to find peace. I also began to paint again, so much vast space and rich scenery to be inspired by. These canvasses have been my best work ever. My daughter Patience, now six, helps me. She is very naturally gifted with a brush. I am sorry I forgot to mention earlier, I came off the ship with childe as well as widowed.

Because of my work and my commitment to serve the Lord, there has been no further intolerance and pressure to marry again and I remain a widow and wish no other state. Except I want to tell you that in the coming month I plan to take the next voyage back to Liverpool and leave this place. I am becoming nervous in Salem. There is far too much talk of witchcraft about and the easy blame of women for ills which are of no cause bar nature and accident. Also, I fear the restlessness of the natives may lead to a rebellion. Some of the native children, who I have converted and now teach have told me many tribes are coming together again from great distances. They want their land back and resent the foreign intruders. Many natives locally have been wiped out by pestilence, brought from the ships, those people having no resistance.

Therefore I intend to amass my belongings, particularly my paintings, and with Patience will return. The booking is made on the Mayflower, (there are so many ships of this name) and my cases half packed. My father will however not be aware of this. We have not communicated since I left. I beg you not to recourse to tell him or Mr Pepys, who I am sure, is still the greatest gossip in London. I am certain the King thinks me dead. But dear Robert, I will say that since being here I have thought daily of you. It has greatly helped my spirit when I am down and perhaps you may wish to visit when I settle. I intend to house somewhere in Liverpool when I arrive mid August, a lively city with growing numbers of theatres so I am told. And I will finish by saying if you do visit and then meet my daughter, Patience, you will verily feel much surprise and pleasure.

With sincerity
Lady Katherine Warren

Maddie had carefully taken this long letter, still in its original envelope with the seal opened, and sat at the far desk quietly to read it. Abby had already identified, from some childhood writing and correspondence which lay on the top of the pile, that Lucinda and Robert McKenzie were not father and daughter but twin brother and sister and were obsessively devoted to one another.

Bel and Zac had gathered a variety of correspondence which they quickly realised were references to Robert's early science interests, but it was the few letters which were signed at the bottom by none other than Isaac Newton, which took Bel's immediate attention. She read the initial paragraphs, her eyes popping with astonishment as history and the first dawn of serious science during the period of the enlightenment unfolded, with names such as Robert Hooke, Robert Boyle, and others including the astronomers, Kepler and Galileo. She was familiar with their names from her physics classes, in which she was doing well and enjoying, but to read and feel a direct connection between some of those great names and her own ancestors gave her a feeling of unimaginable awe. The history behind science had never been discussed in school. Perhaps, she pondered, this could be a great topic for her exam project. The style of language though, as Judy had warned, she found hard going, needing much concentration. Bel was especially intrigued by the clear, black-inked lines and strokes and overall florid style of handwriting, so much more beautiful than anything she or Maddie could do. In fact she couldn't even remember the last time she had ever handwritten anything, and sighed deeply with the passing of a bygone era.

Meanwhile, Ned was leafing through the volumes of diaries of Robert McKenzie and found hunting manuals originally written in 1660, but included as end sections in his first diary. According to the content, these were Robert McKenzie's first serious attempts at writing. Spellbound, he slowly read and enjoyed how Robert and his father, Cameron McKenzie, deferentially referred to as the Master, by his eighteen year old son, with their vast entourage of servants, gamekeepers, dogs and helpers would organise hunts throughout the year, shooting game, deer, wild boar and rabbits. But a final and unexpected chapter caught his attention. He slowly read it and his heart pounded heavily. Ned realised immediately that this information would be hugely significant for everyone.

Bel carefully picked up another letter from Isaac Newton, when she saw the title and stopped in disbelief. It was formally addressed to Lord Robert McKenzie of Orsbrick Hall, Earl of Burscough. Her family ancestors had once been true aristocrats, the very top of the chain of wealthy ruling elites of the land, directly associating with kings and queens. But what had happened? Somewhere along the hereditary pathway, how had the title been lost? She called out to everyone to stop so she could read out this amazing find.

"It won't take long, but what is included I think we all need to think about," Bel said, her voice confident and her mind obviously sizzling with curiosity and excitement.

"Hey sis, these old writings really turn you on don't they, now I know why you've been Judy's best friend," Ned interrupted.

Even Zac glared and shook his head, as Ned held up his hands. "Whoa, sorry everyone — contrition rules, must improve the humour. Anyway, I'm next because this hunting manual will blow your brains out. I want to learn to shoot. Do you think Lynton will teach me Abby?"

"Yes, I'm sure he will Ned, but for the moment …" Abby replied, grinning.

"Just shut it for once please Ned," Maddie interjected, finishing Abby's sentence. Vigorous nodding confirmed the sentiment had a majority vote.

Bel began. "The letter is addressed from Isaac Newton to, wait for it, Lord Robert McKenzie, Earl of Burscough." Everyone looked at each other in astonishment. Ned mouthed a giant 'what?' but Abby thought hard. She had no idea and neither did Vikki or Julian that was for sure. This revelation of a former high family title and what happened to it may be illuminated further in those diaries.

"*My dearest friend Robert. I am now settling in well again at the reopened Trinity College and they have offered me a Fellowship in recognition of my advancements. I would like to take this occasion to thank you warmly for all your past financial support, but request that you finish your kind generosity as I will now become self-sufficient for my needs and studies. I am very mindful that you have five extra young mouths to feed, and hope that your adorable wife, Lady Bella, is getting over her recent bout of illnesses. I understand the latest twins were a difficult birth. However Lady Bella and I are continuing to share thoughts and correspondence about my work on fluxions. We are in* argumentative, but of course as ever, friendly debate about my methods of nomenclature, being as I am drawn by geometric exposition which she says is a stupid and nonsensical barrier to progress the mathematics of the calculus further. She has shown me a different way using dots, inspired by a correspondence she pursues with a prolific German philosopher called Leibnitz. I will of course stick with my pictures which are best for this exposition. The German is a buffoon and like Hooke I will get my way. Bella mentioned an extensive set of papers she found which Lucinda had produced also on the topic of fluxions and extension of my binomial theorem and you were keen of my opinion, when she sent them on. I have to say they are first class and have assisted my endeavours greatly. Lucinda's untimely death, by the flames, at the hands of those murderous cleric butchers has hindered the progress of mathematics one hundred years. I am in comparison merely a nonentity standing on the shoulders of giants, such as your former dear sister.

Alas, I must say Trinity now would not suit you. They want all Fellows to become priests, such an abomination I would never have believed, adding no sense whatsoever to the truths of objective academic and scientific pursuit. I have confirmed allegiance to the Church of England and that has warded off the worst of the zealots but I fear I may not hold out with that forever. Perhaps, in your lead role for the Board of Trade you may be able to speak directly to King Charles on this matter. My mathematics of calculus will improve methods of accurate navigation and mapping hugely, if I am left to it. I am sure the King would sympathise with the academics and rectify such religious profanities. I hear the Dutch are restless again over trade rights in the Indies, *and war may be imminent. I pray you can avert such travesties.*

Your servant and friend, Isaac Newton."

Bel breathed a deep sigh, her face flushed red with the excitement of what she had read. Even Ned looked moved. He had just been doing Newton's laws of motion in technology classes.

"These letters are priceless," Maddie commented immediately. "We must ensure Mum and Dad have them properly preserved, I'm sure Judy will be able to help on that. It's clear to me that Robert McKenzie and his sister were close and that he and his other friends were all quite anti-puritan and anti-religious at the time, as well as being hugely interested in and capable of science at the highest levels. That created the local religious tension, initiating the death of Lucinda, his gifted sister, at the hands of priests. She sounds like a bit of a genius. That coincides with the things I've seen. I think we know the trigger now to the terrible suffering. But where does the bubonic plague come in?"

Zac raised his hand. "I think I've got that one. Judy mentioned Samuel Pepys. He was the famous literary guy in that period who also wrote diaries. In these diaries of Robert McKenzie, between 1666 and 1668, there are lots of references to Samuel Pepys and numbers of journeys and visits made to London in 1665 and 1666, with a huge amount written of what they saw together of the Great Plague. I've cross-checked on my tablet. In fact I've even downloaded Pepys's original diaries as eBooks and correlated the events and happenings with Robert McKenzie's own entries. They were obviously close friends, Pepys was high up in shipping then and close to the King, Charles the second. Robert met Bella through Pepys and it looks like, you will never believe, that Bella could have been one of the King's offspring. He had many apparently ... err ... what's the word?"

"Bastards I think you mean," Ned chimed in with a laugh. "This family certainly has some blue blood, although by the sound of it not exactly legitimate. But hey who cares?"

"And," Bel added, "That period was one of huge change and conflicts especially between Royalty, Parliament and the Church ... that was the spark which lit the flame. What do you think Abby?"

"That's amazing, well done all of you. Yes, I agree." Abby said.

"We're not done yet," Ned interrupted, waving his book of hunting. "Just listen to this ... phew ... I'm glad it's printed." He went straight to the unexpected section and slowly thumbed through various pages.

They sat down at the table and waited patiently.

"Hard to believe but it looks like the occasional hunting of packs of wolves was still being done in the Bowland Forest in the 1650s, possibly the only place left in England. Not only did they use wolfhounds, like Jeb and Kai, but here at Orsbrick Hall, the McKenzie family, principally the father of Robert McKenzie, going by the name of Cameron and known as 'the boss' had a tradition of tying a sort of good luck talisman onto the pack-leader, apparently to ward off evil spirits. There are some amazing engraving prints here, which Lynton often talks about. Wolves of course were associated with the devil. So the wolf element in our psychic mystery can also be explained."

"One thing missing though?" Bel replied screwing up her eyes in thought. "Oh, shit, could it be the talisman?"

"What, the crimson prism of glass?" Maddie said, thinking out loud. "I would have thought that belonged to Isaac Newton, given all his optics experiments with prisms?"

"Actually, hang on all of you. Let me think … I almost forgot." Abby interjected, as everyone went quiet. "When that first piece was found by me and Vikki, we asked Judy, given at the time she was in her first year of studying ancient classics at Oxford. Not only did she say that the glass, called incidentally purpurine, had likely origins from the Roman period but that it also was thought to have magical properties and bring good luck."

"I think you guys have a storyboard, but for what?"

They all turned, startled, to see Lynton grinning at the doorway, obviously listening for the last few minutes to the interplay of discussion.

"How long have you been there? Or more to the point, why are you there? I thought you were staying late for work," Abby cried, smiling, pleased as always to see him.

Lynton bent down and picked up a tray of drinks and large chunks of homemade carrot cake, at which point the dogs perked up from their slumber and also trotted over, waiting patiently.

"Clair reckoned you all needed some refreshments. Julian called me to bring him some fresh clothes and take back his dirty washing, which I've just done …

don't smirk Abby, I do know what a washing basket is … and that's why I left early. He's been a bit concerned about Vikki, now receiving a full drip of this vaccine stuff, but she's gone into a sort of deep sleep. But the specialists have said that's the expected reaction, and all the monitoring indicates not only is she fine but stabilising so it can only get better. They've said we can all visit tomorrow, if Vikki's out of her trance. Shit Abby, I forgot his jeans and pyjamas. They're probably still on the chair where Clair left them."

Maddie shot a glance over to Abby, who made a slight nod in return. They could immediately both feel it, the waves and pulses were back and increasing. Victoria was firing up again in her slumber. The time was coming, exactly like before, only this time Abby would be prepared. She needed to assemble all her Gregorian chants, tarot incantations, spells and repudiations again, but with Maddie only. She had to get rid of everyone for half an hour. At least she remembered where she had hidden them, and stared at the thin black notebooks in the other bookcase, carefully placed at the end of the travel books, hopefully still intact and legible after fifteen years. She wondered, concentrated hard for a moment and looked over at Maddie.

"Actually, Abby, there's something I think you should read over here, after we've had this cake."

It worked. Excellent, Maddie understood. Abby's mind quickly assembled what needed to be put in place, but first, how to get rid of the others? A brainwave came to her.

"Lynton, Can you do me a favour? On your way back to the hospital, can you drop the kids downstairs off at the pub please? Judy is going there to pick them up later. They'll be fine with Adele and Henry, our front of house. Hey, while Maddie and I finish these letters, why don't you lot go with him, make sure he doesn't lose the pyjamas but I'm sure your dad will love to see you. He's done a marathon stint now on his own, and you can at least wave to your mum. I'll ask Clair to do us her steak and kidney pie speciality and then when you come back we can all have a relaxing and well deserved dinner."

"No problem, darling," Lynton agreed, smiling. "Great idea, plenty of room in the pickup."

"That sounds cool, Abby," Ned replied happily. He'd done enough thinking for one day and needed to get out. Maybe he could sneak a beer in at the Red Lion too; Henry and he were becoming mates. "Bel, Zac, let's go. You two can stay here"

Jeb and Kai looked forlorn, until Lynton waved them along as well ... as they loped off happily.

"Peace and quiet at last, I think I'm going to take some headache pills again," Maddie whispered, laying out half a dozen letters which had been separated from the others and wrapped originally inside a pink ribbon.

"No, Maddie, don't. Not this time. I think we need to keep our full psychic strength; in fact I'm sure of it. Do you feel the waves have changed frequency?"

"Yes. Is it ... I don't know how to say it ... time? I'm petrified Abby. Why does this have to be you and me?"

Abby held her hand. "Don't worry, there's three of us now, including Vikki plus Mauveine as well somewhere … but don't ask me where. Now, can you read through those black notebooks carefully, line by line? Try and memorise the paragraphs, especially the ones I've underlined. Last time I did an enormous amount of research to find everything. It worked then and will work again if necessary."

"The language used in these chants and refutations is very old Latin; I remember doing the notation and syntax in lessons. This way of writing and speaking was popular in the fourth and fifth centuries, after the fall of the Roman Empire. One good thing I've inherited from Mum is her photographic memory, all is going in Abby. Gosh, do you sing these, with the music alongside? I definitely can't do that!"

Abby laughed. "And attitude too, you've both got attitude and are very strong-willed. Yes, any singing of Gregorian chants just leave to me. I was a top chorister at school. In another life I should have been a pop star!"

"Okay, that's a deal. I know I'm very like Mum although she never talks much about what she did when she was my age, like she prefers to bury away that time. I get the impression her teenage years were very hard. I still don't even know how she actually got to Rotterdam or why she did her degrees in Holland. In fact … this isn't the time, I know, but I need your advice on something else really important, like a key decision I've made. When we've got through this ordeal Abby, if we get through it … is that okay?"

"I have a feeling I know what that may be, I'm a bit of a mind reader right now remember, especially as you and me are high, and I'm not surprised. Yes, we'll get through it."

Inside however Abby was anything but sure and felt petrified, but she couldn't show it and had to keep very calm and focussed, something at least she knew she could do well in times of stress. But there were so many complications to try and patch together this time. This situation was quite different from Mauveine. Deeper, terrifying unknowns were arising from a far more distant time, and even stranger and more dangerous scenarios to consider, the bubonic plague of Victoria being only one.

Maddie smiled and kissed her cheek. "Thanks Aunt Abigail, I appreciate your advice, as you've been there, done it and got the tee-shirt. Now before they get back, just read these letters quickly."

"Who are they from?"

"They're obviously ... well ... love letters ... between Robert McKenzie and another woman, called Katherine, a Lady Katherine, who seems to have been Lady Bella's sister."

Abby took the first one and read the small, neat handwriting, slowly and carefully. She could instantly feel the distraught emotions and the pain, of separation, a secret love once shared and then dismembered by time, circumstance and distance. The amazing journey across to America, which in that time, for a woman especially, must have been horrific. She could almost hear the waves crashing over the decks, the swell of the ships and the cries of death as one after the other succumbed to terrible illnesses, cold or accident. It was a sad story, especially the early death of Bella, Robert's wife, all too common then in childbirth, and most of his children dying too from smallpox. But the letter was full of hope. What actually happened? Did Lady Katherine land safely in Liverpool? It was pretty obvious that her daughter, the arty Patience, was Robert McKenzie's child.

Enthralled, she picked up the second and third letters which went on to describe Katherine's departure and the careful preparations she was making for another arduous journey. The return trip had been delayed a further month as the Mayflower needed urgent repairs. Katherine was a woman like her, artistic, capable and organised and knew what she wanted and was determined to get it. What was especially fascinating was the way she had lived in that period in an early American colony. Katherine had been marking time, pretending to be a Puritan, but making the most of her situation, learning, developing and still enjoying life as best as she could, given the constraints. Abby reflected on her earlier time with Victoria, in Holland, working at the kebab shop, knowing deep down she wanted to return to her art and fashion work but also treading water until the circumstances came right ... It may have been totally different periods of time but she and Katherine had followed similar paths. The last letter was especially interesting, the only reply to Katherine from Robert, at least in that pile. Part of the letter had been torn, the top and the start were missing sadly, but the gist became clear.

... And I just wish to confirm the joy I felt when I first saw you and your daughter Patience at the Ship Inn, your new residence. It filled me with so much pleasure to see my daughter Emily, only one year younger, playing happily with Patience like they were sisters. I have been lonely and bereft of normal family life for too long. I thought I would die of grief but that dark gloom has been lifted for the first time especially when I saw your paintings. The picture of your school in Salem is now hanging over the fireplace of my favourite study at Orsbrick, so I can happily stare at it every evening over a smoke of cigar.

It has been some years since I was last down Dale Street. So much has changed there with all the splendid young buildings, but I took it upon myself to also first make my journey official and inspect the lay of the ships, docks and cargo. The busy and growing activity in the port of Liverpool, especially as we will fight the Dutch again, is very impressive and well organised. I am now sure of war, as are the French too, but we are prepared to win. It is truly encouraging down there at the port. England will be the greatest trading nation in the world, mark my words. The enthusiasm of the King, to whom I reported my observations for expanding trade, commerce and economic being, is exemplary; the coffers of the Treasury are filling well with gold. But my dearest Katherine, as promised, I have said nothing of your existence or arrival, it will remain our secret.

I am impressed that so quickly you have managed to exhibit in the newly restored gallery at the Gibson Library and Museum. Gibson is an old friend of the McKenzie family and I have already offered him a donation to expand the wing at the rear for commissioned paintings of the new tall trading ships being built in Liverpool. In addition, I was pleased to see you have found time once again to take up your acting career, and already I see the Brown Street Theatre has been reopened, with your efforts. I just wanted you to know that I have booked a Royal box for the opening night of your first Shakespeare play, Midsummer Night's Dream in two weeks and look forward greatly to your personal performance of Titania.

Finally my dearest Lady Katherine, I have given much thought to meeting you again and feel further the uplift you have given me to my depression and distress, and formally I wish to offer you my hand in marriage, if you will accept me. I know this is risky but my life has never been predictable and I truly believe we should take the opportunity of the moment, and of course it will not be the first time that you and I have enjoyed the pleasures of the clandestine. I now have the ear and I believe the good trust of the King, your father, who has become wise and accepting of the changing world and more tolerant with age. And I believe we can take advice and mediation of that old rogue, Mr Pepys, who remains my great friend and confidant, but all will be undertaken solely to your wishes my dearest love. I look forward with trepidation to your reply.

With love Robert McKenzie, Earl of Burscough

Abby sat back, her face flushed with pleasure and wonder, and took a few deep breaths. What a beautiful story. Did Katherine and Robert marry in the end? Did she accept his hand? Hopefully so.

"My goodness, that correspondence is filled with so much emotion, a love story at long last amongst all the tragic readings today. Katherine was a woman after my own heart, Maddie, so enthusiastic and committed to the arts and culture. She must have had a major influence on Liverpool culture at the time, a period I know very little about, I must admit. And of course the library and museum, albeit rebuilt in the 1850s is still standing, just as majestic with those great original Corinthian pillars."

"You've missed it haven't you, rushing through? The true significance of these letters, look again … at the end."

Abby scanned her eyes over the letter down to the bottom, when she saw it. How could she miss such a thing? She stopped dead; in fact she almost stopped breathing forever. That simply could not be … she had to think quickly about her own past, like Julian's, all hazy and winding and fast faded back into obscurity … "Fuck, Maddie. Sorry, but are you thinking what I'm thinking? I simply can't believe it."

"Yes, I am most definitely, because the set of coincidences and comparisons are just too … well … compelling. You and Katherine are similar because you are an actual descendent, another Warren who has equally hit the local world of art and culture with the same impact. Don't you see Abby, this explains something far more fundamental, which has been eating away at my brain since we spoke about our abilities, to psychically see and understand these things beyond most other people. Why you … with me? Not just now but also then, with Mauveine. Because we are all actually part of the same family! The answer to what happened to Katherine is obvious, she did marry Robert and they had more children together and some survived and others carried on. This is the answer to the other mystery in the family that Mum used to talk about. The line of artists as well as scientists … they were all Warrens."

"Oh my goodness," Abby whispered, her head pounding again. "Aunt Eveline must have known too, which is why she and I got on so well. Instinctively I even chose Lydia's dress to marry in. You have remarkable perception Maddie."

"I'm just carrying on the science tradition, same as Mum and before her including Mauveine … right back …"

"Oh my God … back to Bella! This is the key isn't it? The focus of all those hundreds of years of the McKenzie curse, the constant torment and restless spirits. Vikki and Mauveine, together somehow have led us to a conclusion we needed to know. But I don't know how it will transpire … shit!"

"Abby, I'm only sixteen but today I feel so much older. I think we need to keep these facts about your heritage between you and me. I can't fathom how Mum would take it if she knew."

"I agree, for now anyway, then you and I will decide what to do … Hey, I can hear the front door and that smell of steak and kidney pie is tantalisingly wafting through the whole house. Let's get dinner and relax … and then wait."

"Temperature is changing, darling, must be that warm weather front meeting a cold evening … it's become really misty outside. Just look at the shape of the moon, you can barely see it. Brrr."

Lynton rubbed his hands together vigorously, gave her a peck on the cheek and started taking off his coat, whilst the dogs and teenagers ran frantically past to be first in front of the roaring log fire which Clair had stoked up.

"Dinner is on the table, hurry up before it gets cold," Danielle shouted, dishing up, whilst Clair laid out the plates. Ned quickly put food out for Jeb and Kai and soon everyone was enjoying a splendid meal, to be finished off with strawberry cheesecake. Abby even approved one small glass of red Pinot each to celebrate but only eleven percent, which Lynton found, after a rigorous search in Julian's wine cellar, a place he knew intimately over the many years they both had happily spent down there.

Relaxing again in the deep plush-pile armchairs and sofas in the sitting room, Lynton shoved some fresh logs into the dwindling fire, which crackled and spat vigorously to life. Zac pointed to the odd shape of the full moon, now visible through the patio windows and shimmering eerily. A luminescent glow clung around the edge in the mist swirling about outside. He lamented severe disappointment that the visibility had become too poor to use the telescope.

"What's the date today?" Bel remarked, perusing Julian's online plastic newspaper. "The date's gone totally weird on this thing, it says December 666. I really must buy my Christmas presents."

"The 20th," Ned replied. "Five days to go. What are you getting me sis?"

"If you go and answer that door, I'll think about telling you."

They all looked up from playing games on their tablets as Lynton lowered the television sound. A rhythmic knocking sounded at the scullery outside door where they let the dogs out, and continued steadily, with a quiet tap-tapping. Maddie glanced up at Abby, both feeling uneasy.

"Bloody hell, okay I'm coming. Who on earth is knocking anyway at this time of night?" Ned mumbled and raised himself reluctantly off his chair to head out into the scullery. "Funny, I can't hear Jeb and Kai, where on earth are they? I'm going to find them at the same time."

"Do you want this poker Ned?" Lynton said with a grin, waving it in the air.

"You must be joking, I've had boxing lessons last six months. I'll knock seven bells of shit out of them if they look like trouble, sorry Abby, I mean hell's bells ..."

They all laughed, breaking the sudden tension. "Will you get that damn door open then, that incessant knocking is driving me mad?" Maddie shouted.

They heard the bolts slide open and the usual creak of the heavy oak door, followed by a muted "holy fuck," then silence. The door clicked shut again, half a minute went by and nothing. The knocking suddenly restarted but in a different rhythm, tap-tapity-tap ...

Abby put down her newspaper. "What's happened to Ned? Lynton, can you go and take a look? He must have locked himself out. Go on then, if you must, take the poker!"

Once more they heard the door open.

Footsteps returned as a white-faced and silent Lynton walked back in.

"What's up Lynton, you look like you've seen a ghost?" Zac called out, with a laugh. "Where's Ned? Is he with the dogs?"

"I have ..." he stuttered slowly, shaking. "She says she wants to see you Abby."

They turned to look towards the sitting room doorway as Abby got out of her seat. Two people, a man and a woman, hand in hand, stood there quietly smiling, their Sunday attire somewhat more fitting for a hundred years previous. She wore a neat, ankle-length, linen brown dress with clumpy shoes, her mousy hair long over her shoulders, whilst he sported a natty, black suit and waistcoat with a starched, white collar and matching, black boots. Both had on open heavy woollen coats.

"Jesus, Abby, who the hell are they?" Lynton gasped, but having some inner sense he had seen them before, then he realised. Each was the spitting image of Victoria and Julian. She was the woman in the laboratory picture, hanging in the hall.

"Mauveine and Isi," Abby gasped.

Maddie stared at their faces, fascinated with their historic fashion wear, but felt no unease or apprehension, in fact quite the opposite. How similar to Mum and Dad they were but much younger. The likeness was amazing.

Bel mouthed 'Hi' and waved followed by Zac, who had put on his iGlasses, then realised he didn't need them.

Lynton was standing immobile, transfixed, like his feet had become glued to the floor. Abby took his hand and looked into his eyes gently. "You know the day you asked me to marry you outside this house? Remember what I asked you to promise before I said yes?"

"Love me and love my psychic."

Everyone giggled, including Mauveine, and a small …ahh … came from the end of the room, Bel again.

"Good. So now is the time, darling, to honour your promise. Coats on everyone. This is it."

"Err … what exactly is 'it'?" Lynton replied nervously. "Can 'it' for me just be continuing putting logs on the fire? Carry on the good work all you chaps."

"Coat, Lynton."

Outside, both dogs were barking madly and bounded through the scullery towards the sitting room, then stopped, sat on their haunches and whined gently, a doleful and relaxed expression on their faces. They slowly walked around Mauveine and Isi to sit patiently next to Zac.

"Hey you two, you don't have to walk around. You can walk straight through them," he said, stroking their necks.

"Zac, are you so dumb? Dogs see ghosts better than us. It's not respectful to say that," Bel remonstrated, bringing in their shoes from the rack in the grand hall. "More importantly," she continued, turning to the wolfhounds. "Jeb and Kai, where is Ned? Is he still outside? Can someone grab his coat for him?"

But they whined and growled softly, pacing the room, distressed.

"Someone's taken him," Abby cried, visibly alarmed as Maddie winced, her head pounding even harder. "Mauveine, has Ned been kidnapped?"

Mauveine and Isi's expressions turned serious. She put her hand to her mouth and spoke softly, with a distinct echo in her clipped, Lancashire accent, struggling with the effort to communicate across the space and time barriers designed to prevent her.

"Yes, Isi and I were too late, we could not prevent it. But we know where he is. Please, follow me."

Her voice crackled and died on the last word. She waved and the dogs excitedly ran back out of the door, over towards the big barn as they followed, shoving their coats and gloves on hurriedly as best as they could, with Lynton at the rear but already out of breath.

"Just go on, I'll join you in a second. I've forgotten something," Bel shouted and suddenly dived back in, returning shortly with her shoulder bag. Maddie threw open the barn door expecting to find Ned, but instead they gaped up in complete disbelief. Standing patiently, fully saddled up and with belches of steam pouring from their mouths, stood five huge shire horses, four mottled white and one dark brown. Jeb and Kai sidled up quietly and the animals started to sniff each other contentedly. Mauveine motioned for them to get onto the horses. Isi walked to the brown one, patently the lead horse, and led him over, holding his head steady for Lynton to mount up.

"Abby ... are these animals for real? Like I won't fall through if I get on the saddle? This feels so strange." Lynton asked, distinctly uneasy at the thought.

"Lynton, just get on him will you, you've done plenty of riding you'll be fine. The horse obviously knows where to go, and we'll follow."

Mauveine smiled and nodded to Abby, pointing in the direction of the canal.

Isi helped Lynton up as the others mounted a horse each. Maddie noticed immediately that they were sat on a solid but invisible gap, between them and the saddle, the same as holding the reins. She looked towards Abby who smiled back, thankful that Victoria had insisted, ever since the children were small, that they all had decent riding lessons and even took exams. But Abby remembered very clearly. This was her second experience on one of these paranormal horses. The horses were becoming impatient and Mauveine and Isi led them all out onto the drive. It became clear to Abby that Mauveine and Isi would not be joining them, or more likely were unable to, but she felt the directions from Mauveine filling up inside her head, and she could see Maddie was receiving the same message as her horse slowly sidled up directly behind Abby's. The early dusk had grown less misty, the moon was brighter and they could see more clearly through the contorted shadows and shapes of the trees over to the fields.

"Listen up," Abby shouted in between the whinnying of the horses, now ready to fly off. "Lynton will take the lead. All you have to do is just hold on tight and go, the horses will do the work."

Chapter Sixteen

Ned was coming to. His eyes wouldn't open and his head felt like it was splitting apart. He was lying on his back on something soft, his shoulder hurt awful and he could hear water splashing rhythmically in the background, with sounds like someone rowing. He felt the rocking movement; he was definitely on a boat. Someone had jumped him from behind at the backdoor and shoved something over his face, which smelt like shit and he'd blacked out. If only he'd been quicker he could have downed at least two of the bastards. The last thing he remembered was looking at strange shapes, short silhouetted people dressed in dark brown robes and heavy, floppy hoods. But that voice ... the one barking orders in what sounded like Latin, he knew so well, but no way was that possible ... Ade was hundreds of miles away in Dublin. They must have drugged him with something on that rag, he had obviously hallucinated. His left eye gradually opened. His vision was still blurred but he could see tree branches passing slowly above his head and then they went underneath a wooden bridge. Apart from the splashing of oars from the other end, there was complete silence.

He tried to get up but couldn't move. His arms and legs were securely tied to pegs with thick, rough ropes.

As his eyes opened properly, he saw he was at the bottom of the hold on a barge, the sides rising steeply around him. He was lying on large brown, dirty sacks of something that smelled like old tobacco. He realised, he must be on the canal, but where and why? And who were these people? The boat and the wood were unpainted and looked very old and warped, ancient even and was coated unevenly in a black, sticky pitch. Something caught his eye on the far ledge but that something simply couldn't be right. It was a large double edged sword and what looked like an old medieval pistol.

After what felt like an eternity, but he estimated was actually half an hour, the splashing abated and he heard voices whispering at the far end. As he strained to listen, he could make out they spoke English but with the broadest Lancashire accents imaginable, tinged with a peculiar slow drawl, the intonation and stress on many words sounding quite alien. They had stopped and were landing somewhere.

Someone shouted, "Get that heathen Anglican onto land." Four men jumped onto the sacks and he couldn't believe his eyes. They were exactly as he thought he had first imagined at the house, dressed in dirty, brown robes like monks he had watched in old films. Their hair was cut short and fringed, but faces were unshaven and generally they looked dishevelled and definitely smelly, as if they were on the run from something. Quickly, they uncut his bindings and dragged him up a short ladder, holding him firmly.

One hissed in his face. "Don't you struggle noble or your belly receives this dagger, verily, I will hold sway on my promise."

He looked into the man's lined face. They were all a head or more shorter than him, but muscular and strong. His assailant's eyes were bloodshot and evil and his breath stank of foul meat, with a row of yellow and black teeth which grinned back malevolently.

His hands still tied, they dragged him, stumbling along as he tried to look around. It was growing dusk and he saw what appeared to be Harrison's Bridge in the bright moonlight. The mist had cleared, but the bridge was much smaller and all wooden. Some of the landscape was familiar, but there were very thick, old oak trees everywhere and the canal no longer looked like a canal. As he tried desperately to understand, he realised he was seeing the semi-ruins of an old priory on the other side of the pathway. Most of the roof was missing but a small part remained inhabited and intact, with smoke coming out of the top.

This was a moat, not a canal. Where on earth was he? There were a few goats and sheep casually eating in a clearing. His mind drew together the sights, sounds and images which Maddie had described when she had seen her so called 'visions,' and he felt a combination of deep unease and fear.

These people were not of this time. It was as if he had been transported back five hundred years. Two other men, better dressed in breeches, tied at the knees with stockings and short cloaks, grabbed the sword and the pistol, leered at him and jumped off the boat, then walked towards the priory. They were met by another small group of monks or friars, whatever they were, one being much taller than the others, and exchanged words before small leather pouches were swapped. All his belongings, his phone, wallet, keys and coins had gone.

A voice from behind, deep and familiar but croaky, bellowed an order. "Brothers, remove those pagan clothes and burn them, now, before the Abbot comes, quickly."

Ned turned, and looked up at the very tall figure, but horribly gaunt and equally unkempt, and gasped. "Ade? Ade is that you? What the fuck is going on here? Shit man, you look bad. Who are these guys? Ade it's me, Ned, your best mate for fuck's sake. What game …?"

But he never said any more. A blow to the side of the face put a stop to that and made his head spin, the pain shooting across his cheek. "Quiet, heathen. You ask too many questions, just like that whore of a sister, Lucinda. I ate her ashes with porridge. She screamed so loudly and then melted on the fire. We stripped and fucked her of course first. I thought you would like to know that." He laughed, a deep guttural sound, his croaking larynx sounding like an old man. "The great Lord Robert McKenzie babbles the same tripe as that witch. We shall have fun tonight, brothers."

Ned struggled again, but was held firm by five robed monks as a sixth took out a knife and briskly cut and sliced at his clothes, tearing them off in strips, the cold air impelling his bare flesh. In a trice he was naked. They stared and laughed and a sleeveless hair shirt was thrown over his head, followed by a robe. His boots and socks were removed more carefully and examined with interest before being put to one side, whilst a lighted torch was thrust into his pile of clothes.

"Excellent. Get McKenzie fully prepared, I will thence back to finish the woodwork. Brother Arkwright, bring those bolts and rope and a saw from the hold. He is a sturdy lad, I must strengthen the gibbet." He turned and shuffled painfully back towards the priory and exchanged words with the other group who then approached the boat, led by another tall monk in much finer wear. Clearly, Ned pondered, he must be the head of these idiots, the Abbot, whatever game they are up to … But then his blood froze as they approached. More lighted torches were brought around him.

"Dad? Jesus Christ, Dad? What is all this about and why are you wearing that weird garb, like a monk? Is it one of your films Dad? Are we filming or something? Dad?"

The Abbot approached closer as Ned stared intensely. He looked exactly like his father, the build, height and facial features identical but when he smiled, most of his few teeth were black and he had a large, festering carbuncle on his forehead, which he dabbled continuously with a handkerchief. One cheek had deep pock marks.

"Dad, it's Ned, your son. Great costumes and stuff, the makeup and action is brilliant, but you might have warned me. Where are the cameras?"

He was ignored. It was as if a total deafness came over this so called Abbot and the rest of the monks around him.

"Robert, it has been a while since our last meeting. I expect you are sorry you let me escape, but God works in mysterious ways, does it not? It was always ordained that I should be back to claim forever what is ours."

The voice was strange, like Adrian's a broad and heavy Lancashire accent, but clearly he was an educated man. But this was not his father. What was going on?

The Abbot continued. "Life here at the Orsbrick Priory for centuries was excellent until that monster King Henry, defiled the rule of God and the Church and ordained the dissolution of our monastic abodes one hundred and thirty years ago to this day. Your family always understood Robert. It is obvious from your face you don't know the truth, but your great-grandfather defied the ban, kept our community alive and allowed our way of life. And so it went, right through, until your father decided differently, finally siding with the pagan Royalists and allowing our hallowed place to be sacked, and then built his own manor house, his priory, on our former land! Your father, Cameron, was once my friend but he betrayed us and we took our revenge. He begged for mercy but we gave none. I am pleased you saw his desecrated body, riddled with maggots and hanging from the gibbet, his guts and cock eviscerated on the ground. When I escaped I took all of Cameron's remains with me and we fed them to the dogs so they could shit them into the ground and we will do the same to you. Now you know, when you mercilessly despatched my Brothers and regained your heathen home, where the body of your father went."

He spat straight into Ned's face, vile, stinking yellow mucus, which made him almost vomit.

"But we are returned Robert, and today will change history forever and eternally. We have waited so long for this day. Do you think we could have allowed you to continue the McKenzie line, living in that house on our hallowed grounds, with your whore of a wife and bastard children? When they arrive, which they will soon, they will be forced to watch your demise and hear you scream loudly too. Your death will be especially slow and agonising. My brother has created new implements in his workshop to increase the pain ... but your ..."

He was interrupted by another minion. "Abbot Rimmer, we have finished the gibbet and are bringing it out now to the clearing. The torches are lit ... and as predicted the others are on their way."

"Excellent, I must return and drink some mead first."

Ned started to think hard and fast, back to Maddie and ... of course ... those letters in the library earlier, the diaries, why was his brain so fucking muddled? The diaries of Robert McKenzie, Lucinda his twin sister ... of course ... shit ... Maddie's visions were Robert McKenzie, regaining control of Orsbrick Hall after this monster had been routed. He was in the seventeenth century in one of Abby's space-time warps, and this maniac was going to rewrite history in some way ... it wasn't ... it could not be possible ... he had to escape but how? Who were the others? Robert McKenzie's family? His wife Lady Bella? Holy shit ... not his own family?

He struggled hard again, but the four burly monks held him tight. He looked over to the clearing and saw Adrian, or who he thought was Adrian, but obviously the brother of this evil Abbot and clearly the engineer amongst them ... Fuck ... their identities must have been taken over.

With other helpers, Adrian was pulling along a platform on wheels with a wooden structure built on it and a thick hangman's noose, clearly silhouetted, dangled ominously from the top. Fear gripped Ned. He freed one arm and punched hard using his boxing techniques, felling two of them instantly. But immediately others jumped on him and he was thrown to the ground, and kicked and booted viciously in the stomach. They pulled him up, dazed and bloody and overcame his final resistance, dragging him towards the gallows. One monk, with blood pouring from his broken nose, screamed to bring the knives and start the disembowelling and castration immediately, but was sharply reminded that they were ordered to hang Robert McKenzie slowly first, but only enough to choke him, and only when the rest of his family had been rounded up and forced to watch.

Lynton looked back to check that Abby, Maddie and Bel were behind with Zac at the rear. The shire horses were huge, at least half a dozen hands taller than their own horses, Snow and Jet. The two dogs were bounding easily alongside.

"Abby, should Jeb and Kai be coming with us or what?" he shouted.

Zac replied from the back. "Yes, no problem Lynton. They have amazing speed and stamina. They're hunting dogs and you can see, they're expecting to do just that and they're desperate to find Ned."

They set off at a canter, as Lynton nervously attempted to direct his horse towards the canal then quickly realised this horse had a mind of its own and a desire for the fields instead, galloping like crazy unhindered. All, plus the dogs, jumped the first fence next to the pond with ease. The mist and encroaching dusk was still pervasive, but the light from the full moon was sufficient to see the surroundings flash by as they picked up speed. But this was no ordinary ride. There were no roads, only a few dirt tracks could be seen. Lots of open fields with animals were either grazing still or lying down. Small clusters of villages lay in the distance, looking like broken down old farmhouses; thatched, crude dwellings, quite mediaeval with smoke belching out of holes in the roof. But no people could be seen anywhere.

They continued in a huge blur of speed. Jeb and Kai effortlessly kept up on either side as more fences, meadows and forest pathways were hurtled over. Nowhere was familiar, although the general direction seemed to be along the route of the canal, except there was no canal. Suddenly, they slowed and came across some sort of waterway, a fairly shallow but quite wide river with a well worn pathway along the bank. Lynton's horse finally slowed to a canter and they trotted steadily, one behind the other, with Jeb and Kai panting at the rear next to Zac. They followed the path of the river for some miles, dodging under overhanging trees and leaping over fallen branches. The river grew deeper until it was almost indistinguishable from a wide canal, and slowly circled a clearing, behind which some kind of ancient ruin could be seen. Pin points of light became visible through the mist, now thinned out. The horses stopped and Jeb and Kai, still panting hard but clearly in excellent shape, stood still and looked around, before lowering their huge heads to drink from the water.

Lynton and Zac dismounted and helped Abby, Maddie and Bel off their saddles. Everyone looked around, trying hard to make out where they were and what the old monastery type building could be.

"Where on earth is this place? Lynton gasped, incredulous that he couldn't recognise anywhere familiar and he knew these fields and waterways like the back of his hand since childhood.

Abby drew everyone together. "Did you not recognise the types of buildings as we rode over the fields?"

"At that crazy speed I barely saw anything except it was bitterly cold. What happened to the cars?" Lynton shouted, jumping up and down to stretch his legs.

"No cars and no people," Bel replied, shivering and drew her coat tightly together.

"Those houses were so old, like definitely medieval," Zac added, fishing for his iGlasses which wouldn't work. "Hey look at that wooden bridge? Bel? Remind you of anywhere?"

"Crikey," Bel shrieked," See, over to the right. It's Harrisons Bridge, or as it was a very long time back, but it's built over the river now which is much higher up. There's no proper canal, except this funny stretch here ... but at least we know where we are."

Maddie was staring hard over the clearing and at the priory. She spoke quietly and deliberately. "I know exactly where we are? This is what I kept seeing whenever I had those strange visions. This is a moat, not a canal and is surrounding what is or should I say was, Orsbrick Priory."

Lynton followed her gaze and pulled out a tiny pair of binoculars from his pocket to get a better look. He'd been to the Aintree races with clients at lunch time and still had them with him. "Was?" he said, his voice wavering. "Orsbrick Priory, according to Julian, because we talked about this one night after a long session in his rum cellar, was eventually destroyed in the 1660s. Shit, everything we've seen? Are we actually ... back ... back in ... time? Abby?"

"Yes," Maddie continued in a monotone. "All of us have somehow bridged Abby's descriptive space and time universes. This is why Mauveine can't help us now because she's locked into a different time frame. The horses are her means of assisting us to find Ned and try and end the family curse, forever."

"I agree," Bel whispered, as Zac muttered 'cool' and stroked Jeb and Kai. "At least we're all together. But I wish Mum and Dad were here."

Abby nodded, smiling to Maddie. "Correct conclusions. But we must find Ned. My guess is that he's somewhere over where that old ruin is. We need to head that way. Now listen up, this is vital. We may see things which you don't understand or they scare you.

Life was cheap, violent and short then. It's important that we stick together, all of us, including the horses and the dogs. As a group we retain a psychic strength, like carrying our own moat with us. Does that make sense? We will need that strength if we're to find Ned."

"Abby is absolutely right. I know, and I've already seen some terrible things," Maddie added. "You will just have to ignore them. That period of time was certainly pretty brutal."

"Zac and I have strong stomachs after the boat escapade," Bel replied. "Bring it on."

Zac was deep in concentration, fiddling with his iGlasses again, reasoning that if they had jumped a few universes, maybe there was some means of bridging a bit of wifi through too, but no such luck.

Lynton let out a giant sigh. He wished desperately he was still back putting logs on the fire, or in the pub or at the races with Abby and having fun. In fact anywhere would do but not the 1660s. Family curses and time travel were not his thing, either legally or temperamentally.

They set off walking steadily and led the horses away from the moat, onwards through some more trees and quickly reached the edge of the clearing. Lynton was staring through his binoculars at the blobs of light in the distance, when Abby stopped them all with a jerk. Dangling from a rope on a branch were two rotting bodies, side by side and from the fineries they wore, she could see they were once noblemen. She felt immediately sick to the stomach.

Maddie gripped her arm tightly. "Ignore them, all of you. I told you this would happen. Remember, we are truly not of this time, that fact is a strength."

Lynton peered again through his binoculars. "Jesus, there are loads of bonfires everywhere, with people tied to stakes burning. Can you hear the noise?"

As they turned the next corner, loud screams filled their ears, fighting and commotion but no people anywhere, just very frightening sounds. Abby and Maddie realised their journey back into time was distorted. Not all was smoothly connected up, like a crackly radio or a bad electrical junction.

Zac and Bel pulled out the leashes they had stuffed into the horse's saddlebags and secured Jeb and Kai, each holding one tightly. They had got half way across the field when they stopped. Dots of light gradually appeared around the circumference as small groups of men in dark brown robes, and holding large staffs and lighted torches, slowly appeared. They stopped and were watching, but no words spoken. Lynton looked behind and the robed men were there too, cutting off any escape.

"They're monks out of the priory," Maddie shouted. "I've seen them. They were the ones inciting the mobs of peasants and doing the killing of people everywhere, including the burning of witches and the hangings."

Jeb and Kai were now growling, deep menacing and throaty rasps, unlike anything anyone had heard before. The horses were unmoved, probably Bel reasoned, accustomed to warfare and used for fighting.

"No, both of you stay. Quiet." Zac ordered as he and Bel tightened their grip, knowing at least both dogs were highly trained and disciplined. He knew, despite their size, the dogs would be massacred by those monks or whatever they were. There were simply far too many of them everywhere, carrying sticks like huge baseball bats.

"Just keep together, like I said," Abby whispered. "Concentrate on one other. Look, over there walking out of the priory, a group of them are coming towards us. Two are very tall, unlike the others, although the way they shuffle and limp, they're not exactly gym fit."

"I expect that's true of all this lot, given the amount of disease, poverty and inadequate food around then," Lynton added, fiddling with his binoculars. The flame torches everywhere were lighting up the field perimeter as darkness descended. "Life expectancy was about forty but many women never got past twenty, usually dying in childbirth."

Suddenly he shouted hysterically. "Oh my God, I've got to get over there. It's Judy and Julian. We've got to talk some sense into them. Whatever the hell is going on here?"

Abby's heart sank. She suspected this was going to happen, exactly like Mauveine with things taking over people's bodies. Except the whole atmosphere was far more terrifying than the situation she had squared up to in the Orsbrick Hall cellar. They faced an army of the living dead of five hundred years back, and the zombies were monks, clerics, or once may have been ... maybe that even gave them some special protection?

"Dad? Oh my God, it really is Dad, but why is he wearing that stupid robe?" Bel yelled as three robed individuals approached. "I'm coming with you, Lynton."

They strode forward but each was instantly grabbed hard by Abby and Maddie.

"No, Lynton, no, no, no. Believe me," Abby screamed. "It isn't Judy and it isn't Julian. They look like them, yes, but it isn't. Something else has taken them over and adopted their forms. They're a ... shit ... what's the word?"

"A manifestation, they're a sort of distorted apparition," Maddie intervened. "Bel, listen to me and Abby, she's right, I know it too. If it was Dad, I would be the first there ... it isn't. They want to lure you away and split us up. We must stay firm. We have some protection like having a psychic shield around us as long as we stay close and don't break up."

Bel started to sob. "Fuck, Maddie, what on earth is this all about? Where is Dad then and Judy too?"

The dogs were also sticking close and lay protectively on the ground, ears pricked, both on high alert but keeping calm, merely an occasional light growl emitted from their throats.

"Mad's right, guys. Abby, how come Mauveine has got your old iPhone5? Bloody hell that's going back a bit?"

They turned to see Zac fiddling with his iGlasses, obviously seeing something from a normal time period. Abby grinned, a wave of disbelief and relief washed over her. Somehow Mauveine was still helping them. "So that's what happened to it? My iPhone in 2011 just disappeared. I couldn't find it anywhere so I bought another one and then Mauveine confessed by text she wanted to borrow it to start tweeting."

"Tweeting and texting? You've got to be kidding, Abby, ghosts don't tweet?" Lynton said, completely incredulous.

"Mauveine is no ordinary ghost, she's a McKenzie hot scientist, remember," Abby replied smiling, and gave him a quick cuddle of reassurance.

Zeb continued, concentrating hard inside his iGlasses. "Mauveine is using the iPhone to act as a wireless bridge between her time, ours and this one, like a sort of ghost receiver and transmitter. That is so cool. She and Isi are amazing scientists. They've actually worked it out between them. Those three zombies walking towards us, Jesus, the third one is an Adrian lookalike. Mauveine says they are Abbot Rimmer and his brother John Rimmer plus a communal priory whore called Zelda. We have a shield around us which she and Isi are trying to sustain, but once her iPhone battery runs out, and it's getting low, that's it."

"So, what do we do?" Lynton cried, wishing he had his shotgun with him. "Abby, quick, what's up with Maddie?"

Abby took her arm. Maddie was standing, staring into the sky in a trance, a vague smile across her lips "Bel, hold her other arm, quickly, this may be the key."

Maddie was receiving something quite different, at first the familiar throbbing, but then she realised. It was her mother, pumping out a thumping psychic wave after wave, forcing her brain to shut out everything around her until a picture begin to crystallise. Showers of light, then a rainbow, had emanated from inside a large glass prism, exactly like the experiments which Isaac Newton had done in the same period, but the prism was turning a deep blood-red crimson. The prism of purpurine. They needed that damned prism, all the while. This was what the eventual discovery of the individual bits and the piecing together into one whole object had been leading up to. The prism of purpurine had been waiting patiently over all those hundreds of years and generations, for this very day if it ever occurred.

"We need the crimson prism," she cried out in despair, her expression returning to normal. Oh … I wish … I just wish I had thought of that before we left …"

"Ah, but I have," Bel replied, grinning. "It's in my saddlebag." She walked to her horse and fiddled with the flap and eventually after a struggle managed to prise it up. She gasped. "It's sort of glowing, all around the edges. What do I do?"

Zac walked over. "Leave it Bel. Mauveine says leave it, she's like charging it up … with a sort of paranormal radioactive charge. She says leave it until you know."

"How will we know?" Lynton replied, wanting to dive into the bag and throw it at those horrible forms shuffling towards them.

"We just will," Abby said. "Well done Bel. The Abbot is approaching. If anyone wants convincing, he's not Julian, look at his forehead. That bloody great sore on it and those awful black teeth and that shuffling gait. Judy or should we say Zelda, looks like she's just stumbled out of a period whore house, those filthy clothes and baggy eyes and that long matted hair, but the likenesses are remarkable. God, look at the other one, the big lurching ape."

"That will be John Rimmer, aka Ade. Shit, he's in a really bad shape," Zac added. "Now we know why he wanted to become a priest. He must be the priory carpenter and engineer. It all adds up. Mauveine says they are riddled with the plague and Judy has a bad dose of clap. The intention, if we approached them, would be to infect us all by breathing on us or seducing us. Blimey."

"Clap?" Lynton asked.

Abby waved her arms in the air. "Venereal disease, probably syphilis, Zelda looks half crazy. God, those eyes. Maddie bring the horses closer and keep in a tight circle. I think the dogs are aware they can only come so far. But where on earth is Ned?"

Abbot Rimmer suddenly stopped and smiled. That horrible mouth dripped with thick saliva. "Ahh ...welcome to our humble abode, all of you." His broad Lancashire voice had the unexpected lilt, word and letter emphasis of Old English, but he spoke clearly and they understood. Despite his hideous appearance, he projected an aura of being well educated and important.

He stared at them hard, his face contorted with hate and disgust, first at Maddie and then Abby. "Mmm ... but of course, Lady Bella and Lady Katherine are brought together. Obviously, you have both made it up over the years. Bella, we have waited a long time for you, always far too clever. You eluded me the first time, dying much too early before I came back, but I knew my patience and persistence would win out. And you Katherine, you missed the London City plague and the fire by sheer luck. You were smart too, especially unexpectedly escaping to the Americas. I give you credit for that move, but you silly bitch, you came back didn't you. Also, like your foul whore of a sister, far too clever for your own good. But your scheming now ends, here, and forever. And the whole of the McKenzie lineage, ancestors, descendents, all of you no matter how well connected, will now and forever acknowledge the supremacy of the Rimmer family. The McKenzies are finished. Everything could have worked out fine between us Bella, if only that stupid husband of yours, the ever so royal Lord Robert McKenzie ..."

Abbot Rimmer, wheezing, stopped to catch his breath and wiped the yellow pus from his brow. He spat, green and slimy, onto the ground in contempt. "Robert betrayed my cause, Bella, along with his mother. But that cackling crone will shortly be dead from the plague too, no hospital in any time can cure her. Your husband was far too preoccupied with lechery and drink and allowed me to escape. Now he too will pay the ultimate price for his stupidity, with all of you, down in Hades."

The woman suddenly spoke with a very posh voice, exactly like Judy. "My dear Abbot, shall I perform some services? Shall I fuck that ugly footman standing behind these whores?"

Abby turned sharply. "No, Lynton, ignore her."

"I've been called some things before but never ugly ..." Lynton whispered as Bel laughed.

"Mmm ... Patience, the eldest child is here too methinks, excellent, all in one go to die. No, wait awhile Zelda for when the fun really begins."

Brother John Rimmer stared lasciviously at Bel. His six foot six inch bulky frame towered over everyone but with a distinct crooked stoop and a limp. His clothes were even more dishevelled and a horrible smell emanated from his rotting hulk, his skin gnarled and grey. He smiled; most of his teeth were missing and the few left black and broken. "Patience, the artistic Puritan, remains a virgin and all the way from the Americas too. She is verily a true catch of beauty. Before the flames burn off that lovely skin, incinerate her bones and melt away her fat and inners, I think I had better fuck her too, a personal gift before she enters Hell's gates. Would you like that Patience?"

Bel shivered and he laughed loudly, coughing badly with the effort as his towering frame shook with mirth.

The Abbot smirked. "You know don't you Katherine we can't get to you yet. That spirit, the vile whore Mauveine, the one I should have destroyed, is protecting you. But she can't keep it up for long ... ha ... I have waited a long time for you. You saved them all in the cellar didn't you bitch Katherine. You really have been bad, so unforgivably bad. Therefore I have exceptionally interesting things to do to you, personally of course, before you and Bella are tied, back to back, around that prepared stake over there and feel the flames at the same time. But Bella. Are you not wondering what has happened to your dear husband? That fool Robert, always impetuous, a great swordsman, he killed enough of my friars, but now, like his father, his turn has finally arisen. Look, over there."

They turned to the left to see a large wooden platform on wobbly wheels being pulled towards them by half a dozen sturdy monks. John Rimmer went shuffling off, puffing and panting hard up the incline, the remains of the priory visible at the top.

Maddie cried out. "Abby, it's Ned! They've got him tied to that gibbet. He's dressed in those same robes, oh my God ..."

They watched, gaping wide-eyed, as three monks and John Rimmer tore of his robe and then raised his bound and naked body up to the rope and hung it around his neck, so his feet just touched a large block. The position made him choke and cough, as he wriggled vainly to get free, shouting out loudly.

"Your husband looks quite cute up there my Lady Bella doesn't he? Whilst you all have a theatre box view in your temporary enclave, we'll begin a little asphyxiation first, the effect will be immediately apparent ..."

He pulled out a long sharp knife. "But soon to follow with intestines and those over-used reproductives. Such a shame Bella after all the fun you've both had, and finally of course the limbs. Then we may let him die before slicing him into four ... err ... may ... if I stay in a good mood. And then my dearest Katherine, I take my personal revenge, our finale. You and your sister will be next, exactly the same way, plus the burning to finish. But we'll leave your limbs on. More to watch." He laughed loudly. A huge blob of pus fell off his forehead onto the grass.

"Abby, we can't just stand here and do nothing, we have to help Ned." Lynton cried.

Maddie and Bel were sobbing with severe distress.

"No, Lynton, no. We must stay in the circle and keep safe. Now Maddie, start."

They both knew that Victoria was still strong, lying in the hospital with the real Julian and pumping out waves of psychic support, despite what Abbot Rimmer had said. All was not quite going to his master plan; parts were frayed at the space-time edges like him. Now was the time to fight back, but their way, as Abby did with Aunt Eveline, fifteen years before. But could Mauveine and Isi hold those corpses at bay? The shield had to hold.

Abby and Maddie chanted slowly in old 4th century Latin, one ancient dirge after the next, speaking all the incantations against evil which they had each meticulously memorised from notes and tarots. One acted seamlessly as a foil for the other, reinforcing, doubling up, and urging forth the exorcisms. They worked together meticulously as if it had been planned and rehearsed for months.

Bel and Lynton stood motionless and gaped in disbelief, but said nothing. Zac had retuned his iGlasses and stabbed furiously at the screen of his net-watch, knowing that the mobile signal sent down the centuries was weakening.

Abbot Rimmer, his brother John and their whore, Zelda stopped still instantly. They grimaced and conferred also in Latin, jabbering loudly and pointing over to the edge of the fields and down into the woods.

"Lynton, Abbot Rimmer, Abby shouted across. "He must hear this next part in English. For fuck's sake translate will you, quickly, and put that public school education to its best use ever."

Lynton struggled at first with the Latin but concentrated hard as his school classics returned fast and repeated the remaining exorcisms in English. He composed the final refutation in his best legal summary he could muster, slowly speaking it out loud and clear.

"Abbot Rimmer and your debauched heretic followers. Hereby, I proclaim that your power in this universe and all others, past, present and future, will be rescinded by the Holy Trinity and you will burn forever in the flames of your own creation. By order of King Charles the Second, Head of the illustrious Church of England."

But Abby wasn't finished. It was time for the Gregorian chants, her singing echoing loudly across the field, slow and precise, filling the air with the purest of high notes, eerie and compelling. It was the kind of seductive wail that led men to destruction like the mythical Greek sirens on the rocks to lost sailors at sea.

Suddenly the giant carpenter, John Rimmer, backed away and staggered towards the gibbet, spluttering and holding his throat. His head started to swell up like a rubber balloon, his huge body bulging until the robes split and great blobs of grey fatty slime melted away from his bare flesh.

The woman, Zelda, stood still, her petrified eyes turning yellow. Her body shook violently as huge crevices formed in her lengthening face and erupted with boils of stinking pus. Suddenly she pulled her hood down and her long hair frizzled and smoked, transforming itself into a head full of slithering snakes, hissing and spitting that caused her to stumble and roll around the floor as the snakes ate into her face and body.

Maddie looked up at Ned, with a black hood over his head. His guards had gone, leaving him still swinging precariously on the gibbet. The rest of the monks were running and gathering into groups at the edge of the field. But Zac was decidedly alarmed. Mauveine's signal was fast fading and the shield was weakening. Maybe they had only a minute or two left.

Jeb and Kai stood up and growled again, deep and menacing, restlessly pacing within the circle alongside the horses. The animals also sensed their coming vulnerability. Abby was singing her heart out as loud as she could, until she was almost hoarse with the effort, tears streaming down her face.

But Abbot Rimmer stood there unmoved and smiling while he watched his two companions disintegrate but not him. He remained untouched.

"Lady Katherine, you have a most wonderful voice," he shouted, calmly. "Last time, sadly, I wasn't able to appreciate your singing and acting, as you know. However, I'm sorry, I forgot to say earlier. We do learn from history Katherine and of course from our past mistakes. You see, I am a dimension or two behind you, so the game is back to my turn. I've won dearest Katherine and I'm so looking forward to my long anticipated dividend."

He pulled a dirty knife out and looked Abby over, from top to bottom, slathering and drooling obscenely as a cold and fearful chill ran through her body. She had failed, the one individual, the primal cause of all the curses and their manifestations for five hundred years.

The Rimmer of all the Rimmers was still standing, unscathed.

Zac suddenly shouted. "The signal's gone. The shield has gone too."

Abby grasped at Maddie and Lynton and they grouped closely together, huddled up with Bel and Zac. The dogs now were growling fiercely, staunchly defensive and stood protectively between them and Rimmer and the approaching monks in the distance. But Maddie thought hard. She was still tuned into Mauveine and her mother. She turned sharply to Bel.

"Fetch it Bel, fetch the prism."

Bel grabbed at her bag on the horse, tore open the lid and pulled out the crimson prism, shimmering and pulsating brightly with a glowing phosphorescence of changing spectral colours.

"Give it to me," Maddie cried, standing apart. She held it up towards Rimmer, and walked slowly towards him. The dogs growled ominously but moved aside. She began to recant in a strange tongue, a language which went further back, much further back than even Latin; a form of Assyrian, an ancient tongue spoken in early Egypt but which originated, as did the prism of purpurine, in the very distant and ancient civilisations of India.

Abby gripped Lynton, with Bel and Zac hanging onto them in disbelief and totally baffled. Nobody had any idea what Maddie was saying or why. Except Abby knew that something deeply primeval, a force going right back to the very start of civilisation itself, had entered Maddie's psychic channels alone from somewhere else.

Immediately, Abbot Rimmer's leering smile turned into a dark grimace. He reared back and then stumbled awkwardly to distance himself wider from her measured advance.

"Where did you find that?" he roared. "Bella, you pagan bitch … but, it's too late. You can't win Bella because I'm calling them to life now, the ultimate, indescribable and permanent hell of all, the wolves of Hades. They are here to take you, all of you. They are my deterrent and they are immune, the purest of evil spirits. So die, you foul whore."

Maddie's head pounded harder, wave after wave of intense pulses thudded into her brain. The spectral force field of the prism was growing stronger. She had to keep this concentration up …

An eerie, loud wail, like a huge howl of intense pain, echoed across the landscape. They all turned, petrified, to see large black shapes appearing on the horizon, skirting the edge of the field and the priory. They gathered quickly alongside the hundreds of robed friars who had now pulled their hoods ominously down over their heads, waving their sticks in the air and shouting. In the woods, hordes of huge black wolves emerged, stealthy and confident, with bright yellow eyes, their large teeth and fur luminescent in the dusk. They clustered into groups to prepare for the kill, pacing and howling. Jeb and Kai reared up, fur standing on end. They barked continuously, loud and frightening and knew they were vastly outnumbered, determined to fight to the end. The horses had sidled to the side, clustered together and nervous but staying firm.

Maddie finally screamed a long and weird sounding incantation and held the prism up high, the light bathing her all over in the phosphorescence. Rimmer stumbled away, escaping towards the priory whilst the wolves set off running down the field towards them in great packs, howling for their prey. The horses suddenly bolted towards the edge of the other wood.

But a deep and ferocious barking could also be heard, countering the howling of the wolves and ensuing behind from the direction the family had come. Everyone turned, including Maddie, to see hundreds of ghostly wolfhounds, led by one massive beast, black with vivid cream and brown markings, jumping from Harrison's Bridge, running and leaping along the old towpath track. They bounded strongly from all directions, out of the woods on all sides and quickly met with the nearest packs of wolves. The monks were already trying to flee, but were outrun in seconds by the hordes of wolfhounds who jumped upon them and devoured all in their path in a grisly bloodbath. A massive confrontation of howling and screaming had ensued, a ghostly canine battle of ferocious proportions, as the feared wolves of Hades finally met their one and only match, their ultimate nemesis. The wolfhounds of the prism of purpurine had been called up, mercilessly tearing the wolves' bodies apart. Maddie, struggling intensely to maintain her concentration, had finally managed to link up across millennia to Mauveine in time.

In the melee, Lynton took his chance and ran through the battle towards the lone gibbet. Frantically searching from side to side, he grabbed a knife and a robe from the body of a decapitated friar. He quickly cut down Ned, still bruised and battered who tore off his own hood, coughed, and flexed his limbs to free up the stiffness. He had sufficient strength, with Lynton's help, to pull the robe over himself.

"Good job we could cover you up. Don't want to frighten the females, do we?" Lynton jibed with a grin, "Now, run for it!"

Ned slapped his back and they tore off together down the hill, avoiding the packs of wolfhounds devouring mounds of bloodied bodies of wolves and friars, and headed back towards the others.

Jeb and Kai, still on guard, were barking like crazy, torn by indecision of wanting to join the fight but too disciplined to leave their family. Maddie pulled out a pouch from her bag and gently tied it around Jeb's neck, carefully placing the prism inside.

"Now go, both of you. Finish the job."

They hurtled off at a fast pace, followed by the wolfhound pack leader, in pursuit of the Abbot, who with the distorted shape of his bloated brother and their snake-headed whore, were still stumbling desperately together towards the safety of the priory. But it was too late. They turned, frightened and screaming, to see the three wolfhounds, bounding at great speed at them until Jeb, who led the three, leapt fifteen feet into the air for the kill, onto Abbot Rimmer, devouring his face and his head in one great bite. Rimmer's accomplices, brother John and lover Zelda had their throats and limbs ripped apart into a bloodied gore, by Kai and wolfhound leader Caesar, back for revenge.

After a quick jubilant hug from each one and a few sarcastic comments on his new fashion style, Maddie tugged at Ned. "Come on, we've got to get out of here."

Abby shouted, pulling at Lynton. "Head for the horses. Jeb and Kai have done their part, they'll follow."

Dashing to the group of horses, still waiting at the edge of the wood, they mounted hastily. Ned jumped up behind Maddie and they looked back. Jeb and Kai were racing back down the hill with Caesar watching triumphantly at the top, their long legs and agile bodies a blur of motion. They skidded to a halt alongside the horses, panting hard. The vivid sounds of barking and screaming, with corpses and dead wolves littered everywhere, had reached an ear-splitting crescendo.

Without warning, the wind had got up and moaned strongly, the trees bending ominously. A bright yellow light gradually emanated from a ring of suns, hovering over the priory, to encircle everything around and spread over the field and across the woods, covering them with a vast and vivid illumination. The light was so sharp they were forced to cover their eyes, blinded by the intensity, as the horses whinnied and reared in fright.

Three dark, twisted shapes rose slowly into the air. They watched, incredulous, unable to move or speak, shielding their eyes to glimpse a huge crimson ball of flame, at least fifty feet in diameter, roll headlong along the track of the river towpath, past Harrison's Bridge engulfing it in fire, and onwards up the hill. The ball wrapped itself around the rising bodies of Abbot Rimmer, John Rimmer and Zelda, preventing them from floating away to psychic freedom and into the safety of yet another space-time universe. Their terrified faces could be seen trapped inside, pressed against the edge of the ball, contorted, and dissolving into copious streams of fat which ran headlong down the inside, forming a swathe of rainbow colours underneath.

A massive loud eruption, a psychic nuclear explosion finally blew, enveloping them in fire and light, including the horses and Jeb and Kai into a final oblivion with all the rest ...

Chapter Seventeen

Abby stared aimlessly out of the hospital window, feeling like she had gone stupidly into some kind of vacant daydream.

"You know Abby, exactly like when we lived together in Rotterdam, I do sometimes wonder what you think about in that great creative recess called your brain. What on earth are you staring at?"

Abby turned around and realised she was standing in a recuperation room in the Rendezvous Private Hospital, looking at a smiling Victoria sat upright in her bed who positively bloomed with rosy cheeks and was displaying a complete absence of swellings on her neck. A seventeenth century flashback scene of marauding packs of black wolves, dishevelled evil friars, burnings, hangings and the most awful situation imaginable, zipped fleetingly through her consciousness, a reminder, exactly as before, that she could and would remember everything, forever. They, the whole McKenzie family, really had succeeded in destroying the Rimmer curse. This time, what had seemed a desperate and an impossible task, had amazingly worked thanks only to Maddie's last minute and intensely concentrated intervention. Maddie's incredible realisation, heaven knows where from, of the existence of the hidden universe way back into the beginning of ancient civilisation was the key, where Rimmer had sought unassailable sanctuary and immunity from their denouncements. The triggering which followed of the counter-angels of wolfhounds through the purpurine prism, to destroy the hideous devil-wolves from Hades, saved them all from everlasting purgatory.

Never, ever, again would she want to experience such a close death call. The throbbing waves and pulses in her head had vanished and a complete feeling of wellbeing suffused her whole body, giving rise to instant happy thoughts of Aunt Eveline and Mauveine. She stared back and smiled warmly, realising that Victoria's memory was erased of all recollection despite the immense summoning of Victoria's own psychic powers. Now, the seventeenth century happening at the priory never even existed. She was intrigued how the rest of the present space-time they were back in had realigned.

"I knew you didn't believe me. Always trust a scientist, Abby. The specialist confirmed my suspicions last night, after a thorough lab analysis and proper liaison with a research clinic in Cambodia. I'd picked up a bad dose of a very rare form of cryptosporidiosis, a sort of parasite like a worm which had got into my intestines and spread, causing the reaction of that awful rash and the fevers and swellings. The doctors are confident I caught it swimming in a lake at the back of the hotel, a bit of bad luck."

"You really do look well, Vikki."

"A special antibiotic did the trick, although I do wonder sometimes at the imagination of my own children babbling on about bubonic plague? What utter nonsense."

Victoria grinned, her old self was reappearing in spades. "Tell you what though. These last four days of a liquid diet have done wonders for my waist size. I hope you've brought those skinny jeans in. Julian is wonderfully caring but still hasn't got a clue about women's clothes, after all these years of living with me!"

"Of course. All here milady, personal service with a smile" Abby replied jauntily and fished inside her holdall, desperately hoping that whatever it was Victoria was anxious for, they were there. She felt something velvety and pulled out a lovely black pair of very skinny Diesel jeans.

Victoria held them up, beaming. "Great. I told Julian to go back home and get a good shower and change his clothes. The doctors said I could go home at lunchtime, isn't that wonderful? They just want to run through a few final checks first, to be one hundred percent sure. I feel pretty amazing though. Hey, look who's at the door already."

A bustle of people walked in laughing and joking, headed by Julian who gave Abby a quick hug and whispered how pleased he was she had saved his bacon with the jeans. Bel ran forward and gave her mother a first big family hug, followed by Zac and finally Maddie.

"Lynton will be up in a minute, darling," Julian shouted over the racket, relieved the crisis was over. "He's come separately with Ned and brought the dogs in the back of the pickup. Jeb and Kai sensed you were better and are desperate to see you too. I'll wheel you outside for some fresh air before the doctors release you. The air is nice and crisp. You'll be a bit weak I suspect until tomorrow."

Ten minutes later Ned and Lynton rushed inside carrying two big bunches of flowers, a basket of fruit and gave another giant hug each to Victoria.

Abby stood to one side at the back of the room, out of the way, so she could observe discretely. She knew now for sure. The distortion and kinks of the McKenzie curse in the former psychic space-time were healed and they resided now inside another reality, a new continuum which kicked in before Victoria had been rushed to hospital. The event, the horrific 1665 enactment of the Rimmer curse at the Orsbrick Priory from which they had just escaped never happened. So inside their minds, the whole family and Lynton were oblivious ... but was there an exception?

Maddie was stood on the other side, also keeping herself aloof. When she glanced over and their eyes met, Abby knew and saw instantly from Maddie's expression that she was struggling to rationalise the nightmare she still remembered. Thank heaven there had been time for that deeply private discussion between them, to warn Maddie that she may have the same legacy ... the burden of recalling the horror. Now they each understood the reason, being former half-sisters, Bella and Katherine. The two had always been the central fulcrum, the keystone to the entire arch of the Rimmer curse, starting and continuing from the burning of Lucinda onwards, for all those interlinked male and female McKenzie and Warren generations of the subsequent three centuries. As facilitators, the perpetual memory would be their destiny, a fact set immutable in time … to last forever.

But Abby was deeply aware of the incendiary nature that she was an integral spoke in the whole McKenzie family wheel of heritage, as the progenitor of the arts and creative lineage through Katherine's marriage to Lord Robert McKenzie, followed by their daughter Patience. Eventually of course the artistic genes emerged as descendents Lydia and Aunt Eveline. How on earth was she going to explain everything to Victoria? Any approach needed careful and sensitive assessment, although the letters and the facts were already evident, archived in the family library. Once the dust settled and life was back to normal, she would sit down quietly with Maddie and work out a sensible plan. Her instinct, though, whispered strongly that Julian would be quite excited with the notion given his pragmatic and creative character and outlook. Her easy-going Lynton too would likely be delighted … so perhaps the task was not so daunting.

Whilst the hubbub and chatting continued, and Julian, Lynton and the children became preoccupied listening to Victoria and her experience in the isolation ward, Abby quietly beckoned Maddie over.

"Hey everyone," she called out cheerfully. "I just remembered something … I need to give Maddie one of my specialist books for her art in science project. We're just going to the car to fetch it before I forget."

Maddie understood, smiled, and walked across. She was desperate to speak alone to Abby who obviously felt the same. They were happily ignored and were about to turn and go when a movement in the mirror over the sink caught Abby's attention. She nudged Maddie as they watched, incredulous, to see the reflection of Mauveine and Isi, in laboratory coats, smiling and laughing incognito at the back of the others and gazing assiduously at the array of medical equipment alongside the rear wall. The mobile spectrometer was first lovingly caressed before the trolley slowly and quietly moved out of the door. Mauveine and Isi departed with a big smile and generous wave back to Abby and Maddie.

"Oh, gosh, Mauveine has picked up the dermatoscope too," Maddie whispered to Abby, wide eyed as it also floated, unseen, out of the doorway.

"That name sounds familiar, Maddie? Didn't Dr Lee use one to look at those goitres on Vikki's skin?"

Maddie smiled, she had read up the physics again. "Yes, a fabulous optical instrument which the specialist must have used for rechecking Mum's sores and rashes. The lens produces a three dimensional image of patterns through the layers of the skin using polarised light, providing a very accurate diagnosis."

"Hopefully we're witnessing a quick ethereal loan! Let's go before anyone notices," Abby whispered back.

As they reached the door, Lynton suddenly turned and called out, making them jump. "Don't lose those tickets I left for you on the passenger seat, Abby." He walked closer. 'Our trip to Boston,' he mouthed, 'to visit Salem like you asked. Surprise! Happy early birthday!'

Abby looked at Maddie and grinned back, blowing him a kiss and a thank you.

Out in the corridor, Mauveine and Isi had completely disappeared, along with the spectrometer and dermatoscope.

"Looks like they've moved on from iPhones," Maddie said, as both giggled and walked arm in arm downstairs.

"Let's grab a coffee in the cafeteria," Abby replied. "There's hardly anyone in there. I could really just do with some peace and quiet."

"Me too. I reckon we've both had enough excitement for one day. You were right. I remember absolutely everything, as you obviously do, just as you said. But it's only us isn't it?"

"I'm afraid so, and Mauveine of course. We've straightened out the curse kink completely, so history will be rewritten. Half of that was successfully transformed of course when I saved Mauveine last summer. Now all the unknown family distress beforehand will have followed suit, forming a continuous whole McKenzie universe, no splits, tears or unexpected Rimmer wormholes."

They sat down at a corner table with their coffees and some biscuits. A text pinged into Abby's phone. Glancing at the screen, she read the contents then quietly passed it over to Maddie, who giggled.

'Just want to thank you both. Brilliant outcome. Check the news tonight and read Robert's diary of 1666. Isi and I are having great fun with this new kit. Already discovered an unknown dye formula and looking at a wart on his thumb.'

"She certainly does still have my old iPhone but when you try and reply nothing happens," Abby whispered. "What I want to know, Maddie, is how you realised that Abbot Rimmer had tried to hide himself inside the furthest antiquity universe he could possibly run to, and the link with the purpurine prism? I had absolutely no idea."

"It was down to Judy. Like much of Rimmer's concocted environment of evil, not all was, as you hinted at, smooth and straightforward. There were definite imperfections and ragged edges. Mum obviously was one. Rimmer had factored in her death through the plague but she was still soldiering on, unknown to him, with Mauveine providing both of us with sustained mental and psychic support. There was so much for us to fight on all fronts that was just as well. I don't think I could have managed it otherwise."

"Yes, Mauveine is a very special and unique person in the heritage hall of fame. But how does that explain Judy?"

"And the McKenzies and Warrens, sis!"

Abby laughed and patted her hand affectionately. "Yes, I need to work through how to let that great biggie out in due course, because it's an irrefutable fact, both then and now."

"I'll help you, don't worry. A bit of due diligence on some historic research is needed, that's all. I reckon Mum, Dad and Lynton will all be pleased to hear the revelation. Anyway, I suddenly realised, watching the disintegration of Judy's manifestation and of course Adrian's too, that they were not properly aligned to the space-time of Abbot Rimmer, one of the mishaps of his grand plan. Then I remembered, you said Judy had seen the same frightening things as me. Whilst not fully attuned to each other, there must have been an overlap between our psychic universes, with their own connecting wormhole. Judy had an intimate knowledge of the purpurine prism. I concentrated hard to try and connect with her and the moment that awful woman, what was her true name …?"

"Zelda, sounds like something out of a fantasy comic,"

"Yes another mistake probably. Once Zelda's hair went up in snakes, I broke through to Judy and she responded. She knew the precise origins of the purpurine prism, and its powerful anti-evil properties emanating right back to antiquity, in India, where that crimson glass can still be found. Although where I managed to find the ancient linguistics from I have absolutely no idea, the words just came and flowed into my head. Rimmer's surprise at seeing me holding the prism at him confirmed the key, his Achilles heel. He must have assumed it had been lost in time."

"But the ghostly wolfhounds? And those horrible zombie wolves of Hades? My goodness that was terrifying beyond belief," Abby murmured, fascinated by Maddie's deep insightful reasoning exactly at the crisis point.

"I don't know … my head was throbbing so violently, I thought it would burst open. I think Mum knew about the wolves somehow, and the realisation that the prism could trigger the wolfhounds to materialise and destroy them came pounding deep into my subconscious. I had of course also read the other letter from Isaac Newton and about his own brave wolfhound, fighting off the wolves then sadly dying from his wounds, and the breakage of the prism which seemed at that time to be in a transition. I'm certain that massive great leader of the wolfhound pack, the one with odd markings black, cream and brown, oddly similar to Jeb and Kai come to think of it, was Caesar, Newton's brave dog. I bet Jeb and Kai are also family descendents. Robert McKenzies diaries indicated that the purpurine prism had passed first from Lady Bella to Robert, then to Newton, then back to Robert and finally by a quirk to Lady Katherine who took it over to America. In between then and the pieces turning up with Mum's father, my grandfather Jack and Mum's Uncle William, they must have been brought back to Orsbrick Hall."

"Of course, from America, either by Katherine herself or maybe even a future strand of the McKenzie-Warrens who returned it? All absolutely fascinating. Amazing, Maddie, well done and exactly as Aunt Eveline predicted, you're taking forward the McKenzie capabilities onto the next generation. You have an incredible brain inside that young head of yours."

"Hey, I should hope so now, as I must have a mixture of both you and Mum in the genealogical mix!" Maddie replied, laughing. "I've no problem keeping everything a secret. I'm very relaxed because of course I had plenty of practice with those horrible visions beforehand. This last finale is simply an addition to the list."

"Excellent, me too. Life will just move on for you Maddie, as it has done with me. I suppose we'd better get back. I do actually have a book for you in the car too, but we'll have to wing it if they ask."

"I doubt it, they're all far too preoccupied with Mum and doing their own thing ... You missed the girl shyly standing outside the door when we rushed off after Mauveine started wheeling away all the medical gear, didn't you."

"Yes, who was it?"

"Only Nancy. I reckon Ned is already well past any hidden memories of almost being hung, drawn and quartered. Talking of hung, just as well she didn't see him before that robe went back on. Crikey ..."

"Now, Maddie ..."

They both giggled loudly, shattering the silence, the cafe manager glaring across.

Maddie continued. "Actually ... I really want to ask your advice because I've made an important decision, something I desperately want to do and I'm terrified of discussing it with Mum and Dad."

"I wondered about that, you were going to tell me just before everything blew sky-high."

"You know that Bel and I are fast-tracked science students? We're a year ahead of our classmates, in fact more. I can take my final scholarship exams for Cambridge this coming summer if I want to. I've got an online friend in Boston, we've been in a ... err ... friendship for over a year. I speak to her on three-dimensional skype almost every night. She is fabulous, really gorgeous looking and amazingly bright. Janine is at Harvard studying biomathematics along with technology, specialising in artificial intelligence, which I'm really interested in. Look at this?"

She pulled a letter from her pocket and gave it to Abby, who carefully opened it up to read. A smile drew across her face. History in another context was revisiting once again, hardly surprising.

"Maddie, this is a full scholarship offer from Harvard! They've actually offered you a place on the course based on your existing knowledge, starting this January. Gosh, this is amazing."

"Janine tipped me off and I entered a timed online competition a month back for three places. It was like a code sequencing puzzle, to deconstruct the DNA of an alien found on an asteroid. I actually wondered whether it was fact and not fiction, but I came top, with a hundred percent score! I really, really want to go; in fact I simply need to go. The time has come for me to move on from Orsbrick Hall, much as I love Mum, Dad and Bella, Ned and Zac of course. But how do I tell Mum? She will go absolutely ballistic."

Abby went silent for a minute carefully constructing her thoughts. "Actually, I think you will be very surprised when and not if you tell Vikki. She will be much more sympathetic and supportive than you think."

Maddie screwed up her eyes, her fast brain running over scenarios and links. "Is this why Mum has never spoken about her teenage years and how she got to Holland?"

"Yes, and you have a mindset exactly the same; determined, always knowing what you want and ferociously competitive. Vikki too had a special, older friend at your age, her name was Eva, and she was a scientist too. I think your mum should tell you the rest. But don't be afraid. You have one advantage that Vikki didn't have. You have loving parents who care the world for you, support you and want the best for you, and your brothers and sister too of course. And your mum and dad have no money problems. You may have won a scholarship but you'll want a flat and plenty of cash to manage comfortably at Harvard and have lots of fun!"

Maddie leaned forward and gave Abby a large hug and a kiss on the cheek. "I know … Janine's parents are both Senators and even they struggle. Thanks, Abby, I'm so glad we met in a previous life."

Abby laughed. "Me too, sis. Now let's head back. They'll be wondering what we're up to. I expect Julian and the mob are wheeling Vikki around the grounds and then she should be allowed to go home later. It looks, interestingly, like both of us are being drawn over to the US for genuine reasons. Lynton, as you heard, has bought me birthday tickets for both of us to fly over and visit Salem for a week … to be honest, I want to have a good research look around my … mmm … family history now. I'll explain to Lynton about the Warren-McKenzie links when we get there. There should actually be time to book you as well and come with us, and you can visit Janine in Harvard which is close by and check it all out if you can arrange it. Why not? So tell your Mum the news straight away."

"Wow, yes please Abby, what a fabulous suggestion. Funny, as you say, about America looming all of a sudden like there's some divine intervention happening …"

They got up and turned for the door, startled to see Mauveine and Isi, still in lab coats, sat at another table drinking tea and chatting. Mauveine waved and gave two thumbs up.

Abby and Maddie looked at each other … and nodded. There was.

Back home and later that evening, life was quickly returning to McKenzie normality. Clair and Danielle had cooked a giant, special roast for everyone of wild boar, exactly as they would have eaten in the seventeenth century, complete with a big Bramley apple in its mouth. Judy's children had already eaten. Bedtime was looming and they rolled around the large rug in front of the fire, playing happily with Jeb and Kai. Guest rooms were prepared for overnight stays so the adults could drink and enjoy themselves. Victoria had finally been given the complete all-clear and was almost up to her normal strength and vitality.

Whilst Julian was expertly carving up the boar with his new set of knives and Lynton passed around the hot plates of potatoes and vegetables, the twenty-four hour news channel on the wallpaper TV chuntered away in the background.

"Hey everyone," Ned called out, watching the tickertape on screen and holding Nancy's hand tightly under the table. "Take a listen to this. Case is finally shut and closed …"

'An American couple, Herbert and Joyce Springer, who have been on the run in the UK for a month, have been detained at the port of Felixstowe, about to board a ferry to Denmark. Disguised as a priest and a nun, they were ready to flee when security guards were alerted,

as they both started shrieking hysterically, waving knives and baseball bats, and threatened staff and passengers at the ticket office to stop the black crow which had flown in through an open door from attacking them. On arrest, they were found to be high on hallucigenic drugs and have subsequently confessed to the rape and murder of schoolgirl, Sally Savage, two months ago on their former canal holiday cruiser. The burned out boat was found locally, hidden under bushes and reeds, twenty miles further along the canal from where the murder took place at Parbold in Lancashire. The couple have been remanded in custody to face trial early next year.

"Adrian, you must be so relieved this is all over," Victoria called across, passing him the peas. The terrible gash on your arm when you slipped on the deck, once you all found that boat? Is the wound healed up now?"

"Absolutely Mrs McKenzie and I have to say Bel really was a superstar that day with her first aid. They reckoned in the hospital, she probably saved my life and definitely my arm." He grinned at Bel, who sat next to him. They too were holding hands secretly under the table.

"And," Ned added, "Ade … tell them the good news."

"Well, after visiting my cousin last holiday at Dublin University, I've decided to stay on in the Cradwell sixth form with Ned and Zac and do physics rather than go to the tech college. Teachers said I'm easily good enough for A-level double maths too."

"And you'll be in my computing class too Ade, won't you," Bel replied grinning.

He nodded, blushing, looking at Dottie opposite, sat next to Zac and holding his hand firmly under the table. "Dottie's doing English Lit and History though, thank goodness," he muttered, as everyone laughed.

Julian was concentrating at the head of the table, looking for his glasses. His boar slicing had gone somewhat askew with a finger almost joining the big apple, as he struggled putting them on with one hand and then beamed with pleasure. "Excellent … well … what can I say, all this amazing family learning … just the job," and recommenced the carving. Victoria eyed him, wondering whether he was getting even dafter as he got older.

Maddie suddenly piped up, smiling. "I've got some news too, but …"

"I've got a new job and I'm getting married."

A hush spread across the table. All eyes turned to Judy, sitting primly with an uncharacteristically large grin. "I've just been offered the post of Director of Culture with Liverpool City Council and … the Mayor of Southport and I are getting hitched to celebrate. Time I had some fun too." She glanced at Lynton, speechless, his mouth open wide. "He's a widower and an Egyptologist, Dad … you'll love him and his five daughters. Good job we both love kids isn't it."

Abby gripped his hand tightly under the table, digging her fingernails in until it hurt … to say absolutely nothing … progress at long last.

Victoria, sensing the turning point, took charge. "Well everyone, I think we should all congratulate

Judy, what fabulous news. Here's to Judy and a fantastic new future." She raised her wine glass and everyone responded with loud cheers and murmurs of congratulations."

Abby cut in. "Maddie, you were saying?"

"Well, my news is ... but first I'm going to talk it over with Mum, and then you lot can hear it."

Lynton, his head deep inside a seventeenth century replica flagon full of Julian's homemade strong ale, looked over the rim and murmured, "Maddie? You're not ...?" before receiving a sharp kick under the table from Abby, who smiled sweetly back to him ...

Later, whilst Dottie was leading the others in Scrabble, Abby and Maddie wandered back up to the library, to take a look at those old diaries of Lord Robert McKenzie, Earl of Burscough, still up on the top shelf of the far bookcase in the corner.

"There remains the intriguing mystery of when and why the McKenzie family lost all their nobility titles?" Abby muttered, pulling out the 1665 and 1666 diaries. "Same with the Warren's. Katherine of course was also Lady Katherine and her title would have continued assuming she eventually married Robert."

"Maybe she didn't, I mean marry, but she may have continued to have his children. She was a very independent minded woman." Maddie said, pondering hard about the gap period in their knowledge. "Some more research will be necessary there. We need to keep quiet about that bit, until we know."

Abby was busy reading, laughed and passed the diary over to Maddie to read the entries in the week of the 20th December 1665.

'*Following the tragic death of my father, Lord Cameron, and former Earl of this Orsbrick estate in the borough of Burscough, hacked to death at the hands of a small group of religious fanatics living at the former Orsbrick Priory, now so neglected to be almost a ruin, order was quickly restored by my sister Lady Lucinda and myself, on bringing out the King's Guards. It was found that Abbot Rimmer had been living a secret life of sin and debauchery amongst the ruins with a small sect of friars. They had long rejected their vows of meditation, celibacy, prayer and community good. Large quantities of wild mushrooms, hemlock and other potions were discovered in the grounds, the site having been sealed off for some time by a moat.*

After interrogation, the King's Guards and I discovered that my father, always a benevolent friend to the banned sect, maintained their continuance despite the wishes of the King, and had visited quietly with his valet not having been there for some years. Sadly, he stumbled upon an orgy, where the friars were burning the Abbot's own lover, Zelda, believing she was Lady Lucinda. Being off their heads with drink and potions, Abbot Rimmer and the friars were dancing naked around the burning body, obscenely, denouncing her as a witch.

In the resulting melee, my father and his valet were found dead, a knife administered by Rimmer, believing he was Satan himself, plunged into their hearts. Abbot Rimmer managed to escape the fray, as the friars were rounded up and executed on the spot. The mutilated and headless bodies of Abbot Rimmer, along with his brother John, were found a few hours later, mauled to death by a pack of my hunting wolfhounds ... Our next task was for Lucinda and myself, with my new fiancée, Lady Bella Scott, to comfort my poor mother, inconsolable with indescribable grief at the death of her husband ...'

Maddie smiled and looked further, right through and into the year 1666. No entries or engravings for the cellar witchcraft burnings at Orsbrick Hall existed ... because, as Abby reiterated, they now never happened. History had indeed been rewritten, right from the beginning.

As for the prism of purpurine? No mention of that could be found either. In effect, the crimson piece of glass had once more, completely disappeared. There was no sign of it anywhere in the house as Maddie and Abby quietly looked in the observatory and Julian's workshop.

They were about to rejoin everyone back in the sitting room when Maddie's mobile bleeped twice, with a social media tone she immediately recognised. She casually looked at Abby then gazed at her phone in total astonishment before handing it over.

Both of you go and find your destinies. Salem Witch Museum archives are a good start. Hey ho Mayflower! #MissDyeHead

They grinned. Who was it who said ghosts don't tweet?

About the Author

Roy Baldwin was born in West Lancashire and has lived and worked around the UK in various mathematical and scientific guises as an educationalist, civil servant, musician, house conservator and management consultant. Prism of Purpurine, a sequel and the second book in the Mauveine series, was conceived and written during the NaNoWriMo 2014 competition.

Prism of Purpurine is his sixth published novel.

Roy is currently busy researching and writing Flight for Fenella, the fourth book in the Mauveine contemporary ghost story fiction series, following Morag, book three He is a full-time writer, book designer and digital publisher and regularly commentates on the book and publishing industry through Twitter.

In between writing and digital publishing, he also tries to enjoy the fabulous beauty of the Norfolk countryside and seashore where he now lives.

All Roy Baldwin's novels can be bought in eBook and print versions from Amazon and other good physical and online bookstores worldwide.
Further information can be obtained from the author's writer site:
http://www.creativepubtalk.com

In addition, the author hopes you have enjoyed this book and welcomes any feedback or questions on any aspect of the story, characters or settings. Please consider supporting the author by providing a review on Amazon, Goodreads, Twitter or any other favourite online site or social media.

Publishers: http://www.creativegateway.com
Author Twitter: http://twitter.com/creativepubtalk

Have you read Mauveine the precursor?

MAUVEINE: Aged sixteen, wayward Victoria McKenzie flees desperate and confused from home in West Lancashire to a commune in Amsterdam and never speaks to her parents again. Now aged thirty five, single and fancy free, she is settled as a senior polymer chemist working in the ailing Ahrendolie refinery in Rotterdam. Following a serious and unsettling plant incident, she is forced into a long recovery break and plans to take off on holiday with Abby, her best friend and designer flatmate, always up for a new challenge. But Victoria is startled to suddenly learn of an unusual inheritance, Orsbrick Hall, taking her mind back to childhood events and places alongside the Leeds and Liverpool canal she never hoped to experience again. Intrigued by her news, she is summoned to a strange meeting with a Liverpool solicitor and bumps into the quaint Julian, an introverted steampunk writer, all grey hair and flying scarves. But what is it about the creepy Orsbrick Hall that nobody wants to talk about? Why does her past now unravel into an unexpected explosion of crazy scientific revelations and discoveries a hundred and fifty years before, which she would never have believed possible or credible? With Abby and Julian she must track down the source of past family secrecies and find out who the terrifying woman in the purple shawl really is. But will this unleash evil and powerful forces hell bent on her eternal destruction and damnation? And is Julian all he makes out to be?

An excerpt from Mauveine:

… She knocked on the pale green door and Victoria heard a firm but certainly elderly voice, in a very posh accent, reply. "Do please come in."

Mrs Grable held the door wide and Victoria walked into a large and very high ceilinged room, papered with a striped design she had never seen anywhere before and the walls finished off with a marbled Georgian coving. All around the walls were adorned with wonderful hanging pieces of fabrics, again like nothing she had seen, intricately designed and colourful, where she could make out themes of an outdoor nature, trees, water lilies, meadow flowers, orchids. She immediately thought of Abby, wondering why she was taking so long.

A high rear window, from floor to ceiling, which could be opened out, and letting in lots of daylight, especially noticeable with the sun shining in brightly, took her gaze. Standing in front, staring motionless at the view and holding onto two sticks stood a small elderly lady in a mauve cardigan and chocolate brown skirt, her hair white but thick. She turned around slowly, her soft complexion, highlighted with a bright red lipstick and smiled. "Victoria, how wonderful to see you at last."

But Victoria, ready to move forward and kiss her cheek, stopped dead, frozen in her tracks as she looked into the beneficent face and her face dropped. The likeness was so uncanny, she couldn't believe it, it was like looking at herself in the mirror, admittedly a much older face, but Eveline had remarkably few lines, great skin and her thick white hair, cut in a fashionable bob, just a little shorter than her own blonde style. But the eyes and the intense look were identical.

Eveline looked quite amused and didn't seem in the least bit surprised. "Well, my dear, I must admit you have inherited the family likeness and are quite beautiful"

Victoria stared perplexed, who was this woman …?

Other Books by the Author

The Rhapsody Series:
A chronological series of science themed novels that
follow and unravel the complicated emotional journey
and unexpected career ascent of nuclear scientist,
Professor Lauren Hind, through her many
international adventures and relationships. Set in
Belgium and France, the series kicks off in Sicily where
Lauren is taking a reality check on her life as a scientist
who appears to have it all. Global recognition for her
nuclear energy work, a doting designer husband who
she loves and a mega salary in a large corporate so she
can indulge in her joint passions of haute couture and
mathematics.

After leading a prestigious research conference, she
unexpectedly meets up with the mysterious and beguiling
Luis who lures her into a culture she had not experienced.
Fuelled by drink and intrigue, a train of events takes off and
Lauren finds herself desperately buffeted by a seemingly
irresolvable kaleidoscope of emotional and confused
outcomes, which threaten to violently overturn her well-
structured lifestyle and relationship bearings.
Trying hard to salvage her way out of the mess she has
created and save her marriage, new and interrelated twists
and turns throw her into further turmoil, entanglements and

more betrayal as she is forced to question everything she has stood for and make fundamental choices.

But someone else turns up who has the capability, passion and desire to take from Lauren whatever she wants. Lauren needs to find the will and strength to confront this additional adversity and resolve her own complicated needs — but can she overcome the temptations ...?

So Far:

Book 1: Rhapsody of Restraint

Book 2: Rhapsody of Power

Book 3: Rhapsody of Fate

Book 4: Rhapsody of Succession

Book 5: Rhapsody of Moon

And being continued ...

All available in print and eBook versions from online retailers and booksellers worldwide.